MIRROR
MAN

Fiona McIntosh is an internationally bestselling author of novels for adults and children. She co-founded an award-winning travel magazine with her husband, which they ran for fifteen years while raising their twin sons before she became a full-time author. Fiona roams the world researching and drawing inspiration for her novels, and runs a series of highly respected fiction masterclasses. She calls South Australia home.

MIRROR MAN

FIONA McINTOSH

MICHAEL JOSEPH
an imprint of
PENGUIN BOOKS

MICHAEL JOSEPH

UK | USA | Canada | Ireland | Australia
India | New Zealand | South Africa | China

Michael Joseph is part of the Penguin Random House group of companies
whose addresses can be found at global.penguinrandomhouse.com.

Penguin
Random House
Australia

First published by Michael Joseph, 2021

Cover design by James Rendall © Penguin Random House Australia Pty Ltd
Cover photography/illustrations: London Eye by Bruno Abati/Unsplash; seascape by
tanuha2001/Shutterstock; park by Gary Yeowell/Getty Images
Author photograph by Anne Stropin
Typeset in Bembo by Midland Typesetters, Australia

Printed and bound in Australia by Griffin Press, part of Ovato, an accredited
ISO AS/NZS 14001 Environmental Management Systems printer

NATIONAL
LIBRARY
OF AUSTRALIA
A catalogue record for this
book is available from the
National Library of Australia

ISBN 978 1 76089 432 0

penguin.com.au

MIX
Paper from
responsible sources
FSC
www.fsc.org
FSC® C009448

For Nigelle-Ann Blaser, Lesley Thomas and a host of other lovely readers who never gave up hope over the last decade that DCI Jack Hawksworth would return in a new story.

This one's for you.

PROLOGUE

Colin looked at the four girls in his life: all beauties, in his opinion, from his 48-year-old wife to the sixteen-month-olds in the twin pushchair. Each of them shared a golden-headed colouring but his daughter, mother to the twins, was the prettiest of all and had a reddish quality to her hair that in the right light looked like a bronzed rose. This was his only child and she had made him proud from the first squishy kiss she'd planted on her daddy's lips. A spirited child and independent from an early age, she'd impressed him with her decisive manner, taking responsibility for all her decisions, good or indifferent.

Her choice of husband – a slightly rumpled and distracted university lecturer, a decade her senior – had not been who he'd imagined would catch her heart, but he'd proven himself to be not only faithful for the years of their marriage but loving, too. Colin could wish no more for her in her private life. Professionally, he had hoped she would take all that bright intelligence from her double degree and pour it into a career that might reach the highest echelons. But she'd chosen a quieter, less visible life of motherhood, redirecting her interest in medicine into a Master of Psychology. Now she counselled battered women from violent homes and marriages. She hadn't let him down; in fact, she was making him prouder, being one of those silent achievers who didn't go for glory, status or money, but served her community diligently . . . and made a difference to people's lives.

Colin felt blessed by the quartet of females who orbited him. His every waking moment was about them: providing for them, looking after them, offering advice and being the main male in their lives. His daughter was back from the brink of despair at losing the professor to an aggressive cancer, which had taken him to his grave within six months of them learning of its existence. It would be a blow for anyone, but being left behind with twin one-year-olds was daunting, even for his capable child.

He'd suggested she come to live with them for a while, but the offer had fallen on deaf ears. She'd smiled and reassured him that learning to go it alone was the way forward, and would set her girls up to be strong and independent too. She promised to visit often and would consider moving back up to London to be closer to them.

On that wintry day those four sunny smiles appeared all the more vivid for the moody sky, bare trees and threat of rain. They asked him to come but he had some work to get done. All rugged up with beanies and scarves and quilted coats, they looked like a roly-poly gang and he felt touched by the way they all turned to wave from the gate. His emotions swelled and he realised these were moments to cherish, not to avoid due to work commitments. *To hell with those*, he thought, in an uncharacteristic moment of selfishness.

'Hang on, everyone, I think I will come,' he said, laughing at the exaggerated sigh of his wife.

'I told you,' he heard her say to their daughter.

'Oh, Dad! Hurry up,' she said, laughing. 'We want to beat the rain.'

He listened with a smile as his wife distracted the babies, singing about Incy-Wincy Spider and the rains coming down . . . the same rhyme they'd sung to their daughter. That time really didn't feel that long ago. He struggled to pull on his wellies, muttering for his family to be patient as they yelled from the gate. Finally he stepped out, equally rugged up, into the wintry early evening for a stroll to tire the girls out so they'd sleep well tonight.

His wife linked her arm with his. 'I love this smell just before the rain.'

'Petrichor,' he remarked.

His daughter cut him a wry glance. 'Hear that, girls?' she teased. 'Grandpa tells us this smell of impending rain is called petrichor.'

'You can make fun, but I can't help but have an enquiring mind,' he replied in a lofty tone to make his wife giggle. 'It's the ground moistening, releasing various organic compounds and producing that lovely earth scent to tangle in our minds.'

His daughter inhaled. 'Well, I just know it smells like happy childhood.'

'Oh, that's lovely, dear,' her mother said with a smiling sigh. 'I hope our granddaughters will have happy memories to lean on.'

'We'll make sure of it,' he said, squeezing her hand. 'I'm glad they weren't old enough to understand the hard bit of losing their father, but we'll fill their lives with wonderful memories.' He looked over at his daughter and felt suffused with affection on seeing her grinning nod of gratitude. She'd worked so hard to push her own grief down so her children wouldn't feel her pain. 'We'd better not go the long way. It will get dark soon,' he continued absently. 'And the temperature will drop rapidly.'

'You held us up,' his wife accused him, but not meanly.

The road narrowed as they began to skirt the lovely expanse of park they'd arrived at. He could see plenty of dog owners shared much the same idea and were hoping to give their pets a quick run before the impending rain.

'Rather a lot of dogs around,' he warned, noting two large animals gambolling about. Their owners were distracted, chatting. Meanwhile, another dog nearby was barking madly at them.

'Dad, you're always so cautious.'

'You can't be too careful. Don't want to frighten our girls and have them terrified of dogs.'

'All right, let's keep to the pavement, then,' his wife said. 'We can track all the way around.'

He dropped back as the pavement narrowed, allowing his wife and daughter to walk ahead and pausing to study a magnificent rose garden that was now delivering its reward. He was aware of them looking back at him. 'Don't wait. I'll catch up,' he said, and they moved on and away from him.

He inhaled the scent of several blooms and, just as he was deciding life couldn't be more blissful, he heard the screech of tyres.

It happened so fast, he couldn't have reacted, couldn't have done anything to change what occurred, or its outcome.

The four-wheel drive hit his wife at an angle first.

He straightened in horror to watch her loop into the air and hit a wall, coming to rest in a broken splay of limbs and oozing blood. Shocked at the scene that was like a clip from a B-grade movie and frozen where he stood, he looked back open-mouthed to where his daughter and grandchildren were supposed to be, but they were no longer there. Though it happened in a few heartbeats, he felt as though he were taking in events in horribly slowed-down motion. He could see the expensive French push-chair that had held the girls so safe lying crumpled and smashed fifty feet or so away. He could see the pompoms of their beanies poking out from the top where they were still strapped in, no longer safe but motionless, their baby faces rearranged by the scrape of tarmac. Further on, still driving a drunkenly woven path, was the beastly chunk of metal on wheels pulling his daughter beneath it like a rag doll, that rosy hair far redder than it should be, now matted with her blood.

As Colin took in the impossible scene, this same-sourced blood began to flow glacially slow and just as cold in his veins. He could see someone running to a telephone box, presumably to dial 999. They would find only corpses from Colin's family – he didn't need to touch any of them to know that they were dead. There was so much blood, and the four bodies remained inert. But he could see movement in the big car that had wrought this murder.

He began to run, heedless of cars and people but vaguely aware that the traffic had stopped to form a ghastly silence, into which poured the distant sound of sirens. He yanked open the door of the Land Rover and dragged the sobbing man out, pulling him with unimagined strength to flop like a landed fish on the tarmac.

He could smell the fumes of alcohol coming off the man and didn't care what he was screaming – his apologies, or why he was so intoxicated that he had mounted the pavement and killed four magnificent females. He ignored the rough road scraping against the man's limbs as he recklessly hauled the driver around the vehicle to where his daughter lay trickling blood.

Before Colin could force the blubbering man to stare at his broken child and his family's stolen future, he could feel arms pulling him back, and his shocked gaze caught sight of the bottle green of a paramedic's uniform.

'Let me past, sir, please,' one said – a man.

Another, a woman, gently pushed on his chest. 'Let us do our job, sir.'

'That's my child underneath there,' he yelled. 'My grand-children, in that pushchair. And over there' — his voice broke on the words — 'my wife.'

He heard gasps and sounds of sorrow but they were meaning-less. His life was meaningless.

How would he ever give it meaning again?

1

LONDON, MAY 2006

Amy Clarke smiled at the two men on the other side of the bar. She'd not seen them around previously; most people who came into the pub were either locals or obvious travellers on their way through to somewhere else and this was simply a convenient stop. These two blokes looked like neither. One, a few years older than her, she reckoned, was wearing a military-coloured parka, which struck her as an oddity because it wasn't so cold today; most customers had mentioned the delicious spring day. His companion had to be at least twenty years older; unshaven, a smoker, going by the tin of tobacco he slammed on the counter, and there was something shifty about his gaze, the way it scanned the room constantly. They ordered two pints of Carling, which she dutifully delivered with another smile, this time simply to be polite. They paid with coins, which was curious too. The younger one counted them out right down to pennies, not at all awkward about it either.

'What's your name, then, gorgeous?' he asked, raising his remarkable eyes of a clear grey that demanded her attention.

She hated having to go through this dance, found the chat-up tedious but part of the job. 'I'm Amy.' She cut quickly back to business. 'Will you be eating today, gents?'

'What's on?' Grey Eyes asked with a lazy grin, his gaze brazenly roaming her body.

Amy deflected it, pointing to the chalkboard. 'The Guinness pie is a specialty.'

'Expensive,' the older one drawled, looking up from his lager.

'Does anything come with it?' Grey Eyes asked, his tone loaded with innuendo.

'Bit of salad,' she replied, determined not to show any expression other than impatience.

'We'll have two sausage rolls, served with another of those big smiles of yours.'

She gave him a look that said she doubted he could afford the latter, but, not to be deterred, he gave her a wink. Amy wondered how they'd be paying for their lunch, given they were down to pennies, but it wasn't her concern. She would mention it to the manager nearby though.

'Can we pay after, luv? Might have another of these,' the older one said, all but draining his glass, and she noted him leering at her breasts.

Prats! she thought.

As the good-looking barmaid moved away, Davey glanced back at Don and shrugged. 'What?'

'We're supposed to be casing, not flirting.'

Davey swallowed a sizeable draught of his lager. 'Great tits. Makes me horny.'

'Don't let your dick get in the way of business, son.'

'Yeah, you've probably forgotten how to work it.'

'Watch your mouth, kid.' Don made a hissing sound through his teeth but seemed at ease with the gentle insult. 'Besides, she's way out of your punching range. Those tits were brought up around money. She's not your usual choice of slag, Davey.'

'I don't date sluts,' he replied. Don sneered otherwise. 'Did you see how she smiled at me?'

'She's been trained to smile at punters.'

'I guess, but some of us transcend the average punter.'

'What's that word?' Don chuckled. 'Trans-what?'

'I heard it in a movie, looked it up. I like it. Means I rise above the average.'

'You think so?'

'I looked in the mirror this morning, Don. I'm in my prime. Got to take it whenever I can.'

That made Don laugh into his beer. 'You're an arse, Davey. Now focus, eh?'

'I already have. No marks in here.'

Don nodded slowly. 'Just old fogies, I agree. Bad time of day.'

'What about the houses nearby – what's it . . . Oak Walk?' He jabbed a finger in the direction of the side door.

'Nah, they're too open, son. I think we should do a reccy of those big houses at Parkside that back onto the woodland. Much easier to hide; get in from the park. There's got to be some easy pickings up there – jewellery, money, phones that we can lift. Won't take much to snatch and easy to cart, convert.'

Davey nodded. It was well away from Enfield Shopping Centre, where all the action was, but if they were in a hurry, they could run through the park back down to the station and jump on any train. He sighed his agreement as Amy reappeared carrying plates to their end of the bar.

'Careful, they're hot,' she warned.

'You're hot,' Davey quipped.

She gave him a sidelong gaze of fake despair. 'Don't want you to burn your tongue.'

He grinned. 'Depends where my tongue is.'

'Hey, watch yourself,' an older woman said, sidling up next to Amy. 'None of that in here.'

Davey held out his hands in a plea of defence. 'I'm just kidding. No offence.'

Amy blushed, glancing at the older bartender. 'None taken.'

'You can head off now, Amy. Shift's over.'

'Bye, Amy,' both men said in unison.

'Ready to pay, lads?' They won a glare from the middle-aged woman in charge. 'See you tomorrow, luv,' she called over her shoulder.

Except she didn't.

Fate, predestination, the way the chips fall, destiny . . . or plain, horrible luck, Amy would never know what led the two strangers from the bar to turn up at her house a few hours later as the sun was slipping away from the day. She was not followed; she knew that because she stopped to chat to not just to one but two of her neighbours from different streets, and she'd faced the hill they would have had to walk down if they were following her.

So it was chance – random bad luck, she later decided – to have Davey Robbins and Donald Patchett cut through the woodland of Grove's End Park to follow the fence lines of the houses in Parkside that backed onto it. The cover of bushes and trees was perfect for would-be thieves. Her parents were at work, her brother at school, but Gran was home with her.

They were sharing a pot of tea as the light turned a deep golden in the conservatory that backed onto the large, open-plan kitchen that her parents had built onto just six months earlier.

'It's so lovely here,' her grandmother remarked, sighing at her first sip of tea. 'That breeze through those French doors is delicious.'

Amy had to agree. The renovations had added a glass box to the back of the house, giving the family a new living space that opened up the garden into their daily life. Watching the birds go about their business, noting the bulbs pushing up throughout April, now a chorus of bright colour, or spotting a squirrel . . . it was like a whole world they'd been ignoring all these years. 'I'm glad they didn't sell up. I would have hated to leave this house. And summer's going to be brilliant. Why don't you come and live here with us?'

'No, I think your mother has enough on her plate with her busy job and busy life.'

'But you could always be home for Tom after school. He's got another three years, and it must get lonely in that cottage.'

'I'm never lonely, darling. I love where I live, and I have plenty of friends. Are you worried about going off to university?'

'A little. I'll miss it here.'

'You're a close quartet, Amy dear, but broaden your horizons and don't look back. Your parents aren't going anywhere – your dad's clinic just gets busier and your mother's skills seem to be in more demand than ever. Everything will remain as you leave it and you can come home often. Besides, Tom says he likes the idea of being an only child.' At Amy's expression, her grandmother giggled. 'Only teasing. Brighton isn't that far away and it's such a lovely town to be studying in. I'll visit.'

'Promise?'

'Of course,' her gran said, easing herself up to refresh their pot of tea. 'Grandad used to take me there for a naughty weekend.'

The thought of her grandparents frolicking in bed was a thought too far, but the notion was interrupted by a metallic sound that made them both turn and look down the garden, which backed onto the glorious woodland of Grove's End Park enjoying the last licks of daylight.

Davey nodded. 'This one looks like a goer.'

Don agreed. 'Those back doors are just an invitation,' he sneered, a cruel smile twitching at the edges of his mouth, which held a thin, half-smoked cigarette he'd rolled himself. He sucked back on it and flecks of tobacco lit and drifted away on the light breeze as the paper burned down to his nicotine-stained fingers. He flicked the butt carelessly into the undergrowth, ash scorching the dancing head of a bright daffodil.

Davey ducked. 'Fuck!'

'What?'

'Someone's there.'

Don risked a look, on tiptoe on the fence strut they were balanced upon. He squinted to see the woman near the kettle. 'Aw, it's an old lady, Davey,' he grinned. He tapped his friend's parka pocket. 'Nothing this won't fix.'

Davey felt the heaviness of the wrench push against his side. He hadn't planned to use it on a person when he'd grabbed it this morning at Don's nod. He'd figured they'd use it to smash into somewhere if their shoulders weren't strong enough to force a side door.

'We don't know if there are others upstairs,' he hissed.

'There aren't, Davey. We've been standing here for twenty fuckin' minutes and it's getting colder now the sun's going. We need to get going before I freeze.' Don was right; they were not in any position to debate this. 'If we don't pay Big Al, you know what's going to happen, don't you, Davey?'

He nodded.

'Say it, so we both hear it and understand.'

'He'll cut off a finger for each day we're late.'

'He'll cut off a finger *from each of us* for each day. We've only got today if we're going to fence the stuff tomorrow. Big Al is expecting us on Friday. What will happen, Davey, if we don't turn up to have our fingers cut off?'

'He'll kill us.'

'Right.'

Davey hesitated. 'Do you really think he would, over a couple of thousand?'

Don cut him a look of intense exasperation. 'I'll explain this one more time, son. Big Al maims, tortures and kills just on principle. It wouldn't matter if we owed him fuckin' sixpence. To him a debt is a debt. We would be the example he'd use to frighten others. We knew the terms when we took the gear.'

Davey sighed and steeled himself. 'Let's go.' In a nimble move, he leapt up to the top of the fence, balancing briefly before jumping down onto the grass, kicking over a watering can.

'That's done it, son,' Don said in a resigned voice, landing at his side as Davey reached into his pocket and pulled out the wrench.

Amy had to refocus to be sure it was the two men from the pub. She recognised the olive-green parka first before registering that it was the flirt and his dirty-looking sidekick. Before she could stop her, Amy's gran was out on the porch steps demanding to know what they were doing there.

'Gran, get in!' she warned, pulling at her elder's arm.

It was no good. The older woman was already advancing on the pair. 'How dare you! What do mean by—'

Her gran never finished her objection. Amy watched the older guy grab what Grey Eyes was holding and swing it, then watched the woman she loved spin with the force of the blow and crumple onto the stone steps with a crunching sound that spoke of broken bones. Gran fell like a doll made of cloth, as though she had no substance to her body. And as she lay lifeless, the world seemed to still. Both men stopped and stared. Amy's scream was trapped in her throat as she saw a trail of bright blood snake its way from under Gran's head and leak down one step and then another in a slow but determined flow.

The violence was so sudden, so shocking. Her mouth still open with confusion and disbelief, she turned to the men, who appeared as startled as she was.

'Well, that's done it, Don!'

Before Amy could regain her wits, the man she now knew as Don was pointing a filthy finger her way. 'Shut your fuckin' mouth, bitch, and we won't kill you too.' He pushed past her into the house.

Amy moved towards her grandmother but Davey grabbed her, squeezing her arm fiercely to spin her back towards the house and shoved her in his friend's wake.

'I have to call an ambulance,' she pleaded, her voice high, panicked.

'No point,' Don said with remarkable heartlessness, as he opened drawers and cupboards, rifling through her family's stuff, tossing the contents onto the floor.

'Let me at least get a blanket for her, please!'

'She's not fuckin' cold, luv,' he replied. 'She's dead.'

★

Tiring of the conversation, Davey pushed Amy backwards against the kitchen bench, noticing how, as she grabbed it to steady herself, her shirt stretched against the breasts he'd admired.

The itch, which he hadn't scratched in a couple of weeks due to being troubled by Big Al's threats, reasserted itself. Sex would calm him. Right now, the need to relieve that particular desire was only adding to the stress. If he could get rid of that, he might think more clearly. He needed a woman's body against his own; something soft and real to pound out his fears against.

'I know what you're thinking, boy,' Don cut into his thoughts, growling next to Davey's ear for only his hearing, 'but right now, we must do what we came here for. But I'll tell you what, Davey, if you can find me at least two thousand quid's worth in five minutes, I'll let you do her. Find the goods!' He flung a backpack at Davey. 'Fill it.' Don turned his attention to Amy, and Davey was further aroused to see his friend grab the girl by the breast. She sucked back a breath of pain. 'I'll stop if you help me find what we need. Phones, laptops, jewellery.'

'My granny,' she began, realisation pushing past the shock, tears helplessly streaming. 'Er . . .'

'Got any cash, luv?' Don pressed. 'We only need two thousand.' He squeezed harder. 'Get going, Davey!' he snarled over his shoulder.

Davey ran upstairs to begin ransacking.

Don smiled his hideous sneer. 'Listen, darlin', I'm cold and tired. I don't care that your granny's dead; a man's going to cut off my fingers if I don't give him two thousand quid.'

'My phone's over there.' She nodded to the coffee table.

'Good, we'll do this together, shall we?' He grabbed her convenient ponytail and watched how it bent her with pain. He pulled harder and she straightened. 'Nice and obedient, Amy, that's how I like it. Now, phone into the bag. Oh, good, that looks new. Now, Mummy's jewellery?' Amy led Don upstairs to her parents' bedroom and into her mother's walk-in wardrobe, which Davey had already discovered. Don gave a low whistle. 'Fancy,' he cooed. 'I told you, boy, about those tits, didn't I?'

Davey grinned, watching Don let go of the girl, knowing she was too frightened to disobey them now.

'I'm thinking Daddy might have a safe stashed somewhere, eh, luv?' Don wondered.

She looked back at them bewildered, her thoughts wandering again. Davey backhanded her with vicious speed and force. Amy collapsed to the plush cream-coloured carpet, her snotty nose leaking onto it. Davey picked her up and over the top of her sobs explained what she needed to know. He was privately enjoying watching her fear; it was making him hard . . . and he knew she could see his arousal.

'Listen, Amy. Be sensible. Help us and this will be over.'

'Not for Gran.'

'Yes, that's a shame. But she was old and you're young and gorgeous . . .'

'Aha!' Don said, gleeful. 'I knew it. Here's the safe,' he said, pushing aside her mother's long coats and gowns that hid her father's safe. 'Okay, luv, I need the code. If you don't give it to me in your next breath, my friend here will not only rape you, but I will kill you afterwards. Are we clear?'

She nodded, looking sickened. A welt on her cheek had begun to deepen in colour. It was probably fractured.

'Zero eight four eight nine two,' she said.

Don felt the door of the safe click open. He rummaged inside it, tossing aside documents and files, before giving a whoop. 'Cash, Davey. Delicious cash. Count it!' He threw it at Davey, who duly counted it while Don fixed Amy in place with his narrow-eyed leer.

'Just shy of eighteen hundred,' Davey said, sounding joyful.

'Well done, Amy,' Don praised her, reaching back into the safe to upend ring and bracelet boxes.

'Doesn't my phone make up enough with the cash?'

'Ah, luv,' Don said, almost sounding sympathetic. 'This is just some extra security for me and Davey here. Aw, look at this beautiful stuff, son. We're done.' He glanced at Davey and checked his watch, returning a resigned nod. 'There's just one more thing, luv. My friend really likes you.'

She looked back at Don, sullen but defiant.

'Ooh, Davey, watch this one. She's going to fight you.'

'Not if you hold her down, Don.'

After wriggling free of her bonds, Amy made a teary nine-nine-nine call on the home telephone. Two ambulances and a couple of police response cars arrived with flashing lights and sirens squealing. A police dog unit was in tow and headed off to find the trail of the men, but the two criminals were by then already on their way, using the parklands to get as far from the scene of the crime as they could before changing into a new set of clothes they'd hidden earlier that morning; they'd figured it would be a good way to dodge the street cameras. The dogs and their handlers found the domestic bins on the street where the clothes were thrown but then the trail went cold, after Davey and Don had split up to make their separate ways into central London and to its east.

With Davey wearing a bandage on his cheek, they'd paid their dangerous creditor a visit a day early to settle their account. Big Al had nodded, impressed; told them he'd do business with them anytime they needed. Their mistake was to fence the jewellery a day later, by which time an accurate description had gone out on the missing goods and the usual suspects were raided.

They'd also underestimated Amy's fighting spirit and her good memory.

She'd been badly beaten, her face unrecognisable. So many bones fractured because she'd fought them with every ounce of strength she possessed. She'd been raped by both men and left in her parents' bedroom, bleeding and broken, but with three nails full of DNA belonging to Davey Robbins. They also had no idea that Amy was an artist; in her rage she had drawn very good likenesses of both men. Don's illustration was particularly illuminating. The police had them locked up within forty-eight hours, their fingers intact.

Nothing was intact for Amy again.

2

He opened the new bag of coffee beans and inhaled, relishing the toasted aroma that his favourite brand of arabica gave off. Tipping the contents into the grinder's basket, he enjoyed the satisfying clatter of the oily rubble, awaiting the revolution of the burrs that would allow them to perform the alchemy that hot water and their grinds could achieve.

This was a ritual for DCI Jack Hawksworth. Ever since his last trip to Australia to see his sister and her family, now living in Melbourne, coffee had taken on a new dimension for him. No longer did he swallow the muddy slurry from vending machines for something warming; now well-brewed caffeine had become a passion. Having tasted the delicious version of a piccolo in the Italian quarter of Melbourne – where unshaven men stood behind hissing, steaming machines twisting buttons and pressing levers that ultimately delivered a shot like liquid liquorice, topped by a layer of caramel-coloured crema – he now prided himself on attaining a similar magic at home.

He sat back now at the small breakfast table, satisfied with this
morning's brew. His laptop was open to read the news but he
ignored the screen and instead stared out of the window and across
the concrete complex of his temporary home. He'd worried this
place might turn him melancholy but contemplated instead that
life was looking up. Moving into this apartment while he decided
where to live had been wise. And while its architecture seemed to
contradict everything he might normally respond to, he enjoyed
its convenience and ease. These last few weeks had been coloured
by a watershed sense of arriving at peace. Two relationships in a
row with intelligent women, both characterised by bright personalities and beauty, had ended horribly. How could one person
have such poor luck as to have two lovers who were enmeshed in
crime? Anne McEvoy had notoriously emerged as a woman on a
revenge spree for a gang rape in her childhood; she'd killed all but
one of the perpetrators but in the process had effectively changed
Jack's life, especially as he'd never stopped loving her.

Then along came Lily. The sensuous florist had entered his
world by chance and a sense of hope had begun to simmer. He
had liked Lily enormously, although they both knew the relationship was doomed. Her Chinese parents had arranged a suitable
marriage to a surgeon, but that was not the pain in his heart. The
hurt that would never leave was that Lily never got to live her life.
It had been snapped out by the sinister fiancé, and Jack had spent
a year now trying to regain his faith in himself; he felt he had
failed both these women.

He sipped the coffee, allowing its richness to fill his senses and
move him away from the past. Tapping the space bar, he watched
the screen brighten and he read the headlines and their articles.
Most disturbing was the report that a three-year-old child called
Madeleine had gone missing during a family holiday in Portugal;
he couldn't imagine a more terrifying scenario for a parent. He

wondered how the Europe Desk that he headed up at Scotland Yard might be drawn into the case. There would be a media circus to contend with, and Jack began to imagine the emotional energy building within police from both countries, which would be about to explode. Moving on, he scanned the usual depressing facts: Manchester United had won yet another Premier League final, and Britain had come joint second to last in the Eurovision Song Contest. He sighed.

Jack shifted to the newspaper; if technology continued the way it was, he imagined that one day he might read the news via his phone – now what a crazy world that would be. He shook his head, feeling old, and kept turning the pages; he was now simply scanning, thinking about a second coffee, knowing he should probably get to work. He'd only had the briefest of sleeps, having left the Europe Desk in the small hours and not been able to drift off happily, so he'd been up by five for a run. He checked his watch; it was nearing eight. He was about to close the paper and start his day when a brief caught his attention.

Jack's forehead knitted with disgust, the good buzz of just moments ago beginning to ebb away as he read that Rupert Brownlow had been released a week earlier; that he was *not giving interviews, had done his time and now just wanted to get on with his life.*

'Rupert, you bastard,' he murmured, recalling the case. He hadn't worked on it, but the detectives who had were broken for a while; certainly, the paramedics first on the scene had been collectively traumatised. Four children, two forty-something adults, two seniors – one in her seventies and an older man in his eighties – plus a couple of beloved dogs had died that day, not quite eight years ago, because spoilt, rich, arrogant Rupert Brownlow had been enraged that his girlfriend had dumped him for some other pimply private-school sixth-former. He'd taken some drugs and swallowed more alcohol from his family's drinks cabinet than a youth of eighteen should at ten in the morning. Then, in his drugged, drunken teenage version of wisdom, Rupert had taken his father's tomato-coloured Range Rover and gone wheeling around London, a police car and a police bike ultimately on his tail. They finally caught him but not before half-conscious Rupert had ploughed into a suburban street in Potters Bar, ending lives through his selfish hellraising. He'd served just over three years of his appallingly short seven-year sentence.

'Amazing what money and a lenient judge can do, eh?' Jack remarked to the universe, feeling a punch of despair on behalf of the families who had lost their loved ones and would now know the killer was back out to pick up the threads of his life, repair the gaps and move forward in his twenties . . . contrite perhaps, but still wealthy. Meanwhile those families would likely never escape their loss and move forward, as Brownlow could.

Jack gave a growl, knowing the police would bear the brunt of public scorn, when in fact it was the legal system that had let folk down.

He stood, resigned to get on, hopeful that today they might get news on the careful operation presently underway in Brussels, which was a joint effort by British, French and Belgian task forces. This was an important one for Scotland Yard's counterterrorism unit, of which he was second-in-command for the International Liaison Section.

As Jack was rinsing the shampoo out of his dark hair, in need of a trim, which he would tame with a firm brush, he heard his phone ring. He reached for the Nokia that was balanced on the basin and stepped away from the showerhead, his other arm grabbing a towel. Eyes stinging slightly from the suds, he answered.

'Morning, Jack?' It was his old super, Martin Sharpe, now Acting Chief Superintendent of the Homicide and Serious Crime Branch at Scotland Yard.

'Morning, sir. This is a surprise.'

'Have I caught you at an awkward moment?'

'No, sir. Well . . . just showering. Hang on.' He put his head briefly under the water again to rinse properly and then, in a slightly muffled tone as he dried his face, he returned to Sharpe. 'Are you well, Martin? Family okay?'

'All fine . . .' He sounded hesitant.

'Except?' Jack encouraged him, turning off the water.

'I've got something.'

He waited, but Martin was prepared to wait too, it seemed. Jack began towelling dry. 'All right, spill it, sir.'

'Three corpses. All murdered, we believe.'

'Related?'

'Not as far as we know.'

'Where?'

'Finsbury Park, another in Eastbourne, a third in Birmingham.'

'So . . .?' Jack frowned, perplexed.

'Two different counties as well as London and we can't tie them together, I admit. However, their bizarre nature has set off alarm bells. Heads of CID have agreed that the Met should coordinate investigations rather than risk another Ripper.'

Jack blinked with surprise at the mention of Sutcliffe, who still haunted police ops and indeed changed the way they approached major investigations. He decided to leave that alone. 'Bizarre in what way?' Jack opened the mirrored cabinet and reached for the deodorant, before filling the basin with hot water. 'Sorry, sir, hope you don't mind if I keep getting ready.'

'Not if it gets you in faster.'

Jack winced. So it wasn't just advice being sought. He should have known it was coming.

'I'll need you on this one, Jack.'

'Martin,' he began, hoping to appeal to the mentor he treated with the same affection as a father, on the slim chance he could wheedle out of whatever it was that his old boss was about to lay at his feet. 'I'm at the pointy end of a huge operation that's taken almost a year to come to fruition. I've been working on—'

'I know about it . . . not the Secret Squirrel stuff, of course, but I know you've been doing a sterling job as deputy head at Counter Terrorism International Liaison. I know your French counterparts especially enjoy working with you and, in particular, Mademoiselle Bouchard at the embassy is impressed by you.' Sharpe let that hang. So, Martin knew about Sylvie. Jack smiled. Couldn't hide much from the old fellow. He soaped his face and began shaving. He waited. 'Are you there, Jack?' he heard his superior ask.

'I don't want to return to my previous role, sir, to be honest.'

'You wouldn't be returning to your previous role.'

'I see,' he said, relieved. 'What did you have in mind?'

'How does Detective Superintendent sound?'

That was unexpected. Jack didn't know whether to feel elated or cornered. 'I hadn't put in for a promotion.'

'Don't be coy, son. You've earned this and deserve it, but I need you heading up this operation.'

His super was playing with semantics. Not precisely the identical role because he'd have more status, but still heading up a major murder investigation . . . if it was one. 'There must be half a dozen qualified—'

'There are,' Sharpe interrupted, becoming testy. 'But none as experienced as you.'

'For what?' Jack genuinely couldn't see why he was the best fit.

'For taking on a serial killer.'

The words hung between them. Jack flung the razor into the soapy water and gave an exasperated sigh. 'You've admitted there are no similarities.'

'Not with the actual killings, no. And not with the MO either.'

'I'm sensing a but,' Jack said, realising he was not going to win this one. He stared at the man in the mirror, the former poster boy for Scotland Yard who had caught two serial killers in back-to-back dramatic operations that had almost claimed his life and that of his best DI, but had also carved away a chunk of his heart and his faith in humanity. 'Where's the similarity, Martin?' he demanded.

'The victims. They're all convicted criminals.'

Jack's expression changed to one of intrigue. 'Dead cons?' he said.

'It's the only link we can make. But I have a good nose, you'd agree?'

Jack nodded. 'And you're smelling something bad.'

'That's right. My office, soon as you can.'

Sharpe gestured to a seat once they'd shaken hands. 'Good to have you back, Jack.'

'Am I officially back? This is an order, is it, sir? I have no say?'

'It is and I'm sorry.' His boss had the grace to look genuinely sympathetic. 'We need you on this one.' He pushed a couple of files across his desk.

Jack opened them to look at crime scene photos, pathology reports, all the other relevant documentation, taking time to have a cursory glance through the material. Martin didn't mind the brief silence, even fielding a call – one that involved Jack.

'Yes, he's with me now. We'll start the ball rolling this afternoon. No. Absolutely no media. Not yet – we're not ready to discuss anything outside of these walls . . . unless some wily journalist makes a connection. But as I've told you, sir, there's nothing to join the dots yet, in my opinion, but we'll see what our boy turns up. Yes, I've mentioned that to him, sir. No, I doubt it did.

You know Jack.' He smiled humourlessly as the person on the other end spoke. 'No, sir. Nothing yet, other than my twitching gut, Commander,' he confirmed.

Jack looked up, waiting for Martin to conclude his conversation.

Sharpe put the phone receiver down. 'He hopes you're happy with the promotion. So?' he said in a weary voice, nodding at the files.

'You all right, sir?'

'Just a bit tired. I thought I'd hate retirement. My wife assures me she'll keep me busy . . . there are cruise brochures stacked next to our bed.'

Jack smiled in sympathy.

'Curiously, I'm feeling ready for it now – retirement, that is, not the cruising. Can't see myself in slacks and plimsolls.'

'They're called sneakers these days,' Jack quipped.

Martin chuckled. 'I like to use those words to annoy the grandchildren. Seriously though, can you see me in a polo shirt, strolling a ship's deck and impatiently awaiting happy hour?'

'I really can't.' Jack grinned. There was a poignant pause between them. 'You'll be missed, sir.'

Martin nodded. 'Until then, we have this problem,' he said, gesturing towards the files in Jack's hands. 'I am not going anywhere until this is sorted. Talk to me.'

Jack blew out his breath. 'Nasty,' he agreed. 'Julian Smythe, in for manslaughter . . . only got five years for beating his wife senseless. He was out in less than three years. Got off lightly,' he remarked, his eyebrow lifting.

'Well, I agree until you find out he was killed by being all but cooked to death.' Jack flipped over the page as Martin spoke. 'The coroner summarised the pathology report that the perpetrator likely poured several litres of freshly boiled water over his head before setting him on fire.'

Jack shook his head, giving a low whistle of awe. 'That goes beyond vicious. Even the heavy guys in Vice wouldn't be bothered with that . . . unless they were torturing him for information.'

'From all we can tell, he wasn't connected with any known crims.'

'The dead men weren't in the same prison, were they?'

'No. And Peggy never made it to prison.'

'Doesn't sit right with you, sir?'

'Does it feel odd to you? One of London's well-known madams, who we're certain was running an even bigger online prostitution racket, apparently commits suicide with an overdose while sitting next to a tree in Finsbury Park?'

Jack waited, as he could tell that Sharpe was just drawing breath.

'. . . in the middle of November!'

'All right, I'll admit that's beyond odd, but I'd have to study the victim, understand the circumstances.' Jack frowned, pondering. 'So no prison involved here?'

'Should have been. Peggy Markham was acquitted two years ago for the crime of procuring a girl under sixteen for unlawful sexual intercourse.' At Jack's frown, he explained. 'She was accused of allowing a client to practise his particular deviancy on a fifteen-year-old. The girl died.'

'That's a long bow you're drawing, putting Markham in with these two.'

'And yet I am. From all I've dug up, I can't find a single reason for Peggy Markham to end her life. If anything, her empire was flourishing. She wasn't sick, had no troublesome family – a son in Spain running a hotel keeping as much distance as he could between himself and his criminal mother, not to mention his criminal father, long dead. Meanwhile, she'd just dodged a prison cell that had her name on it. She should have been celebrating, not contemplating suicide.'

Jack blew out his cheeks. Martin was right; it was curious, but privately he wondered if his superior was simply reaching, keen to go out on a triumph. Even thinking that made Jack feel disloyal. Martin had never been someone who sought out the limelight, but he could feel the passion exploding from the other side of the desk.

'What about Alan Toomey? Remember him?'

Jack shook his head.

Martin threw a file in front of him. 'Read what happened to him.'

Jack obeyed and was soon enough looking up with an expression of disbelief. 'So, where do I come in?'

'I have to be sure, Jack. I'm not leaving for the great yonder knowing there's unfinished business. Just take a look, would you?' he appealed. 'The oddity of these deaths and the vague commonality I sense in the victims are sticking in my craw. You've run the two most notorious murder cases in living memory, you've got the cred and the knowledge, and I want to put that to good use. So, I've been given permission to follow my hunch. Are there more dead crims we are yet to find or haven't connected the dots to?'

Jack looked back at him, trying not to show his despair at being cornered into accepting the task, as Sharpe sat forward in earnest.

'Jack, do you agree that these look and even sound like murders?'

'Yes, to the two men.' How could he not agree? No one would inflict those injuries on themselves. 'But Peggy Markham . . . I'd need more time.'

'Take it. These deaths have occurred over three years, so there's no panic. Put together a small op – we don't need the usual dozens. Keep it tight.' The phone rang and Martin looked vexed. He pressed the button to the loudspeaker on the unit. 'I said no—'

'You'll want to take this, sir,' his secretary assured him. Martin glanced through the glass to where she sat, and Jack watched her nod firmly. Martin visibly sighed and picked up the receiver. 'Sharpe here.'

Jack watched the man's brow crease before he leaned his elbow on the desk and supported his head as though the burden of it was suddenly too heavy.

'Where?' was all he said before nodding. 'All right, I appreciate the early information. Thanks, Doug.' He put the phone receiver down and glanced at his secretary with a slight nod of gratitude before he looked at Jack. 'Rupert Brownlow?'

'Out last week, I heard.'

Sharpe nodded. 'No justice there for the people he killed because he was dumped by his girlfriend.'

'Does the Met think we should keep him under supervision now that he's out? He's an obvious target who's going to be hounded by reporters and angry civilians.'

'Yes, well, he doesn't have to worry about being chased any longer. His corpse was found near Portsmouth seafront. Dragged behind a car like a ragdoll for quarter of a mile . . . or so the bloodstains suggest.'

Jack stared at his boss, eyes narrowing, taking a moment to process what this meant. 'Hardly an accident then, sir.'

'Believe me now, Jack?'

'Is Joan available?'

Sharpe stood and grinned. To Jack it looked like a grin of relief. 'Already moving in. Seventh floor. You know the pack drill.' He extended a hand. 'Thanks.'

Jack shook hands with the senior officer, knowing the gesture sealed his fate in regard to the European operation he was in charge of. 'Who'll take over upstairs?'

'It's all in hand. Seriously, Jack.' Sharpe hadn't let go of his hand yet. 'I appreciate your help on this one. Then I can retire and know I left things tidy.'

'Until the next time,' Jack murmured but in a lighter tone.

'That's someone else's watch,' Sharpe replied. 'Joan's waiting for you.'

Jack nodded, fully resigned, and began his journey down from the senior corridors to the seventh floor, where his new operation was apparently already underway.

3

Sitting and waiting for his appointment, he amused himself by reliving the Rupert Brownlow killing. Amazing that he was like two men in one body. One half was perfectly respectable and leading a good, sound, empathetic life. But the darker half, which had emerged since the bleak day that changed everything, was capable of inflicting a terrible price on people whom he felt deserved it. He now considered these halves a team: two minds, two voices, one body. It wasn't that he didn't have a conscience – quite the opposite, in fact. It was his good conscience that led him to consciously partake in bad acts.

The news had only reached the papers this morning, but Colin knew his victim had taken his last breath two nights ago. Since he'd been old enough to hear stories and tell them, Colin had been able to live them with great detail and authenticity in his imagination. He used to make up games for himself and his friends to act out in the woodland around Enfield. He could see it all in rich colour: landscape, characters and action in minute detail. He was like a film director, giving his actors a brief and then they'd be off, he and his friends, scattering into their roles as spies, or soldiers, or cowboys and Indians. He could describe rivers to cross or mountains to scale, castles to storm or prisons to escape from, and his band of friends would listen wide-eyed and excited, because he was able to make each scene come alive for them.

Curiously, even though that talent nourished this new and murderous role, it was now occurring in reverse: Colin lived it first in the real world before he allowed it to unravel in his imagination. In real life it was always quick, focused, with no time to think on it other than to be sure tracks were covered, no clues left. It was only later that the replay could be watched, a movie unfolding in all of its lurid detail. There was no enjoyment in the death but there was satisfaction, which rode on a sense of relief and even a sort of evangelical righteousness.

And Rupert Brownlow had deserved every moment of his fate because he'd never shown contrition. What the court had witnessed was the hollow repetition of a scripted apology delivered by a criminal who, even in that period of supposed regret, managed to let his arrogance born of privilege ease through. Eight human lives had been lost because of his selfish joyride. It should have brought eight life sentences.

However, Brownlow's sentence, when handed down, was lenient enough to shock the public, but that too was halved when he was let out early . . . quietly. Prisons were full, the pressure on the public purse was enormous, and all the do-gooders were riding on their high horses to let people like him out. He was young, good-looking, saying all the right well-rehearsed words of remorse, with all the ticks from prison psychologists to say this was a prisoner who deserved a second chance. *Rehabilitated? My arse!* No one had made Rupert Brownlow pay anything close to the debt he owed the victims' families and friends, or indeed society itself, which shouldn't feel safe as long as the justice system kept allowing people like him out early.

Would he reoffend? Who could tell? Probably not. Most could grasp that at the heart of the crime had been teenage irresponsibility fuelled by substances. But the do-gooders could only truly understand if one of their beloved had been a victim of Rupert's casual disregard for others' lives. Only then would they understand the depth of grief, the relentless pain, the life sentence that those left behind were now living. Why did a murderer who took one life go to jail for thirty years, while another who snuffed out eight lives only grind through a few years in an easy prison?

The rage Colin had felt a dozen years previously had turned inward, provided fuel, given permission for him to take the vengeance for private pain.

'Won't be long,' the receptionist said. 'Doctor's just having to take a phone call.'

A nod, a bright smile. He distracted himself by continuing the film unfolding in his mind of the day when killing that whinger Rupert Brownlow had been the sweetest of revenges. It had all fallen into place. Brownlow had been released on a Saturday and his wealthy family had organised to have him whisked off to the seaside. The darker self had called in sick on the day of Brownlow's release, but he was owed so many days leave that they'd sounded almost pleased. It had taken a couple of days of stake-out but he didn't mind; he rather liked the fresh seaside air as he observed the comings and goings of the house, until he saw Rupert emerge alone as evening was arriving. He noticed that the newly released prisoner had buzzed his hair to change his looks and had pulled up the hood of his nondescript dark sweatshirt, beneath which he wore a beanie. Jeans completed the ensemble that allowed Rupert Brownlow to look like every other callow young man who walked around Portsmouth seafront. Brownlow had been loaned, or perhaps had rented, a small Japanese car and drove with some awareness, sticking to the speed limit. Made it easy to follow him.

The plans were never elaborate but he'd learned with experience not to be too locked in. He'd discovered that flexibility was the key: being able to respond to the situation that rarely followed a script, no matter how carefully one might plot.

The silly bugger had handed him an unexpected gift by wandering along the seafront late that evening, with no idea that he was being followed. And here on the shingle beach – a fair trot from the popular Southsea pier – made for a perfectly distant and lonely killing ground. The houses were all set back from the beach behind the tennis courts, model village and golf club. The former inmate had made it as easy as he could by being alone on an otherwise deserted beach, on a particularly windy evening in spring when the nights were still dark and cold. *Confidence is the key*, he'd told himself so many times. *Act like you're meant to be there and it might mean any observer's gaze slips over quickly.*

He approached the youngster, crunching over the shingle to announce himself before he arrived. 'Hello there. Are you all right? Forgive me for interrupting, but you looked a bit lonely and I couldn't walk past without checking that you're okay.'

'Yeah, I'm fine. Just want to be alone.'

'Right . . . right. Aren't you cold?'

Brownlow gave a low half-laugh. 'I am actually, but I just wanted some peace and quiet.'

'And it's not my intention to spoil that, but out here you're a bit exposed, lad. Can't have you catching your death, can we?' He chortled at that jest, which was purely for his own benefit.

Brownlow looked up and shrugged. 'Your fish and chips will get cold.'

Good – he'd noticed, and the wind was blowing in the right

direction to make sure he did. 'Well, you couldn't have picked a lonelier spot.'

Brownlow nodded absently.

'Here, fancy a nip?' He offered a flask. The liquor was laced with something that would help Rupert sleep.

'No, thanks. I've sworn off the booze.'

'Really? Awfully young to be making that promise.'

Brownlow gave a soft snort. 'Yeah, well, if you knew why I wasn't drinking, you'd understand.'

He'd risked sitting down, not too close to scare him off, but close enough to be friendly. He'd try again with the liquor if the moment presented itself, but he had a backup. 'Is that so? Well, I'm a good listener. My name's Peter,' he lied.

'Rupert. I'm one of the most hated in people in Britain.'

'Why would you say that?' He kept his voice light, amused, as though what his companion was saying was impossible.

'Well, you clearly don't recognise me?'

'Night is falling, young man, and I haven't even looked you square in the face yet.'

Rupert turned to look directly at him. 'Recognise me yet?'

He had shaken his head, pleased that Rupert didn't recognise him either – but then why would he, out of context? Plus, he'd taken the precaution of the hat, the glasses. 'No, but should I? You just look like a sad youngster who's lost his way. What's up?'

'Who are you?'

'I told you, Peter . . . Peter Jones. I answer phones for Lifeline, do my bit with Meals on Wheels and the like . . . I'm a community-minded person, and anyone sitting alone on a cold, windy beach as night draws in catches my attention. Here – the fish and chips are fresh and way too much for one. Want some?'

The lad shrugged. Who could resist the smell of fish and chips? Not Rupert, apparently.

'That is a lot of food,' Brownlow said as the paper was opened and the powerful smell of vinegar and salt hit them both.

'I know. My eyes are always bigger than my belly,' he said amiably. 'And the odd thing is, the moment I bought it, I got indigestion. Here, you hold the food. I need to take a pill.' He'd eased out a small bottle into which he'd put some harmless tiny sweets. 'Eat up, Rupert.'

'C'mon, they're yours, man,' Brownlow said, trying to pass it back.

'No, really, I feel a bit ill. I'll just have a nip of medicinal whiskey here to wash down my tablets,' he said, pretending to swallow a swig but barely letting any of it touch his lips. He gave a sighing sound. 'I should feel brighter in a minute or two. You have it.'

'Are you serious?'

'Yes. Maybe it will cheer you up and I can go home knowing I did my bit for the community this evening. Here, I bought a bottle of Coke too. It's yours.' He twisted the cap open.

'Really?'

'Check for yourself, untouched.' That was another thumping lie. The soft drink was fizzing with Rohypnol.

He watched Brownlow eat the food, carefully ensuring he ate all the fish that had been doused with Rohypnol-laden vinegar too. Now it was just a matter of waiting for the drug to take effect. He watched with fascinated glee as Rupert drank the Coke as well. Double whammy. Wouldn't be long now. The whiskey would have to be thrown away – a pity to waste it, but it too contained Rohypnol. He had backups for backups. That was his tidy, thoughtful way.

He'd need to kill some time before he killed Brownlow.

'Tell me why you're hated, Rupert.'

'I made a mistake behind the wheel. The mistake cost lives and

I've done my time for it but I'm not sure how to come back from the years I've spent in prison.'

'Good grief. How long were you there?'

'Nearly four years.'

Six months per death, he thought with disgust.

'I was let out before my sentence was complete,' Rupert explained, 'and I just want to get on now, but I'm down here because my family thinks the newspaper and TV reporters won't leave us alone. We have to let my early release die down a bit, wait for some other catastrophe to happen to distract people.' He'd begun to slur.

'Well, I'm not going to judge you,' he said, enjoying his lies. 'But you must give yourself some adjustment time, Rupert. Can't be easy.'

'I just feel as though everyone's watching.'

Not for much longer, his stalker thought as he watched Rupert politely hold a hand to his mouth before taking a long draught of air; well, prison hadn't removed his manners.

'Wow, that food is hitting.'

'You okay?'

'Yes, I feel suddenly tired.'

'Come on, lad. Let's get you off this beach. Did you drive here?'

'Yeah. My aunt's car.'

'Up on your feet.' He helped to hoist him upright. 'Here, give me that. We don't want you in trouble for littering the beach now that you're out of prison.'

Rupert actually laughed as the man who intended to kill him took the remains of the fish and chips. He would need to dispose of that away from here.

'I can't in all good conscience let you get behind the wheel, lad.'

'I think I'm going to be sick.'

'No, you're not. You'll be all right. Listen, let me drive you home. It's the least I can do.'

'I can cab it.'

'There aren't any, son. This isn't London. Most of them hang around the station, and on a night like tonight there won't be many, and they won't pick up someone like you who's swaying. You look drunk.'

'What's wrong with me?' he asked. 'I feel like I'm just going to fall asleep right here and now.'

'Come on, my car's just here. I'll get you delivered safely – it can be my community service for today,' he said, enjoying another private play on words. 'I hope you can remember your aunt's address?'

Careful to keep his head lowered against the CCTV cameras that looked out across the seafront, he pulled up his coat collar, the cap hiding most of his face, and helped Rupert into the car, out of the CCTV camera's shot . . . not that the car would be found in time to connect him.

Rupert mumbled the address in Southsea, but Colin was no longer listening. Now it was time for payback. He would do what the justice system had been unable to do for the families of those victims who had died senselessly because of Rupert Brownlow's behaviour. If he was honest, he didn't believe the 22-year-old was a threat any more, but did that matter to the families? The most generous of them might nod, but deep down they'd hate him – because they all remembered his smirk, his expensive legal counsel, the leniency of Judge Leland, and now the horror of knowing Brownlow was back out to pick up the threads of his privileged existence. No, the only way to make everyone feel better was to rid them of Brownlow. Rupert was fading fast and he had to stop the car a bit sooner than planned, but he'd already checked this street as a potential killing ground. Clarendon Road was a quiet stretch in a particularly subdued street that had no CCTV until it hit a particular kink and then bent around towards a roundabout which would be watched over by cameras.

He parked at the end, got Rupert out – who was fully confused and compliant by now – and toppled him into the boot, quickly gagging him. He'd probably choke on his own vomit before he could kill him, but the man didn't mind – so long as Rupert was dead within the next few minutes, the job would be done. The rope was already prepared, and he slipped the noose around the victim's neck without him even realising.

He closed the boot and checked the street. There was no one about on this frigid night and the rain was beginning too, so that would ensure people stayed under cover. Excellent. It was actually a half-decent shower. Lights were on behind drawn curtains but there was no twitch of those curtains, as far as he could tell.

This was the moment. He'd need to be quick. Opening the boot again, it took all his strength to urge and then haul Rupert out of its cradle. The youngster was already lost to most of his senses but he hoped there might be just enough consciousness left in him to feel the friction and killing power of the tarmac. He allowed Rupert to slump to the road. The other end of the rope was tied quickly to the bumper as he'd rehearsed tirelessly.

'Bye, Rupert,' he said casually, before he got into the car and drove, trying not to let the tyres squeal on the newly slicked road. It wouldn't take speed – the bump and grind of bitumen against the skull, and fragile bones breaking as the noose tightened and tightened around the neck of someone deeply drugged and fully gagged meant death was certain.

As the man who called himself Peter reached the kink in the road, he climbed quickly from the idling car, sawed at the rope with a sharp hacksaw, then carefully but swiftly headed back down the street, avoiding what might be blood and without so much as looking back at the huddle of the corpse that had been Rupert Brownlow. Turning into a side street that again had no CCTV, he found a spot to leave the car to be picked up another time.

It was as though he and that darker person parted company once the killing was done and he became himself again to walk off into the night, taking every back road towards the railway station. A soft smile creased his expression while a sense of satisfaction took over but with no pleasure attached as he made his way back to London. A good night's work on behalf of the victims of Britain's crime and the legal system that didn't punish the perpetrators.

The receptionist was calling his name. He hadn't read a word of the magazine he had open on his lap. He blinked back to the present. 'Lost to the fairies,' he admitted with his best smile, and she returned it.

'Doctor's ready. You can go through,' she said, beaming.

4

Joan Field lifted an immaculately shaped eyebrow, covering everything from a welcome to 'how do we find ourselves here?'

'Mother,' Jack said, using the affectionate nickname he reserved
for the implacable Joan, who would now field calls, people and
dramas for the forthcoming op. He kissed her cheek. She had lost
none of her matriarchal glamour – if he could term it that way.
She had to be well into her sixties and he noticed she was no
longer colouring her hair but allowing the grey to silver through
what had originally been a true blonde. She was not especially
tall, but she kept herself lean and wore simple column-like dresses
that lengthened her appearance. She was of the breed that liked
to carry beautiful handbags to match impeccable shoes. How
she kept them unscuffed and polished through a single day in
London was a marvel, but these were simply aspects to admire in
an all-round splendid person who he knew every major operation
would benefit from having on its team. There was no finer gate-
keeper than Joan.

'Wicked boy. You haven't visited in so long,' she replied in the tone of a lightly vexed parent. She risked squeezing his hand in a way that asked so much more than her next question. 'You look very fit and tanned. Some might say unfairly so.'

'Cap Ferrat,' he answered, deflecting the compliments.

'How dashing . . . a yacht, I hope?'

He grinned. 'I have a friend who moves in those circles.'

'Yes, so I hear.'

He cut her a look of mock despair.

'How are you getting along, Jack?'

'I felt pretty good this morning, Joan.' He knew what she was really asking but he'd got by this last year by being vague. He had no plan to change tack.

'But I'm guessing Martin's news didn't thrill?'

She was the only person in all of Scotland Yard, Jack was sure, who addressed everyone by their first names.

'It didn't.'

'But someone has to do it. Congratulations, by the way,' she said, beaming.

'For what?' He looked back at her, puzzled.

'Your promotion.'

'News travels fast. When did you hear?'

'The day before yesterday. You?'

'Today,' he said, looking pained.

Joan smiled indulgently. 'I'm glad Martin leaned on you. I hear there's a fourth death.'

'Joan, how do you know these things before anyone else?'

She tapped her nose as if to say she couldn't possibly reveal her source. 'I've taken some liberties.'

'Tell me.' He wandered over to the window and gazed towards Big Ben. From the European Desk he could see the famous clock and most of the landmarks of the city, but down here on the seventh floor, it was only other tower blocks that stared back at him. 'Well, at least no one will be distracted by the view,' he remarked.

'Now, now,' Joan admonished him. 'Look, we even have a newfangled coffee machine. No other operation has one.'

Jack gave an unintelligible grumble.

'No, look, Jack. Pretty little capsules.' She held up a tiny purple pyramid. 'Now everyone can be a barista.'

'You're joking.' Jack leaned in to stare at the capsule.

'I know you're a coffee snob and I told Martin we had to pander to your weakness.'

He plucked the coffee pyramid from her palm and sniffed, then shook it. 'Joan, I think you should run MI5 for your ability to gather information. Are you sure this works?'

'George Clooney thinks so.'

'What's this one?'

'Purple, for royalty − that's you, Jack, in police terms. Only the best. A combination of Central and South American arabicas offering roasted cocoa notes, I'm assured.'

'Wow.' He laughed.

'Care to try?'

'Only if you go first,' he said, with feigned trepidation.

'Back in a tick.'

He couldn't complain about their digs. Martin had been generous to accommodate them in enviable surrounds, spacious enough for a proper incident room and an office and partitions. For such a small, under-the-radar operation, it was obvious that it had serious intent. He heard curious mechanical sounds and gurgling from the back and within moments Joan returned, carrying a pair of steaming brews.

It was hot, he'd grant her that. Jack sipped. He wanted to hate it with all of his heart. 'Actually . . .'

'I know.' She grinned. 'It's not half bad, Jack. It will do.'

He nodded. He allowed himself to luxuriate in his second sip as he considered the next steps, although Joan was ahead of him on that path.

'Cam Brodie is going under cover up in Scotland so I've let him be, but Malek Khan is on his way,' she explained, ticking off notes on her pad. 'They were contacted yesterday.'

Yesterday. He gave an expression that said *I give up*. 'Sarah?'

'DS Jones is returning early from her holidays but is still a week away. Wild horses wouldn't keep her from this one. Besides, who else can manipulate the database as well as she?'

'No one.'

She briefed him on some constables. Then only one name hung between them. Jack knew he would have to say it.

'What about Kate?'

'I haven't reached out to her yet,' Joan said with caution. 'I thought it should be your call. Do you see her?'

He gave a casual shrug that he knew Joan would see through immediately. 'On paper we should run into each other frequently as we're both headquartered on the sixteenth floor. But I've been away in Australia, as you know, and then when I returned to head up the European Desk, she'd already been sent over to her new base at Heathrow. Anyway, she's doing a very good job over at Special Branch.'

'So I hear.'

'Maybe we shouldn't disturb that.'

Joan nodded. 'Maybe. Although Kate will surely feel affronted not to be asked.'

'Do you think so?'

'My big nose tells me so, especially if the old gang is back with you.'

'All right. I'll contact her.'

'Good. But do it this afternoon – she's in this building for a meeting, and then you won't have to traipse over to Heathrow.' At his open mouth, she gave him a smug look.

'What about here? When can we be set up?'

'Desks, phones, mobiles, computers . . . all that gear will start arriving in about an hour. Apparently, we have top priority. Seems your name opens doors, Jack.'

He gave a snort. 'Flattery, Joan.' He waggled a finger at her.

'I know. That grey at your temple is just splendid. You look strong again.' He knew she was finally getting around to referring to his history, to how broken he'd looked the last time she worked with him. She gave him another caring smile that reached right beneath his defences, and a hug. 'You doing all right?'

'Better, Joan. Much better.'

She didn't hesitate now, and he admired her courage. 'And have you seen her?'

He knew she was referring to Anne McEvoy, the woman he'd fallen in love with only to discover that she was Britain's modern-day female serial killer. 'I try not to. It hurts us both, to be honest.'

She nodded her understanding.

'Her little girl is probably getting on for two by now,' he added. 'I suspect they'll be taking Samantha away from her very soon, if they haven't already. I know how much she loves her.'

'Most mothers do, you know,' Joan said gently. 'And Anne McEvoy, despite her history, is probably a very good mum, given her own sad childhood.'

'She's also an incredible person, who is deeply damaged and . . .' He didn't finish. There was no point in justifying the notorious murderer. The fact that he'd fallen in love with her alter ego was irrelevant.

'Where is she now?'

'Still at Holloway.' He pulled a face of embarrassment. 'It's where, on paper, she deserves to be but I hope she'll get out of that hideous place and into a different facility. She's got her whole lonely life ahead of her behind prison doors, so . . .' He shrugged, knowing it was a pointless hope.

Joan managed to convey pity without turning her expression sympathetic. Perhaps she, more than all the others, knew how fond of Anne he'd become in his ignorance, though once he'd learned her true intent, he'd pursued her with relentlessness until he found her. He could tell that Joan understood all of this. 'I don't see her, but I keep in touch with the governor; she's very understanding. Tells me that Anne's a model prisoner. She's taken it upon herself to teach the youngsters better writing skills, among other activities, I gather. I had no idea she had a master's and PhD in criminology. She told me when we met that she'd studied business and commerce at university.'

'I suppose if she had told you, it would have been a striking talking point. Your two worlds would have been instantly closer in all the ways she would not have wanted you to appreciate.'

'I suppose. In prison she's managed to persuade a top psych to supervise her through her practical. She's working with the inmates as an in-house clinical psychologist.'

'Good grief.'

It felt powerful to surprise Joan, and he grinned. 'I know. She's set up one-on-one sessions, group sessions and special community activities that she's designed to help her patients.'

'She might as well. There's only a prison cell to look forward to.'

'Exactly.' He shrugged again.

DI Kate Carter had been working at Special Branch for the last fifteen months. The career shift had been deliberate, to take back control of her life after having nearly died on her notorious previous case; bad dreams that the Beijing-born surgeon was removing and stealing her face still chased her around some nights. But after the breakdown of her romantic relationship – the one she'd so wanted to work, with a man she admired and respected, certainly laughed with – she'd felt adrift.

It had ended in a dignified manner over a curry at their local; no shouting, no hand-wringing, no tears. A conversation had begun over a balti and ended with a foamy twist of sweet ice cream from a van doing a summer night run. As the driver had driven off, the familiar 'Greensleeves' had sounded its tinny tune into the night, taking their affections with it and haunting their frank discussion about calling it quits. Even now, seven months on, she could still shake her head in surprise at how maturely they'd arrived at the decision to part. DCI Geoff Benson had been good to her, but their important, time-demanding jobs had kept them apart too much.

Alone again, she thought, as she scattered the instant coffee granules into a mug and reached to depress the bubbling urn's handle to make another hideously ordinary cup of coffee. It would be her second today and it was only ten; had she really been here since seven? Much too eager!

'Kate?'

'Yeah, hi.' She swung around to see one of her junior colleagues. 'Won't be a mo.'

'Someone in reception for you.'

'Who is it?' She frowned. She had no appointments today.

'No idea, sorry.'

She sighed and poured the steaming black liquid down the sink. Didn't need the caffeine anyway. Kate made her way across the seventeenth floor, threading her path around desks that were now occupied, with phones ringing and computers whirring. She preferred it here at Scotland Yard than her new base at London Heathrow, had even thought about quitting when they'd asked her to transfer there, but she hadn't . . . Instead she'd obediently moved because even she could see that what she needed now was stability. Trips back to Scotland Yard were treats and she would be here for a couple of days. She was looking forward to them.

She fielded the nods and wearied morning greetings from her Special Branch colleagues but nearly stopped in her tracks when she saw who her visitor was. She kept walking, though, trying not to show anything more than a bright smile. Inwardly, she was appalled at how he could still unnerve her normally tight composure.

'Morning, K—, er, DI—' The receptionist didn't finish because Kate spoke over her.

'Jack.'

'Hello, Kate.'

She hadn't heard that voice in too long.

He stepped forward and made it tough by kissing her cheek and then made it even worse by kissing the other. 'You look fabulous as always.'

She found a smile in spite of the way he managed to make her insides clench. 'You look tanned.'

'The mark of the Australian sunshine lingers . . . I also had a weekend recently on the French Riviera – Cap Ferrat.' He paused and refocused on Kate. 'Time for a coffee?'

'Here?' She gestured over her shoulder, surprised.

Jack grimaced. 'No, but I promise not to keep you long.'

'I'll grab my bag,' she said, moving in a slight blur. She knew all her body language was suddenly awkward and far too brisk.

'Enjoy your coffee,' the receptionist said, beaming at Jack. *Hot!* she mouthed to Kate, who returned a look of deep exasperation.

★

Kate would never walk this far for a coffee, but Jack insisted and now, seated at a small table by the window, he looked like a man who had just found nirvana.

'Not bad,' he sighed after his first sip.

'I don't get it.' She smiled.

'I know. You're part of the heathen pack that would accept coffee that looks like a tequila sunrise, served in an Irish whiskey glass.'

'So why are you visiting this heathen?' she asked, liking how the mellow quality of his voice could put her at ease.

'I need you.'

She breathed out, enjoying his directness and also how it landed; it made her feel special on a morning when she couldn't imagine anything more perfect being said to her by this man in particular. 'Tell me, Jack.' She pushed her hair behind her ears, smelling the Moroccan oil that she'd lightly run through to stop it frizzing.

He did, quietly spilling everything he knew to date and giving her a sense of dread that was echoed in his expression. 'The Brownlow death convinced me that the Super's onto something.'

'And we've got to keep a low profile?'

He grinned gently. 'So . . . you're in?'

'I can hardly say no when you spoil a girl with expensive coffee.'

'Let me woo you more properly, then. Dinner?'

'Woo?' She tried to make it light, teasing. It didn't come out that way and she saw his spirited expression darken. Kate knew she needed to reverse, couldn't have Jack worried that she still had feelings. 'I don't need wooing. I enjoy what I've been doing at Special Branch.'

He nodded. 'I know, but I need your experience and clarity.'

'I suspect the Chief views you the same way,' she said, enjoying the compliment from him but not allowing her pleasure to show too brightly.

He sighed. 'Yes. I was in the midst of a big European op, but Martin wouldn't let me see it through. He needs all his best people on this.'

'I trust him as you do, and none of this sounds good – not that I care much about the victims, but it means there's another killer out there.'

He drained his coffee and looked up expectantly. 'So that's a yes?'

'To dinner? Anytime, no rush. To your new op?' She knew this should be a no because it only meant heartache to be working alongside him, but she shrugged. 'Definitely. I'll have to clear my desk – it will probably take me today to hand over to DCI—'

'Hand over to your team. But don't worry about the DCI – I can fix that. It's Jeffries, isn't it?'

She nodded with a questioning frown.

'I'm Detective Superintendent as of yesterday, apparently.'

'Wow, Jack. Congrats. You don't look thrilled.'

'I just don't know if it's what I want.'

'Bloody hell. Of course you do. We need people like you in charge. Everyone wants to work for you . . . you're a good manager of people and you get results. Jeffries is a lot of bluster and he doesn't listen to what his team wants or needs.'

He grinned. 'Heathrow getting you down?'

'I hate it.'

'Well, from this moment you are now officially based here on the seventh floor. Joan's waiting for you with a new coffee machine and a sense of carte blanche that we can have whatever we need. They don't want this blowing up in the media.'

She nodded. 'All the old gang?'

'You, me, Malek. Cam's undercover. But Sarah's rushing back from Jordan.'

'Of course she is. Everyone else goes to the French Riviera but Sarah's probably in her anorak right now stomping around Petra.'

'Don't be mean. I was sorry to hear about you and Geoff, by the way. I thought you two were a brilliant pairing because you were such opposites.'

She grinned sadly. 'You're right about opposites. Geoff wanted a family.'

'And you don't?'

'Well, it's not that. Firstly, I think I'd be rubbish at motherhood, but more to the point, I was honest about my career aspirations. Geoff wanted family but didn't plan on compromising his work to do so . . . and I was fearful that all the responsibility would have settled on my shoulders.'

'To address the first, you doubt yourself too much. It's like learning to drive, according to my sister – very scary but the only way is taking that wheel.'

She nodded, appreciating the sentiment. 'But one can stop driving. One can enjoy being driven by others or take public transport. Children . . . very frightening business.'

He chuckled. 'As for careers, I understand – Geoff's senior and is only going to become more senior, because he's a seriously good policeman.'

'And I didn't want to ruin his trajectory or dreams by being that harried wife who demanded he be home to read the bedtime story. I also worried that I might not be happy always being the person to tuck the children in. I remain genuinely suspicious that motherhood won't be enough for me, but admitting that in the open is to welcome criticism. I want to be a good mum, if I do have children . . . and I don't want to blame them for me not realising my potential and all that stuff women wrestle with today. I wasn't sensing a similar compromise in Geoff.'

'No rush,' Jack said and she was grateful for his neutrality on this point.

She revealed her pressing fear though, because if not to Jack, then who? She had no best girlfriends to unravel this sort of emotional knot with. What was wrong with her to not have a trustworthy pal? She smiled to herself though, realising she did have someone – him. 'I'm thirty-two. Time is ticking.'

'He loved you with every ounce,' Jack said, and it struck Kate that he said this hesitantly, as though he knew he was taking a risk airing the notion. But he and Geoff were the best of friends. Poor Jack . . . bestie to both of them and probably why he had avoided these friends in recent times.

'I do know that, I promise.' She shook her head. 'I really worried that I was going to hurt him.'

'You did.'

'It could have been worse if it was complicated by marriage, family, pets, property.'

'And that's wholly true. Maybe it's all of that responsibility that makes you reluctant.'

She looked at him in query.

'Looking up and realising you've followed tradition and that the career isn't everything that motivates you.'

She didn't know what to say to that, so she changed the subject. 'So . . . Cap Ferrat, Jack? Know a few millionaires, do you?'

'A few.' He grinned.

She knew he wasn't going to give her more information, but she suspected a woman was involved somewhere. There always was with Jack.

5

The oncologist, Dr Monkhouse, looked back at Colin with a baleful expression. No doubt this was the default arrangement of his features when delivering bad news, Colin thought. 'We did prepare for this,' the clinician said, using his soothing voice.

The man nodded. 'Yes, we did,' he agreed, sounding resigned as he watched Monkhouse switch off the lightbox that had lit the CT scan of his body under attack.

'Bladder cancer is a tricky foe. You can't test for it, you can't take much precaution against it . . . other than the obvious of eating, living healthily and not smoking.'

'Right.'

'It's not choosy, although having said that, it does seem to prefer men.'

He nodded. 'So I gather.'

'I know you've come to me for a second opinion, and I can't help but wonder why you didn't act upon the diagnosis when the early signs were detected?'

He wanted to tell the oncologist to mind his own business;

instead he smiled in a guarded way. 'There was some emotional trauma in my life that prevented me from taking action when I first noticed the blood in my urine. The fact is, we can't go backwards.'

'No, that's true. I mention it only because treatment can be effective in those early stages, especially with urothelial carcinoma. I presume this has all been explained?'

'Thank you, yes. I have a full understanding of my ailment.'

'Good.' The doctor nodded, returning to his seat behind his desk where he sat in front of an impressive array of framed certificates.

An old-fashioned clock ticked time away and his patient was sure his heartbeat had synchronised with the clock to remind him that his life's end was likely in sight . . . that he might even count it in months – even weeks – rather than years. He would need to escalate his plans, take as many as he could before he too checked out. 'And now?' he asked. 'I mean, is there a next step?'

Monkhouse attempted a smile. It didn't quite work. 'There's always a next step. You've had the urogram and retrograde pyelogram; next I'd like you to have an MRI together with a bone scan and a chest X-ray. I want to know exactly what we're dealing with here.'

'Gosh, and there I was thinking it was serious.'

The oncologist's gaze flashed up from his file.

'Gallows humour.' He shrugged.

Monkhouse sucked his lips. 'Oh well, sometimes that helps. I'm ordering all of this so we can get a proper fix on the stage you're at.'

He nodded. 'Whether it's spread, you mean?'

'I do. Ignorance is not bliss in my profession. Armed appropriately, we can use our weapons better,' he said. 'So let's get all of that completed as a matter of urgency. The receptionist will make all the necessary appointments for you.' He held up a finger to stop the patient leaving as he buzzed through. His nurse's voice answered. 'Er, yes, Beth, would you organise . . .' Colin couldn't be bothered to listen. Tuning out the raft of tests being ordered, he scanned the ordered room; he appreciated that it was hugged by warm timbers and leather-covered books.

The doctor returned his gaze to the patient he had no idea was a serial murderer. 'So, I'd like to see you in . . . let's say four weeks, and we'll formulate how we go forward with treatment?' His patient nodded. 'In the meantime, I would urge you to refrain from alcohol and any recreational drugs. You look strong for your age.'

'I exercise daily, a brisk few miles, do weights twice a week and some yoga most mornings.'

'Well, I wish more of my patients would keep up their end of the bargain. The seesaw is always unfairly weighted at the medical team that is supposed to perform miracles.'

'I'm not anticipating a miracle, Doctor Monkhouse. I'm simply keen to know how long I have.'

The oncologist gave a nod. 'I'm sorry, that really wasn't directed at you. I believe you're in excellent shape to fight alongside the medics.'

'Good. Thank you, Doctor. See you in a month, then.'

Colin stepped out onto one of the most iconic streets of London and into a cool spring day, glad that he'd taken the precaution of an extra layer beneath his raincoat. It would surely rain today but he might get home before the cloudburst. Opulent Harley Street was synonymous with top medical care; even Florence Nightingale had opened up her practice in the late nineteenth century in one of the houses in this delicious sweep of Georgian terraces.

All this private care was costing him a mint, but what did it matter in the greater scheme of his life? He had no one to leave it to, no family left to mourn him. So using it to prolong his ability to continue his important work felt worthy. Ensuring criminals paid their dues, while answering the need to empty prisons; his was a neat solution to a modern dilemma. Justice. If he could believe that Britain would rally for more justice in the system, then he would let go and let the cancer have him. There was no joy in life left anyway. Not even this sparkly spring day could make him smile within. He couldn't remember the last time his mouth had lifted with genuine pleasure . . . he would have to dig back many years to a time when smiling had been as natural for him as breathing.

Even so, his mind was occupied with whether the police had made any connections yet. Doubtful. While Brownlow's release and subsequent death would likely get a fair run in the media, Peggy Markham's death had been moved over swiftly, as had Toomey's, and that hideous wife-bashing professor barely rated a mention. The others hadn't yet been discovered — there had been a year or more between some of them — or hadn't made the national news reports. But he wasn't so naive as to believe no one had noticed.

Well, he couldn't worry about that now. He'd set his path and he was on a deadline. He had no intention of taking his foot off the accelerator now; who knew when his strength would fail him or the pain would overwhelm him, or when he might simply lack the ability to move around with such ease?

He walked in the direction of Euston Road. He'd come by Underground to Harley Street, but he didn't feel like a subterranean journey home. Instead he'd take the bus and watch London go by. It would take nearly half as long again, but there were no changes requiring a dash through the crush of people to another platform. He could wait for the number 29 bus that came on the hour, and then it would be a full hour between Warren Street and Wood Green stations. Perfect time to think and reflect on who might be next on the long list of people who deserved his attention.

Given how cool the day was turning after a promising start, he was glad to see his bus lumbering up Euston Road. He was pleased it was a double-decker, as they seemed to be phasing in those articulated single-deckers on this route. Something about the lovely London double-deckers helped him to keep memories alive. He nodded for a middle-aged couple to go first and then held back again, bowing politely as a woman using a walking stick tried to hurry.

'Don't rush,' he said, 'I won't let it leave without you.' He winked.

'Thank you, young man,' she said and they both laughed. She had a couple of decades on him for sure, but he was still middle-aged.

He stepped on board and used the newfangled Oyster card, smiled at the driver and found himself a window seat. Excellent. He tucked himself tight against the wall so he wouldn't have to shift for a fellow passenger. The seat beside him was soon filled by a wide-hipped woman carrying two bags of groceries. He smiled in greeting and then looked away, satisfied now that he could get lost in his thoughts.

Reaching beneath his coat to the inside pocket, he pulled out a list he'd been given the previous month. The list was adjusted regularly, making sure it was across all the new paroles and changed sentences. It was time to get a new one, now that life was moving towards May. The bulbs in his garden were heralding spring's arrival, even if the temperature was yet to acknowledge it. He stared at the list that was kept to ten; as one disappeared in any calendar month, he replaced it. Right now, the fifth name – Davey Robbins – should be a priority. Rupert Brownlow would be at a funeral parlour by now, as Colin was sure the pathology team and the coroner were finished with him. He looked up briefly as they lurched to a halt and he saw someone carrying a bunch of sunny daffodils down Camden Street. His wife had loved daffodils and his garden had drifts of them. He thought, without regret, of those Brownlow had left behind; at last Rupert's family could join the families of his victims in a lifetime of grief.

He looked down at the list again. Davey Robbins. He must be twenty-three; strong, he guessed, after time in prison. Davey hadn't done it tough, though. His barrister had argued for rehabilitation, suggesting he'd been coerced by the older and more threatening Don Patchett to rape that beautiful young woman. He remembered it clearly: Davey intermittently crying, admitting that his uncle had threatened him with violence, had said his fingers would be cut off if they didn't do this.

'He has learning difficulties, my lady; he was vulnerable and in awe of his elder who used coercion through fear. He was a victim . . .' and all the other tried and true plaintive cries of defence counsel.

Learning difficulties? My arse, he thought. Davey was a streetwise kid who had grown into a rat-cunning young adult and while, yes, his thug of an uncle had led the nephew from petty thieving to rape and a murder, it was obvious from the trial that Robbins possessed a sort of perky arrogance and knew exactly how to take a brief from his defence team.

Eight months ago, when Davey Robbins had been released from Wakefield Prison to a halfway house for sex offenders in Yorkshire after serving only two years, he'd found his way onto Colin's death list quickly. Research was well advanced: Davey was driven to and from a local farm where, with a group of Polish seasonal workers, he picked vegetables.

His fellow pickers lived in caravans nearby, but Davey was returned each afternoon to the house that accommodated other young sex offenders whom authorities believed could be rehabilitated and released. These men were warm, well fed, allowed plenty of TV, even game consoles. They had table tennis and were allowed to cycle to a small grocer just over a kilometre away. They had access to computers and, according to his research, each was being tutored in something that could help them 'on the outside'. He got to live again – to reinvent himself if he followed the rules. His victims, in the meantime, no longer had that wonderful life they once had.

His dark friend brimming in his mind, he'd caught the train north and sleuthed out the muddy farm on the hilly slopes of Yorkshire where Davey now moved among more sheep than he did people in his daily grind. Through binoculars he'd picked out Davey in his beanie and overalls – easily the youngest and skinniest, but the lad looked healthy. He would have to factor that in to whatever trap he was going to lay to kill him, for Amy and for her grieving family.

Heading towards Finsbury Park, the bus trundled up the slope of Camden Road before forking into Parkhurst Road, where the looming building of the famous women's prison cast its shadow. He stared out as they passed the Holloway Prison, which had struck so much fear into women through the decades. Horrible place. He thought about some of its famous serial murder inmates of recent decades: Maxine Carr had been here briefly, Myra Hindley, Rose West . . . and who could forget Anne McEvoy?

He was getting distracted, he realised. *Focus on the list.* Davey Robbins needed attending to. Forgiveness was not appropriate, and rehabilitation was offensive, given the lad had all his faculties. He might not have intended to kill that girl's grandmother, but he certainly intended to rape young Amy once he'd broken into her home – and the jury had seen through him. Davey thought he'd won, though. Just five years' prison, assured by his defence that he'd be likely out in three into the arms of carers, but he was out in eighteen months, albeit into the system that made mockery of justice. Couldn't everyone see the heinousness in how the system worked?

He was Justice. And he would bring justice to Amy and to her grandmother. Davey's days were now numbered; he could count

them on one hand. As the bus rumbled towards Manor House
Station in North London, he made the final decision he'd been
wavering over: Wednesday next week would be when Davey
Robbins took his final breath . . . and another family could feel
a sense of relief.

6

Few people in and around Hastings knew much about Bernie Beaton. None who looked at the slightly dishevelled little man could know that he'd once been one of Britain's wealthiest music magnates, known simply as 'Bard', who used to pay more for a haircut than his fortnightly food bill of today. But his world had imploded with the arrival of the digital revolution in his playground, and given Bernie had not responded swiftly enough, it had only taken a few years for the fall. Coupled with the fact that he played hard and overgenerously with property, in casinos, in nightclubs, with his car dealers and his drug dealers, this sophisticate had once had the freedom of the city's clubs and hotspots; restaurants could always find a table for him, and his jet-setting lifestyle was fodder for cheap gossip magazines. Now he lived in a tiny flat on the south coast, designed for old, needy residents. It was hardly flash, given this was sheltered housing, but it was a roof over his head and a more than reasonable one at that.

Today, Bernie's schizophrenia from chemical abuse was under control with regular medication in the right dose, and he felt lucky to call himself a recovered druggie and alcoholic. Those twin towers of addiction had dominated his 1990s and by 2003 he had been wandering the streets, sleeping rough for two years straight. He'd finally awoken, pushing through the fog of his strange life, to find himself shivering and sweating, screaming for help in the addiction unit of the Whittington. It had taken another sixteen months but with all the right help and a kindly nurse referring him to a specific charity, Bernie had moved into his Beaufort Court flat. A long way from London, it was provided by the local council as part of a special program for recovering addicts, far from the glitzy, and sometimes ugly, life-style he'd once led.

These days Bernie moved around his two small rooms and could admit to feeling at peace with his world. He led a group of recovering addicts in a weekly meeting at a local commun-ity hall, he called bingo on a Thursday morning for the local pensioners, and he had a Monday slot on community radio doing talkback about everything from the price of fish and chips to whether or not Hastings would get a faster train service through to London. Now and then on a weekend evening, he could be called upon to do a turn as MC for small bands performing locally. If really pressed, Bernie had a good set of tonsils and would join in some rousing karaoke at his local pub. But that was rare. For the most part Bernie was a shadow of the man he'd once been: gaunt, with a stubbled chin most of the time, known for his orange beanie and the MCC scarlet and yellow tie he wore as a belt to hold up patched jeans, but also for his good heart towards the addicts he was helping to rescue along with himself.

Bernie had few memories of the time when he would have given a limb for a hit of something that could make him forget all he'd lost. The schizophrenia and panic attacks fed into the fog

of those years, of him mostly out of control, often engaged in
rants towards anyone who might listen and usually people shying
away. The streets of North London had become dangerous for
him too, and he'd had to learn how to become invisible, which
he achieved effectively by casting off his impeccably tailored
Savile Row suits to wear a drab ensemble from Oxfam, including second-hand shoes, pawning the few items of jewellery he'd
hidden, letting his hair grow wild and, above all, not showering
often. The resulting shabbiness and overpowering smell meant
most people gave him the wide berth he wanted, even the louts
who went looking for someone to pick on.

There was one memory, though, that no hit of heroin could
shake out of his mind. This vivid recollection had stuck with
him despite the fact that his misted mind mostly forgot what it
had seen. It was the memory of a woman. He knew her, had
used her extremely high-priced services once or twice in his
heyday and she hadn't let him down . . . he had certainly got
what he paid for. Peggy Markham's girls were curated with
astute care and thought for her special clients. Madam Peggy
had few enemies, in his opinion, and so it was with confusion
and horror that he had watched this woman – who had wealth
that should have kept her safe – being propped up against a tree,
wide-eyed and terrified, as a man brazenly plunged a needle
into her neck. The stranger had not even waited to check on his
deed; he had simply walked away, confident in his kill, melting
into the wintry night.

It was Bernie who had checked on her, using his remaining
matches to illuminate the familiar features, which held some of
the grimacing quality of her final moment as the drug had forced
her heart to stop beating. Bernie knew better than to touch her,
or the syringe still stuck in her neck, around which oozed a
pinprick of her blood. He had retreated to his safe place to watch

the commotion that ensued the following morning when the stiff cadaver of one of Britain's wealthy criminals was found sprawled in Finsbury Park.

The remains of his withered conscience had got the better of him, and two nights later he'd found himself shambling into Hornsey Police Station, when he knew there'd be fewer people around, especially police people.

He waited patiently while two officers finished a conversation, from which he gathered that the night shift had just come on duty, as he'd hoped. Bernie recognised the detective who was speaking to the reception officer, whose name tag read 'Phil'. He glanced at the clock on the wall, which was showing seven minutes past ten; his timing was perfect.

'Crime reports all checked,' the detective said, 'and I've just put the phone down on the custody officer – no prisoners of interest to us. So we're off to Tottenham then, Phil.'

Bernie cleared his throat and they glanced his way. Phil gave him the once over. Bernie was well aware that with his unruly look he was the polar opposite of the fellow behind the counter in his crisply pressed, blue, pinstriped shirt with the Met logo sewn on the left breast.

'How can I help you, sir?' Phil said. The words were polite, but the tone sounded ever so slightly mocking.

Bernie was used to it and he decided to be direct. 'I wish to report a murder.'

'Murder, is it?' The reception officer whistled as he tried unsuccessfully not to grin at the detective.

'Blimey. Bernie Beaton, what brings you here? You're normally asleep by now, aren't you? I'm Detective Sergeant Coombs, in case you don't recall.'

'Thank you.' Bernie said, ignoring the sarcasm. 'I'd like to make a witness statement, please.' He was, by nature, helplessly polite, but he was making sure he observed all his best manners so they might take him seriously. He owed it to Peggy.

Coombs grinned. 'Have you taken your meds, Bernie?' he asked loudly.

Bernie was used to this, not just the increased volume as though he were deaf, but the sarcasm too. Most of the police considered him one of the crazies . . . and if he was honest, he couldn't blame them. 'I have.'

'When was the last pill you took, Bernie?' Phil asked, catching on.

'This morning.'

'And before that?'

'Yesterday.'

'Good. And you wish to report a murder?'

'I do. I saw it happen two nights ago in Finsbury Park.'

Phil sighed. 'Who did you witness being killed?'

They knew damn well who had been found. 'Peggy Markham,' he said simply. 'I saw it happen.'

Now he had their attention. DS Coombs turned back. 'Bernie, are you sure, mate, or are you just amusing yourself with that imagination of yours? We're on the nightshift here and always stretched. I'm about to head to Tottenham.'

His colleague chimed in. 'We cover the whole district from here, Mr Beaton. The whole of the boroughs of Haringey and Enfield. A big area, in other words.'

Bernie nodded. 'I understand. I won't take up too much time. I just wish to do my civic duty and give a statement, that's all.'

'All right, Phil.' The detective nodded at his colleague, but Bernie didn't miss the wink. 'Something for Lisa, I reckon.' He also wasn't deaf. 'This should liven her evening up,' Detective Coombs murmured. He turned back to Bernie. 'You have ten minutes.'

'I won't even need that much,' he admitted.

Phil shrugged, picked up the phone receiver and dialled an extension. 'Ah, DC Farrow, we have a witness statement to be taken.' There was a pause. 'Yes, Bernard Beaton. No, I know, but John said you should . . . ten minutes and then Tottenham. Yes.' He put down the phone and cut Bernie a smile that didn't feel at all welcoming. 'She'll be right out.'

'Thank you.' He shuffled away from the counter.

'Mr Beaton?' She came out of a side door, surprising him, but then he noted that his appearance took her by surprise too. He watched her slide a look to the snickering men behind the counter. 'I'm DC Lisa Farrow. Would you follow me, please?'

Bernie hoped she was older than she looked, which to him was about seventeen. Clearly they weren't taking him seriously, or the DS would have listened to his story. Even so, he dutifully followed DC Farrow into a small interview room. As soon as they were seated, she was back up on her feet and reaching to open the door. 'Excuse me,' she said, managing to look horrified and apologetic at once.

'It's all right, I'm used to it,' he said and saw her surprise deepen at hearing his cultured voice. 'I sleep rough, and baths are hard to come by,' he said, telling a small lie to cover his embarrassment and the real reason he didn't bathe often.

Sympathy chased away her initial disgust. 'Can I get you a hot drink, Mr Beaton?'

He hadn't been shown such a kind gesture in a long while. 'I was told there was no time,' he replied, uncertain.

'Always time for a quick cuppa.' She smiled warmly.

'Thank you, DC Farrow. Tea would be grand.'

She blinked, surprised again by his polite manner.

'Back in a tick.' She disappeared for a couple of minutes, returning with a steaming plastic throwaway beaker of strong, dark tea. 'Careful, don't burn yourself,' she said, pointing towards the double layer of plastic.

'It's fine,' he said, sipping and giving a sigh of pleasure.

'So, Mr Beaton, you say you witnessed a murder?'

'I did.'

'All right. Why don't you tell me everything you remember?'

Bernie proceeded to recall the detail that was still imprinted like a short film in his memory. She made careful notes, nodding with encouragement. When he had nothing more to say and had swallowed the rest of his tea, she looked up, frowning.

'Mr Beaton, this is a powerful claim. Are you sure? I mean, how can you prove—'

There was a sharp rap at the open door and they turned to see DS Coombs looking agitated. 'Pardon me,' he had the grace to say. 'I'm sorry to interrupt, but we've just got a suspected rape victim over at Edmonton. There's only us, Bernie, who can respond. I'm sorry, we have to go. Come on, Lisa, shake a leg, eh?' He nodded his head towards the hallway.

DC Farrow looked apologetically at Bernie. 'Okay, Sarge. Thank you again, Mr Beaton. If we need more—'

Coombs pointed a thumb behind his shoulder in an impatient gesture. 'Yeah, we know where to find you, Bernie. Thanks for stopping by. Find your way out, matey?'

DC Lisa Farrow watched the curious tramp as he shuffled out of Hornsey Police Station.

Behind her, Coombs smiled. 'And how did that go?'

'Actually, he sounded sincere. I believed him. Is there really a rape?'

He nodded. 'Apparently – we'll find out more shortly. No rush, though. The victim is in hospital. We're going over there now.'

Her shoulders slumped slightly with exasperation. 'I hadn't finished, Sarge. What about the witness statement?'

'Look, love, I've known that fellow for years. He's a known drunk and a schizophrenic. Even if he's on his meds, which he often isn't, then he's blurring their effects with whatever hallucinogens he can get his hands on. Used to be LSD but more recently he's had to settle for ketamine – stolen from vet surgeries and sold on the street cheaply enough. Were his pupils dilated, did you notice?'

She shook her head. 'I don't believe so.'

'Well, even so, let me assure you that Bernie believes aliens from another planet are hunting him, and he "feels colours" sometimes,' DS Coombs said, gesturing inverted commas in the air. 'He is paranoid a lot of the time and suffers panic attacks. You can't rely on him, luv. He's read the headlines and they've sunk in to his addled mind.'

She didn't look amused. 'You're saying he's not a reliable witness, Sarge.'

He grinned at the gentle sarcasm. 'That is indeed what I'm saying, DC Farrow. Leave your notes with Phil at the desk. He'll put them in the file. I doubt they'll ever be read, let alone relied upon. But you've done your bit.'

'Right, Sarge.'

'Bet you feel like taking a bath now, eh?' He winked.

'Not really; felt a bit sorry for the old guy.'

'Okay, well, we leave in two minutes. Make sure that interview room is sprayed with air freshener.'

Phil tossed her a can with a wry grin.

As they departed for the hospital, the station doors groaned open and a man wearing an Arsenal sweatshirt arrived, a crying child in tow. She was in a tiny version of the same hoodie.

'Oh dear. What's happened?' Phil asked kindly, giving the weeping girl a sympathetic smile. 'Very late for you to be out, little one.'

'Missing dog,' the father said, picking up his daughter. 'Her name's Trixie . . . er, the dog, that is.'

'Trixie, eh? And what's your name?' he said to the girl, who was staring at him through red but now wide eyes. The reception officer reached beneath the desk and retrieved a small basket of lollipops. 'Why don't you take one of these and tell me everything?'

Bernie Beaton was forgotten within moments, and his witness report was dutifully yet haphazardly filed as handwritten notes. The ripe smell of his visit was also forgotten, courtesy of a determined spray of lavender-scented air freshener.

7

Jack leaned against the desk with his tie loosened. It was cool in the office, but the heaters were either already off for spring or dodgy on this floor. He would have preferred to have his jacket on, but he wanted to give the impression of getting down to business – that he was rolling up his sleeves and he too would be getting elbow deep in this operation rather than simply being a chieftain. He scanned the room where his team had assembled for the first official day of Operation Mirror; the Met's book of names for operations had randomly assigned them yet another vague op name. Jack, long used to the bizarre titles that bore no relation to the crimes being investigated, was comfortable to be working with this one, although, honestly, he'd be happy to call it Operation Doing-Us-All-A-Favour or Operation Who-Cares.

The familiar faces gave him a boost of confidence, while the few new faces were looking back at him eagerly; he would need to say all the right stuff to settle the first-day nerves. He smiled. 'Morning, everyone.'

'Morning, sir' was spoken in a chorus.

'I see you've all made use of our clever little machine in the kitchen.' He got a round of cheers in return. 'We have Joan to thank for that blessing,' he said, using this to introduce her. She waved away his comment as he slid her a broad smile. 'Joan is going to keep us all on the straight and narrow, so please keep her in the loop about your movements. "Ask Joan first" is the best piece of advice I can give you.'

'Hello again, everyone,' she said, before turning towards reception. 'I'll be here. Pay your dues into the swear tin, keep the kitchen tidy and we'll all get along.'

Jack chuckled as she departed. 'Okay. So, welcome to Operation Mirror. For those who haven't met me previously, I'm Detective Superintendent Jack Hawksworth and I've been appointed to spearhead this new op, which is going to do its utmost to fly at speed but as low as we possibly can. We're a small group and that's deliberate; we've been pulled together quietly and quickly to test whether a trio of deaths from our criminal underworld have any relation to each other.'

He pushed away from the desk so he could move freely as he warmed to this important initial briefing. 'Our task is to either disprove any correlation or to find evidence that links these deaths – and if we can find it, then I suspect we have a serial killer on our hands.' He paused, letting his gaze land on each of them for impact. The younger members of the team sat notice-ably straighter. 'But' — he held up a finger — 'to begin with, our remit is to gather information. We've been entrusted to see if there are any other deaths connected to the criminal underworld that have passed without raising any sort of flag within the Met.'

'That's broad, sir?' Malek said, turning it into a question.

Jack was pleased that the more experienced detective was making the query. 'You're right, Mal. Criminals who kill other criminals are usually either efficient for expediency, or they're messy to send a message. What they aren't is elaborate or bizarre, and you'll know what I mean when we work through the examples that have brought us together. What we're looking for is some commonality, no matter how small – a sort of invisible current flowing through them all . . . if there is one.'

Jack had been walking and talking. Now he halted to face them. 'You've all been selected because we trust your resourcefulness, diligence and especially your discretion. We tread lightly wherever we go. Please understand this: we are not pointing fingers at other police officers for their work on past cases. We're after cooperation at every turn. However, if something's been overlooked or people have been sloppy, this group of smart people have to find it and note it – within these walls only. If there is someone out there killing and thinking they're getting away with it, Operation Mirror is now underway. Our work, if we can prove there are links, will ultimately set off the hunt for that person or persons. But we're not about to broadcast it.'

'Why, sir? Wouldn't the media be a help?' One brave newcomer, a PC, was finding her feet.

'The media can be a brilliant help, but we have to be strategic about what we make public and when. To simply let people know that we might be hunting another serial killer in Britain will potentially cause unrest. And—'

'Only in criminal circles, surely?' the PC wondered. He liked her courage to interrupt him with another question while he was answering the first.

'Yes, you're undoubtedly right, since this killer would be targeting only criminals, but we don't want to create grisly interest that becomes addictive and thus unhelpful. All we'll do is drive the perpetrator and their accomplices, if there are any, into hiding. Right now, if there is a single killer, they are operating under the presumption that the deaths are not drawing attention, or they could be wrongly believing that no one particularly cares about a group of crims getting their comeuppance.' He let that remark sit among them for a couple of heartbeats, so they were in no doubt of his intention.

Jack grinned again. 'I am reassured to see so many of our old team reunited. Thank you for making yourselves available.' Malek and Kate nodded back. 'Welcome to the new troop of constables we've pulled in. We're pleased to have you here and you are not to feel reluctant to ask questions. If you're thinking it, someone else surely is. What's more, we've got some experienced officers working here – DI Kate Carter and DI Malek Khan, who has returned from an op in Europe . . . serious thanks for coming back, Malek.' Khan gave him a thumbs up. 'We're awaiting the final member of our team, DS Sarah Jones, who should be with us later this week. Please introduce yourselves, and convey your strengths and background to each other. No thought is a bad one, so share it; the more we talk, the better informed we all are. Don't ever be afraid to chat to me or any of the senior officers about even the smallest matter in connection with the cases we're about to go through together. We're not infallible and this is to be a tight team that looks out for each other, so share your ideas, expand on your thoughts. There's a file for everyone at the end of this initial meeting. Study it. Familiarise yourself with every detail of each case. I've promised our superiors that we'll have some answers within a week or so.'

There were a couple of gasps and he held up a hand, with mock guilt.

'I know that's not much time, but we're going to work hard, fast, smart – all of us. Now, I'm going to hand over to Kate, who has come over from her important role at Special Branch to help us. Kate and I have worked on two major investigations together and I trust her judgement implicitly as my next-in-command, so please help her in every way. I've asked her to walk us through what we know so far. Kate?'

'Thanks, sir.' She stood and joined Jack at the front of the room.

At Jack's introduction, a feeling of comfort swept over Kate. For the first time in a year or so, she felt like she belonged. This building, even this room, the familiar colleagues, a killer potentially on the loose, the hunt . . . and *him*, of course. Jack standing nearby, encouraging her. Most, she guessed, would see this situation as either dangerous or exciting – certainly thrilling – but to Kate it was akin to a hot bath. It calmed her to know her place, her role; she felt confident as DI Kate Carter. It was the other, less confident Kate Carter – who was deeply and helplessly attracted to Hawksworth – who struggled . . . the one who had a string of dates that led nowhere and one broken relationship with the brilliant Geoff Benson.

Geoff was kind, funny and generous, and he understood her prickly manner, but the problem she couldn't allude to with Geoff, of course, was Jack Hawksworth, his best friend – the one she needed to entirely rule out as a prospect. For a long time she'd felt safe and in control of the unrequited romantic affection she had felt for Jack since they met. He wanted friendship and to be reliable colleagues and so did she, of course, but she hated how he unintentionally weakened her. His presence produced an electricity around her. Even so, she was older and wiser now; definitely more capable of holding her emotions tight. So long as Jack didn't show her any sympathy or special attention, she was going to enjoy working alongside one of her favourite people in the world and would not allow it to tip into that more destructive feeling that could derail her.

That was the firm promise she'd made to herself in the bathroom this morning as she readied for day one of Operation Mirror. She'd chosen her clothes carefully: a plain, elegant pencil skirt for the first day so she achieved a feminine appearance, but muted in charcoal grey, with a simple white shirt and lighter mercury-grey cardigan. Marks & Spencer's latest cashmere range was exxy but fantastic. She was planning to steadily invest in each colour, starting with the neutrals. Barely any make-up – just a tinted moisturiser, a dust of blush and a soft sweep of natural-coloured lipstick – and her dark golden hair in a ponytail. Neat and professional.

She gave a sympathetic, slightly crooked grin and cast a look Jack's way, where he'd taken a seat on a nearby desk. At his encouraging nod she began, delighted that he'd given her this task. He could have kept it for himself, could have been the big guy in the room, but this was typical Jack – he managed his team with a skilled hand and a heightened awareness of what they needed. After a year of hating her world, she needed this.

'Morning, everyone, and welcome. I've spent the last year working with Special Branch, but wild horses wouldn't keep me away from this op when Jack asked.' She used his name deliberately and the women constables' eyes snapped to hers. They now knew she had his ear. 'This op is as intriguing as it is challenging, and by that, I mean that the victims are criminals who perhaps we all feel deserve what they got. I understand that it's human nature not to care much about these people who create so much misery for others . . . but we're being asked to set that sentiment aside and work on these cases as we would those of any innocent victim. That's our role as police in any capacity, so let's work hard at doing what we all set out to do when we first joined the force – to protect without prejudice.' Kate moved to the board where she'd neatly pinned up photographs of the victims.

She pointed to the image of a bespectacled man with unruly pepper and salt hair. 'Julian Smythe, forty-five, university lecturer in astrophysics and inmate at Pentonville Prison prior to his death. Smythe was a wife beater. His bashings were vicious enough that on one occasion Eleanor Smythe, a teacher-librarian at a local school, died of her wounds on the floor of their family home.' She could feel the fury rising off the other women in the room while the men looked down momentarily as one. 'Smythe got five years. He was out in three.' She waited a beat. 'He's on this wall because he died under suspicious circumstances after his release. The reason we don't have an image up here of the crime scene is because his features were unrecognisable and the detectives had to rely on dental records. Mr Smythe was found in a warehouse building in Eastbourne back in 2004 but his death remained a cold case . . . until now. The warehouse was used as government storage only and did not have people coming and going, so Smythe's body was badly decomposed by the time it was found. The coroner's report concluded that he died from third-degree burns to his head and face, most likely from several litres of boiling water being poured over him repeatedly.'

Sounds of disgust rippled through the group.

Kate nodded. 'I know. Before he died he was burned a dozen times – quite deeply, we gather – using a car cigarette lighter. Full details are in your file. Even those who believe he deserved to pay wouldn't wish that end on anyone and, as our boss has just mentioned, this is not a typical execution-style death. It's torture, yes, but he had no history of any other criminal activity, no links to any criminals that the investigation team could find. I might add that every family member of his wife's had a solid alibi and, frankly, not one of those people would strike you as a revenge-taker. You'll see that most tried repeatedly to help Eleanor escape her husband, but she consistently refused. Three of her close family members live in the US, and their only child, a son – who was perhaps the most outspoken against his father – took a teaching exchange in Asia for two years just over a month before his father was released. He did not leave Singapore during those two years and has since extended his trip. He only returned briefly – for around thirty-six hours, apparently – to bury his father.'

'In other words, no suspect?' Mal queried.

'Correct. The case remains open. Clearly a suspicious death.' Kate waited for any further questions before pointing to the next photo. 'Moving on. Here we have Peggy Markham, fifty-nine, whom some of you might know of. She's reputed to have run a chain of high-end brothels across our city that many suspect were linked to drugs and human trafficking, but to date police haven't been successful pinning any of that on her – not even tax evasion, although that was probably going to be our only way to escort Peggy Markham into a prison cell.

'She never married but had a son to one of the city's well-known gangsters from the sixties – he died during the late eighties. We finally got a charge on pimping; within the right circles it was known that Peggy could acquire the right girl, or boy, for any pleasure. The case in question was an underage girl – fifteen – sent as an escort for a Turkish businessman with a particular sexual deviancy. The girl died as a result. Peggy was acquitted, as her legal team proved that the escort was a contractor who lied about her age and that Peggy had merely introduced the pair at a party. There was no evidence to prove otherwise.' Kate pointed again to the picture of Peggy, features slackened on the pathology table at the morgue. 'She died as a result of speedballing – that's a mixture of heroin and cocaine. Hers was an overdose of about two grams, which is big.'

She looked towards Jack; she felt it was time for him to take over again. He took the cue and seamlessly returned to the presentation.

'The thing is,' he began, pushing off the desk, 'Peggy had absolutely no reason to overdose.'

Kate watched him hold up slim fingers to count off what they knew. He looked good today . . . strong again after all that nasty business a couple of years ago. The tan would fade soon, like the darkness around the hair at his ears, revealing a few dabs of silver. She looked away.

Jack held up the last finger as she tuned back in. 'She had money and was essentially laughing at the police trying to pin her down to any crime. She'd just dodged prison on a charge that was the closest we'd ever come to putting her behind bars. Acquitted. You'd think Peggy would be out celebrating, not contemplating suicide. Her son, a squeaky-clean family man running a hotel for a reputable group in Spain, assured police that his mother was in good spirits and he'd spoken to her the day before she was found dead. She'd been planning to visit him and the family. They hadn't seen each other in years – while he admitted to loving his mother, he wanted distance from his notorious parents – but they were in touch regularly.'

Kate took over again. 'So . . . why would Peggy, with every reason to live, kill herself in this way? If you're going to overdose, presumably you'd inject into a vein in your arm; you wouldn't stick yourself in the neck, would you?' All of those watching shook their heads or murmured. She opened her palms. 'And certainly not in a public parkland.' The others agreed. 'If someone from the criminal underworld wanted Peggy dead, they'd have so many other less public, less weird ways to finish her. Whoever did this wasn't a professional because professionals minimise all risk. This guy – if it is a guy,' she said, not meaning to glance Jack's way but doing so anyway and feeling herself blush at the memory of Anne McEvoy, 'simply wanted her dead, it seems. It could also be more than one person. Anyway, she was stuck with the needle and left under the tree with no further interference. Whoever did this is pretty slick, because there's little trace of their presence.'

'Winter?' Mal asked.

'Yes,' Jack said. 'Around nightfall. No one in their right mind is strolling through Finsbury Park on a wintry Tuesday night at dinnertime.' He shrugged. 'But maybe we can find another reason . . . another connection.'

'You'll read in your files that she was propped up against a tree off the main pathways in a lightly wooded area,' Kate added.

'And no sign of sexual abuse?' PC Ali Johnson asked, as if Kate's earlier explanation was not enough.

'No, as I said, no additional interference,' Kate admitted, without any vexation in her tone. 'That in itself is an oddity too. If this was an angry punter, some other sort of criminal who was offended by Peggy, then presumably they'd have used her criminal activities symbolically in her death. But she was tidily murdered.'

The group let out a collective sigh as Kate stepped across to point out the third death.

'Finally, we have Alan Toomey.' At the murmurs, Kate nodded. 'Yes, most of you will have heard about it in the news but let's go through it. Alan Toomey, forty-two, went down for killing a pregnant woman who was just four weeks away from delivering her child. Jennifer Shaw was riding in a bicycle lane towards the nursery school to pick up her daughter. Toomey was speeding and took out Ms Shaw as he misjudged a slip road outside a Morrisons supermarket. She was declared brain dead, her baby was delivered by caesarean section, and now her two daughters are being raised by her husband and their two grieving families.' Kate couldn't entirely hide the disgust in her tone.

'Toomey served just nine months – the length that her pregnancy should have been – because he had excellent legal representation and he presented very sympathetically at his trial, showing extreme contrition. His wife and four children, including a baby in arms, attended court daily and that certainly helped him. After serving his short sentence, he moved with his family to Norfolk but was found dead by the side of a country road. He used to take the family dog for a walk along a particular route every night after dark, and it was the dog arriving home without its owner that sounded the alert. He'd been run down and driven over a couple of times.' She watched people look down in shock, but she sensed a quiet sense of justice floating around them all. 'No witnesses have come forward despite numerous call-outs.'

'Kate, may I?' She nodded at Jack, who continued. 'Again, you might be tempted to think he got what he deserved, but please remember that Alan Toomey was convicted of involuntary manslaughter. At the trial, witnesses testified that the victim had swerved outside of the cycle lane. I'm not saying she was culpable, but there were some mitigating reasons for how it all unfolded. The speeding was actually misleading; he was driving six miles above the limit but he was on an incline coming off the motorway; his blood showed no toxicity for any form of drugs or alcohol. Importantly, and what we're about, is that the person who snuffed out Alan Toomey is potentially guilty of first-degree murder. And as police, we must treat each death with the same care, no matter the victim's history.' He nodded to reinforce this cautionary note, and Kate suspected Jack had also sensed the moral dilemma that some in the room were wrestling with. 'One more that we received news about yesterday, and this will no doubt be in the media by tomorrow – do you all recall Rupert Brownlow?'

There was joint agreement and a sense of shock that he was on this killer's hitlist.

'Well, he could be our latest victim if we have a single perpetrator. He was murdered two nights ago in Portsmouth. We're waiting for the forensics and the post-mortem to tell us whether he was dead before or after he was dragged by the neck from a rope attached to a car. I'm sorry, I didn't have details of this to pin up. We only heard about it yesterday, but Joan is getting the files for each of you on this most recent slaughter.'

It was Mal who aired what Kate suspected everyone was thinking. 'A vigilante?'

She gave a small shrug. 'It's not for us to judge, though I think we'd all agree that's how it looks. These deaths are scattered . . . London, now Portsmouth, Norfolk and Eastbourne. The acting chief wants to know if we can link them. That's our job, first and foremost: to find evidence that supports there being a single perpetrator committing these murders. Any questions?'

Silence met her gaze.

Jack gave a nod. 'Thanks, Kate. That's a lot to take in, I know. I suggest all of you take time this morning to read the files fully and absorb them. This afternoon, you start hitting your contacts, working your networks, following every clue, compiling every ounce of knowledge. We'll break the workload into individual murders to follow and then compare notes. I want every detail you can hunt down pertaining to each of these deaths by Wednesday, and then we'll work out our next step. Hit the caffeine, everyone, and today, morning tea is on me, because I don't like anyone working on an empty stomach.' Sounds of approval accompanied Joan's arrival with a platter of muffins.

'Don't get used to this, boys and girls,' she said, smiling.

8

Kate took Malek aside as the group broke up. 'Can you set up who works on which case?' He nodded. 'Spread the skills, keeping in mind that Sarah's back any minute and will need at least one slave.'

'Righto,' Mal agreed. 'I can organise that. Um, I was thinking about putting the word out through our snitches. I'm out of touch with the word on the ground though.'

She nodded. 'Yes, that's smart. Any intel we can gather from anywhere, even from the crims themselves, is vital. We'll run that by Hawk, as he'll need to get us access via the handlers. I'll mention it but you can follow up.'

He gave a finger salute. 'I might also have a word with my contacts in the Turkish community, see if they know anything about this Ekrem Çelik fellow who hired the escort. If the chief wants us to hunt down every avenue . . .'

'That's a great thought, Mal. Good stuff,' Kate said. 'Go for it, we don't have long. I'm going to speak with my contacts at Special Branch too. I don't care where tip-offs come from. Take a couple of days, but any leads, let me or Hawk know.'

Mal departed to his desk and Kate went looking for Jack. She found him scowling at a charcoal-coloured foil pyramid in the kitchen area. She laughed. 'Are you offended by it?'

'Deeply,' he admitted.

'They do look pretty, though,' she replied.

'Fancy the real thing?'

She didn't hesitate and liked the upbeat feeling that overtook her when they both settled back into the black cab's leather seats.

'To Soho, please. Berwick Street,' Jack said to the driver.

'Just before the markets okay, guv?' the driver said, looking at them in his rear-view mirror. 'There's some roadworks.'

'Anywhere around there is fine,' Jack said and winked at Kate. 'You okay to walk a minute or so?' he said, glancing at the heels on her boots.

'I can run in these.'

They sat in an easy silence while the taxi began to slow tediously in the bottleneck of traffic. 'And how about you these days, Jack? Anyone special in your life?'

He grinned at this. 'No. I'm seeing someone but for both of us it's simply . . .'

'Convenient?'

He laughed. 'I was going to say simply companionship. Neither of us wants anything more from the other than the good times we enjoy in the moment when we're together.'

'Good grief. What kind of amazing woman is that?'

'A busy one,' he said, and something in his tone told her he would not be enlightening her further.

'And Anne McEvoy?'

He seemed to know this was coming as he didn't strike her as unduly awkward at the mention of his former lover.

His phone pinged in his pocket. He reached for it and read the message, returning his phone to his pocket. 'Anne is surprisingly in control of her incarceration.' He told her about Anne's work as a psychologist within the prison. 'She's very good too, I gather. Keeps her busy and engaged for the long road ahead.'

'Over 'ere okay, mate?'

'This is great, thanks,' Jack said. He paid the cabbie and gave a good tip, Kate noticed, as she bundled out into the cold morning.

She shivered. 'I hope you're not planning to walk me far, Jack?'

'Just over there.' He pointed. 'Welcome to Flat White,' he said, pointing to the shop's name above its large window. Kate had to look closely at the sign, created as though from an old typewriter, thin and white in the simplest of Courier fonts against an all-black shopfront. She'd miss it if she was hurrying past. 'One of the best coffee spots in London,' Jack assured her.

She noted a long bar running the length of one wall and tiny tables up against a bench seat that ran along the facing wall and around the corner. Jack pointed to that corner. 'My favourite nook,' he grinned. 'Go get comfy.'

'I'll have . . .' she began.

'Allow me,' he said. And she shrugged her acceptance that he knew his coffee. He returned with two thickish Italian-style cups in a Mediterranean blue; he didn't sit in the chair opposite, but next to her on the bench. She could feel his warmth through her thin sweater. She focused on the elegantly wrought pattern of a tiny heart picked out in steamed milk against the rich caramel colour of the coffee's crema. 'No froth?' she said to tease him.

He gave her a look of disdain and she enjoyed the mirth his horror instantly provoked in her. 'Taste it,' he urged.

'Gosh, you're so intense, Jack.' He waited, impatient. Kate sipped and blinked. She sipped again and raised her gaze to him.

He gave a smug nod. 'You now understand the secret to the universe. This café was opened by an Aussie who was troubled, presumably, by what we have been claiming for years to be Italian-style coffee.'

She laughed again. 'All right. This is delicious, I'll grant you.'

He smiled. 'Everyone happy back at base?'

'Excited, I think.'

You were good this morning, Kate.'

She hoped she wasn't blushing because a compliment from Jack meant so much more than one from most others. 'Thanks. Listen, Jack, just for the record, I don't think we're dealing with any of London's known criminals here. Nothing gang-related, I mean.'

He nodded. 'My instincts say the same.'

'Good. I thought I might be out on a limb.'

Jack sipped his coffee, savouring it. 'The deaths are too contrived, too messy, too dangerous for me to believe these are hits by any of the known criminal groups, but they are also too bizarre to all be random crimes by a variety of individuals.'

'Don't believe in coincidence, Jack?'

He slid her a wry gaze. 'Martin hammered into me years ago that the suggestion of coincidence is ninety-nine per cent wrong. And every time the thought bubbles, it should drive us to look harder.'

Kate waited a beat. 'So . . . can we treat this as a serial killer?'

'Between us, yes, that's my position. I wish I could stop myself thinking it. I really do not want to be heading up another serial killer op.'

'And yet here you are,' she said, sounding resigned. 'A vigilante, do you think?'

He looked troubled at that. 'I really don't want to believe we have one of those on the loose. The media will make it a circus and the public will subsequently panic. I can't think why one would exist for the deaths of known criminals.'

'One death, maybe, as payback. But none of these seem related. How is one person offended by all these people? The crimes are inconsistent in victim, method, setting . . . there's no pattern and few forensics.'

'No pattern we can discern immediately,' he pondered aloud. 'But if we're right, we'll find the pattern and the connection. Sarah's the key to that. The message in the taxi was from her – she's planning to be in tomorrow morning.'

'Great. I do hope she brings her anorak as well.'

'Now, now, Kate.'

She smiled. 'We'll need to brief her carefully. The more strategic her search, the faster and better the information.'

He sighed. 'I really just want her to input *bizarre deaths in Britain's criminal underworld* and give us some answers.'

She smiled, finishing her coffee. 'Yes, wouldn't that be simple? We'll need help getting permission to contact handlers of police informers – the problem is it will be across all divisions, presumably.'

'Let's start with Vice. I'll make the call and the team can take it from there.'

She nodded. 'Mal is going to talk to the Turkish community to find out more about the fellow who used Peggy's services. Can't hurt.'

'I agree. I think starting as broadly as we dare is wise. What about you?'

'I'm going to put the word out through Special Branch, but I thought I'd talk to the various police stations that were involved in each of the crimes. There are the files, but then there are all those aspects that perhaps get overlooked and never reach the files.'

'Wet memories . . . powerful. Yep, that's good, Kate.'

'Jack, don't jump down my throat, but how often do you see Anne McEvoy?' He looked at her with a sense of exasperation and she apologised, holding up a hand. 'No, wait, hear me out. It's about our op.'

'What has Anne got to do with this?' His gaze narrowed and she felt she'd left the safety of friendship and was now on a tight-rope. Anne always was and probably always would be his tender underbelly.

'Look, it's a wild idea but why not ask her . . . get her perspective?'

'On what?'

She remained patient. 'I doubt you ever had the chance to meet Anne the killer; you were spending time with the lovely woman walking around as Sophie from your apartment block. Why don't you go meet the prisoner serving all those life sentences and ask her about her planning for those kills?' He looked horrified but Kate pressed on. 'Jack, how often do we get the sort of opportunity you might have to get into a serial killer's mind? I'm not suggesting you're trying to find out what makes *her* tick, but more about the logistics and the practical side of planning a kill. We can guess at it, or we can speak with a profiler, but blimey, Jack, she's done it enough times to enlighten us on . . .' — she shrugged — 'on just the nerves alone. How do you go through with it when the moment comes? You've just applauded the idea of wet memories, experience. Well, anything we do is based on dry fact. Even a profiler can only brief us based on information lifted from recorded detail. We have a chance to leap into those wet memories with McEvoy.' She risked squeezing his arm, not sure if it was to reassure him or simply to touch him under the guise of making a persuasive argument. 'The murders suggest a serial killer. This person is not an opportunist. If we agree that these are not random deaths, then the intention comes with planning. Remember, the McEvoy crimes ranged over southern England and we took a while to connect them to one killer. You've just told me all about McEvoy's work as a criminal psychologist. Surely she'd have some insight . . . She could be an amazing yin and yang kind of counsel – offering up both sides, you know?' She frowned. 'Am I being stupid?'

He frowned back, perplexed. 'I don't know if it's stupid or inspired. I don't really want to see her, but it does bear thinking on.'

'Then think on it.'

He sighed. 'Let's head back. But I owe you dinner.'

'You bought me a great coffee. Consider us square,' she offered.

'No, no, I mean it. How about Friday night? Are you busy?'

She hadn't been on a date since she'd farewelled Geoff, but she reminded herself that this was not a romantic date. 'Probably cleaning the fridge or something. Actually, that's a lie – I never clean it. Sorting out my underwear drawer, then.' She immediately wished she hadn't said that; damn, he made her say stupid things.

He smiled. 'Friday evening it is, then, Operation Mirror permitting. Seven okay?'

'It's fine. Where?'

'My place,' he said.

'You're cooking?'

'You get to taste my chicken risotto. And if you can hold off getting cranky with me between now and then, I'll make a dessert.'

'Cranky?'

'I know I vex you.' He grinned.

'All men vex me, it's not personal,' she said in a droll tone. She let him help her back into her coat. 'I don't know where you live, by the way.'

'I'll text you. Come on, Mother will be getting impatient with us. And I've just thought of something.'

'What?'

'Something that's been nagging at me, and you just loosened it from the crevices of my mind when you mentioned Anne.'

She waited, refusing to move.

'I'll tell you in the taxi.'

'Tell me now, Jack,' she insisted.

He sighed. 'The original crimes. The victims all went to trial. Where were those original sins committed?'

9

Lauren Starling stared at the computer screen and the new masthead for *My Day*.

'What do you think?'

She let go of her sneer and turned to see the newly appointed features editor staring over her shoulder. Rowena had only worked with the magazine for just over a week and had transferred from the parent company, removed to the shitty rag of a magazine to inject fresh life into something Lauren felt should be allowed to die.

'It's okay, I suppose,' she replied with care.

'It works.'

Lauren shrugged, not wishing to wholly compromise her honesty. 'Hot pink is so . . . er . . .'

Rowena didn't wait for her to finish. 'Doesn't matter what we think. That colour screams. And while you, dear Lauren – how old are you? Thirty-two? – prefer to move around in perfect monochrome, women of the demographic we're after wear purple, pink, cyan blue, mauve and the like. They notice this colour in supermarkets, in stationers, in newsagents. The danger is thinking we work for *Vogue* or *Time*, or Condé Nast.'

'I wish!' Lauren grinned, all too aware that her presentation screamed fashion magazine, not gutter press, as Rowena perched herself on the edge of her desk to look at her face to face. 'I'm thirty-three.'

'You should be working for *Vogue*. You don't look like you fit here.' Lauren knew her superior wasn't being mean; the truth was obvious. 'I know you were employed by *London Talking*, which has serious cred. Whatever are you doing here?' Lauren sighed and Rowena gently touched her arm. 'No, really. I want to learn about the whole team here. So why do we have you, the square peg . . . I mean, I suspect we're lucky to have you – you're a seriously good writer, but why, Lauren? You dress like you wouldn't be caught dead in Primark.'

'I wouldn't.'

'So?'

'I needed the work, and quickly,' she admitted. She didn't want to explain about the failed engagement, the promise of a fabulous new life in New York, the bastard she'd fallen for and sold up for . . . and lent all her savings to. 'I sold my flat, took a working holiday to the US, did some travelling . . .' That was a lie, unless a trip to Washington DC and a weekend in Florida was 'travelling'. 'I thought I'd be gone a lot longer but it didn't work out and when I came back, I had rent to pay in a hurry and no job lined up.' She dredged up a smile to help the comment sound sardonic, despite the reality that its anxiety woke her up in the early hours most mornings. 'I took the first opportunity offered.'

'Here, though? The people who read our rag shop in Asda for the most part, not the M&S Foodhall.'

'It's just a way back in,' she explained. 'Suits me for now, truly.'

This was no lie. It wasn't where she wanted to be, but it was still a magazine with pages to fill and deadlines to meet.

'All right, Lauren. I doubt I'm hearing the full story, but I accept it's not my business. What *is* my business is getting revenue into this magazine.'

Lauren looked back at her with a gaze that said *you're joking, right?*

'I know, I know,' Rowena continued, palms up in defence. 'In these digital times the days of print are numbered. However, forecasts suggest that really high-quality magazines will survive, while the myriad glossies in the middle range will most likely disappear.'

'And ours?'

Rowena shook her head with surprise. 'Ours? That's the curiosity. It's the ordinary cheap reads with crosswords, recipes, agony pages, misery stories, celebrity rubbish and sensationalist crap with a royal beat-up every few weeks that will keep ticking on through the revolution.'

Lauren sighed audibly.

'So it's the latest Brad and Ange fight, how to lose five kilos in five days, and the newest trends in wedding cakes and plastic surgery, that sort of thing, that will keep selling our pointless magazine to thousands of women who don't seem to mind being told what to think, how to live and so on.'

'But why?'

'Why what?'

Lauren pushed back on her chair so the castors rolled her away and she was no longer looking up the editor's nostrils. 'Why can't we lift our game?'

Rowena stared back at her, bemused. 'Why would we?'

'To broaden our reach?'

Rowena laughed. 'You're not dumb, Lauren, so don't act it. The success of *My Day* is that we know exactly who our demographic is and we don't try to elevate it or widen it, or—'

'Educate it?'

Rowena wasn't expecting that. She blinked at Lauren, taking her measure. 'You want to educate our readership, who are looking for escape, titillation and distraction from their really very ordinary lives?'

'I can't see any harm at all in tackling either some issues or some news more regularly. It's all about how we do it . . . keep it appealing and they'll still devour it.'

'Issues? Like mental health?'

'Why not? Why can't we do a feature on anorexia or anxiety? If we write it in a way that isn't overly depressing, or too academic, perhaps we can get a conversation going.'

'You think they'd want that?'

'Look, I'm not trying to win a Pulitzer here, but I think we're disrespecting our audience. They're not dumb, though I accept they're not academic either. They're everyday women, not in careers, but working hard, running homes and families, making ends meet. I get that. Their lives are a very long way from mine, even, and a world away from glamorous. Most of them are living tougher lives, but they still have interests, dreams, hopes for their children. Their ordinary, salt-of-the-earth lifestyles don't mean they're disengaged from the news, for instance.'

'Lauren, we come out once a fortnight. We can't do news.'

'But we can do interesting news features, surely? We can take a subject and still keep that titillation and escapist approach you want.'

'Give me an example.'

Lauren looked to the ceiling, desperately searching her mind for something to win her editor's attention. 'How about Britain, ten years on from Diana's death? How has her impact affected attitudes to motherhood, fashion, feminism, et cetera? We package it in the way our readers like, but we tackle interesting angles that actually deliver something.'

Rowena cocked her head to one side as she considered this. 'Give me one that isn't about the royals but is titillating.'

'Give me fifteen minutes and I'll send you a proposal.'

'Make it half an hour – I have a call to make. My office, with your idea. Bring us a coffee each, and not instant.' She dipped into her trouser pocket and pulled out a ten-pound note. 'My buy.'

Lauren took the cash and found herself smiling inwardly. 'How do you take it?'

'White, no sugar. I have sweeteners in my bag.'

Seated in a hot-pink bucket chair and wondering if it was from this piece of furniture that Rowena drew her inspiration, Lauren pitched. 'Have you heard about Rupert Brownlow?' she began.

Rowena frowned. 'Should I have?'

Lauren lifted an eyebrow that suggested perhaps she should, but it didn't matter, she'd enlighten her anyway. 'Went joyriding in his father's four-wheel drive and killed—'

'Oh yeah, yeah, I remember . . . horrific! Whole families killed. Right . . . and?'

'And he got a pathetic sentence that created massive controversy a few years ago.'

Rowena didn't look impressed. 'What's your point?'

'Daddy's rich, can afford the top barrister in the land to argue anxiety, rehabilitation, youth – all the usual stuff – and take the focus off the fact that eighteen-year-old Rupert, angry from being dumped by his girlfriend, recklessly killed four adults, four children, two family dogs and ruined countless lives. To make it all even more heinous, the prison system has seen fit to release Brownlow early to get on with his indulged, wealthy lifestyle.'

'And you want to do a story about what? Lenient sentences?' Now Rowena sounded bored.

Lauren piled the energy into her tone and sat forward. She needed to get this over the line. 'In part, yes. But there's more . . . and this is where the titillation comes in.'

'Surprise me, Lauren, because the earth hasn't moved for me yet.'

'Rupert Brownlow was murdered last week after his release.'

Rowena had the grace to look surprised. 'All right . . . where's this going?'

'This isn't gangland, Rowena. He was an uppity, pathetically immature sixth-former with no connections to the world of crime. He committed one, did insufficient time and then out of nowhere he's murdered horribly . . . dragged behind a vehicle on a rope around his neck.'

'Fuck!'

Lauren nodded. 'Titillating, isn't it? It gets better. I have a friend in the police force and, when I mentioned this idea for a story, she told me of a case along similar lines. A man beat his wife to death, was jailed for it with a relatively lenient sentence, got out and apparently was murdered with boiling water tipped over his head repeatedly. It remains a cold case. Most of his face had melted.'

Her editor gave a look of horror. 'Bloody hell.'

'Gruesome, titillating, fascinating . . . and there's a story there, I can smell it.'

'What's the story?'

Lauren shrugged and finally took a sip her coffee through the plastic spout. 'Er . . . criminals get their just deserts. Or how about, "Do you feel sorry for these crims?" We could engage with domestic violence victims, or ask how people feel about rich people moving through a different justice system. That sort of thing. If we can get chatter going, I'm betting we can bump sales; then we could argue we're tackling issues and not just the sewer end of publishing.'

Rowena sighed. 'The sewer end, as you call it, makes money, Lauren. Nothing dirty about our graphs around the big table, but I like the idea of delving where we haven't, so long as features stay fully in touch with the readership. I'm not interested in anything that makes any of our audience skip the pages.'

'Death, and particularly grisly murder, sells just as well as sex, Rowena.'

'Okay, I'm intrigued. This friend of yours in the police, are you close?'

'We used to share a flat,' Lauren replied, dodging the truth.

'What else does she know?'

'Rupert Brownlow was killed recently, but the other case is older.'

'Well, the police must be looking into these murders.'

'I suppose so.'

'Maybe the angle is along the lines of, do we want our tax to be spent looking into the deaths of criminals when . . . oh, I don't know, find some angle . . . hospitals, creches, education, something that matters to our readers, needs more funding. But keep it upbeat, keep it relevant. Find a rapist who's been killed and then ask that question: do we care? Find more recent cases so we jog their memory of them.'

'So I can work on this?'

'Let's see what you can do and if you come up with something special – I'll need photos and people to quote. If you can do that, I'll give you a double-page spread and a front-cover teaser.'

'I want my own column and a proper byline with photo.'

Rowena chuckled. 'Of course you do. Impress me and we'll talk about a regular column and your new status.'

Lauren felt herself ignite with a thrill she hadn't felt since Dan had asked her to marry him. She hadn't been expecting his proposal as they'd only been dating for a couple of months. He was a catch to be going out with, let alone to wear his ring – all her friends had envied her. He'd said the ring was his mother's – something to propose to her with – but he'd wanted her to pick out an engagement ring she would want to wear for the rest of her life. 'We'll choose it at Tiffany's in New York,' he'd promised.

The closest she'd got to Tiffany's was lurking on the opposite side of the road to Fifth Avenue and 57th Street, wondering whether they would let her pawn his mother's ring. As it turned out, visiting a seedy pawnshop on the Upper West Side confirmed that the family solitaire was in fact a worthless cubic zirconia. She'd had to ask her sister for the cost of the airfare back to Britain. He'd used all of her savings to start up yet another of his new ventures, which, she only discovered upon arriving stateside, followed a string of failures. The present innovation was to set up a podcast platform, but Apple was leagues ahead of Dan and her money drained away like rain into the New York sewers. The few friends remaining felt sympathy and perhaps relief that 'Dan the Bastard' hadn't turned his attentions on them, because they'd have fallen for him just as she had. Dan was a con and Lauren hoped one day he'd get what he was due.

'Sound okay?' Rowena prompted.

She flicked the memory of Dan away. 'Yes, of course. I was not expecting you to react like this. That's terrific, thank you.'

'Good. Don't take your eye off the other stuff; we still need your top ten cheap versions of impossibly expensive handbags for next issue, and that feature on which dog breeds make the best companions for single women.'

Lauren nodded. 'On it.'

'Keep me updated. How long, do you reckon?'

'Well, it needs proper investigation. At least a month.'

'Maybe an early summer feature, then?'

'Thanks, Rowena . . . and for the coffee.'

★

'Are you losing your marbles?' her flatmate from a previous life hissed.

Lauren imagined poor Ange cupping her mobile phone so no one else could hear her, although she suspected she was outside, shivering as she smoked. 'You owe me.'

'How much longer are you going to leverage that?'

'This is the last time, I promise. Listen . . . at Scotland Yard—'

'I'm just admin! I should never have mentioned that cold case. It broke all the rules but I thought I was talking to a reliable mate,' her friend growled.

Lauren pushed through the guilt. 'Admin doesn't mean you're not privy to information. You access stuff that others don't. I just want to know if there's an operation underway or being assemb—'

'I can't! How many different ways can I say this?'

'Ange, this is my chance.' Lauren waited, taking the silence to be encouraging. 'Please. I'll never lean on you again.' She held her breath for a heartbeat. 'Meet me for a drink. My treat,' she urged. 'A couple of questions, that's all.'

'You get two questions, Lauren. And I'm warning you, I won't tell you anything about any operation underway within the Met.'

'I'll text you where. Tonight, all right? Six . . . a quickie.'

Lauren heard the line go dead. She felt nausea erupt that she was burning a friendship, although she had to admit it had been foundering since she'd learned about her former flatmate's betrayal.

Later, at a wine bar, she waved to Angela, who seemed agitated. 'I'm sorry, Ange.'

'No, you're not,' her companion said, sitting down in the seat opposite. 'I know you're starting again, Lor, but taking advantage of your mates is about as low as it gets.'

'Are we still mates?' Lauren tried with hope in her tone.

'Not once I leave here.'

'That's tough,' Lauren said, having anticipated this outcome but hating it anyway and despising how far the repercussions of Dan stretched. His actions were forcing her hand on something she didn't think she was capable of. She poured her companion a drink from the bottle of wine she had sitting between them. 'It's a nice chardonnay.'

Angela took the glass and at least clinked cheers with Lauren's. 'Here's to goodbye, Lor.'

She swallowed. 'Do you have to be so nasty?'

'I do actually, because I made a mistake, you know that. Just like you did.'

'Ange, I didn't sleep with my sister's fiancé, like you. My mistake was simply making a bad choice for one, but he wasn't attached. The only person I hurt is me.'

'It was a long time ago after a drunken night out and I'm not going to feel guilty any more. She's my sister, yes—'

'And my close friend,' Lauren pressed, reminded of the awkward and heart-wrenching position Ange had put her in when she'd found her flatmate curled up with Michael after his stag night.

'I don't think for a minute that you would tell Lucy but if you choose to, fuck you!' Angela had nearly finished her glass and was reaching to top it up. Until this evening, Lauren had never uttered anything about Ange and Michael's treachery. It was only Ange's guilt that led her to believe Lauren would be two-faced, but right now Lauren needed what Ange knew and if that meant letting her believe her secret was under threat, then so be it.

'We'll never speak of this again,' Lauren promised.

Ange shrugged as if she couldn't care any less than she did right now. 'You've got two questions, and hurry, because I'm walking after this glass.'

Lauren took a breath. 'Over the last few months I've been looking back at old cases . . . all of them murders – anyway, you know this from previous conversations. But with today's news I now have four, and I think I need one more juicy murder. That's enough to build a story from.'

Her friend nodded unhappily. 'There is a cold case from 2001. A district nurse who helped people on their way; she argued compassion, but the jury saw it differently – as a murderess who enjoyed selecting her victims and playing executioner under the guise of empathy. Her name was Annie Wilcox. Second question?'

'I don't really have one . . . I figured how you answered the first would give me my second.'

'Good, then I'll be on my way. Bye, Lauren—'

'No, wait . . . wait! Okay . . .' Lauren frowned. 'Surely the police are looking into these deaths as suspicious.'

'That's not a question.' Angela drained her glass.

'All right. Are the police looking into the killings I mentioned as a collective series of murders rather than individual cases?' Lauren blinked, surprised at just how targeted that sounded.

Angela actually smirked. 'Are you asking me if we're investigating a serial killer?'

Lauren didn't realise until this moment that this was precisely her question. 'Have I hit on anything, Ange? I will never divulge a source. I will never say anything to your sister. I will never phone you again if that's your wish. I swear on the lives of my twin nephews that I will not bring any trouble to your door.'

She watched Angela breathe out as she weighed up how much to reveal. 'I'm not going to discuss police operations with you, Lauren. Here's my farewell to you – and you'd better keep faith with what you've just promised.'

Lauren nodded. 'Deal.'

'There's a newly promoted Detective Super called Jack Hawksworth. He's worth a look.' Angela stood, slung her bag over her shoulder and eased out of the bench. 'Thanks for the drink. Hope never to see or hear from you again, Lauren.'

'Jack Hawksworth,' Lauren repeated, frowning, pushing away the cut of Ange's words, and then looked up to see her friend's back as she shouldered a path away through the crowd of early evening drinkers.

10

'Jack, look who's arrived,' Kate said, as he picked up his messages from Joan.

He turned and his face lit up. 'Sarah! Thank you for coming home early.'

She looked embarrassed by the fuss. He glanced at the familiar brown anorak she wore, and his gaze shifted to Kate, who winked from behind Sarah's shoulder. He kept his features even. 'You look well.'

'You looked tanned, sir. Congratulations on your promotion.'

He walked towards her, smiling. 'I can't tell you how pleased I am to see you and just how much we need your help. Can I get you a coffee?'

'Er, I don't drink coffee, sir.'

She'd lost none of her awkwardness over the last year or two, he noted. He hoped Kate had warned the newcomers that Sarah possessed a curious manner; it could often be interpreted as Asperger's but he didn't believe she was anything more than simply shy. She lacked the usual raft of social skills but was mostly supremely focused on her work. If he was honest, he felt like hugging her, but he knew that would be greeted with fright.

'Well, grab a cuppa of something if you feel like it and let's have a quick briefing in my office.'

She nodded. 'I'm ready now.'

Of course she is, he thought, even though she hadn't yet shifted out of her anorak. 'Right.'

Sarah picked up a pen and pad, and followed him into his office, not bothering to ditch her outerwear, which made a familiar swishing sound. She sat down where he gestured and pushed her owl-like glasses further up her nose. 'Thank you for asking for me to join this op.'

Jack smiled reassuringly. 'I wouldn't dream of not asking you,' he admitted, his words true. She found a crooked smile that conveyed how much those words meant to her. 'Has Kate had a chance to give you an overview?'

'I've read the files, sir. And Kate answered my immediate queries.'

He anticipated that she would have read everything she could before pulling her backpack off her shoulders. 'Good. And you know that we've put Constable Beck at your disposal?'

'I work better alone.'

'I know, Sarah, but she's there if you feel overwhelmed.'

'I don't.'

He held up a hand gently, then dropped it quickly, shrugging instead. 'You may need an errand run, a file fetched, a phone call made . . . a cup of—' He glanced at her. 'What do you enjoy?'

'Honey and lemon in hot water, sir,' she said, slightly defensive.

Jack relaxed his shoulders deliberately so she could note the gesture and his widening smile. 'Perfect. All I'm saying is, she knows the system and is keen. I think she would be worthy of learning at your elbow and, as Detective Sergeant, it won't hurt you to pass on some of that vast knowledge, encourage a newcomer. We need more people like you.' Sarah blinked behind the large lenses of her glasses and Jack couldn't tell if it was because she felt complimented – as he'd intended – or irritated that her territory might be invaded. 'She won't be breathing down your neck, of course, but I want you to know you have some back-up.'

'Thank you, sir.'

He moved on, sensing her desire to do just that. 'So, how do we make the best and swiftest use of HOLMES?'

Sarah predictably looked relieved to be getting down to business. Her forehead creased as she became immediately focused. 'As it stands, we have disparate cases that, on the surface, bear little relation to each other. The time difference across the four victims we know about is around eighteen months.' She paused.

He realised she was waiting for him. 'Is that important?'

She gave him a look that suggested it could be. 'Perhaps not. However, if we are dealing with one perpetrator, then he or she has been busy at the business of killing.'

'One every four months, approximately.'

'That we know about, sir. These are the bodies we've found . . . the cases we've picked up on.'

Kate had appeared at the doorway. 'Do you mind if I join?'

Jack gestured to another seat but Kate remained in the doorway. 'Why hide some if the ones we know of were left in the open?' she asked Sarah, to broaden the discussion.

'I agree,' Sarah replied. 'And unless we find a hidden grave, it seems our killer doesn't mind these bodies being discovered. But other bodies could be anywhere and not yet found, not yet reported, or reported but not yet connected. I think we need to also look at which crims might be inexplicably missing. I'll need to get onto the MISPER Index – we simply can't rule it out that more victims might be missing persons.'

Jack nodded, frowning. 'Unless their families have let police know they're missing, we won't know.'

'Not officially, but if we do, I'll find them. Perhaps someone else could speak with other divisions . . . find out the word on the street?'

'We're on it,' Kate said.

'That's good. On the surface, certainly, it appears that the killer wants his victims noticed.' Sarah looked up to the ceiling, frowning. 'Or maybe the killer simply doesn't care if they are.'

'Then we need some help with this,' Kate said. 'We don't have the time between now and our self-imposed deadline to ponder the mindset of this killer. Let's get a professional opinion.'

'A profiler?' Jack frowned.

'Why not? Or you could follow that other suggestion of mine,' Kate offered, pointedly.

Jack looked away; the thought of meeting with Anne felt daunting. 'Sarah, anything else before Kate introduces you to the rest of the team?' he asked.

'Just that if he's killed four, then I would hazard he's killed others,' she said.

'Kate, let's get a message out immediately on the PNN.'

She looked at him with caution. 'Our police national network isn't necessarily as secure as we'd like to think. I thought we had to work under lock and key?'

'I know, but I agree with Sarah that there may be others up and down the country. We're not helping ourselves if we can't warn our own to brief us on any suspicious deaths of people who have been convicted.' He sighed. 'Keep it vague. The Met does lots of statistical research all the time, so we could veil it beneath that sort of information gathering. Put my number as the contact.'

Sarah looked at Kate. 'Have we got Brownlow in London?'

'No,' Kate admitted. 'He's with the Hampshire coroner.'

Jack frowned. 'I think under these circumstances we can have him brought to London.'

'Best idea, sir,' Sarah admitted. 'Then we have continuity.'

'I'll have his body brought down today. We'll ask the Chief to make the request. Actually, hang on, I'll do that now.' Jack removed himself, returning less than a minute later. 'It's done. Kate, can you get down to the morgue today? Make sure Brownlow is in and given top priority.'

'Consider it done.'

'Anything else?'

Sarah hesitated and Jack looked at her. 'Go on.'

'Sir, Kate mentioned that you believe we should go back to the original crimes.' He nodded. 'This has to be our starting point. Without them, we simply have the unconnected deaths, which don't really point to a single perpetrator. In fact, it's only the hairs on the back of our necks right now that are suggesting these are linked.'

He grinned. She'd summarised their situation perfectly.

Kate bit her lip. 'We have nothing to go on, to be honest, but we'll leave no stone unturned. We'll find the link if there is one.'

Sarah nodded. 'We need the original crimes collated and then we can look into any potential commonalities with the deaths.'

'All right, Sarah, you focus on hunting the original crimes and collating that information. How fast?'

She looked at her watch. 'Er, end of the day, sir.'

'That's excellent. Don't let me hold you up.'

'It's, er . . . it's lovely to be working with you and all the team again, sir,' she said.

Jack let the full warmth of his smile fall on her. 'Sarah, it was pure relief when I heard you were cutting your holiday short. And I'm sorry you had to do that. How was Petra, by the way?'

'Very pink,' she admitted and found a rare smile. 'Gob-smacking, sir.'

'Jack?'

He turned to see Joan pushing past Kate at the door. He nodded at his two colleagues and they swiftly departed.

'Sorry to interrupt.'

'Something up?'

'Possibly. There's a journalist who has rung three times looking for you.'

'Why?'

'She won't say.'

'From where?'

'*My Day.*'

He frowned. 'What's that?'

'One of those dreadful rags that you pick up at supermarkets.'

He stared at her. 'You're joking.'

'I'm afraid not. Her name is Lauren Starling.'

'Why me?'

'Jack, she's caught your scent.'

'The op?' Dismay laced his query. 'How can she know?'

Joan shook her head once. 'Not the op; I reckon she's digging to see if there is one. But perhaps she's somehow onto the murders.'

'Bollocks!'

'You're forgiven for that.' She smiled. 'Swear tin behind my desk for the next one.'

'Fuck!' he added and immediately began jingling the coins in his pocket to dig out the penalty.

'Well, that's going to cost you a pound coin, Jack,' she said, leading him to her desk. She shook the empty tin. 'First one . . . lovely. We'll have cakes every day for morning tea if you keep this up.'

He dropped the pound coin through the slot and Joan nodded at the satisfying sound of its arrival. 'You need to nip this in the bud.'

'When did she call?'

'This morning at eight-thirty and twice since. It's now nearing half-ten and she's decided to visit you.' He drooped. 'Afraid so. She's also savvy; got in using a false ID for one of the major newspapers but came clean to me the moment Harry called up from Reception.'

'He's signed her in?'

'No. Mercifully, he rang me first. I told her my name is Margaret, so hopefully she'll never find me again. She's spun him a tale of talking with the media department – even quoted a name. She quoted yours too. Are you sure you don't know her . . . slept with her, perhaps?' He gave her a look of unbridled exasperation and she squeezed his arm. 'Lighten up, Jack. We've got a serial murderer to find. A smartypants journo for a two-bit magazine is really not that important. Get rid of her. She's waiting downstairs.'

He sighed in frustration. 'Right. Joan, please call me in about fifteen minutes and make up something urgent that drags me away.'

'Certainly. Are you coming back here?'

'No, but I'll only be about half an hour away.'

'How mysterious. Although I suspect I can guess.' She smiled kindly and in a way that made him wish once again that Joan was family. He would give a limb to spend weekends with her, enjoying the full force of her personality, which could shift from acerbic wit to warmth; it felt like remembering a good childhood with a special family member. This particular smile of hers wrapped around him like a reassuring blanket. Of course she knew exactly where he was headed.

He grinned his goodbye to Joan. 'Kate?'

'Yep?' his DI said.

'Let's see who might have been recently released and who is up for imminent release.'

She raised her eyebrows. 'Can you narrow that down a bit?' she asked.

'Yes.' He held up a finger. 'Who was sent down with a sentence that the public or the media felt was too lenient.' He raised a second finger. 'Who has been given an early release from prison in the last few years from that list of lenient sentences . . . and . . .' He held up a third finger, his eyes narrowing. 'Who is about to be released early in a surprise reduction of their sentence due to the government's decision to cull numbers in our prisons.'

'Right,' she said, looking no less daunted.

In the lift he closed his eyes to find his equanimity. How could a writer from a rag be onto them already? As the lift dinged to tell him he'd only made it to the fifth floor, his instincts, ever present, told him someone in the Met was chattering.

He took out his Nokia again and dialled Joan once more, only to achieve further frustration because there was no service in the lift.

Lauren didn't feel welcome in the slightest, even though the person behind the reception desk had greeted her cheerfully and gestured towards a seat. She wasn't asked to sign in, so there was obviously no chance of clearing security and being invited upstairs. Detective Superintendent Hawksworth was on his way down to see her. She hadn't expected that, so it was a win of sorts. Leaning back against the couch, she tried to imagine who was descending towards her: he'd be overweight, probably balding, irritable. He'd talk down to her, use official language peppered with acronyms and do his utmost to speak around all the questions she wanted direct answers to.

The lift gave its chime of arrival and she watched several people emerge. She wished her bloke was the tall, dark-haired fellow with the good-looking, greyish glance in her direction. He was likely selling photocopiers. He moved past her to the security desk while speaking on his mobile phone.

She caught, 'Hello, me again,' and then he was out of earshot. Pity. She scanned the others and, oh yes, here he came. An older guy, breathing audibly, staring at her – at her breasts, actually. And then he too was gone. She watched him pass her by, limping slightly through the revolving doors.

'Lauren?' She was taken aback to see Photocopier Man staring down at her, his sharp gaze glinting like sunlight off a stormy sea. He didn't look thrilled.

'Er, yes,' she said, struggling to get up out of the deep bucket seat and onto her heels. *Damn!*

'Detective Superintendent Jack Hawksworth.' He held out his hand and surprised her by smiling. He was even better-looking close up; even the lines on his face were attractive, and now she couldn't tell – were his eyes green or dark grey? 'Shall we?'

She looked back at him, disarmed. No, this wasn't right. Why did he have to look like this? Why was she wearing a deliberately distressed denim miniskirt with opaque cropped leggings and her thick belt with all that metal? Okay for the magazine – sexy, even, to go for a drink after work – but now she wished with all of her heart, staring at his conservative clothes, that she could have looked a bit less raunchy. Nothing powerful about the way she looked today, with no make-up and two-day-old hair scraped back into a ponytail. *It shouldn't matter*, her internal voice screamed . . . but, of course, it mattered very much to her. In her previous days as a reporter for *London Talking*, she would never step out of her flat unless appropriately attired, head to toe.

His smile widened, and an eyebrow curved up in query. 'I was heading out to grab a coffee. Do you want to walk and talk?'

'All right,' she said, distantly disappointed that he didn't offer her a coffee.

He gestured politely and let her walk first. 'Lovely morning. Thanks for dragging me out.'

'Did I?' As she looked at him, the wind caught his neat hair and, because there was plenty of it, it shifted like a rich wave of nut brown and caught glints of the sun. A policeman? Really?

'All very boring up there,' he assured her. 'And you work for *My Day*, is that right?'

'Yes.' It was the best she could do.

'I must admit, I've never read it, but I think I've seen it around. It's for women, right?'

'Aren't all magazines?' she said, feeling slightly more in control, although his long strides meant she was stalking rather than walking and her heels were sounding a loud tattoo on the pavement.

She watched him frown. 'I disagree. I read *Architectural Digest* as well as *Gourmet*, for instance, and I doubt *Playboy* has ever been published with a woman in mind.' He gave her a sideways grin.

'Do you read *Playboy*?'

Now he laughed. 'No. I prefer *Architectural Digest*, to be honest.'

He'd walked her to St James's Park tube station and pointed to the park itself. 'Over there's a bench in the sunshine. Shall we?'

'What about your coffee?'

'I'll grab it soon. Now, how I can help you? I'm a little confused as to why you wished to see me.'

Go for the jugular, she told herself. *Push him off balance.* 'Rupert Brownlow.'

His perfectly proportioned forehead knitted into a frown. 'The teen who went joy-riding and ended up killing a lot of folk?'

She nodded. 'The same one who was released from prison and then murdered just two nights ago in Portsmouth.'

He shook his head, confused. 'And?'

Okay, so she wasn't even cracking his cool facade. 'And Julian Smythe. Remember him?'

'I do. What do you want me to say?'

'That you're as intrigued as I am that he too was murdered not long after his release.'

'As a policeman I'm obviously interested in any crime.'

'But are you linking them?'

'Me personally? No, I haven't linked them.' Something about the careful, specific way he answered, literally interpreting her question, flagged in her mind. 'Ms Starling, why are you asking me these questions?' That greyish, greenish gaze began to look irritated.

'I am writing an investigative piece that I believe will link these crimes, and others, to a vigilante.'

She watched him carefully but he barely flinched. His phone rang in his pocket and, in an act of courtesy that she had to admire him for, he didn't react to it immediately. He was rubbing day-old stubble that she could hear and for a moment wondered what it would feel like against her skin. It made her angrier to think she was falling under a spell.

'For *My Day*?' he qualified. She nodded, embarrassed. 'To what, be featured alongside Paris Hilton showing off her midriff yet again? Or will you insert this exposé alongside the big question of whether to wear a frayed or non-frayed denim miniskirt?'

Lauren hated that he nodded towards her expertly distressed skirt, which had cost her a cool fortune at All Saints. She might be down, but she wasn't out yet. They both looked at her opaque tights, which ended at sharply angled ankles. 'For *My Day*, yes,' she said, in a tone to match those ankles.

'Excuse me, Ms Starling. I have to get this,' he said, reaching for his still-ringing Nokia. 'Hawskworth.' There was a pause. 'When? All right. Where is she now? Okay, I'll be back in a few minutes. Thanks. Yes. Bye.' He gave a shrug. 'I have to go.'

'So I gather.'

'Why me?'

'Why not?' she said. 'You have the cred for hunting down the last two serial killers our country has been troubled by. If I were the Commissioner, I'd drag you in as a matter of priority.'

She knew her reasoning was rock-solid but he wasn't giving anything away.

'What exactly do you want from me, Ms Starling?'

'Please call me Lauren. Look, Jack . . . may I call you Jack?' He didn't answer. She pressed on. 'I'm going to write this story and I'm going to be digging into these crimes. I thought I'd inform you.'

'Why do I need to know?'

Give him something . . . use it to unnerve him, she told herself. 'Because a little birdie tells me you too are digging around in the same series of crimes. I just thought we could collaborate – you know, scratch each other's backs.'

He laughed and it was a lovely sound. She wished she could share that laugh over pasta and chianti. 'Well, thank you for thinking of us . . . and of me, specifically.'

Lauren bristled. He was gloriously impenetrable; what a lovely challenge. 'I'm not being generous. I'm warning you of my intention.'

'You sounded magnanimous a moment ago. Now you sound threatening.'

She stood up from the bench, hating that he wasn't taking her seriously. 'Well, thanks for at least giving me your time.' She pulled out a card and offered it. 'If you feel like talking . . .'

'To *My Day*?' He shook his head. 'I don't think so.' He took her card anyway to show good manners. 'And apart from this amazing piece of investigative journalism, Lauren, what else are you working on?' he said, standing too.

She would never know why she was candid in that moment, or so self-effacing. 'Well, it's a searing piece about which breed of small dog in 2007 suits the single woman best.' She didn't blink as she said this and met his amused gaze head-on.

He laughed with delight. 'Excellent!'

She joined him with a smile. 'I know, it's powerful stuff. Sort of thing that keeps me awake at night.'

'Have you always worked at this magazine?'

'No, I was with a major news magazine – and I do apologise for trading off that, but I had to reach you somehow.'

'I admire your tenacity, but I'm not your guy. What happened to bring you to *My Day*?'

Again, she was shocked at her honesty. 'I met a bastard, fell for him, lost my flat, my job, my friends . . . and I suppose I'm easing myself back into the game, but it's costing me.'

She watched sympathy light up his eyes, as though he understood something about her now. 'Well, I'm wishing you luck with your endeavours. I'm sorry I was no help.'

'I appreciate your time. Most wouldn't have bothered, so thank you.'

They parted, him back in the direction of New Scotland Yard and wherever his local café was and her into St James's Park tube station.

As the slight breeze was blowing in the right direction, she thought she heard him mutter a cursing word of despair.

Kate was at the morgue where Rupert Brownlow's corpse had arrived.

She'd been expecting Rob Kent, a pathologist who liked to make any observers suffer, especially if he sensed they were particularly squeamish. But Rob was on sabbatical and a new senior pathologist now looked up as she arrived, and with a nod acknowledged her witnessing his study of the body. He was dark-haired, slim beneath his scrubs, and had a neat ducktail beard she'd glimpsed before he pulled on his mask. His gaze was as striking as it was unnerving, with blue eyes the colour of ancient ice.

'Morning. I'm Dr Cook.'

'DI Kate Carter.'

He switched on his microphone, preparing to work.

'So . . . do they call you Cookie?' she said, hoping to get off to a bright start.

'No.' He blinked behind his face mask.

'Oh.' She gave a nervous chuckle. She couldn't tell if he was smiling behind his mask but felt it was safe to say he wasn't. 'Er, thanks for getting onto this so fast.'

'I was told of the urgency. Shall we crack on?'

'Please.' Kate moved closer. She had never got used to the business-like manner of post-mortems; Kate understood there was a job to be done and the pathologists she'd known had been respect-ful towards the dead. But Kate's mind always reached to the family beyond, and this was someone's son. He was a convicted criminal who had served his time whether anyone thought it was appropri-ate or not, and he was surely loved and mourned by people on the other side of the door. In here, though, she had to be objective, alert, and not allow empathy too much room in her mind.

Brownlow's body was still relatively fresh, so the smell wasn't overwhelming. She'd taken the precaution of wearing a mask but it couldn't fully protect her from sensing the unpleasant gaseous odour coming off Brownlow. She was grateful for the tall ceiling and excellent ventilation.

'You're not going to pass out or anything, are you?'

'Absolutely not,' she replied, her sharp tone obviously amusing the pathologist, as she could see the edges of his eyes wrinkling above his mask.

'Good.' He paused for a heartbeat, looking at her, then returned his attention to Brownlow. 'So, Portsmouth has done a very good job, presenting our victim with bagged hands and head, so we have a fighting chance of preserving any trace evidence.' She nodded. 'Right, I'll just do the usual broad brushstrokes,' he warned and began. 'The victim is identified as Rupert Brownlow, a 21-year-old male. There are no tattoos or distinguishing marks. No needle marks in his veins.'

Kate tuned out, allowing her thoughts to roam. When the pathologist found something she didn't already know, she'd hear the difference in his tone.

The crime scene investigation team in Portsmouth had done a professional job too. The information had been emailed promptly, almost as the body had arrived at the morgue in Westminster. She'd been able to walk down to the coroner's court in Horseferry Road, to which the morgue was attached. She wouldn't linger – this was more a courtesy to thank the pathology team for getting onto this pronto – but had wanted to lay eyes on Rupert Brownlow.

She'd never seen a lonelier figure than the one lying on the mortuary bench. He appeared a skinny, pale kid, who looked all the more forlorn and somehow pathetic on the stainless-steel table as his corpse was pushed, pulled and scrutinised by Dr Cookie. She couldn't think of him any other way now.

He'd just glanced her way again.

'Pardon?' she said.

'Did you read that they found footprints at the scene? They're not our victim's. He's a size eleven.'

'Yes, nine and a half, I gather.'

He nodded. 'It's a start for you, because Mr Brownlow isn't giving us much outwardly. Shall I call you when it's done?'

She realised that he was letting her off the uglier scrutiny to come.

She felt gratitude. 'Thanks. That would be great. I can come back down.'

'Or I can ring you,' he said. 'Why don't you leave your number with my assistant?'

She nodded. Dr Cookie wanted her well away from him, it seemed. 'Er, you probably have it on your phone from my call this morning,' she offered.

'I probably do,' he replied, without looking up from scrutinising Rupert's toes. 'Except you called me on the landline. Leave it anyway. I'll put it into my mobile.'

Yes, Dr Cookie wished her gone while he worked. She couldn't blame him for starting at the feet. Even from where she stood she could tell Rupert's head and torso were a mess. Obviously, Portsmouth did everything well, including killing.

11

Her Majesty's Prison Holloway had daunted prisoners for decades. Jack had been intrigued to discover that when it originally opened its imposing doors in the early 1850s, it had taken both sexes; one famous inmate was Oscar Wilde. Demand for a women-only prison meant that it switched its priority at the turn of the century and for the next threescore years and ten, it had held adults and young offenders alike behind its fortress walls.

As another new century approached, the government had decided to bring it up to date; the general agreement was that the makeover was a dismal failure, and Jack could see why if the entrance alone was an indication. It was a brief study on how to make someone feel despair from the moment of arrival. As a person who was intrigued by architecture, he couldn't find anything about the hideous red brick blocks — which looked straight out of the communist Eastern Bloc — to fascinate him. An architect could have used their freedom and budget to bring about something that might at least feel restorative for the inmates. It hunkered down in the middle of inner Islington,

although the prison was big enough to command a neighbourhood all of its own called Holloway.

After he'd shown his warrant card, Jack handed over his phone
and received a tag with a locker number. He passed through a
gate that bleeped and then triggered a search. He was frisked by a
granite-faced prison officer who checked his pockets and scrutinised his shoes.

'I'm a detective superintendent with Scotland Yard,' he said,
making the point.

'Oh, you'd be surprised,' she said. 'Mouth?'

'Pardon?'

'Chewing gum? Say *aaah*.'

He opened his mouth, bemused.

'Thank you, Detective Superintendent. Straight through.' She
gestured ahead.

Another guard smiled. 'Welcome to Holloway. I'm supposed
to give you a stamp on your hand,' she said, 'but I think we can
waive that.'

'Thank you.'

'Go through. The desk will get you sorted.'

Drifting down, as though carried on the wind that was
seeping into the corridor through cracks in windows and under
doors, Jack could hear the shrieks of women. He knew there
was something in the order of four hundred and fifty prisoners inside, and it sounded like every one of them was presently
screaming.

At the desk, another officer gave him the once-over before
rewarding him with a curt smile. 'Oh, you'll be popular,' she said,
and he ignored the backhanded compliment.

'I've only been here once previously. Is it always like this?'

'All day, every day. You get used to it.'

'Get used to women screaming? I doubt I could.'

She said no more. Her colleague arrived. 'Detective Super-intendent Jack Hawksworth?'

'Yes.'

'The Governor told us to expect you. Seems you're liked,' she said. 'Anne McEvoy is just finishing up one of her group sessions. I can take you over. We haven't mentioned to her that you're coming.'

'No, that's all right,' he said, trying to calm the nest of snakes suddenly uncoiling in his belly at the thought of seeing Anne again.

They began walking through bleak corridors of scuffed lino that squeaked beneath the prison officer's rubber soles. Fluorescents flickered on the low ceiling above, and the walls were a colour Jack could only describe as a poor attempt at aquamarine. Someone – no doubt an inmate who fancied herself an artist, but wasn't that good – had painted murals along the long tunnels and, somehow, instead of brightening them had made them seem darker, more melancholy. They were like galleries, these older prisons, so the warders could easily see from end to end and there was nowhere for prisoners to hide or leap out from.

'I'm taking you to a room we use for group meetings,' the warder said over her shoulder. Another mural of a tree only made the place feel more depressing, if that was possible.

Anne was serving several life sentences here and he hoped, for her sake, that she could be moved to a brighter, healthier prison, away from London, perhaps. 'I hear they're talking about closing Holloway.'

'You hear right,' his squeaking companion confirmed. Keys jangled from a large clip on her belt, which was holding up blokey trousers.

'Must be time,' he muttered.

'Yeah, but what about our jobs?'

'True,' he agreed, not wishing to inflame her mood. He'd heard horror tales of bashings by the guards, and her hands looked like they'd ball up into a bigger fist than he could make. 'Thank you very much,' he said, as she slowed in front of a door.

'McEvoy's in here. You've got forty-five minutes.'

Jack nodded.

'I'll be at the back of the room, out of earshot.'

'Thank you.' He stared at the door.

'Go in, mate. She doesn't bite.'

He gave her a sick version of his smile, not that she'd know it.

'No touching.' That last was said sarcastically.

Jack turned back to the door and looked in through the narrow window. There she was, as attractive as he remembered, and busy moving chairs around. He knocked and she looked up, but either she didn't recognise him immediately or couldn't see properly, because she simply beckoned. He opened the door and stepped across the threshold.

'Hello, Anne.'

She stared, looking like someone trapped in time, which in many ways she was. 'Jack,' she muttered, her voice gritty. 'What?' Then she half smiled, half sighed. 'Really?'

'May I?'

'Yes, yes, of course. Come in.' He watched her hand fly to her hair, push it back nervously around one ear. It was clean and slippery, still glowing its bright blonde. 'Er, would you like to sit down?'

'Thanks.' He sat where she gestured, and they stared at each other before both looking back at the prison officer, who was far enough away and reading the newspaper. Jack glanced back to Anne. 'You look surprisingly well. Thinner.'

'Food's horrid here. And thin can't be a bad thing.'

That voice. It brought back so many memories of the briefest time in his life when he was ridiculously happy. 'Is that prison garb, or . . .'

'No, we're all allowed to wear our own clothes.'

'I should have brought you something, er . . .'

She shook her head. 'It's fine. I'm amazed and intrigued as to why you're here, actually.'

He sighed. 'Wow, we're awkward, aren't we?'

'You certainly are.' She chuckled and began pulling her hair back into a ponytail as she seemed to relax. 'Are you well, Jack? You must have brightened up the day of those prison officers.'

'I felt like an insect being pinned to a board.'

She laughed at the image. 'Yes, well, we don't get tall, dark, handsome strangers around here.'

He let the compliment pass by. 'You sound good, Anne.'

Her smile broadened. 'Given my circumstances, I have to admit I'm enjoying my role here. I mean, I hate prison, but I feel like I'm achieving something, giving others confidence and motivation. The prison team believe it's worthy, so I'm given a lot of rope, you know. It's weird, but I'm a better person on the inside than I was walking free.'

'I don't know what to say to that.'

Anne shrugged. 'I had a choice. I had to decide to live or die here. It's easy to die. It's much harder to live, to survive, to turn one's life around. I chose the harder road and I suppose it's giving back some reward now.'

He nodded, again finding it hard to think of anything worthy to say to that. 'Samantha?' It slipped out before he could stop himself.

Pain danced across her features and she swallowed and closed her eyes momentarily. 'Sorry,' she said. 'I didn't know you even knew her name.'

'That was brutal of me. I didn't know I was going to mention her. I've kept in touch with the Governor . . . er, just to make sure you're both, well, coping,' he struggled, annoyed with himself for lacking his usual grace. If Martin Sharpe knew he was here without his express permission, he'd skin him. But then he probably already knew, as Joan had likely implanted some sort of spy tracker on his clothes – in his phone, maybe, or in the heel of his shoe. The skinning awaited him, but he would argue that with his promotion surely came the power to make this sort of decision, especially due to its urgency.

Anne's injured gaze found his. 'Why wouldn't you mention her? I'm pleased you have. To risk a dreadful cliché, she's the light of my life, Jack.'

'Is she still . . .' He shrugged, gesturing awkwardly by sweeping his hand towards the wall lined with books.

She shook her head. 'No. It's been twenty-three days and . . .' Anne glanced at the clock on the wall. 'And six hours, thirteen minutes since my child was taken away.'

It was his turn to swallow.

'Don't say anything,' she said, saving him the torture of bolting together the right words of sympathy. 'Nothing can stop the pain and it's mine alone to deal with; I brought this on her, on myself. But you should know that she's beautiful and bright, and I hope whoever is fortunate enough to consider her their daughter will love her as much as I do.' Her eyes welled with tears.

'You know, I was secretly glad when you dodged us,' he said, shifting the topic. 'I hoped you'd stay lost forever.'

'Really?' She smiled back sadly.

He nodded. 'I will admit my heart was crushed when I got the call to say you'd been found and were being sent back to Britain. I'm sorry it was me who—'

'No, I understood. You had to finish your job. You were very cold that day though. You barely looked at me.'

'I was only just holding myself together to have to escort you to prison, but perhaps you read about the case I was on?'

She nodded. 'Hideous.'

He decided not to tell her about his relationship with Lily; hoped she didn't know. 'It was awful, Anne. Worse than working on your case, to be honest. I think if we walked in your shoes, we could all understand your motive. But that guy, Chan? It was arrogance and money that drove him. And his victims were all hand-chosen innocents, selected for their faces and murdered for them. He's a monster. You never were.' He tried to smile but couldn't. 'But now you're a criminal psychologist?'

'Unfortunately, it took the monster getting out to allow me to become myself.' She shrugged. 'Here I am, normal Anne. Almost surprised that I was capable of such brutality and terror. I was always a fully qualified clinical psychologist, Jack, I just didn't tell you. My specialty was criminology. Now at least I'm putting that knowledge to good use.'

'No wonder you were always one step ahead of us.'

'I've never apologised . . . never had the opportunity.'

He stared at her. They were at the precipice.

'But I am sorry, you know. If I have one blinding regret through everything that's happened, it's using you.'

He nodded.

'And falling in love with you.'

He blew out his breath audibly. 'I hope they don't record conversations here.'

She smiled. 'Not in this room, no.'

Jack finally shook his head. 'We have to both live with your regret.'

'Yes. I have the heartache too of letting my child down. But when I took my revenge, I didn't know the pain of parenthood existed in the world. It was getting pregnant that got me caught. Anyway, suffice to say, you two are the big pains in my heart.' She tried to smile but looked more likely to cry.

'Can I get you anything?'

'No, I deserve this. And it's good to cry sometimes. Better than screaming.'

'I can't believe the noise here.'

Anne nodded. 'It's dreadful, a constant reminder of the pain of where we all are . . . the children, families, dreams we've all squandered.' She tilted her head from side to side as if weighing something up. 'However, the pain reminds me I'm alive and that I can repay my sins by helping others who have a chance at rebuilding their lives.' She checked the clock again and a pause lengthened between them as she straightened in her chair, looking helplessly attractive in old Levis and a slouchy, soft grey crew-necked sweater. 'Why are you here, Jack? It's been so long it can't be because you're curious.'

'No, I do have a reason.' He paused. 'If I'm honest, I'm utterly shocked to find myself sitting here in front of you.'

She frowned. 'What is it?'

Anne McEvoy sat back and regarded Jack, seemingly stunned by all that he'd just told her about what sounded like a series of revenge murders.

Her scrutiny weighed on him. Was this a mistake? Had Kate miscalculated? Had he simply used this as an excuse to see her again? Perhaps all three, but he had to admit it was thrilling to be looking upon the first and only woman to hold his heart. There had been plenty of women before Anne, and it had taken six months but he'd begun dating again after Lily's death, needing company, knowing he also needed to rebuild a life.

There had been some other dates of surface interest and Sylvie was his current attraction; she was always fun and especially easy to be with because all she wanted from him was laughter, sex and companionship. There was no threat of it turning serious, so that was empowering, and why he always returned her calls to action . . . the trip to Cap Ferrat being a fine example. She was currently talking about a mini break to Prague.

'Am I your Hannibal Lecter?' Anne sounded amused.

'You can view yourself that way, if you like,' he replied with a laugh.

'Then you're my Clarice Starling.' She chuckled, reminding him of the conversation he'd had with the attractive, unfulfilled journalist.

'I have no doubt I'm crossing some unspoken but obvious boundary in even asking, but we figured you might be able to give us some insight into the mind of this killer.'

'We?'

'DI Carter made the suggestion.'

'Ah, Kate. She's on this case too? Dangerous.'

'Why do you say that?'

She looked back at him as though he were a simpleton. 'Because Kate is fond of you in a way that is unhelpful to everyone, especially herself.'

'She's fine.'

'If you say so.'

'Will you help me?' He made it a personal plea.

'What's involved, Clarice?'

'No idea. Never done anything like this before and it's off the record, Anne. I dare not even let the powers that be know. Nothing official.'

'I feel I owe you.'

'I didn't say you owe me anything, nor would I.'

'But you agree?' she asked. He just stared back. 'Am I allowed to look at anything?'

'Files? Absolutely not.'

'Photos? Pathology?'

'No, sorry.'

'So your explanation alone is supposed to assist me to help you unlock where you should hunt for this killer?'

'It's crazy, I agree.'

Anne smiled and he tried not to let that all-too-familiar warmth reach far enough in to touch him. As it was, hearing the soft tones of her voice was hard on his emotions, which were crashing around within – guilt, desire, horror, sorrow . . . regret as much as pleasure just to look upon her, all colliding.

'It's not crazy, Jack. It's unusual but it's also irresistible for all the obvious reasons.'

'So that's a yes?' He grinned with hope.

'At least share the name of the operation. I'm sure you told me when we first met that operations always have odd names. Amuse me.'

He figured it was safe. 'Mirror.'

'Operation Mirror?' She laughed. 'I like it.'

'We're not admitting to having an op underway, of course.'

'No one will hear about any of this from me.'

'I appreciate it.'

'Where do we begin?'

He checked his watch. 'You're on board?'

'I do have a caveat.'

'Of course you do. Don't ask me to get you a reduced sentence, or days on the outside . . . or a file or shovel,' he joked. 'Before we discuss your caveat, do you have any initial thoughts?'

'Well, from what you've told me, my gut feeling is that you are dealing with a male.'

'Why?'

'Women killers tend to know their targets quite well; they have some sort of relationship with their victims that has an emotional link.'

'Like you?'

'Exactly. Men are far more capable of killing strangers. I'm not saying these victims are not known to the killer, but they are not connected in time, location or modus operandi, so there is more likelihood they don't share a relationship with the killer, as such. Plus, what you're up against is calculated killing over a stretch of time, and given that the most recent you mentioned . . .'

'The lorry driver and the careless drunken teen driver,' he offered with no names.

'Yes . . . given their deaths are barely six weeks apart, he is escalating.'

'My thought too. Why?'

She shrugged. 'Anything from his age or health, to him feeling the heat of the police, or the heat of the weather.' At Jack's frown, she smiled. 'It's easier to kill in winter – there are fewer people around, the cover of darkness from late afternoon, and just the sheer cold keeping people indoors.'

'This killer is not feeling our radar yet. And I'm not buying the weather as the reason.'

'Okay, age and health, then.'

'Thoughts on that?'

She shook her head. 'Your killer has avoided capture by being smart. There's a level of intelligence here, but there's patience too, and from what you've said there's no need to glorify the killing, no weird messages left.' She frowned. 'No sexual component?'

'None.'

'Okay, that's interesting.' Anne stood and took a few paces before turning back to him. 'The deaths are swift, by all accounts, so it's a job being done . . . it's not a hobby, no pleasure apparently derived. I'm going out on a limb here, Jack, and would prefer to study some more information . . .' She glanced questioningly at Jack, who just gazed back with an implacable expression.

'All right. But this is my take based only on what you've told me. I think this is an older person rather than younger because of the maturity required to be absolutely in control.'

He nodded. 'Any other reason that you think it's calculated?'

She looked away from him as though running through all that he'd told her. 'Well, I am sensing no heat in the killings.'

He was surprised and must have shown it, because she continued.

'Don't get me wrong; there's rage, for sure, but the various deaths are so disconnected that – on the surface, anyway – this feels like someone taking cold retribution, as opposed to someone like me, who took passionate and personal revenge.' She glanced back at him helplessly. 'Without more detail . . .'

'I understand.'

'A male is likely because we rarely happen upon a female serial killer; often they're accomplices – so don't rule that out – or if they're acting alone, they tend to be nurses who kill patients, or wives who kill a string of husbands. Most hunted serial killers are sociopathic or psychopathic men.'

'Other than you?'

'We're not talking about me, Jack.'

'Well, we are drawing on your experience as a serial murderer.'

She sighed and he could see what it cost her each time she had to acknowledge this fact. 'Mine was targeted vengeance for a single wrong. The average person on the street was safe from me. I had a specific list of people to pay for the savage murder of my dog and my repeated rape, as a helpless, innocent thirteen-year-old. It was opportunistic. When I was the perpetrator, though, no one innocent got hurt.' Her voice shook slightly, and she pushed back a few strands of golden hair that had flown loose from her ponytail. She cleared her throat and took control again. 'Perhaps you could term it as having a psychotic episode, but if

I'd not been found, I swear I would be living quietly on a Greek island in near enough to perfect happiness, and no one would think I was anything but a blonde Brit chasing the sun. And I would have lived and died peacefully as that person, raising my child, never upsetting another soul, because my rage was spent. Unless your team finds some extraordinary link that ties these criminals together into one original crime, then my initial assessment is that this is a man, on a mission, whose rage is prevalent and has no intention of dissipating.'

'The mission?'

She laughed and shrugged. 'Oh, Jack, it could be so many things. He could believe they're all demons from the Underworld. He could have a grudge against these people, although my suspicion is that these aren't the only deaths you may end up attributing to him.'

'We've reached a similar conclusion.'

Anne shook her head, searching for more ideas. 'My instinct says he's not killing criminals for kicks. If he was getting his rocks off, then the deaths might be more elaborate . . . Oh, any trophies taken?'

'None to our knowledge.'

'So he really isn't aroused by these deaths. This feels personal to him, nonetheless. A vendetta, or a path of . . . I have to say it . . .' Jack looked at her expectantly and with an expression that gave permission. 'Vigilance,' she said.

He dropped his shoulders. 'We were trying to avoid the vigilante label.'

'It feels like a fit though.'

'But we can't find connections. Vigilantes must have a *raison d'être*, something that makes all the killings meaningful, right?'

'And so will Mirror Man, I promise you. There is a connection, Jack. Find it, or you'll never find him.'

'Mirror Man. I like it.' He grinned. 'So . . . your caveat?'

She looked hesitant.

'Try me,' he encouraged her.

'Samantha.'

His gaze darkened.

'Look, I know I can't see her, and I spent the time I had with her promising myself I wouldn't interrupt her new life with her adopted mother.'

'That's quite a promise.'

'And one I intend to keep, because I'm trapped here and nothing I do or say will change that. She really doesn't need the burden of obligation to visit a mother in prison with no chance of release. I hope she never looks for me or even knows about me. But that doesn't take away how much I love her or need her in my thoughts.'

'So how do I fit into this?'

'Find out where she's gone.'

'Anne—'

'Hear me out. Discover her whereabouts, but you don't have to tell me, and I give you my word I will never ask. I know I owe you, Jack; I know you all but let me go that day when you were chasing me in Brighton, so this is part of that debt. I will never make you feel awkward, but I want you to have the knowledge of where she is and I want to know that you will somehow stay in touch with her life on my behalf.'

He blinked, hurting for her. 'That's no small responsibility.'

'We loved each other, Jack. Samantha could so easily have been a daughter we were now doting over together. I'm not trying to make you responsible for another man's child, but we're connected in ways that are hard to verbalise. So keep an eye on her for me. Just knowing you know how she is, where she is, is enough.'

He looked trapped. 'I'll try, Anne. That's all I can offer.'

Anne smiled. 'And that's enough for me. Thank you.' She glanced at the door. 'Your minder's ready.'

He motioned that he was coming. 'I'll see you again soon.'

'I'll be here.' She smiled. 'Bring chocolate!'

Jack left Holloway feeling like a moth easing out of its cocoon, desperate for escape from the prison, but mindful of who he was leaving behind and the effect she still had on him. Now he'd agreed to what felt like an impossible task of finding out information about her daughter. On the plus side, Anne's agile mind had already started to range on Operation Mirror's behalf, and so much of what she had said, even as casual comment, rang true in his mind. There were no definites in this cat-and-mouse game but already he was beginning to see their prey as a man on a mission, as she'd described. It helped to have her objective clarity. Nevertheless, Mirror Man would remain purely reflective until they found something . . . one tiny link that could convince him there was a single person on a killing spree.

His phone rang while he was in the taxi on the way back to Scotland Yard. 'Hi, Kate.'

'We've got a shoe size for our killer. Size forty-three . . . that's nine and a half in old money. If I said Saloman to you, would you know who or what that is?'

'No. If I said Mies van der Rohe to you, would you?'

She laughed. 'Idiot. Saloman is a brand of outdoor shoe.'

'Excellent, I shall bring that up in dinner conversation soon. Mies van der Rohe is the architect who coined the phrase "less is more" and introduced the world to what we now call minimalism. I take it our killer was wearing these Sultan shoes?'

'Salomans,' she corrected, amused. 'Yes. X-Pro Trail.'

'So we need to check for that with all the other forensics from all the other crime scenes.'

'Already got the team on it. Where are you?'

'On the way back.'

'From where?'

'I'll tell you later. Anything else?'

'Sarah is working like a crazed terrier. I think she might have a sniff of something.'

'Already?'

'She won't say, but she still hasn't taken her anorak off.'

He grinned as he clicked off.

12

As Jack was sitting in a taxi thinking about Anne McEvoy, Davey Robbins was scrolling mindlessly through the songs on his iPod, wishing he'd never met Amy the barmaid, whom he blamed for ruining his life. Conveniently, he chose not to think about his own criminal lifestyle that had led him there. As far as Davey was concerned – and as he'd whinged to his court-appointed solicitor – that was all on Don. And the rape was instigated and forced upon him by Don too. He knew it was a lie but he needed to get out of a harsh sentence. Let Don take the rap – he was old. Turning on his partner was the only way, according to Davey's counsel, and then using every excuse, from him being a slow learner to having been raised with a shocking childhood of crime and lack of care. It was all lies but, frankly, it was easy to spin them – from the outside his life did look tragic, but he had never complained. He was good at burglaries. It was Amy and her flaunty tits that had brought them down.

Anyway, now here he was, working his frozen fingers to the bone alongside a pile of immigrants. He thought he was getting out

when they'd released him from prison; couldn't believe it when he
was told that his sentence was being reduced. He hadn't really paid
much attention; he would have said yes to anything to get away
from the clank of cell doors and the hideous routine of the jail,
scary blokes at every turn, each trying to out-threaten the other.
But he hated this life of hard labour outside in the elements.

He tucked his iPod back into his pocket and looked at the
chunky black watch on his wrist. Mr Chingford was running very
late today; it was already darkening, and a light drizzle had begun.
But he didn't dare move from the spot. This was where he was
dropped off and picked up every working day. He was never to
deviate – those were the rules – and Davey had no intention of
breaking any rules . . . he had zero desire to be locked up again.

'About effing time,' he murmured as headlights picked out the
hedgerow in a ghostly amber.

But the car that drove up wasn't Chingford's. The window
rolled down and a different guy leaned across from the driver's
side. 'Are you Davey Robbins?'

He pulled out one earphone to reply, frowning. 'Yeah, that's me.'

'Get in, son. I'm what they call a relief minder.'

'Where's Mr Chingford?'

'He's had to go to hospital. I'm taking you today.'

'What happened?'

'Gallstones, they said. Lots of pain. Hop in before we both get
soaked – I want to wind the window up.'

'Who are you?' Davey asked, climbing into the passenger seat
of the small hatchback. He pulled out his iPod again to switch it
off, placing it in his lap and disconnecting the headphones.

'Hang on, I'll just get us back on the road. Don't want to get
bogged on the verge. This is a bit of a dangerous bend. Ah, that's
better. Are you always picked up here?' He frowned at Davey,
who nodded. 'Odd spot.'

'Yeah, well, it's usually still light enough.' He wondered at the wisdom of getting lippy with the stranger, but the man was concentrating on the road.

'All right, now,' Davey heard him say, almost to himself. He watched the new guy check the rear-view, look in his side windows and then back to the rear-view like a typical oldie, Davey thought. 'I'm not familiar with these roads, so give me a tick. Let's just lock these doors, as it's quite dark out, isn't it?' The man pushed a central locking button.

'No one's going to mug us,' Davey said, exasperated.

'You never know who is around the corner, Davey. Can't be too careful,' the man said, cutting him a benign smile in the dull light.

'It's straight down there and turn left.' Davey pointed to get them moving.

'Righto. Just a quick errand to run, won't take a few ticks.'

Davey sighed. At least he was out of the rain. 'Warm in here. Feels like you've been driving a while?'

His driver frowned. 'Oh, yes. I, er . . . I've been running all these errands for everyone. When you're a relief minder, they seem to think they can give you a list of all the stuff to do that no one else wants to. Now, just let me concentrate here.'

Davey stared ahead but mentally he was rolling his eyes with impatience. It had been made clear to him that only Chingford was responsible for his transport but this dithering man seemed to know all about him, and Chingford, too. Davey was happy to be away from the bastard vegetables and the filthy Poles, and he really just wanted his working day over. Tomorrow was Saturday. Football, video games, a chance to go to the shop, sleep in – all of those normal things.

'So, Davey, were you originally in the sex offenders area at Wormwood Scrubs or Wandsworth? I used to work in the nonces' wing at Wandsworth Prison.'

'Wormwood, and then I had some time at High Point Prison.'

'Ah, near Newmarket, the old RAF base. I know it.'

'Yeah. But then I moved to HMP Wakefield, which is a category C prison.'

'Fortunate.'

'Yeah, pretty low-key there and they had schemes for us. They put me in a training unit for outdoor cultivation. I didn't think they'd send me up here though, but I took it because they had an opening. I just wanted out of the cells, and the home in Selby for sex offenders seemed an easy gig.'

'Far away from home.'

'S'okay,' he mumbled. 'Not forever. And it got me out of the jail system.'

'And how are you getting on?'

'I hate it up here. It's always cold, always raining, they've got stupid accents, and every northerner seems to hate anyone from the south.'

'I rather like Yorkshire.'

'Well, this place I work at Sherburn is the arse end of Britain, I can tell you. But I know I have to keep my nose clean for a bit longer and look like I've really changed my ways, and then I can get back down to London.'

'And have you changed your ways, Davey?'

He shrugged. 'I don't plan on doing it again, if that's what you mean.'

'Getting caught, you mean?' The guy actually winked but didn't wait for Davey to answer. 'Do the crime, do the time,' he continued.

Davey didn't like the man's smugness. 'Yeah, well, that girl I was supposed to have raped was a pricktease at the pub, really coming on, you know.'

'Well, Davey, the jury saw it differently. *That girl*, as you describe her, was employed to be welcoming to customers.

There is a reliable witness to say she was polite and appropriately friendly, that's all. Your interpretation of her being some sort of tart doesn't wash. She came from a good family, was a talented creative headed for university, and she'd only had one boyfriend through school. She was a virgin when you raped her.'

'You seem to know a lot about my case,' Davey snarled.

'That's my job. If I'm going to be your minder for the next few weeks until Mr Chingford is well enough to return, it would be remiss of me not to have read your file, don't you agree?'

'No. I don't think it's any of your business. I thought your job was to see I go to and fro each day, that's all.'

'Well, it may look simple to you, Davey, but I take my role seriously. And you need to take responsibility. And by the by, there was no *supposition* about it. You broke into her house, your companion killed her grandmother and you raped the young victim while your mate held her down. That's a very long way from consensual.'

'I dunno what that means,' Davey lied. 'Mr Chingford doesn't judge.'

The man laughed. 'No, and that's fair enough. But there are some who might think your victims didn't get justice.'

'I don't care.'

'What about your work here? Are you making a good fist of it? It all bodes well for you if you work hard and don't complain, right? Now, we just have to go up here, I think.' The driver squinted through his large glasses and the light drizzle that danced in front of the headlights. 'Yes, right here, I believe.'

'I hate the immigrants I'm with. I'm the only English bloke and I don't see why they have to be here, taking our jobs.'

'Immigrants?'

'Polish, Lithuanian, Russian, Czech . . . I dunno. They all sound the same to me, talking their rubbish language and living in their filthy caravans. All the men are benefit scroungers and all the women I pick vegetables with look like men.' Davey laughed scornfully. 'They blather in their stupid talk – they all sound Russian.'

'You sound angry.'

'Yeah, I am. It's a fuckin' disgrace that I have to work with people who don't even speak English. I'm going to join that Combat party.'

'Don't they have links around the world to Neo-Nazis?'

'So?'

'Not a good idea, Davey.'

'No? In prison, right, I listened to a lot of fascist talk and now it all really makes sense.' He knew he was getting worked up, but this guy had a way of getting under his skin. 'I didn't see these people in my neighbourhood in London, but they're everywhere, and not just them; it's everyone . . . no one's English any more, are they?'

'Looking to find your tribe again, are you?'

Davey wasn't sure what that meant but blocking out the Eastern Europeans was why his iPod was everything to him. He could disconnect from their babble and escape his horrible life in the cold mud of Yorkshire by listening to an endless loop of music, particularly the song that had sat for seven consecutive weeks at the top of the English rock and metal charts the previous year. His iPod was precious. He'd saved every penny he could to buy the electric blue second-generation model. Apart from his clothes, he didn't own anything but this tiny piece of tech; he didn't count his watch, a cheap digital they'd given him at the home. He usually just put the song from My Chemical Romance on repeat . . . sometimes it played all day into his head and helped to keep him angry – and it made sure the others gave him a wide berth.

The car turned off the main road. 'Where are we going?'

'I have to pick up something from one of the filthy caravans, as you put it.'

Davey frowned. 'The Polish ones? Why?'

'Are they Polish? I wouldn't know. I have two errands: picking up a parcel from the only caravan in Leveson's top field . . . ah, there's the gate now. I'll need to check which direction, so we don't search in the dark . . .' the bloke said, reaching to pull out an envelope from the glove compartment. '. . . and pick up Davey Robbins and deliver him . . . and deliver you, we shall.'

We? Davey didn't see the syringe that the fellow pulled from the envelope, but he felt the needle stab into his neck.

'Ouch!' he yelled. 'What the f—'

'You're a lucky boy, Davey. I'm showing more kindness than you showed Amy or her grandmother before you hurt them.'

'The fu—?' Davey repeated in an angry voice, feeling something cold begin to ease through him from where he'd been stabbed. He began scrabbling at the locked door. It wouldn't open; the man kept relocking it from the central console each time Davey released it. He tried to swing a punch, but his fist seemed to move in slow motion.

'Don't fight it, Davey. Amy fought you and it got her nowhere. I can assure you that you'll get no further than the roadside. So do me a favour and settle down . . . let it work.'

'Why?' Davey wasn't sure but he thought he might be crying.

'Why?' The man laughed, hugely amused. 'Why did I just give you an enormous dose of propofol? I'm sure you're already feeling drowsy . . . we'll just give it a little longer.'

'What do you want?'

'I want you to die, Davey, so I plan to stop your heart with a much bigger dose of propofol. Right now it's keeping you sedated but it will wear off unless I top you up, which I'll do shortly. The world is going to be a much better place for Amy and her family without you in it. In the meantime, however, seeing that you haven't learned your lesson and still bear Amy and the world a lot of hate, I think we need to teach you something before you drift away. I might even chop your old fellow off as a special courtesy to young Amy. But don't worry, I'll snip that off with very sharp shears after you're dead. No pain, less blood . . . no screaming.' The man laughed again.

'Please . . .'

'No, Davey, that doesn't work. You know that – Amy pleaded with you and you ignored her. Fair's fair. By the way, the Polish keep their caravans spotless, from what I hear. Righto, you're looking very sleepy. Let's get you sorted.'

Davey's last immediate thought was for his electric blue iPod as it slipped from his lap.

When Davey stirred, he was able to work out that his mouth was taped up heavily, his hands were cuffed and he was on his knees with his arms above his head leaning against a tree. He looked up to make sense of it all in the murky, intermittent moonlight. When that pale light next emerged from behind the night clouds, he could see rope attached to the cuffs that bound his hands; he followed its path to see it was slung over a sturdy branch and then pulled taut, tied to the bumper of a car. *How did he get here? Who did that car belong to? What was going on?!*

'Crude but effective,' a voice that some primitive response told him to fear said from behind him. 'Welcome back, Davey. You've been out for twenty minutes.'

He whipped his head around, trying to see the man who spoke. The man came into view and regarded him, almost studying him. Davey looked back wildly.

'Ah, yes, I was warned about this. The drug I've used does cause memory loss. Do you remember me picking you up, Davey?'

He shook his head.

'Not to worry. And I must thank you for staying semi-conscious and helping me by getting yourself out of the car and into the woods. You were most compliant . . . saves my old back a bit.' The man chuckled. 'Now to answer the question burning in those frightened eyes of yours – what do I want? What I want is you dead. That's what I explained to you in the car.'

Davey whimpered.

'Justice was never served with your sentence, Davey. I know you haven't forgotten that you're a heinous law-breaker of the cruellest kind. Accidents happen, and I can forgive accidents. But what you did was deliberate, and calculated to cause harm. Your sentence was always too lenient and you clearly haven't learned much at all from incarceration. I think you'd go straight back to your bad ways in London.'

Unable to speak, Davey shook his head violently.

'You'd say anything at this point. I don't trust you. And besides, I don't like you. I don't like what you did. I don't like how you sneered in the court. I don't like how you performed your part like an old pro for your defence counsel, when even right now I know you harbour intense hatred for people around you. I don't like that you never showed an ounce of genuine contrition towards the Clarke family. You will rape again, Davey. You are a lowlife and a threat to society.'

Davey moaned. He tried to beg but the masking tape was too firm. It just came out as a pathetic squeal.

'Justice, Davey. That's what this is about. Can't go back and serve your time properly, so let's just go forward and you can pay for it all now.'

Davey began to scream, but it was really just an animalistic sound, and the man who planned to kill him spoke over it.

'So, I went to some trouble to learn how to insert this cannula into your vein. See? Just here.' He shone a torch into the dimming light and Davey only now saw the butterfly clip and the sinuous plastic tube that curled away from his arm. 'And then we'll attach a syringe full of propofol. That will fix you up nicely, I think.'

Davey began to cry in a long silent sob, eyes clenched in terror.

'Oh dear. I'm sure Amy could sympathise with how you feel right now. Anyway, let's crack on, shall we? There's just one thing to do before I allow you to go to sleep, my friend. The longest sleep, that is.' He gave a low chuckle. 'It won't take long if we just go at it. It's not your old fellow that's the problem − your hands are the offenders. Hands that thieve, hands that grip a girl and ravage her and touch her in places you have no permission to touch. Now, there are still some places in the world today where they cut off the hand of a thief. And you are a pathological thief, so we'll take a hand off for that. And then you thieved something precious from Amy, so for that I'm going to take off the other hand.'

Davey let go. His bladder emptied through his jeans and the air about them filled with the unpleasant, slightly sweet and acrid smell of urine.

His killer tsk–tsked. 'Awful to feel that frightened, isn't it? This is how Amy felt. I think it's valid that you feel this fear. I'm proud of you, even. Now at least you know.'

Davey couldn't even feel the cooling dampness between his legs. He pleaded with his eyes, shaking his head, hoping to find some mercy. But the man looked as distracted as he was impervious to the pleas.

'I'm no surgeon, of course, so we'll do it the quickest way.' He pointed to an axe that Davey only now noticed. His eyes widened in understandable horror. He began to struggle, his actions hysterical. 'Not worth it, Davey. The more you move around, the less accurate I can be. I used to be a pretty good wood chopper when I was a lad, so I suggest you trust my aim and strength. Be still and we'll whip those hands off in a jiffy and then I'll press that syringe and you'll be off to find your maker somewhere in hell, I hope.' The man reached for the axe. Davey did his best to scream, tried to stand but only now realised his ankles were bound and so were his knees. He was too weak anyway.

'Righto, Davey. Here we go. This is what we call justice for thieves who steal people's lives.'

The man measured the blade against Davey's wrists, then swung the axe back, and Davey lifted his chin and screamed through his already raw throat.

13

Jack arrived back at the incident room and could feel the electricity that was crackling invisibly through his team members.

'Here he is,' Kate said to Sarah, nudging her. Kate gave him a nod and he understood immediately.

'All right, everyone. I gather Sarah's got something to share.'

The room quietened and people moved closer, giving their full attention.

'Are we missing anyone?'

'All present,' Kate confirmed.

'Over to you, then,' he said, gesturing for Sarah to take the floor.

She'd removed her anorak, Jack noticed, and now she stood, pushing her glasses back up her nose. 'Er, well, there's not a lot to say, but I believe HOLMES has arrived at what is certainly one commonality that simply cannot be ignored. This is not going to deliver us a serial killer immediately . . .' She paused, unsure now that she had everyone's focused silence, but took a breath and pressed on. 'So, we all know the four victims were either convicted or certainly charged with a serious crime. Each crime involved a death. Each received a lenient sentence and in one case no conviction. Those who went to prison served only a partial sentence.'

Jack hoped everyone would hold onto their patience; Sarah was telling them stuff they already knew.

'But the database has told us that each of the original crimes was committed in the Borough of Enfield, and every one of those original court cases was heard at North London Crown Court.'

Her words were met with stunned silence.

Jack broke it from where he sat on the corner of a desk. 'Good work, Sarah!'

She gave him a nervous beam of pleasure.

'Excellent,' he continued. 'All right, everyone. Now we have something. This is great policing and a fast result. Our superiors will be impressed. So, we focus on Enfield. We need to talk to the court and see what the staff remember about these cases and any others that smack of any similarity. Kate, can you get Mal to handle that and to work out who does what?'

'On it,' she confirmed.

'Sarah, I want you breaking down those old cases for us and with special emphasis on the courts, so we can target them properly like a wolf pack.'

'Yes, I've begun that, sir.'

'Good stuff.'

'Kate, perhaps you can focus on scrutinising the original crimes – I'll help with that. Which police teams were involved, and original investigating officers, et cetera.'

She nodded. 'Yes. Everyone, I know we're not ready to call it yet, but we do have a shoe size from the Portsmouth killing and it doesn't belong to the victim. So at this point we are presuming the person who killed him was wearing a size nine and a half trail shoe, if that helps any of you with your enquiries.'

'So, Enfield is potentially where our killer hails from. What else?' There was a silence as the group pondered this. Jack broke it. 'Commonalities in pathology?' He looked at Sarah.

'Er . . . hang on.' She tapped on her keyboard, scrutinising the screen. Everyone waited expectantly. 'Of the four we have, we're waiting on toxicology for Robbins and Brownlow, but Peggy Markham had traces of propofol. No sedatives with Toomey. No drugs at all, in fact, which is refreshing for a long-haul truck driver.'

Jack nodded. 'Let's keep a watch on the propofol.'

Mal frowned. 'If he is using drugs to make victims compliant, then it might be worth having a chat to our local street pharmacists in the Enfield area.' The incident room people chuckled at his polite term.

'Okay, you can handle that?'

Mal nodded. 'Easy.'

'Right,' Jack said, sighing as he drilled down into his thoughts. 'We're moving a click back into the original crimes. I want us sifting through every aspect of those crime scenes, forensics, pathology, investigation and trials – nothing left unchecked, okay?' He won a series of nods. 'That's a lot of work, so call it early doors tonight and get a good night's sleep, because we'll be hauling through the weekend. No partying, folks.'

Kate began ushering people away. 'Go on, you heard the Chief. Have a good evening and see you all tomorrow. Sorry to ruin your Saturday.' She checked her email and then tapped on the glass that separated Jack's office. 'I've just heard back from Pathology on Brownlow. His full report will be in overnight – they were just a bit late for our briefing.'

'And?'

'Brownlow may well have taken his last breath on the end of that rope attached to the car, but his fate was already sealed by a hefty amount of Rohypnol that was in his final meal – mostly fish and some chips, plus a cola soft drink. Our killer made sure he would have died from that overdose alone.'

'Dragging him up the road was a flourish?'

She shrugged. 'A final certainty, perhaps, and certainly symbolic if we go with the vigilante theory.'

'Which I'm not prepared to do yet.'

'Just saying. Are we still on for dinner?'

'Yes. Seven?'

'I still don't know where you live.'

He pulled out his phone. 'Doing it now.'

Kate emerged from the Barbican tube station. Jack didn't live that far from her place at Stoke Newington, but here? This maze of inner-city accommodation didn't feel like Jack at all. He was known for preferring creaky buildings that were centuries old, or elegant, cutting-edge glass and steel. This felt cumbersome. She couldn't stand the thought of hunting around endless pathways, so she sent Jack a text.

I'm standing by the central pond and near a waterfall.

She waited a moment or two and, right enough, he was back quickly. *I'm coming out onto the balcony.*

She waited, glancing around for movement among the various backlit windows that gave her the impression they were eyes looking at her. There he was. He lifted a hand in welcome and she felt something give inside. Wouldn't it be so easy and lovely if this was her coming home?

Dream on, Kate, a voice inside cautioned. *Don't be a drag. He'll shut you out immediately if he senses it.*

She smiled, waved back and texted. *See you in a mo.*

He was waiting at the open door of his apartment in slippered feet and navy trackies, although she noted the brand, which probably contributed to how well they hung from his narrow hips to cover those long legs. He'd finished off his casual ensemble with a mid-blue crew-necked sweatshirt.

'Well, you look comfy,' she said.

'Forgive the slippers. They're my guilty secret.' He grinned. 'Come in.'

'I wouldn't have placed you here at the Barbican,' she said, handing over a bottle of wine.

'Thank you for this, we can have it later. I've got a pinot open.' He helped her to slip the coat off her shoulders and hung it on a hook.

'It's hardly you, right? All these people, all this concrete; the sheer scale of it seems to fly in the face of what you enjoy.'

'And yet isn't there something splendid about the way the water runs, the ponds carry lilies and birds visit? No vehicles . . . easy pedestrian routes throughout.'

'So you can run, I suppose. Don't you miss your park running?'

'Indeed, I do miss the big breathing expanse of green.' He gave her the glass of wine he'd poured for her, lifted his own and they clinked.

'Cheers,' she said, sipping and sighing her pleasure. 'What do you call this sort of architecture?'

'Brutalist. Now Grade II listed. A principal landmark of London architecture of its time.'

'Which is?'

'Late sixties, early seventies.'

'I think you should grow a porn-star moustache and wear bell-bottoms to go with it.'

He laughed delightedly. 'It belongs to a friend who is on a year's posting overseas. Made it easy for me returning from Australia because I rented my place out, then the tenants extended and I haven't got the heart to throw them out. Plus, I'm in no rush; for now, this place is convenient. I can walk to work.'

'Well, that's gold, I'll admit.'

'I'm going to keep cooking.' He pointed to the open kitchen. 'Stay comfy and chat to me from there.'

She wasn't just comfy . . . it felt so easy to be here, with him. 'And so the concert halls and everything are all around?'

'Yes,' he said from the kitchen, stirring a big pot. 'The arts complex is massive, sort of hugs the rest – the tower blocks, thirteen terrace blocks, two mews and a few courts thrown in. And, of course, I really enjoy that adjacent is the Museum of London, the Guildhall School of Music and Drama, the—'

'All those schoolgirls whistling at you when you dash out in your running gear.'

He laughed. 'They haven't found me yet.'

They will, she thought. 'This is a very large apartment. Must cost a bomb.'

'A maisonette, and of course that view is everything.'

She smiled. 'It's wonderful to look out, I'll admit, even though it's all concrete in front. Amazing, really, how the designer achieved . . . well, beauty.'

'It's the lighting, the water, the way the night falls in and all the apartments illuminate from behind their curtains and blinds. And it's quiet, believe it or not, for all these people among approximately two thousand living spaces. I find it extremely easy to live here.'

'You certainly look relaxed. What are you stirring?'

'Risotto.'

'Can I help?'

'No, we're eating on our laps – nothing to do but hold a bowl and a fork.'

She couldn't think of anything nicer. Sitting at a table made it formal and potentially awkward with too much eye contact.

'Ooh, it's a good brew, Kate. Avert your gaze, I'm going to

toss in a pile of butter now.' He covered the dish with a flourish. 'Now we just leave that to do its alchemy.'

He came back to sit with her, putting down a bowl of fat roasted cashew nuts.

She took one. 'Your wine is delicious.'

'Glad you like it.'

Their gazes held and Kate looked away first, unable to meet the challenge she'd set herself to be cool and easy around him.

'I saw Anne McEvoy today,' he said.

Kate was taking a sip of her wine and had to prevent herself from spilling it. 'You did? What happened?'

He shrugged. 'Not a lot. It became easier as we talked and forgave each other silently.'

'You have done nothing to forgive.'

'No . . . but I do feel responsible for her being behind bars for the rest of her days. She was as much a victim as Amy was.'

'Except Amy didn't kill anyone. Anne McEvoy murdered those men in cold blood. Do you still feel . . .'

He gave an abrupt shake of his head. 'No. But there's a tenderness, a sort of sorrow, if I'm honest, that this is where she's ended.'

Kate blinked. 'And how is she?'

'She's resigned, accepting that she needs to pay her debt for the crimes she committed, and making the very best of herself as she can.'

'And her child?'

He looked uncomfortable at her query. 'I don't know. Her daughter's been adopted. Shall we eat?' He smiled, getting up and moving around the small kitchen again.

'Yes, please,' she said, noting his shift away from the awkward question. 'I'm starving. I only realise now as I smell that delicious risotto that I forgot to eat today.'

He made a tutting sound, returning with a small lap tray with a napkin and cutlery laid on it.

She laughed. 'When you said a bowl on the lap, you really meant something else, didn't you?' As he turned, self-conscious, she kept smiling. 'It's lovely, thank you. No one's done anything like this for me in a long time.'

'That's your fault, Kate. You're beautiful, intelligent, witty . . . a bit prickly sometimes, but essentially we both know men would fall over themselves just to have a drink with you.'

'Oh, yeah. Where are they, then?'

'Everywhere, but you have to pay attention.'

'Not quite ready, Jack,' she admitted.

He nodded. 'Well, I'm glad you feel spoiled. Here,' he said, handing over an attractively plated bowl of risotto with basil leaves as garnish and a light sprinkle of freshly grated parmesan.

'Wow, yum.'

'Made with my own stock – don't laugh.'

'Go on, tell me what I'm eating.'

'This is chicken, sweet potato and tomato risotto with a lovely hum of saffron and chilli.'

He sat down opposite her with his tray and watched her take a first forkful. 'Bloody hell, Jack,' she said, after chewing for a moment or two. 'That is fantastic. If you ever give up police work, open a takeaway.'

'I only cook for people I like.' He winked, and together with the pleasant heat of chilli, his words warmed her.

'So is Anne helping?'

He nodded. 'From what I told her, which wasn't much.' He sighed. 'I tiptoed with care.'

She gave him an understanding nod back.

'She is convinced this is a single killer. She believes it's a man and she spoke the word we've been avoiding with some assurance – this is a vigilante's work.'

'All right, let's say it is one. What's his reason for killing a wife-bashing academic, a brothel owner, a careless driver, and a stupid kid who unintentionally killed a lot of people due to his emotional episode?'

'It doesn't add up. But Anne assures me it will.' He traced a path through his risotto with the fork.

'Mal called while I was making my way over here.'

Jack looked up sharply. 'Anything?'

'Nothing new, but he confirmed that Peggy Markham had no known reason to top herself. The night before her death she was dining at Marcus Wareing's restaurant in Knightsbridge – chef's table, no less . . . with all the theatre that the Michelin-starred restaurant could bring,' Kate said, one eyebrow lifting. 'According to Mal's source, there were about ten of them, on her tab. One was an acquaintance of the guy who took out the young escort who died.' Jack sighed. 'The acquaintance – an Egyptian man – said it wasn't a celebration; Peggy called it her relief dinner. She was happy, drinking but not drunk, full of good spirits at being exonerated, with no evidence to suggest that she was responsible for the girl's death, which incidentally involved a lot of cocaine.'

Jack considered the implications of this. He forked another mouthful of his risotto as Kate hungrily enjoyed hers. Finally, he shrugged. 'Martin made it clear to me that Peggy was not a candidate for suicide, and while she lived on the fringe of the serious criminal underworld, she didn't openly commit any crimes that we could pin on her. Her real crime was to be a friend of that underbelly, providing what others couldn't. She even paid her taxes.'

'So we're back to someone with a grudge sticking a syringe of heroin into her neck,' Kate said. 'But he's also got a grudge against the wife basher and the sixth-form kid.'

Jack nodded. 'Who might that person be?'

Kate ate and thought. 'Someone who loved someone who was collateral damage?'

'But if you wanted to unleash your rage upon the boy who killed all those people, why would you also kill Peggy?'

'Well, because she was associated with the death of the youngster.'

'All right, then why the professor?'

'Because he was a bully?'

Jack smirked but more with helplessness. 'But that means logically you or I, or ten million others, could be easily motivated to go out killing too.'

'I know. I'm just trying to think this through.'

'Skin in the game.'

'What?' She was finishing the last mouthful.

'To be this driven, you'd need skin in the game.'

Kate stopped chewing. 'Who has a vested interest in such a diverse range of deaths?' she asked, finally swallowing.

'Well, that's what Anne was getting at: when we can establish that, we might be getting much closer to our guy. He's got pain that's connected to all of these people.'

'To all these victims?'

'Somehow, yes.'

Jack's phone rang from the kitchen counter and Kate sighed inwardly. Couldn't they just have this one evening uninterrupted? She watched him audibly show his disgust and quickly scoop up the last couple of mouthfuls before he stood and reached for the phone. She stood too, gazing longingly at her bowl and wondering if she could run a finger around its remains.

He pointed with pain at the phone and mouthed *sorry*. Then he spoke aloud. 'Hawksworth.'

Kate waited, noting his expression darken. 'You're one hundred per cent sure?'

She felt a claw of tension, followed by a dozen others sinking into her as he began running his free hand through his hair.

'Right. I want the body brought down from the York District Hospital mortuary to London immediately. I'll get the authorisation tonight.' Another pause. 'All right, tomorrow latest, please. I appreciate it and, listen, thank you for moving so fast on this.' The person on the other end spoke and Jack seemed to cringe. 'I can't say any more. But what you've done by contacting me tonight is, how can I put this . . . a massive favour.' He smiled as he listened. 'I'll let you know. Thanks so much. Bye . . . yes, bye.' He rang off and looked at her. 'Davey Robbins has been murdered.'

'Davey Robbins,' she repeated. 'How?'

'Kidnapped, mugged, sedated, hands and todger chopped off.' Kate gasped. 'He bled to death, left outside a caravan that was parked in a field not too far away from where he picked vegetables. The killer apparently rang it through to police, even providing the address.'

'Bloody hell. What now?'

'Dessert,' he said, somehow looking focused and distracted at once.

'Really? Shouldn't we be . . .'

He looked at his watch. 'It's nearing nine.'

'I thought you'd want to go in.'

'No. I promised everyone a night off and that goes for us too. I don't mind talking about the case, but we are not going to live, eat and breathe from that incident room, seven days a week, twenty-four hours daily. That's how we all got trapped last time. We'll think better if we step back, like now.'

'I guess there's not much we can do tonight anyway, until we know more about how Davey met his end. SOCO will be working through the night, presumably.'

'I'll take the first train to Yorkshire tomorrow. Can you hold things down here?'

'No problem. Book it now.'

'Yes, okay. There's pudding in the fridge. I know you like chocolate, but I hope you like it rich and dark and chewy.'

'Ooh . . . may I?' He grinned, nodding at the fridge as he moved to a desk in the corner of the room where his laptop blinked into life. 'It's mousse but for grown-ups. Get the glasses out, let it warm up a bit.'

She pottered around his kitchen, noting how tidy the drawers were and wishing hers were similar. If he ever walked around her kitchen and snooped like this, he might form a new opinion of her. *Don't worry, Kate, it's not going to happen.* Kate glanced over at Jack tapping away at the keyboard while he made his reservation. She took the opportunity to open the wine she'd brought and pour them each a fresh glass. It was an excellent Chilean merlot that she knew he'd enjoy.

'Here,' she said, placing the glass at his side, feeling the warmth of his body next to hers as she leaned over.

'Oh, thanks.'

She nodded, smiling, then moved away for fear of doing something extremely silly, calming her crazy intentions by swallowing a slug of the merlot. It was as good as she'd hoped and as she turned, she heard him make a sound of satisfaction.

'Delicious.'

'You're welcome.' She sat again and realised something was nagging.

Jack turned. 'Done. I'm leaving on the six-fifteen to York.'

'Oof, that's early.'

'It is but it means I can be there around nine and come back same day.' He stood. 'So, mousse?'

'Yes, please,' she said with genuine eagerness, staring out at the flickering view of lights on the long stretch of water from the central ponds. Jack came over with two champagne coupes of mousse and she greedily accepted the dessert. 'Cream as well?' she noted.

'Needs it, trust me,' he said.

He was right; it was the richest, chewiest mousse she'd eaten in a lifetime. 'Jack, this is so good,' she said, hardly swallowing before she shovelled in the next mouthful. She deliberately smiled at him knowing there was chocolate covering her teeth. He stopped eating and stared before exploding into laughter, exactly as she'd hoped.

'Sarah should see that! I'm sure she believes you haven't a playful bone in your body.'

'I'll call you a liar if you ever mention this,' she threatened, swallowing quickly. 'Jack?'

'Mmm?' He sounded suspicious, as though she were going to ask him a difficult question, like *shall we spend the night together?*

Whether that thought had even subconsciously crossed her mind was irrelevant. That was not what was on it right now. 'If you were a clever murderer who managed to kill people almost under the noses of others, leaving no subtle forensic clues, why would you be so stupid as to leave behind a nice, firm impression of your footprint?'

He gusted a chuckle. 'It's a good question.'

'Odd, don't you think?'

'Not alarm-bells odd.'

She shrugged. 'No hair, no fibres, no trophies, no fingerprints, no blood or bodily fluids, no giveaway bits and bobs that most crims don't even think to check for . . . but a lovely bold set of footprints.'

'It's clumsy, but he probably knows it's such a broad clue that it's all but generic. Imagine us having to hunt down who, in the whole of England, wears Sultan trail shoes and could be a serial killer.'

'Saloman. How about deliberately clumsy?'

He turned to her, scraping the final morsel from the pudding. 'A false sultana trail?'

She laughed and tried to keep him on point. 'We have nothing else but this at two sites now. I think we might scrutinise that footprint for weight, tread and all those other clever things they can measure . . . just in case.'

'All right. No stone unturned, we promised.'

'Who usually picked up Robbins? I mean, how did he persuade Robbins to go with him?'

'The boys up north say he posed as a relief minder, having incapacitated the usual guy who escorted Robbins to and from his work. No doubt it will all be neatly pieced together before my arrival tomorrow as to how Mirror Man trapped him. Let's leave it to the locals.'

'Mirror Man?' She sounded impressed.

Jack smiled. 'How I think of him now.'

'The hands? Why go to that trouble and risk the mess, the extra time? We've been busy establishing that he's not a torturer but we also have Smythe killed by burning.'

'If it's the same killer who killed Smythe.'

'Sounds right, though. It must be symbolic.'

He nodded, chewed, swallowed, taking his time. 'In Saudi Arabia you lose a hand if you are convicted of repeated theft.'

'Okay.'

'Hear me out.' Her shrug told him she'd give him all the time in the world. 'Davey Robbins was known for thieving in and around London. He was a petty burglar, but the Clarke family case was him moving into a much darker situation. The murder I accept he may not have planned, but the rape was probably at his instigation. They ransacked the Clarke household of phones, cash, jewellery.'

'So you're thinking this killer decided on some gruesome medieval punishment for Davey Robbins?'

He nodded, unsure. 'It's a notion.'

'And removing his dick has resonance, right, to the original crime?' Jack tried to avoid her gaze. 'Don't deny it.' They were standing too close. 'The vigilante tag gets weightier. Chopping off the weapon of a rapist says only one thing.'

He sighed. 'Yes. Seems to be what we're staring at. I can hardly believe we're in this deep again with another serial killer.'

To her he looked suddenly forlorn, just busting to have his hair ruffled and arms thrown around him. 'Right, listen. I'm going,' she said, her only defence.

'I haven't made you a coffee yet.'

'And if you had, I'd be hating you by two in the morning when I couldn't sleep. No, you have to get up with the birds and I suspect it will be a big day tomorrow for both of us. Let me head off with sincere thanks for a delicious meal. Really, Jack, you're such a show-off,' she said, clasping his wrist briefly.

'Well, we must do it again,' he said, and Kate wondered if that was genuine or the sort of thing people said with no intention of doing it again. Gosh, she was paranoid! 'Let me get your coat. And also let me call a taxi.'

'What? No need. The tube station is right there,' she said.

'I know where it is, but you are not taking the Underground home . . . not tonight. This is on me.' He picked up his phone. 'Same address in Stoke Newington?'

She nodded, impressed he remembered. 'Thanks.'

He organised the taxi as he helped her on with her coat. 'There, done. I'm sorry this was so brief, Kate. I didn't want it to be a working dinner, but it turned out that way.'

'It's fine. What else were we going to talk about? We'd have been a couple of sad sacks sharing failed relationships over our wine and risotto and mousse – all delicious, by the way.'

He pecked her cheek. 'We will do this again properly.'

'Good,' she agreed, not knowing what *properly* meant.

His phone pinged. 'Taxi's here. Downstairs, turn left, first right and go into the small lane.' He paused. 'Thanks for coming. It was nice to cook for someone.'

Awkward! Don't do anything stupid, she pleaded inwardly. 'Call me from Yorkshire.' She risked a familiar but wholly friendly kiss to his cheek and smelled his cologne. It was Chanel Homme Sport . . . a favourite that she could instantly recognise.

And then she fled.

14

Jack had clambered into his paper forensic suit; he always carried a spare, and although the North Yorkshire scene-of-crime team were deferring to him – even offering a suit before he dug his out of the backpack – he could sense their collective grimace that the south was here to bully the north. He stood in front of the caravan, in a field that had had a sizeable portion cordoned off by the scene-of-crime team and police constables. His shoes were covered in plastic, and he was pleased to see that the North Yorkshire team had followed all the right protocols, even halting him at the top field gate to hand him the booties and gloves.

A Detective Inspector Lonsdale had greeted him briefly on arrival and had given him a file he was yet to study.

'I thought you'd come from Northallerton HQ,' Jack remarked, purely to make conversation.

'York CID is closer, sir,' came the curt reply with a handshake that felt just as unwelcoming.

Jack wasn't surprised. Apart from the north–south rivalry that still permeated all facets of life, no police team took kindly to the big boys walking in and using their Scotland Yard status to take over a crime scene. DI Lonsdale now returned to where Jack stood. 'You're sure this is your guy?' His accent sounded as though he was from Bradford.

'As sure as I can be,' he said as cheerfully as he could muster, snapping on the gloves.

The detective grinned without mirth. 'Which means nothing concrete, right – all instinct?'

Time to push back. 'Listen,' Jack began, making sure just enough appeal was in his tone. 'You were briefed on the confidential message sent out through the PNN to all heads of CID, right?'

DI Lonsdale nodded.

'It's not my wish to take over anything. I realise this is your turf, and your people have done a great job – I mean that. But I do need the body sent to London today.'

'Is this part of an op?'

'I've been asked by the Acting Chief to gather—'

'Yeah, so I hear, Detective Superintendent Hawskworth – I mean, I hear that it's coming from the top. But that's not what I asked . . . sir.'

Jack's gaze narrowed. He really didn't want to make any enemies up here, even though he was far more senior. 'DI Lonsdale, this is the fourth newly released prisoner who has turned up dead. Davey Robbins is not a local, he's a London lad who's ended up in a halfway home having got off lightly for a violent burglary that resulted in the death of one victim and the rape of another. I'm just trying to work out if there are connections between him and the others. Beyond that, I'm comfy – as I'm sure you are – that another lowlife is off our streets.' He shrugged. 'Anything you and your people can do to help me tick off that we've done our due diligence is appreciated.'

Lonsdale held Jack's gaze steadily for longer than was

comfortable. 'Then may I respectfully request, sir, that everything in connection with this murder is copied to my guys in York?'

'Agreed,' Jack said with a firm nod. 'I'll ensure you get a full copy of the pathology report in the same way that you'll be providing me with all the forensic evidence. How's Mr Chingford, the usual escort – you said he was mugged?'

'He's doing fine; it's all in there,' he said, nodding at the file Jack held. 'How else can we help?'

'You can get rid of that local reporter hanging around. How did this get out?'

'Hard to keep something like this quiet, sir. The workers saw the ambulance and uniformed cars arriving. There were sirens, lights, the full works, set off by the guy's phone call, which suggested Davey Robbins could be saved. There are always ambulance chasers around. Someone's tipped off the local TV and newspaper. He's from *The York Gazette*, as I understand it.'

'Must have got a very early tip-off.'

'Blind luck. He and his girlfriend were staying over at a guesthouse not far from here.'

'I see,' Jack said, unable to hide the disappointment. 'Well, it hit the national news late last night.'

DI Lonsdale shrugged. 'I don't know how to help that, sir.'

'You can't. Can you run me through everything we know?'

A constable arrived with two takeaway coffees. 'Sure,' Lonsdale said, gesturing for Jack to grab one. 'Thanks, Al,' he said to the young uniformed officer. Jack hesitated only for a heartbeat; a bridge had just been built, so to risk smashing it down over a nasty coffee was unwise. 'Just what I needed, thank you.'

'Cheers,' Jack said, lifting his coffee to Lonsdale as Al wandered away. 'Have you used dogs?'

'Yep. We wanted to establish where he was brought from because there's insufficient blood for him to have died here.

At this stage, we have him getting out in that small wooded area over there.' He tipped his head. 'The dog has tacked a point from where you can see that marker.'

'Tyre tracks, footprints, drag tracks?'

'All captured.'

'Dragging Robbins, that would need strength,' Jack said. It wasn't really a question but not a statement of fact either . . . more his thoughts out loud to be explored later.

DI Lonsdale moved his head in a manner to suggest it wasn't necessarily so. 'The victim is small and wiry. Killer wouldn't need a lot of muscle. Although that would depend on whether he was drugged, but still, he'd be a dead weight.'

'Have we got anything on the killer at all?'

'He's apparently invisible because he's left no trace,' his colleague said, sounding baffled. 'Apart from some footprints.'

Jack would come back to that. 'The call to Emergency. No use?'

'He changed his voice using some cunning method.'

'I'd like to listen to that, all the same.'

'Of course. We'll send that today.'

'Car rentals in the region?'

'We're looking into it, but I suspect he drove up to Yorkshire from another county. We're going through CCTV of the main train station, too.'

Jack nodded. 'That's great, well done. Tedious work.'

'And lengthy. And of course,' DI Lonsdale said, sounding resigned, 'he could have got off at a different station, caught a bus, hitched a ride or picked up a car he'd already had in place.'

'All true.' Jack frowned, even though he'd considered all of these factors on the journey up. 'All right, what do we know?'

DI Lonsdale pointed. 'We know this caravan was rented by a Polish guy, Kacper Bartek. He's clean, as far as we can tell, gets a good report from the local farmer as a reliable guy, hard worker, honest and helps with organising the others.'

'Why this caravan?'

'Bartek tells us he moved out nearly three weeks ago and moved in with his girlfriend where most of the other seasonal accommodation is.' DI Lonsdale pointed in the other direction. 'Over that rise.'

'Why would he live here if all the other seasonal workers live over there?'

'Bartek's a musician; says he likes the silence to compose and play his music.'

'What sort of music?'

'Er . . . guitar, I think, but we can check if you think that's important.' Jack didn't, but he nodded anyway. 'Either way, sir, he seems reliable. The farmer said this caravan would have been let in the next week or so. In fact, he's already had an enquiry, was planning to see the guy at the weekend. So he'd had it all cleaned out and ready.'

'Convenient,' Jack muttered.

Lonsdale shrugged. 'Sometimes we have to accept coincidence. It was empty for more than a fortnight.'

Jack waited but as Lonsdale didn't say any more, he continued, returning the DI to their only witness. He wasn't about to be fobbed off with a dry report in a folder. 'Tell me more about . . .' He glanced into the file for the man's name. 'Alan Chingford. He's important, given he survived a killer's touch.'

Lonsdale shrugged. 'I don't think he was important to the murderer. Chingford is the formal escort who took care of Davey Robbins since he arrived in Yorkshire. He's forty-six, been doing this work for fifteen years; ex-prison guard. Mr Chingford has not missed a journey to or from work for Robbins since he was appointed as his escort.'

'Until now. Is he really okay?'

Lonsdale nodded. 'Yes. Took a blow to his head, but no serious concussion, luckily. The killer clearly wasn't trying to hurt him so much as distract him. He hit him with a three-quarter-full plastic lemonade bottle. We think his head snapping back is what made him momentarily unconscious – just long enough for the killer to restrain and gag him.'

Jack gave a wry smile. 'Sounds like an experienced killer.'

'Yeah, my point.' Lonsdale grinned and Jack sensed the tension easing. 'He just wanted to stun him a bit, I reckon. It gave him a chance to pull a black bag over Chingford's head and tell him he was holding a knife. He threatened to hurt Chingford's wife, who was indoors, if he didn't do as he said, but he promised he was not going to enter the family home if Chingford cooperated. He was tied up, handed over his car keys and fully expected the car to be stolen. It wasn't, but the keys were tossed in the garden beds and two tyres let down. To me that simply suggests the killer was fully expecting us to be called and on his tail.'

Jack nodded.

'And then he left Mr Chingford still tied and gagged in the garage; his wife found him nearly forty-five minutes later when she expected him home. Apparently she was on the phone for that whole time and couldn't see the driveway from the kitchen where she was chatting to her sister.'

'So she didn't know he hadn't left.' Jack nodded. 'Can he remember anything about his assailant?'

'He assures us he didn't see him. But he's probably worth talking to because he's an experienced prison guard – he's got that sixth sense.'

Jack nodded. 'I'll do that. Thanks.'

'So,' Lonsdale continued, 'my take is that the killer posed as a relief escort, picked up Robbins, made some excuse to come up here to the caravan and it all unfolded badly for the kid, not that anyone's going to feel particularly sorry for a convicted rapist.'

It echoed Jack's thoughts. He sipped his horrible coffee because Lonsdale was drinking from his cup, reminding him to do the same and not appear ungrateful. 'All right, so, how do we believe Robbins was convinced to come up to the caravan?'

'He was likely heavily sedated. The blood near the tree suggests he wasn't already dead by then. I'll let our pathologist confirm what we already suspect, but he has estimated that by the time the emergency team arrived, Robbins had been dead for approximately two hours, so he was likely overpowered soon after pick-up, which was scheduled for five thirty-five each afternoon. The call came through to Emergency at . . .' He double-checked his notes. 'At seven forty-three yesterday evening.'

'By overpowered, you mean drugged?' Lonsdale nodded. 'Do we know with what?'

'We will shortly. The doc said Robbins was alive when his hands were removed but most likely dead before his killer hacked up the rest.'

'Any trophy taken?'

'None that we know of. His bits were left next to him on the grass.'

Jack blew out a breath of disgust.

'He's neat, I'll give him that. There are rope marks around the wrists but no sign of the rope used. We think he suspended the victim's arms using that rope around a branch – there are marks on the branch to confirm this – and then tied it down, perhaps to the car. The pathologist said the dismembering was done with two firm blows, most likely from an axe. They were accurate and there are chop marks in the bark of the tree consistent with an axe blade.'

Jack grimaced at the thought. No one would wish that on anyone, but then he decided that maybe Amy Clarke and her parents might. The thought stayed front of mind. 'You mentioned footprints?'

'Yes, sir. Size nine and a half, we believe, but again awaiting confirmation. They're trail shoes – big four-wheel-drive tread, if you get my meaning.'

Jack didn't let on, simply nodded. 'Clear prints?'

'Very. For someone who left no forensic evidence of himself on the body or in the woods, he was careless here.' He watched Jack. 'You don't think so?'

'Get your guys to check that print in every way possible – weight, et cetera. I don't trust it.'

'You've seen it previously?'

Jack nodded. 'Like you, I sense a careful killer here. But the prints are too obvious.'

'Okay, will do. Your people are doing the same, presumably?'

'Yes, something else we can share.'

'Thanks.' Lonsdale shrugged. 'Nothing much else except he made the call to Emergency, as explained.'

'Tyre tracks?'

'All they tell us is this is a small hatchback. Again, we'll confirm the make when we know more.'

Jack closed the small notebook he'd written a few reminders in. He found it cathartic to write down facts alongside his thoughts to let it all blend and percolate. He'd scribbled *killer's voice, shoe size* with several question marks and he'd underlined the words *recording of emergency call*. 'I'll talk to Mr Chingford. Is he in hospital?'

'No, he's at home.'

'Have you spoken to the young offenders' home?'

'Yes, I did it myself. Nothing unusual, although you're welcome to go over it. It was a normal day as far as the staff are concerned. Robbins left the breakfast room at twenty-five past eight or thereabouts with his small backpack. We have that, and it gives us nothing of any use, just the usual crap – near-empty wallet, a scarf and a beanie, half-eaten bar of chocolate, headphones, penknife. Nothing else of any interest. According to a staff member who checked him out, Davey Robbins put on his headphones and walked outside as he saw Chingford arrive to take him to work in the morning. We've questioned his housemates and they're shocked, obviously, but said all was normal: no arguments, no dramas, no sense of Robbins being anything but the usual Davey Robbins who talked about a concert he wished he could go to in Manchester, his upcoming apprentice tests and the new life he was headed for in London. According to them, he had no obvious intention of running away or anything. He hated the immigrants he worked with, talked a lot about joining a Neo-Nazi group, but the staff said he was just spouting rubbish he'd heard in prison more than anything else. He showed no indication of being violent.'

'Other than raping helpless teenage girls,' Jack remarked, unhelpfully.

Lonsdale nodded with equal despair. 'He'd not broken any house rules. Nothing out of the ordinary occurred yesterday morning and he did a full day's work, speaking to none of his fellow workers as usual, just listening to his music.'

'Thanks.' They shook hands. 'We'll stay in touch, eh?'

'One of our guys will give you a lift to Alan Chingford's place and then back to the train station when you're ready – the constable who brought the coffees.'

'Al?'

'Yeah, good memory. He'll drive you.'

Jack looked up. 'Looks like it might rain.'

'Always looks like that, sir.' He grinned. 'This is Yorkshire.'

★

Beryl Chingford looked at Jack with a pained expression when she answered the door. He could tell she did not want to let him in, despite his warrant card.

'Just a few minutes, Mrs Chingford.'

'Look, he's answered all your questions already.'

Jack gave her his best smile of sympathy. 'All of York CID's questions, Mrs Chingford. I'm from Scotland Yard.'

It didn't impress her. She breathed through flaring nostrils and her husband arrived behind her.

'Hello there,' he said, smiling at Jack. 'I don't mind at all. I'm devastated about that lad. Come on in . . . er . . .'

'Detective Superintendent Jack Hawskworth,' he answered.

'Alan!' his wife despaired.

'Come on, Beryl. A youngster was murdered horribly on my watch,' he appealed. 'I'm not hurt — more embarrassed than anything.' He shook Jack's hand.

Beryl sighed and stood back. 'Can I get you a cup of tea, Mr Hawksworth?'

He didn't correct her. 'Only if you both are having one.'

'Yorkshire tea is the best tea,' Alan boasted. 'Yes, let's have a pot, Beryl, thanks, luv.'

She disappeared into the back of the house and Jack was ushered into a sitting room where a small gas fire guttered.

'I feel a bit chilled today,' Alan admitted, giving a shiver.

'You must be shaken up?'

'I am. But as I said, I'm mostly embarrassed.'

'Don't be,' Jack said.

'How can I help, Detective Superintendent? How come Scotland Yard is involved?'

'Davey Robbins is a London criminal and we're just making sure we do all our due diligence.' It sounded convincing enough and Chingford seemed to accept this rationale.

'What can I tell you that hasn't already been said?'

'I'm mostly interested in any small aspect you can remember about your attacker.'

Chingford's face creased into a deep frown. 'I told them everything I could. I don't think he had any intention to do me harm.'

'A kind attacker?' Jack smiled.

'Well, nothing kind about a fellow who does what he did to Davey . . .' Chingford sounded sad. 'I know most would have no sympathy, but my role was never to judge. I like to see my lads get through their worst times and make good – repay the society that gives them another chance.'

'You're generous, Mr Chingford.'

'Call me Alan, please. I try.'

Beryl bustled in with a tray, pinched-lipped. 'Let it brew, Alan. Can I offer you some cake, Mr Hawksworth?'

'Er, no, thank you. This is perfect.'

'Right, well, if there's nothing else, I'll leave you both to it.'

'I won't hold your husband up for much longer,' Jack said.

Her lips thinned further but she nodded and departed.

'I'm sorry, Detective Superintendent,' Alan said. 'She does worry too much. This was frightening, I'll admit, but prison life taught me to stay calm in any confronting situation. I realised he didn't want anything from me other than the car, but when he left without it, I'll be damned if I could work out what his intentions were in coming to my home, tying me up, threatening he'd hurt Beryl!'

'Tell me about his voice, Alan.'

'His voice? Well, now, that's interesting. Er . . . nothing particularly unusual about it. I wouldn't say deep or high, mellow enough. He spoke calmly, although I think the cold weather up here was giving him a workout.'

'What do you mean?'

'Well, he sounded cold, sniffed a bit. He spoke quietly though, and while his words were threatening, he didn't put any heat in them. A man in control, I would say.'

Jack nodded. 'Accent?'

'Definitely a southerner.' Alan grinned. 'No real accent at all . . . I could pick someone from the West Country or even Sussex.'

'Did he sound like a Londoner?

'Well, he wasn't cockney. He had a cultured accent but wasn't overly posh.'

'Educated, then?'

'Yes, definitely. The way he spoke held no cursing, no slang. He spoke in full sentences and in excellent English.'

'Could you take a stab at his age?'

Alan leaned forward to pour the tea. 'Age . . .?' He pondered this as he prepared the tea with milk and handed a small mug to Jack, gesturing towards the sugar if Jack wanted it. He sat back with his mug and sipped. 'Not young, but his voice held no tremors. I think if I was cornered, I would guess he might be in his fifties.'

'Any clue as to why?'

'Just something he said that made me think he might have gone to school in the late fifties, early sixties.'

'Ah, good. What did he say?'

'He offered me some water, because he warned I might be left tied up for a while.'

'How is that a clue?'

'He offered a beaker of water. That's what we all called the cups in school. I haven't heard the word used in a long time and certainly not from someone younger than myself . . . it's only us boomers who use that sort of language.'

'Okay,' Jack said, sounding enlightened. 'That's a help. You didn't happen to see what he was wearing on his feet, did you?'

'I did, actually. How curious.'

'Why do you say that?'

'Well, he was wearing a pair identical to ones I used to wear when I was all day on my feet in the prison. I still like them but now I wear them in brown, like his . . . my prison uniform meant I wore the black version.'

Jack blinked at all the information. Alan liked to talk, but in truth he was being more helpful than Jack could have hoped. 'Would it be an imposition to see your shoes, please?'

'Not at all. They're just out in our boot room. Give me a moment.' He hauled himself out of the chair with a sigh and, while Jack felt bad for causing the exertion, he sensed this was important. He watched Alan return, padding in his slippers. 'Here we go. He was wearing a pair just like these – except his were a sort of warm tan, not this dark brown.'

Jack looked at the bland cushioned shoes. 'Hush Puppies.'

'I swear by them. Really comfy and they don't set off metal detectors in airports . . . or prisons.' He grinned.

'Do you know the name of them, by any chance?'

'Oh-ho, now you're testing me, Detective. But Beryl being Beryl will certainly know.' He called for her and Jack inwardly sighed, knowing another disapproving look would be coming his way.

Right enough, it arrived, creasing across her stern expression. 'Were you leaving, Mr Hawksworth? Can I show you out?'

'Er, yes, in a moment, Mrs Chingford, I—'

'Listen, dear,' Alan interrupted. 'What are these shoes called?'

'What on earth—?'

He stopped her again. 'Darling, just answer. Do you or do you not recall the name of these shoes?'

'Yes,' she replied, bristling at his interruptions. 'Of course I do.'

'Could you write it down for the Detective Superintendent, please, dear? It's important.'

'Yes, well, give me a moment.'

'*Is* it important?' Chingford asked as she disappeared again.

'It could be. The footprint we have does not belong to a smooth-soled shoe like this. In fact, it's the opposite – it's got the deep grooves of a trail shoe.'

'Oh, I see. Well, he was in formal shoes just like these. I remember clearly because I was on the ground and they were all I could see just beneath the pillowcase he pulled over my head. I gave that black pillow slip to the police. They were going to check for DNA.'

'I doubt they'll find any. He's cautious.'

'Not if he's leaving footprints. He could have changed to avoid his shoes getting muddy.'

'Yes, he could have,' Jack agreed, but for different reasons.

Beryl was back. 'I've written down the name that was on the side of the box. We bought them in Leeds two years ago – the receipt is taped inside if you need.'

Jack smiled. 'That won't be necessary, but you've been most helpful, both of you.' He pulled out a card. 'Alan, if anything else strikes you – any small recollection from your attack – don't hesitate to call.'

'Righto,' Alan said and then grinned. 'That's what he said when I pointed to where I'd put the car keys down. He really was quite polite about it all.'

Jack smiled kindly once again, shook Alan's hand and nodded his thanks at Beryl. 'Thank you again. Nothing beats Yorkshire tea.'

15

Lauren had risen in London at about the same time Jack had to catch his train. She had seen the late-night bulletin reporting the discovery of a mutilated body outside a caravan in Yorkshire that evening and her internal radar was beeping madly. She had been restless ever since, and it hadn't taken much to convince herself to call *The York Gazette*, which had broken the story first. It wasn't yet six but pigeons outside her flat window were busy, so why not her?

'Congratulations,' she said to a fellow called Angus Hartley. 'You must be the darling of the newspaper.'

'Oh, well, for today anyway,' he said, sounding understandably chuffed, and young – that could help her.

'How on earth did you crack the story?'

He laughed. 'My girlfriend wanted to do one of those farm experiences, you know?'

'Yeah?'

'We took a Friday off and drove down to a farm that offers it. We'd had a good day and decided to have a pub meal before driving home and I heard sirens. Then I got a call from my editor, who wanted to know if I was anywhere near Sherburn.'

'And, of course, you were,' she said, ensuring she sounded enthralled but hoping to hurry him along.

'Yeah, pure chance that I was able to get to the scene fast. I was there before the TV crews.'

'Good for you, Angus. Are you still covering the story?'

'Yeah. My newspaper's paying for the accommodation for last night and tonight, and I'll be going back to the field and the caravan where he was found. I'll leave in an hour.'

'Listen, Angus, if I make it worth your while, would you do me a small favour?'

'Depends. I can't—'

'No, it's simple. Can you just ring me later and tell me one senior policeman's name who's in charge? Just a name. Then I can do my own sleuthing. I'll pay you one hundred pounds for that information.'

'A hundred quid? Are you joking?'

'Not at all. You see, I'm writing a feature about ex-criminals, so it's got nothing to do with daily news. Davey Robbins was sent to prison for a serious crime against a woman. And we write for women, so rape and domestic violence, these are important issues, you know?'

'Yeah, yeah, I hear you. Plus, he had the jewels cut off, so that should keep your readers insanely intrigued.'

She didn't reply to that.

'So, just a name, is it?'

'That's it. Ring me the moment you have it. Can you text me your postal address? I'll send a cash cheque today. No one has to be any the wiser.'

'Cheque's in the mail, eh?'

'I'm good for it, Angus. I promise. You have my name and phone number so I'm hardly going to dud you.'

'No. Okay, then, talk later.

Lauren was pleased to discover that Angus was as good as his word. He rang her four hours later while she was putting the finishing touches on her feature concluding that the Jack Russell terrier was the best dog companion for a single woman today.

'Got that story, Lauren?' Rowena reminded her.

'Just about to hit send,' she called back over the bent heads of the other two writers. 'Hang on, my phone's going. I have to take this.' She grabbed her phone and moved quickly to the corridor. 'Angus?'

'Yeah, hi.'

'How's it going?'

'Crazy up here. Full crime-scene drama and plenty of police guarding it.'

'Who's in charge?'

'Well, from York CID it's Detective Inspector Ian Lonsdale.'

She grabbed the pen she kept habitually behind one ear and scribbled it on her hand in biro.

'All right, that's great, thank you. I'm going to—'

'No, wait, it got very interesting.'

'What do you mean?'

'Scotland Yard turned up.'

Lauren opened her mouth in surprised delight, but no sound came out; her mind was racing now, confirming that her hunch as the pigeons began cooing this morning was right. 'Are you there?'

'Yes, yes, sorry. You dropped out momentarily,' she fibbed. 'You said Scotland Yard?'

'Yeah, and the local lads weren't happy, I can tell you.'

'Do you have a name?'

'Big shot. Detective Superintendent Jack Hawksworth. Pretty boy. They all hated him on sight.'

She smiled. *Hello, Jack.* 'Angus, this is perfect.'

'You got my address?'

'I did. I'll go to the post office at lunchtime. Thanks.'

'Any time,' he said. 'Good luck with your feature.'

'Good luck with your story. Bet *The Yorkshire Post* hates you.'

They both rang off to the sound of each other's chuckles. Now she had to explain to Rowena about needing a one-hundred-pound cash cheque.

Lauren was on her third coffee, the Pret a Manger soup she'd hungrily consumed at eleven-thirty a distant memory, and she was beginning to feel cold leaning against the wall, watching the incoming-trains information changing on the flicking arrivals and departures board. All she was feeling right now was frustration. Everyone else seemed to find what they needed, surging forwards to a platform gate as their train's time was confirmed or an arrival platform verified.

She'd carefully watched all the trains arriving from York from around two in the afternoon. Unless Jack Hawksworth flew, which was unlikely, she was convinced she could meet him off one of these trains before he could disappear into the well-secured clutches of Scotland Yard. The tension building in her gut was about whether he would sneer and march straight past her. That too she considered unlikely; he probably wouldn't be rude to a woman's face. She was counting on that quality she sensed in him.

The board told her that the train arriving just before four had pulled in. Tired as much as stiff, she strolled over to the entrance of the platform, casting a hope that she'd see him because she couldn't stand the thought of waiting for the next one. Her mouth felt thick from too much caffeine and she dug in her bag to find a mint.

Looking up after finally finding a battered old packet of gum, she slung the two remaining oblongs into her mouth and scanned the barrier where passengers were streaming through.

Chewing determinedly, she couldn't see him and was sighing her disappointment, twisting on her heel to head back to the main board, when she caught sight of a familiar tall shape disappearing ahead on the long strides of his ever so slightly bowed gait. He loped like Colin Firth as Mr Darcy, striding down the long gallery corridor of Pemberley. She pulled her bag's straps high on her shoulder as she legged it after him, cursing the heels she wore.

'Jack!' she yelled. She couldn't let him dip from her sight and leave the station. '*Jack!*'

He swung around as her cries finally reached him. He was frowning as she rushed up, breathing slightly hard. 'Sorry, sorry . . . I, er . . . I couldn't call out "Detective Superintendent" or everyone would have turned.' As it was, people were glancing their way.

'Lauren, right?'

'Er, yes,' she confirmed. Today she was dressed more formally but curiously didn't feel any more confident beneath his greyish gaze. No policeman should be this distracting. 'From—'

'From the fabulous *My Day*. Yes, how could I forget?' It was dryly said but somehow he managed not to make it entirely scornful. If anything, he looked amused . . . and somehow that was worse; now she felt like a joke. 'Are you following me?' he asked when she didn't reply.

'Not technically, no.'

'Ah, coincidence?'

'No.' She couldn't lie to him, for some reason.

He gave her a grin she desperately hoped was genuine. 'So, what are you doing?'

'Waiting for you?'

'I see. How nice.'

She laughed now, fresh mortification spilling out of guilt and despair and making her feel like the worst kind of annoying journalist. 'I'm sorry.'

'For what? I can hardly complain about a greeting party at King's Cross . . . that would be churlish, surely?' It was said kindly but with the slightest hint of warning.

She looked at him, unsure of where this could go. Was he cross? Was he disgusted? Was he simply laughing at her?

He checked his watch and she got ready for the polite excuse. 'Do you feel like a drink?'

Had she misheard? She stared a moment longer than seemed intelligent, making sure she hadn't. 'Yes,' she lied.

'Good. Do you mind a walk?'

Lauren shook her head, taken by surprise, and felt herself smiling as she tried to keep up with Hawksworth's distinctive Darcy stride.

'Been to The Queen's Head?'

'No.'

'Well, I think you'll like it. It's a rather old-fashioned pub from Victorian days.'

'You don't care for gastropubs?'

'Well, no, I'm not a fan, but to be fair I think some of the newly renovated pubs have breathed new life into dying places. I'm all for not losing the pub culture, but I do yearn for the old kind of slightly grubby pub with its sticky bar and cosy atmosphere.'

'You sound like my dad,' she admitted.

'Please don't tell me I'm old enough to be your father,' he bleated.

She laughed. 'No, not at all. My dad's sixty-two and you're what . . . thirty-five, thirty-six?'

'You're kind,' he said in a tone of disbelief. 'Add a couple.'

'I've dated men my own age who look twice yours. You could step in for James Bond when Daniel Craig gets tired of the role.' Did she really just say that? *Lauren . . . oh, Lauren*, she thought. *You idiot!*

He gusted a self-conscious laugh. 'You know how to flatter, Lauren. Come on, here we go,' he said, slowing to open the door of a cute-looking pub with a cloud of second-hand nicotine hanging over the drinkers.

'Do you smoke?' he asked.

'No. Hate it. My grandad smoked like a train and my father did for the first few years of my life.'

'Good. I can't wait for the law to go through that forbids it.'

'Do you reckon they'll be able to enforce it?' She looked doubtful.

'By the end of this summer, there'll be no more smoking allowed in this or any other pub in England. Imagine that – a clear atmosphere.' His certainty made her feel optimistic, but she wasn't sure why. It wasn't because of pub smoke . . . more his truthful manner. She doubted Hawksworth made a promise he wouldn't keep or held an opinion on something he didn't believe wholly in – or even said anything without consideration. That was refreshing. The last man who'd caught her attention had been a liar, a thief, a full-on rogue and a cheat. 'What's your poison, Lauren?'

'Er . . . a gin and tonic would be great, thank you.'

'Are you happy to find us a seat and I'll bully my way through to the bar?'

She nodded.

'I also have to make a call. I promise to make it quick.'

She guessed he must be making a call to the woman in his life, explaining that he'd been waylaid by work and would be home soon. She wondered where he lived, what sort of partner was waiting at home; he would probably make a good dad, but she sensed he wasn't one. So, a professional couple maybe? She'd either be in health . . . perhaps a GP, or she could see him with an artist. Someone who sat at home in their airy, glass-filled villa that let loads of sunlight into one of the rooms they'd designated a studio. She'd be a modern artist . . . abstract, lots of colour. Lauren could picture her barefoot, in slim jeans and a baggy pastel sweater, golden hair carelessly scooped up. No make-up because even in her mid-thirties she was still fresh-faced and far too pretty to improve upon her features. They'd have a dog called Buddy that they called Boo just between themselves. Bugger it, she felt envious of someone who may not even exist. She peeped through the pub-goers and could see him speaking on his phone while paying for the drinks. He looked hassled. Was she the cause?

A few moments later she watched him shoulder his way through the drinkers to find her tucked away at a small table.

'I asked for a slice of lemon. Hope that's okay?'

She grinned as he handed her the gin and tonic. 'It's perfect.'

He sat. 'Cheers,' he said, clinking her glass with his before sipping on a small beer. He gave a soft sigh of pleasure as it seemed to hit the spot. 'So, Lauren. Why the stake-out?'

Straight to the point, then. *Be direct back, Lauren*, she urged herself. *No squirming.* 'I know you've been north to visit the crime scene where Davey Robbins was murdered.'

She watched the formerly amused grey gaze turn troubled. 'I can't talk about that.'

'Well, I'm writing about it.'

'What do you know?'

'Probably as much as you do.'

He paused and she could see he was thinking back over his day. 'Ah, the nosy reporter from *The Yorkshire Gazette*?'

She grinned. 'You make a good detective.'

'And I have to hand it to you, you're a wily journo.'

'Thank you . . . if that is a genuine compliment.'

'It is. And meeting me . . . how does this fit into your plan?'

'To be honest, I thought if I could catch you off guard – you know, surprising you at the train station where you least expect to see media – you'd accidentally spill something to me,' she said, not sure if she was trying to be amusing or just candid.

'You have caught me off guard, which is why we're here, drinking like friends, and I didn't just stomp away. But that doesn't mean I lose my focus. I don't like being followed.'

'If I apologised, I wouldn't be sincere because now I know I'm onto something.'

'Why?'

'Because of you! Why would such a senior guy from Scotland Yard make a trip to freezing North Yorkshire unless the murder victim was of interest to him and the case he's working on?'

'I'm not working on a case.'

'I think you're lying.'

They both paused to sip their drinks, like two fencers touching swords and testing each other.

He smacked his lips and put his beer down. 'I'm not lying.' She believed him. 'I'm not working a case.'

Semantics. *Try again*, she forced herself. 'An operation, then.'

He said nothing but his eyes narrowed.

'An operation?' This time it was loaded with query.

'I can't say anything, Lauren.'

'I knew it!'

'It's actually not what you think.'

'Then set me straight.'

He considered again. His pauses were awkward for her but apparently not for him; he looked at ease as he pondered his internal battle to tell her more.

'Set you straight? Okay, then, I think you're extremely talented; few would have sleuthed out what you have as agilely and swiftly. And I also think the magazine you work for is insulting to that talent.'

Lauren grimaced at his words. 'Tell me something I don't know,' she said as a throwaway line so she could look away awkwardly and not confront the truth of what he'd said.

'All right,' he said, pausing. She waited for some sort of placation. He picked up his glass again and looked at it. 'I'm drinking a beer called Old Speckled Hen. Now, this beer originated from the Morland Brewery in Oxfordshire to commemorate the fiftieth anniversary of the MG car factory based there. Curiously, it was named for one of the old MGs that the workers used to run errands in and around the factory and the town. And because its regular and somewhat careless use resulted in it becoming covered in random flecks of paint, it won itself the nickname of "Owld speckled 'un" and that morphed into Old Speckled Hen – the first brown ale brewed by Morland.' He stopped talking and stared at her, waiting for her to say something. When she didn't, he grinned. 'I'm guessing you didn't know that?'

Lauren couldn't help blasting out a laugh of pure joy. 'Tell me something else I don't know.'

'Er . . .' He grinned, searching for another item of trivia to share. 'This area is believed by many to be where the legendary battle between Queen Boudicca and the Roman invaders took place. The story goes that the final resting place of the warrior queen of the Iceni is under one of the platforms here.'

She stared at him. 'You should go on *Mastermind*. Are you always like this?'

He shrugged. 'You asked me to tell you something you didn't know.'

Lauren laughed helplessly. 'Detective Superintendent Hawksworth, you're fun.'

'I'm pleased, because I sensed we were about to disappear into a melancholy conversation.'

She studied his expression, which was far too kind in this moment, then nodded. 'I hate my life,' she admitted.

'So change it.'

'That's easy to say.'

'It's easy to do, Lauren,' he replied as fast as a whipcrack on her words. 'It's all up here,' he said, tapping his temple. 'Make a decision to make a change and you'll find yourself on a new pathway. All it takes is one simple decision . . . to take control. And, of course, if you can choose the right pathway, you'll change your life for the better. If you don't choose wisely, then at least you tried and you can shift pathways again. Stagnating is what will do you in.'

'He took all of me . . . all that I owned, all that I was.' Jack waited, didn't comment. 'I fell for everything about him. I really loved him. What I realise now, with the clarity of pain, poverty and humiliation, is that I loved the character he projected; it was all acting. He was good at it too: romantic, affectionate, support-ive, exciting, fun . . . I was all in and I'd never been in love until I met him. My girlfriends used to joke I'd be the old spinster among them and always available to babysit. And then Dan came along.'

She sipped her drink, tasting the pleasantly sour tang of the lemon, and hardly noticed that her companion hadn't spoken but was watching her earnestly. She felt slightly mesmerised by his gaze and, without planning to, kept talking. 'He was such a catch. His lifestyle was thrilling, you know? He called himself an entrepreneur, and when we met, he was involved in a new tech start-up, which was exciting. He was on the brink of leaving Britain for the US – headed for Silicon Valley, but planned to buy an apartment in New York.' She sighed. 'Fuck! I fell so hard for him, his lies, his promises. We got engaged – it was a whirlwind. My family was astonished and so happy for the old maid; my friends were all jealous because he was handsome and charming and apparently loaded. He drove the right car, he had the right address, dressed like a mannequin . . . clearly worshipped me.'

'All smoke and mirrors?'

She nodded, wiping away helpless tears. 'I'm sorry.'

'It's all right. I'm sensing you don't talk about this much.'

'You're the first person I've revealed my feelings to since I came home from America. I've avoided all my old pals. They're embarrassed for me but probably think he dumped me, when in fact I had to escape him, borrow money to get home.'

'Your family?'

'It's a terrible disappointment for them. I don't want sympathy, but I also don't want them to know how deeply angry I am for being so gullible.'

'Can I get you another drink?'

'Oh, it's my round,' she said, As she reached for her bag, she felt the warmth of his hand on hers.

'Let me, Lauren. I'll put it on the Met's expense account.' He stood before she could protest. 'Same again?' She sniffed and nodded. He was back surprisingly fast with a refreshed pair of drinks.

'Another Hen?' she asked, trying to lighten her own mood.

'Ah, no. This time I'm having a London Pride.'

'Will you be sharing its history with me?'

'I think I've bored you plenty already.' He grinned. 'Cheers again.'

Their glasses clinked. She shook her head. 'You are far from boring. Tell me something else I may not know,' she said, harking back to their previous conversation, wishing she hadn't deflated their happy atmosphere.

He watched her over the top of his half pint as though reaching a decision. 'That you are onto something that is a long way from simply titillating.'

The glass was halfway to her mouth. 'Are you playing with me?'

He shook his head once, slowly.

'How close?'

'Enough that you're stepping into dangerous territory.'

'Shit! Tell me.'

'No. It doesn't work that way. Tell me what you know. If, after I hear it, I deem it's permissible, I'll talk to some people and see if we can let you in on some stuff.'

She sat straighter, hardly daring to believe they were having this conversation.

'But Lauren . . . this is not a discussion to be having with *My Day*.'

She shook her head in confusion.

'I've spoken to the man at the top of our media team about you.'

'What, just now?' She frowned.

'Yes, that was the call.'

So much for the gorgeous artist waiting at home and Boo the dog.

'What did he say?'

'I've told him you're not going to let this go.'

'Did he believe you?'

'He did when I told him you were my welcoming party at King's Cross.' He smiled and she gave a self-conscious chuckle. 'The head of our press office is a genial sort of fellow.'

'What does that mean for me?'

He shrugged. 'I don't know yet, but at least I'm following protocol. If you do too, then it might mean that we can offer some sort of exclusive briefing.'

Her mouth opened in surprise.

'I'm not promising anything, Lauren, but if you follow my suggestions and you respect confidentiality, then just maybe you'll get your scoop.'

She nodded.

'I need to know if I can rely on you, though.'

'I promise.'

'Someone had to tip you off,' he remarked.

She looked down. 'I can't talk about that.'

'You're going to have to.'

'I really can't.'

'But you want me to share highly confidential material?'

It felt like a stand-off. And Lauren could tell he was in no mood to negotiate any further – and if she was honest, he had been more than generous in not simply giving her the finger at the railway station.

'It was a friend,' she said finally, knowing he needed her to capitulate. 'Well, actually she made it clear I'd burned that friendship by cornering her for information.'

'Cornering?'

'She thought I would leverage an indiscretion of hers from years ago that could bring grief to her family.'

'You'd do that?' He looked disappointed.

Lauren was surprised by how much his disappointment hurt and indeed mattered to her. 'No, never. I was just pressing for information.'

'She works for the Met, presumably?'

'I won't give you her name because, in her defence, she told me nothing connected to any of the crimes; she doesn't have that sort of access.'

Jack sighed. 'What did she give you, Lauren? If there's a leak at the Met, I need to know because it could endanger lives.'

Lauren took a swig of her drink, which was losing its spritz. 'Well, if she did know anything, she refused, absolutely point blank, to discuss any case, any operation, any files.'

He stared back at her, saying nothing.

'She works in admin, nothing sexy. And all she did say, to get me off her back, was your name. That was it. Jack Hawksworth.'

He breathed in and breathed out audibly. 'I see.'

'All the rest is on me. I hunted you down, I began to put things together myself. But I sense I'm out of my depth on this unless I can get in on some background.'

'Listen, Lauren, if the Met is going to cooperate, we're going to do so with a reputable media outlet that will handle this properly, sensitively, with all the right research and a balanced view.' She began to speak but he cut over her words. 'Davey Robbins was a violent rapist, but the person who killed him showed equal violence. Now, a part of me believes it couldn't have happened to a nicer bloke, but the policeman in me says all victims are due the same treatment, all murderers earn the same scrutiny and unforgiving hunt.'

'I hear you, but are you admitting that there's a killer at work picking off the bad guys?'

'I'm not admitting anything yet. I'm simply saying that if you want me to talk to you about what I'm spending my time on, I will not talk to *My Day*. Otherwise it turns into sensationalist rubbish written purely to sell another week of cheap thrills to people looking for distraction rather than real news.'

'But I work for *My Day*,' she said, feeling helpless.

'Well, I think we should address that. Maybe it's the first of the changes we should make in your life.'

We. 'How?'

'Just leave it with me for the time being.'

'And what do I do?'

'Promise me you won't write a word in your crap magazine about this. If you can't give me your word, I walk away now. You'll have to chase me all over Britain and I will never acknowledge your presence, will have you removed at every chance.'

She nodded.

'No, you have to say it. I'm trusting you; dozens wouldn't.'

'Why are you doing this for me?'

'Well, hopefully this will help you to forget the blip in your life, and fast-track you back to where you were . . . perhaps beyond.'

'You shouldn't feel responsible for me.'

'I don't, but perhaps if you counterbalance the bad experience with a good one, you won't lose faith in men.'

She smiled. 'I won't. And I promise that I won't write anything about what we've discussed until I hear from you.' She waited. 'Okay?'

Jack nodded.

'But help me now – make it a bit worth my while. I have an editor breathing down my neck.'

'Put her off. I will never give you anything that might find its way into *My Day*.'

'I hear you, but give me something, Jack!' She put her glass down, slightly shocked at herself. 'May I call you Jack?'

'You just did. Tell me what you know.'

She didn't hesitate, tears forgotten. She sensed he was turning over the wheels in his mind about how to break her out of her dead-end job, and maybe help her get a role that had some cred again. Lauren leaned forward. 'I've been collecting bizarre deaths for probably six or seven years now, long before I started working for *My Day*. I had no real purpose for them to begin with, but they intrigued me, and I was actually storing them for a serious story on lenient sentences. But they are titillating, as you say, and when I got back to Britain, feeling sorry for myself, it struck me that my bizarre death stories could be handy for some sort of salacious piece that might just win me some notice – my own column, that sort of thing.'

He nodded.

'So I did some more hunting in my spare time. I had nothing better to do,' she admitted.

'And?'

'There was a district nurse convicted of killing several patients in their late eighties, all with terminal illnesses. She claimed she was helping the families, who she said didn't care about their elderly relatives nearly as much as she did. She apparently came across sympathetically at her trial.'

'I remember the case. Are you telling me the nurse is dead?'

She nodded. 'Dead in her lounge in—'

'Brimsdown,' he said, the name dawning.

'Good memory. According to her daughter, nothing was taken, nothing disturbed, and there were no signs of a break-in. What wasn't revealed is that she died of a drug overdose. One policeman I spoke to – a senior-enough guy – said that a former nurse would have had connections for getting those sorts of drugs, although he never told me what sort of drugs, and that nurses who worked with the very ill, or very elderly, could get depressed, blah blah. The evidence was watertight that she helped several old folk to their last breath and, while they were mercy killings, they were still death by her hand. I never believed she topped herself. So if someone did kill her, she perhaps knew her killer, or certainly she trusted the person.'

'How long had she been out?' Jack was already reaching for his phone.

'Er . . . she died a few months after being released from prison, but she only served a short part of her sentence before she was released on licence . . . served maybe eight months of a three-year sentence.'

He held up a finger to stop her talking and lifted the phone to his ear. 'Sarah? Yeah, got back about an hour ago.' He listened. 'First thing, I'll be in. Listen, are you around for a bit longer?

Okay, good. I'll ring you shortly. Can you run a couple of names for me?' He nodded as she spoke. 'Great, thanks. Back soon.' He rang off, looked back at Lauren. 'Any others?'

'Am I helping the police now?'

His gaze seemed to darken further, though that seemed impossible.

'Okay, er, one more off the top of my head, although I'm on the trail of another.'

He waited.

'There was a lorry driver who was distracted and also tired . . . he'd been swallowing yippee pills to stay awake and was doing a long haul round the M25. He dozed momentarily, swerved and cut up a family car carrying parents and three sleeping children.

'I recall it. One parent dead, one consigned to a wheelchair and only the infant in the baby seat unharmed. He was convicted for death by dangerous driving.'

'That's the one. Well, he was killed in the Midlands somewhere, but he was originally from North London . . . Clay Hill, from memory. He was given a light sentence because the defence team was able to provide sufficient doubt about how secure the kids were. Apparently, two of the children had unclicked their seatbelts and the mother in the passenger seat had distracted their father driving, as she had turned around to help clean up a spilled drink.'

'But the lorry driver was still culpable.'

'Correct. Blood tests confirmed he was driving on a mix of amphetamines, concentrated caffeine and an anti-narcolepsy drug. They held him responsible, but not entirely, so the sentence was lenient. The lorry driver's death was unsolved. Seems he was the casualty of a hit-and-run when he pulled into a truck stop. Happened at night on a motorway exit. No witnesses. He left behind a wife and two children.'

It seemed to her that Jack's somewhat tanned complexion had become paler. Now she saw only the gravely serious senior detective.

He stood. 'Lauren, I have to go.' He pulled a card from his jacket pocket. 'Here's my direct number. I know we have yours. I promise to call.'

'Give me something, Jack, please. I'll keep my word – we made a pact, but I just need to keep my editor on a string. She's in no hurry.' She dug into her bag and ripped out half a page from a small notebook before rummaging for a pen. Finding one, she scribbled hurriedly. 'Look, here's my home address and my personal mobile. If you'd rather keep it all away from *My Day*, contact me privately.' He took the scrap of a note and pushed it into his wallet. 'Is there any clue you can give me, no matter how vague, so my boss believes I'm making progress?'

He regarded her carefully and sensed how earnest she was. 'Think about where all the people you've researched have committed their crimes,' he said, giving her a searching look.

She stared back unblinking, her thoughts racing, invisible fingers in her mind picking through the files she held in what she liked to think of as her vault. When she returned her attention to the noisy pub, she realised her lovely senior detective from Scotland Yard had left.

But something important had just clicked into place.

16

Martin Sharpe looked apoplectic behind his reading glasses, which were sitting far down his nose. 'You did what?'

No point in repeating it; the chief's question was rhetorical . . . a shocked response to a shocking admission. In the morning light angling through Sharpe's office, the idea no longer seemed so inspired. 'You heard right, sir,' Jack replied, anticipating the outburst and the subsequent dressing-down that was surely coming.

'And what didn't you understand about words like "covert", "under the radar", "no media", "hush-hush" . . . or even straightforward "confidential"!' His voice had risen with each word.

'Careful, sir, you'll spill your tea,' Jack said calmly. Sharpe opened his mouth and closed it again, banging down the cup and saucer, spilling the tea anyway. 'Oops,' Jack murmured.

'Don't make light of this.'

'I'm not. Did you hear my explanation?'

'I'm retiring, not deaf! But perhaps you're the one who didn't hear clearly.'

'Sir, she's onto it . . . and us. I've already disentangled myself once from her but this woman has a nose for a story. She's bloody good at her job—'

'Jack, are you out of your mind? We're not talking *Time* magazine here or *The Guardian* . . .'

'Ms Starling and I have had that conversation. It's why I called Mike.'

It didn't seem possible to shock him further but Sharpe looked like he might need smelling salts. 'You've called the head of our press office?'

'Last night. I wanted us to try and get ahead of her and stop it finding its way into the gutter press. I sought his advice and also wanted to ensure he knew what I was doing, so there would be no back . . .' He couldn't find the right word and ended up saying 'flushing'. It made no sense, but Sharpe didn't seem to care.

What *did* make sense to him was what he was focused on. 'Why wouldn't you speak to me before Mike?'

'Sir, with all due respect, if you choose to elevate me to the rank of detective superintendent, you need to allow for all that goes with it; I did not overstep the line. I felt it right to brief Mike immediately. It's all you would have done, and there seemed little point in upsetting you at the end of the day and asking you to contact Mike.'

'But you should have told me!'

'I'm telling you now.' Jack stared at Sharpe, who simply quivered with vexation. 'I know the protocols, sir, and I followed them. Right now, I've got her under control and waiting for us to guide her, rather than defending ourselves against the circus tent that was potentially being built around our op.'

'Who's the leak?'

'She refuses to say, and the leak only gave my name, nothing else.'

'And you believe that?'

'I do, sir. She is candid about this. It cost the friendship.'

'Good!'

'Sir . . . Martin . . .' he appealed. 'It is Starling who put it all together, not the leak. She's a talented journo in the wrong job, just trying to claw her way back to a level where she can be taken seriously. Why don't we use her – point her in the right direction as we need? Lauren— Ms Starling actually shows some depth of conscience and would much rather be doing a serious piece that consults with the Met.'

'What's being proposed?'

'Mike rang this morning and said we could probably offer her an exclusive once you're satisfied with our findings and the op is closed.'

'What are my chances, Jack, of my big nose being wrong?'

Jack risked a grin. 'Slim, sir.'

'Tell me.' He did. Sharpe leaned back in his big chair, in his big office, which made him look smaller and somehow older and more ready for retirement than Jack thought possible. 'Bloody hell,' he murmured as Jack continued, grateful that Lauren Starling was mercifully becoming a distant problem. When Jack finished, Sharpe rubbed his face for several seconds. 'We have a multiple murderer in our midst.' He said it as though it seemed implausible, as though he was shocked, even though it was his instincts that had set up this covert operation to establish that very fact.

'A serial killer, yes,' Jack agreed, deliberately blunt. 'He's been at it for years, if Ms Starling is correct. There are probably many more deaths we are yet to link. And we do believe this is a male, sir, so we're referring to the killer as such. I was almost ready to believe when I was up north, but after what Lauren Starling said last night – and my subsequent research – I'm convinced, sir.'

'Have you briefed the ops team?'

'Just about to. Um, one more thing.' Jack looked sheepish.

'Do I need to be taking my ulcer tablet for this?'

'Yes, sir.'

Sharpe closed his eyes momentarily. 'Why can't you just be obedient, Jack, like other members of the police force?'

'You wouldn't find it at all stimulating if I was, sir.'

'What's happened?'

'Anne McEvoy.'

'What about McEvoy?'

'I went to see her.'

'When?'

'Earlier this week.'

Sharpe's expression clouded. 'Because?'

Jack explained.

'You astonish me,' Sharpe said, sounding beyond frustrated.

'Well, the idea, sir, was about stealth. I figured if Anne McEvoy could give us some insight into how a multiple killer might think, plot, act . . . it might just give us a speedier answer to the question you posed.'

'And did it?'

'Yes, sir. And then some. Her experience—'

'As a serial killer?' Sharpe snarled.

Jack remained calm; he deserved this. 'I was going to say in criminal psychology, plus the people she mixes with daily . . . and, yes, of course, being a serial killer herself, she's got a perspective we could never have.'

'And what's in this for McEvoy, pray tell?'

'Nothing, sir,' Jack lied.

'Just for old times' sake?' Sharpe couldn't disguise his disgust.

'A favour for a former friend.'

'And what do you think your new *friend* – the journalist Ms Wren—'

'Starling, sir.'

'Whatever! What do you think she'll make of this irresistible titbit when she discovers that a serial killer serving four life sentences at Holloway is now Scotland Yard's go-to consultant?'

'Blood pressure, sir.'

'Oh, be quiet, Jack!' He opened a drawer, took out a plastic sheath and popped out a small pill. 'One conversation with you and I think I'll need heart surgery!' He flung the packet down with disgust and swallowed the white pill with a sip of cold tea.

'Don't say that.'

'Why?'

'Because I want to see you in those deck shoes, heading off for your cruise, sir, when we solve this case.'

'*Solve* it.' He gave a mirthless laugh of frustration.

'Operation Mirror needs a green light to pursue its findings, sir. In my opinion, and in the opinion of the senior members of our team, we are hunting a vigilante. You were right, Martin . . . and I'm going to make sure that you retire with no loose ends trailing behind you.'

Sharpe wagged a finger at him. 'You'd better keep that promise.'

Jack had asked everyone to gather. Even Joan leaned against the entrance to the incident room to hear progress. He could see Kate had been busy setting up photographs in chronological order of death and wondered if she was aware that the neat array was about to be disrupted.

'Okay, settle down, everyone,' he said, with a smile to set the tone. The room quietened. 'All right, let's get an update on exactly where we are with our enquiries, although I should probably pre-empt this conversation with news that I feel sure you're all anticipating anyway.'

Kate straightened. 'No longer a look and see?'

He nodded. 'Upstairs has given us the go-ahead that this is now officially a hunt and catch. But—' He raised his palms to quell the murmurs. 'I want us to remain as lean as we can. This is not about money; this is about keeping the operation tight. We've already had a leak.' His team looked understandably shocked and immediately began denying their involvement to each other. 'No one from here, or else that person or persons would already be giving out parking tickets on the Isle of Skye.' That won a chuckle, but he could hear the relief too. 'No, I'm sorry to say that one of our admin team has been loose-lipped.'

Kate looked vexed. 'How much was revealed?'

'Very little. Just my name, actually, but a wily journo has been following my tracks and met me off my train at King's Cross Station.'

'He knew you were in Yorkshire?' Kate looked instantly guilty as people around her slid glances her way. 'I mean, how could he—'

'It's a she, actually. Her name is Lauren Starling and rather embarrassingly for all of us, she works for a rag called *My Day*.' He glanced at Joan, who raised a single eyebrow, which could mean anything, he realised. Jack took a minute to explain about Lauren, how they were going to try to work with her. Kate looked especially annoyed and he anticipated a prickly conversation with her later. He continued. 'The point is, we'll control what goes out and when. And to be honest, while I imagine Sarah already has some more unsolved cases that fit our criteria, Ms Starling has had nothing but her internal radar and she's well ahead of us. She's put this together herself over a few years, and I think we should show some respect for that and not underestimate her. So, the plan is to keep this journalist on a short but exclusive leash.'

'Who holds the leash, sir?' Mal wondered out loud.

'Our press office is fully up to speed, but essentially I will hold it, very tightly. Can I add, she's savvy and knew well before the leak that she was onto something. If she approaches any of you, for any reason, just shake your head and smile. You have nothing to say to Ms Starling. However, don't judge her for being from *My Day* – she's got the goods' — he tapped his head — 'and the smarts to work for top-notch media. So if you do find yourself suddenly chatting to a good-looking girl in a pub, think Lauren Starling, and be aware that her antenna is always alert.' He took the liberty of pinning a blown-up photo of Starling onto a corner of their board. 'Can't miss her.'

Jack thought Kate looked uncomfortable at the mention of Lauren but chose to let that thought go. 'Right, onwards. Let me tell you about my trip north yesterday.' He gave them a comprehensive update. 'So I suspect by the end of today we'll have some pathology and SOCO information, but the body should arrive in London today and we'll hear back from that post-mortem of Dr Cook's by tomorrow. Kate, you stay on that as he's familiar with you now. We need to corroborate that Robbins was drugged, and with what.'

Kate nodded.

'Why the hands?' Mal asked.

'I think it's to do with being a thief,' Jack replied. 'Just a theory.'

'But his real crime was the rape, sir.' Sarah frowned.

Jack nodded. 'Yes, I suspect our killer is subtle of mind. Usually the penalty is one hand for repeated theft, but he's taken both, and my bet is he's suggesting taking Amy Clarke's virginity is every bit a theft of property . . . And the other dismemberment is obviously more symbolic.' His team looked numbed. 'Okay, we should have Sarah brief us on her progress next.'

He was relieved to have the news of Lauren Starling's involvement out of the way and his team fully diverted onto more important matters, but he still refused to look at Kate or Joan in case their gazes held questions. Instead he took up his usual position, leaning against a desk, arms crossed.

'Thanks, sir. All right, well. I hope all of you are ready for the roller-coaster. Together with the information Ms Starling gave us, I have now found nine unexplained deaths of criminals over the past four years.' She waited for and got the collective gasp of surprise. 'Nine that we know of . . . potentially there are more.'

'Can you link them?' Mal asked.

She smiled. 'Not in an obvious way, with the killer's calling card, trophy-taking, even his MO. Each died wildly differently and up and down the country. But,' she said, pausing, 'every one of the cases I have now put into your files committed their original crimes in the Borough of Enfield.'

This prompted looks of astonishment, as a vital piece of the puzzle found its home.

'Excellent work, Sarah,' Jack said, clapping once. 'So, everyone, our killer has been at his craft for several years, selecting victims from in and around the Enfield area. What does this tell us?' He stepped back and indicated for Kate to take over.

'Part of the criminal scene?' one eager constable said, trying to get noticed.

'Potentially but not necessarily,' Kate said. 'Naturally that's our first thought, though, and why we've asked various divisions to let us know what they're hearing on the streets. What's happening with the North London Crown Court?'

'There are fourteen we're looking at,' Mal confirmed.

Kate looked surprised. 'Right, well, that's a lot of ground for us to cover. Mal is designating tasks and we need all the admin staff to be quietly interviewed. We're looking for regular visitors to the gallery, anyone who is particularly lippy about lenient sentences. Let's get looking for blogs and articles about lenient sentencing. We probably need to look into any judges who are known for their liberal approach, too. Give me that list. Mal, perhaps you could tackle judges' clerks. I'll speak to any judges, or even you, sir . . . they might prefer your rank.'

Jack stepped back up. 'Good. All right, let me know what you need. Yes, Sarah?' She had her hand up and he smiled.

'Er, my uncle was a clerk of the court over in Somerset. Because they're out front, they're very aware of the comings and goings of the court. I think it would be advisable to give that group of people a special focus because they'll have eyes and ears on everyone within the court, whether they're criminal, voyeurs, journos, the curious, students and so on.'

'Okay, good,' Kate said. 'As you know the role, why don't you handle calls to the clerks of the court and I'll handle judges. Sir, perhaps you can take up the conversations with the judges if we find anything interesting?'

Jack nodded. 'I don't mind helping out at the courts as well, anyway. The more of us covering off those interviews, the better. That is on top of everything else we're focused on, which is stripping down every case we know of and rebuilding it. We're looking for gaps, stones that have been left unturned, essentially. Sarah, I want to know in how many of these cases propofol was used.'

She nodded.

Kate gave him an expectant look and he sighed. 'My office.'

She had the grace to bring him a coffee before she fixed him with a look of accusation. He gave a defensive gesture with both palms facing her. 'I didn't invite her, Kate.'

'Why couldn't you get rid of her?'

'Do you mean when she was waiting downstairs, or meeting me at King's Cross?'

'Why not? She's only a rag writer.'

He gave a small look of pain. 'She'd have just bobbed up somewhere else. She's so much more than just a rag writer.' He watched Kate's hackles rise as she caught the sniff of something only another woman might. 'What I mean is,' he said, now trying to throw her off that particular scent, 'she's talented, and none of us should underestimate her.'

'No, you've made that clear to all of us.'

'She can run circles around most. She's really a bright kid.'

'How old is she?'

He shrugged, hoping to make it appear as though it wasn't important. 'I have no idea.'

'Take a guess.'

'Why?'

'Why, Jack? Because on the two major cases I've worked with you, a woman involved catches your interest.'

'I'll stop you there,' he said, an edge of warning in his tone. 'I didn't know Anne McEvoy, I knew a person called Sophie. And Lily was a victim. I don't need reminding of the personal pain to me over previous cases, and I certainly don't need cautioning from you about my romantic involvement with anyone I choose. I don't particularly like it that Ms Starling's involved, but I'm not going to spit in her face because she is. She was there first. She has more cases to scrutinise than we do. We're on her coat-tails and she just may be able to help.'

'How?' Kate wasn't backing down. He admired her terrier-like determination and that was why, as her senior, he was indulging her despite the rebuke he'd like to give.

'She can fly under the radar in a way that no member of the police can. Nosy journalists are tolerated, swatted at, anticipated, even . . . but the minute you have plain-clothes police involved, a new set of tongues begin wagging.'

'You're going to use her?'

'If the right set of circumstances present themselves, I might.'

She looked back at him with dismay.

'You're a hypocrite, do you know that?'

Kate blinked, wounded. 'Why's that?'

'Well, you're quite happy to suggest manipulating Anne McEvoy in prison for anything she can tell us, but bring on the good-looking journo and suddenly your hackles are up.'

She put her hands up defensively but momentarily they looked like claws . . . if they had been talons, he suspected she'd have plunged them into him. 'Are you saying I'm jealous?'

'No, I'm saying don't have double standards. We need all the help we can get on this case because right now we don't have much.'

He knew Kate hadn't heard much since he'd accused her of being insecure. He had to make it right. 'Kate—'

'That's fine, sir. Bring in whoever you choose, sleep with whoever you like.'

'I will . . . and I do, DI Carter, and I don't need your permission to do so. Are we clear on that?'

'Yes, sir.'

'That will be all.'

17

Kate left Scotland Yard unsure of where to go but wanting to get as far from the incident room, and especially her boss, as possible. What was wrong with her? Now he was irate in all the ways she'd hoped to avoid. How could he trust her if she managed to reduce them to this familiar stalemate?

What did that say about her – was she a nutcase or simply someone who felt deeply? Being labelled emotional was not the best badge of honour to receive as a detective inspector with aspirations of moving to DCI over the next couple of years. For a woman, showing emotion at work was often the antithesis of what was admired. Kate knew she covered her feelings by being brisk; her dry manner could come across as cruel when all she was trying to do was to keep people at a distance so they wouldn't look too far inwards at the girl who was looking for love.

She'd thought she'd found it – so good for a while – but it was sadly with the wrong man. That was not Geoff's fault. Jack had only responded to her in that charming, inclusive way that was his method for running a team. Geoff had once said she'd got

Jack wrong from the start and had misread his manner as romantic instead of just his way with every woman, which was to be gracious, amusing, generous.

'He's like an old-fashioned knight. Chivalry is alive and well in my buddy, and he makes the rest of us look and feel like cavemen by comparison.' Kate had heard the clear ring of truth. Even so, Kate knew she and Jack shared something special. Not even Jack could deny it, not even Geoff, and that was the real reason their relationship had foundered. Geoff had been so good for her . . . but he was not Jack and that was her whole problem.

Kate sat on the Underground carriage, rumbling through the belly of London, lost in a mind devoid of thought but filled with guilt and embarrassment. Jack could be forgiven for thinking she had found some perspective, but she felt so very stupid now for showing him that she hadn't; she could fake it, but she couldn't make it stick for long. She'd been so proud of herself after their dinner, at how casual, amusing and capable she was of being alone in his house without making him feel awkward. But all he had to do was give her an inkling that there may be some romantic interest in his life and she became unreliable.

He was right, she reasoned: she was jealous of him taking an almost proprietorial interest in this journalist. It was identical to how she'd felt when he'd fallen for McEvoy and then Lily. Dislocating from Jack had been the best move for her heart but now, back in his orbit, she could feel that sense of despair, that desire for ownership creeping up on her again. Every smile he cast someone's way, every wink, any attention . . . she wanted it to be hers, not theirs.

Kate, you are grieving for a relationship that was never real and will never be, she told herself in the darkness beneath London. It was not an unfamiliar piece of advice but, this time, clattering towards a destination she now realised was Enfield as she glanced up at the blue Piccadilly line's route, she made a firm promise that she would let go of this daydream, which was holding her back from finding what she wanted.

The automated woman's voice announced their imminent arrival at Finsbury Park Station and, given it was the middle of the morning, it was not too crowded. She emerged at street level where the National Rail, London Underground and two major bus stations connected.

A lot of tracksuits and way too much leggings-and-sneakers action, she thought, noting the sloppily dressed pedestrians moving around the concourse. She couldn't help but be aware that she stood out in this neighbourhood, even in her working garb. And no one could be oblivious to the fact that this was the home of the Arsenal Football Club . . . there were Gunners logos, signs and souvenir shops all around and many wearing Arsenal gear. She would be careful not to mention that she was a Manchester United fan, she thought grimly.

Football was not the reason she was here, though. She'd come to see where Peggy Markham had been found, plus a walk around Finsbury Park seemed a good way to clear her head of today's misstep. She moved away from the busy streets around the station and the stadium and followed her nose towards the green expanse that formed one of London's oldest parklands in the neighbour-hood of Harringay, a once proud and verdant landscape of the Victorian era. The British Lottery Fund had quite recently awarded it a ton of money, which had enabled much-needed renovations including cleaning the lake, building a new café, adding an updated children's playground and resurfacing tennis courts. She recalled attending an Oasis concert here. When was that? She couldn't be bothered trying to remember. Right now, it was host to dog walkers and mothers with babies in prams, but it was so large an expanse that it felt deserted.

It took Kate a further five minutes of strolling, realising she was headed in the wrong direction and turning back on herself before she found the huge old tree where the brothel madam had been found slumped. There was still a small snag of police tape on the tree to confirm this was the spot – Markham's final resting place, where her killer had injected the lethal dose of propofol that had snuffed out her life at fifty-nine.

The space was open but not entirely naked to the public eye. A small copse of trees would have given some cover, and it was not a place that many would wish to be in the darkest, most silent hours of a wintry morning. Close by was a timber shelter over park benches; it seemed incongruous to Kate as she looked around, wondering why that spot in particular had been chosen, but she didn't dwell on it after giving it a cursory look, noticing that the slats of timber that formed the ceiling had been ripped away. She frowned, wondering distractedly why bored teenagers got their kicks from destroying things . . . any structure seemed to be fair game. She imagined they'd wearied of the effort because the enclosure looked solid and well-made and only a few slats had been tampered with. She kept walking, doing a couple of revolutions of the tree where Peggy had been found, but she couldn't find anything that inspired her to linger. *Head back, then?* No, she was still embarrassed, still angry with herself; they'd made a promise of no stone unturned, in which case, it was off to Hornsey Police Station for her.

She took a ten-minute taxi ride to Crouch End and pushed through the doors of the police station, surprised by how busy it was. Flashing her warrant card over the heads of the people waiting to be dealt with, she was let in through the side door past the reception counter where two officers were fielding enquiries, various complaints, one lippy drunk and an angry woman demanding that the police do something about the driver who had sideswiped her car and driven off. An officer approached, introducing himself as DS Helm.

'DI Kate Carter,' she said, matching his smile. 'Bit of a circus out there?'

He shrugged. 'Pretty normal for us, ma'am, although it is pension day and that always seems to get people stirred up.' He walked her past the custody suite where she could just see through the porthole that a recorded interview was underway; this unit seemed swamped. He showed her into a small meeting room. 'Our senior detectives are at court today, ma'am. How can I help?'

Kate didn't feel like sitting but did to be polite. 'Thanks. Um, I'm actually just doing some due diligence . . . making sure we've locked down everything we know about a particular case.'

He frowned. 'That Hornsey's involved with?'

'Yes, but it happened about six months ago. Got some media attention.'

It dawned as soon as she said that. 'Peggy Markham.' He nodded and so did she. 'I wasn't here then, but what can I do to assist?'

'Well, we've read the files uploaded to the database. I just wondered if I could see the original material; it helps to eyeball it all, plus I can tell my chief that I've ticked this box.'

'Of course. I thought the case was all squared away as suicide, though?'

She sighed inwardly; she had anticipated this. 'Yes, it was, but there may be some connection with a new case. I'm sorry that I can't say more about that right now but, as I say, this is just me making sure we've done all the right legwork.'

'No stone unturned,' he said with a smile.

'Exactly,' she said, ensuring there was a note in her tone that suggested it was tedious but necessary.

'Right. Sit tight, I'll fetch what you need. Coffee?'

'Coffee would be great,' she said.

Later, engrossed in the file, she realised the coffee was far from great, but it was hot and filling her belly, which she'd overlooked feeding for breakfast, and she suspected lunch would pass her by too. She was down to the last couple of sheets; she'd already decided there was nothing new to learn here but at least felt satisfied she could report to the team that they knew all they could from the original crime reports.

Just as she was reaching for the mug of tepid coffee to take a final swallow, she turned over some handwritten notes tucked into the back of the file. The detail at the top told her it was a DC Lisa Farrow interviewing a man called Bernard Beaton. She frowned, then realised it was a witness statement. Her breath caught as she quickly scanned the neat handwriting. Beaton had claimed he'd witnessed a murder; that Peggy Markham had been brought to the park and killed by a man with a syringe of something lethal. Kate knew she was reading the same lines over and again, also that her mouth had opened slightly and she could swear her heartbeat was audible.

'What the hell?' she finally murmured. 'Killed!' she spoke to the empty room with disbelief.

DS Helm chose that moment to tap and open the door a chink. 'How are you getting on, ma'am? Can I get you anything else?'

'Does a DC Farrow still work out of this police station?'

'Not to my knowledge. Could be before my time he worked here.'

'It's a she,' Kate corrected gently. 'What about someone called Phil Brown . . . the reception officer?'

He looked pleased that he could assist. 'Phil's still here, ma'am. He's on his break.'

'Could you ask him to give me a minute when he gets a chance?' She was glad she could still sound polite, because she wanted to growl at everyone in this police station. She was sensing a massive oversight. 'I'll wait, thank you.'

He nodded and she reached for her mobile phone, dialling Jack without hesitation.

'Hawskworth,' he answered.

'It's me, sir.' Horrible pause. 'I'm . . . er, I'm at Hornsey Police Station.'

She wondered if he was frowning but he immediately replied, reminding her he had a mind like an efficient filing cabinet when it came to cases. 'Peggy Markham?'

'Exactly. I've found something.'

There was a pause and she let it hang. 'Are you going to tell me it wasn't suicide?'

'There's a witness statement here that attests to watching a murder take place in Finsbury Park.'

'Bugger me!' She heard Joan distantly claiming he owed a coin. 'How come it . . . actually, don't bother explaining now – you'll need to brief us all shortly. What's next?'

'I'm going to talk to the officer who was on the desk that night and I also need to hunt down Detective Constable Lisa Farrow. She took the witness statement.'

'I'll sort that and have her call you.'

She heard voices. 'Sorry, am I interrupting?'

'No, I've got a few of us at the North London Crown Court.'

'Anything?'

'Not yet, early days.'

'Well, good luck. Oh and, er, Jack . . .'

'It's all right,' he said, obviously guessing where her next words were headed.

'No, it's not. I was so far out of order, I'm disgusted with myself. I want to apologise on a personal level as a friend, but more importantly as a fellow officer. I had no business questioning your intent. I'm truly appalled. I can barely face coming back.'

'We need you back,' he said, and she was reminded of Geoff's insight about Jack's endless grace. 'You're forgiven,' he said. 'Talk soon.' He clicked off before she could say more, his mellow voice with that slightly gritty hitch in it still echoing. Typical Jack. She couldn't tell from that easy charm over the phone whether his forgiveness ran deep or whether the damage was permanent.

There was a knock at the door again and this time it was an older officer. 'I'm Phil Brown, the reception officer. Jim Helm said you wished to see me, ma'am?'

She pushed through the warmest of smiles, needing this fellow to cooperate and not feel cornered. 'Oh, thanks – I know you're very busy.' She stood. 'DI Kate Carter . . . Kate,' she offered as well as a handshake.

His brow wrinkled. 'Jim said something about the Peggy Markham case.'

'Yes.' Kate sighed and explained again about dotting i's and crossing t's, keeping it light, making it sound tedious again. 'Do you mind if I get your take on that evening? I can see from the file that you were on reception that night.'

'Not on the night of her death, I wasn't,' he said. 'The only reason my name is in that file is because a local fellow, a rough sleeper called Bernie Beaton, staggered in one night on my shift and claimed to have witnessed her death a couple of days previously.'

She nodded encouragingly. 'His statement claims she was murdered.'

He shook his head, looking weary. 'Yeah, that's Bernie. He was well known to us at Hornsey as a schizo and a druggie; barely knew what day it was.'

'Ah,' she said, understanding the police attitude now. 'So he could have been lying, is that what you mean?'

'Not lying. Bernie's a nice enough fellow. Harmless. But he has episodes, you know? There are times when he's been delusional, believes wholly in whatever Bernie's World is showing him.'

She frowned and nodded. 'So where is Mr Beaton now?'

Phil shrugged. 'As far as I know he's found some proper accommodation, but not around here. Er, hang on,' he said, stopping another officer who was passing. 'Hey, Bill, whatever happened to Bernie Beaton?'

'Didn't we hear he'd left London, gone south?'

Phil looked back at Kate. 'I'm sure we can find out more if . . .'

'No, that's okay, thank you. You've all been helpful.'

'You can dot your i's and cross your t's now,' he offered.

'Hope so.' She stood. 'Thanks again for letting me look through this file.'

'You're welcome. Pleased to assist.'

They shook hands, Phil with finality, and Kate, unbeknown to him, with a handshake that said *I'm just getting started.*

18

Jack clicked off from Kate. He wasn't angry with her so much as disappointed . . . in both of them. She'd let him down by revealing that she hadn't managed to stare down the monster who seemed to lurk in the corner each time they were together. After their dinner, he'd felt elated that maybe she had moved past whatever quirk lived within to keep some tiny light on in her heart for him. He had told her previously that they were colleagues and they were friends and he wanted it no other way, but he despised that being friendly with Kate only seemed to make it worse for her. She was a fine officer, destined for greater things within the Met, but no matter what he did it appeared he compromised her. He couldn't have Kate feeling awkward around him.

He put his phone away distractedly as Mal nudged him. 'Here come two of the clerks of the court. They're the ones available right now.'

Jack nodded. As they arrived, he smiled and introduced the team to the clerks. 'Detective Superintendent Hawksworth,

Detective Inspector Khan, Detective Sergeant Jones and Constable Johnson. We're sorry to interrupt your day.'

The two clerks made pleasant sighing noises that this was not a problem.

'I welcome the change,' the thin middle-aged woman called Shirley Attlee said, smiling.

Her colleague, Brian Jarvis, agreed. He was probably around the same age in his early fifties, with a genial smile that touched his eyes. 'If you had to sit through the session that I did this morning, chatting with you gentlemen and ladies is a pleasure,' he said. 'Shirley, why don't we go to the canteen?'

'Ooh, yes. In fact' — she checked her watch — 'let's have an early lunch, shall we? Do you mind, Superintendent Hawksworth, if we eat? We've both got long afternoons ahead.'

'Not at all,' he replied.

'I can assure you they do a marvellous bacon sandwich here.' Jack watched Brian look instantly horrified. 'Oh, my apologies, DI Khan. I hope I haven't offended you?'

Mal laughed. 'No, Mr Jarvis, I'm a lapsed everything. You have no need to fret on my behalf.'

Brian placed a hand over his heart with relief and won a look of admonishment from Shirley. 'Thank you. Here, it's this way . . .'

Jack brought up the rear, his thoughts still teasing at his waspish conversation with Kate; he hadn't fully finalised his thoughts but his disappointment in himself still niggled. While Kate had no business saying what she had, she'd obviously hit on something to make him lose his cool. And he rarely lost his cool. The private truth was that there was something about Lauren that had got beneath his defences. He wanted to help her escape *My Day*; hated that someone clearly fun, talented and intelligent had fallen for someone who had treated her hideously. He imagined she'd been on a sharp trajectory in her career, and to see her moving around in the gutter, having to trick her way through rebuilding it, was not right – not if a word in the right ear could help her. So, yes, Kate might not have read his intentions correctly, but she'd hit her mark that Jack was still playing Sir Lancelot to damsels in distress.

Sarah cleared her throat.

He blinked back to the present. 'Sorry?'

Shirley smiled. 'I was wondering if our conversation might be confidential, in which case, I would suggest we sit in that far corner beneath the windows.'

Jack nodded. 'I agree. We probably should take precautions.'

Jack had expected a swanky café for all these lawyers, but a canteen was truly the only way to describe it, he realised as he regarded the chequered lino floor with a curious wine red and faded black that now just looked blue-ish. This was teamed with strange charcoal and canary-yellow table arrangements of hard plastic and melamine with narrow timber tops. The weirdly high ceilings perhaps spoke of its original use as a Masonic Institute for schooling the young of Freemasons, especially with the heavy timber beams and the odd circular window at the apex that looked like a ship's wheel. Adding to the confusion were cherub pink and white paper Chinese lanterns hanging six feet from the ceiling.

'Over here?' Shirley offered, oblivious to his offence.

'That would be fine,' he agreed. At least at one end of the room was a traditional canteen where chips and toasties, pots of steaming tea and terrible coffee were being made. Plenty of men and women from the legal fraternity, wigs off and at their sides, stared at phones or at laptops, unmoved by the room's clashing horror, plus he noted all the men were eating bacon sandwiches. 'And please, let Scotland Yard buy your lunch for giving us your time.'

Brian and Shirley looked at each other, surprised. 'Are you sure?' Brian asked. 'Shirley here can eat a lot.'

She poked him. 'Oh, you rogue! But Brian's right; you don't have to. We're both very pleased to help, as any of the clerks here would be.'

'It's my pleasure. Make yourselves comfy.' He withdrew a credit card and handed it to the constable. Sandwiches and tea were chosen from the sparse menu and PC Johnson left to place the order.

'Before I forget,' Brian said, 'I believe the clerks of the court for numbers six and eleven will be available in about twenty minutes,' he offered, glancing at his watch.

Jack nodded. 'Mal, take Ali and perhaps go and meet . . .' He looked at his list. 'Hugh Pettigrew shortly and . . .'

'John Fraser,' Shirley answered for him.

Mal nodded and joined his constable at the counter, leaving the two clerks to return their attention to Jack and Sarah. Jack took their measure. They were like a sweet couple of opposites who had attracted. Shirley Attlee was rake thin, with glasses she could take on and off easily because they hung from a gold chain around her neck. She wore neatly applied mascara, eyeliner and rouge brushed lightly and high on her cheeks, with a rich red lipstick that younger women might think twice about applying.

Her colleague was like a dormouse in comparison. He wore dun brown trousers and varying shades of beige to go with them. He was of average height, with a long body but short legs, and his garments seemed too big for him, as though he'd been much plumper at some stage and hadn't updated his wardrobe. Smiling eyes looked back at Jack through owlish glasses that hooked behind equally large ears, where tufts of gingery hair needed a trim. Jack could see daylight through what was left of his once full head of hair. He wasn't fooled by his mild appearance though; he knew only too well the power of these people once they were robed and managing their courtroom responsibilities.

'Let me explain what this is all about,' Jack began, realising they were used to being patient and listening. He told them everything he could — which wasn't much — and watched their eyes grow bigger, their expressions more concerned and then their frowns deepen to straight-out shock when he finished with: 'and we've narrowed down all the original crimes as being tried in North London Crown Court.'

'Good grief,' Brian exclaimed, glancing at Shirley, whose hand was now placed across her chest in surprise.

'I understand this is a shock.'

They both looked back at him, confused. It was Brian who led. 'So you are talking to all of the clerks with a view to finding out . . . what? How can we help?'

'Not just the clerks of the court, Mr Jarvis, but all the administrative people too. We've begun with the clerks because we respect your knowledge of your courts.'

'Judges?' Shirley asked, glancing again at Brian as though they were tiptoeing into hallowed territory. 'That could be tricky.'

'Leland's the one to consider talking to first, perhaps?' Brian mused.

'Why do you say that?' Jack asked.

'Brian's right,' Shirley said. 'Judge Leland is notoriously lenient. All very precise and within the letter of the law, mind.'

'Just errs on the side of less rather than more,' Brian explained.

The first of the bacon sandwiches arrived and the smell distracted everyone.

'DS Jones, I hope you don't mind me mentioning this,' Jarvis said, as he offered her the tomato ketchup, 'but you remind me a lot of my daughter.' He smiled.

'Do I?'

He nodded. 'Uncannily so.'

'What does your daughter do?'

'Well, she used to be a psychologist but she gave that up to be a full-time mother. A very good one, I might add.'

'How many grandchildren?' Sarah asked.

'She gave me two beauties.' He grinned, and Jack noted the softly indulgent smile that Shirley passed his way. It briefly flickered in his mind that these two might be an item but that was of no concern to him.

All munching happily, Jack led them back to the matter at hand. 'In terms of the public gallery, are there any regulars?'

'Yes,' they both replied at the same time, laughing in a way that only close friends did. Jarvis dabbed at his lips politely with a paper serviette. 'Mmm, we do. All the courts would have regulars.'

'Really?' Jack frowned.

'It varies, of course,' Shirley explained. 'Some cases are more interesting than others and can attract media, some have more family members who attend each sitting . . .' She shrugged.

'And then there are those for whom the courtroom itself becomes a favourite, but I can't tell you why. That's the quirk of why they are the regulars,' Jarvis remarked.

'Can you give us an example, Mr Jarvis?' Sarah asked.

'Well, there's a fellow called Horace Pickering . . . Horrie, we know him as. He's about – oh, what would you say, Shirley?'

She shook her head. 'About seventy, wouldn't you think?'

'At least. Horrie's been coming to my courtroom – that's number seven – and number twelve for at least the last decade. Don't ask me why just those two courts.'

'So it's not about the cases themselves?'

'Well, yes, he's very interested in them, but it wouldn't matter to Horrie whether we were on trial for a murder or for embezzling funds. He's interested in every case, but he's mostly interested in sitting at the far end of the public gallery and woe betide anyone who gets to his seat before him.'

'What happens if someone does?' Sarah wondered, intrigued.

'Well, the first time it occurred, there was shouting. The second time, about a year later, an actual scuffle broke out. Horrie's older, wiser now, since we told him if he creates a problem for a third time he'll be barred from both courtrooms.'

'How would you describe Horrie's disposition?' Jack asked, although he didn't think this fellow of seventy was their man.

'I would say he is obsessive. He makes endless notes about cases he has no link to or knowledge about, and he has plenty of conspiracy theories he likes to share. I've never seen him order anything in the café but a cheese and ham toastie plus Horlicks . . . always the same, no matter the season. And he reads the same book while he eats – the same book, cover to cover, and has done for years.' Jarvis shrugged with a look of sympathy. 'I think he's single . . . Do I think he's dangerous, though – I presume that's where our conversation is headed?'

Jack nodded.

'No, he created the scuffle by trying to take the fellow's place when he stood up to stretch during a break in proceedings. There were no punches flung around. I wouldn't ever think of Horrie as violent, just intense and locked into his mind, his needs, his rituals.'

'And what about you, Shirley?'

'Oh, plenty of regulars but they're all locals, seniors, coming in from the cold, nothing much better to do and a chance to catch up in the canteen.'

'Anyone can come in here?' Sarah wondered.

'Yes, it's open to the public,' Brian said.

'Any other regulars, Mr Jarvis, who might seem a little "off" to you?'

'Off?' he repeated, as if considering what that implied. 'Well, I suppose there was one chappie who was coming regularly but I haven't seen him for . . . ooh, now, it has to be six, maybe seven months. Much younger, not the sort coming in from the cold; he did pay attention and he was one of those people who never missed sentencing, I remember that.'

Jack and Sarah sat forward. 'Would you know his name, Mr Jarvis?'

He shook his head. 'No,' he gusted, as though it were a silly question. 'I have no contact with the public as such. I'm sure you've attended court and understand that the public gallery is like being at the theatre. The players are on the stage and seemingly oblivious to the audience.' He made the sign of inverted commas in the air. 'We try not to break the fourth wall.'

'But you notice them, Mr Jarvis?' Sarah asked.

'I do. I'm sure Shirley and every other clerk of the court subconsciously makes a mental note of who is in the gallery.'

Shirley nodded. 'Yes, I'm aware who is in, of course, but I pay them no heed when the court is in session, just as Brian says. We simply can't risk involving the public.'

Brian reinforced this. '*Seemingly oblivious* was my phrase. We give the impression that we are entirely remote from the gallery but of course we do take a quick measure of who is in the court. And people like Horrie and this other fellow I mentioned who are regulars become like furniture. You see them and the eye glides past, but the brain makes a mental note somewhere. Put it this way: we'd notice if they weren't there. You recall that big bearded fellow, don't you, Shirley?'

She grinned. 'The one we nicknamed Mr Bear?'

'That's the one,' Brian said, smiling back at the police team. 'He was a big man.'

'Big as in broad,' Shirley added. 'Not especially tall, as I recall.'

'Big as in overweight?' Sarah pressed.

They both shook their heads. 'Brawny,' Brian explained. 'I don't think I ever saw him smile. He was quite an intimidating presence in my court, but he didn't really bother anyone. He was mostly silent.'

'No name?' Sarah asked.

'No, I'm afraid not.'

'Well, thank you both for your thoughts, and I agree, that bacon sandwich deserves pride of place,' Jack said, smiling at them both. 'Mr Jarvis, perhaps you won't mind if Sarah takes a description from you of this bear fellow you mentioned.'

'Do you mean now?'

'At a time that suits you,' Sarah assured him.

'Righto!' Jarvis smiled.

Jack stood and shook hands with the clerks. 'Sarah will leave her card, and here's mine. Please feel free to call either of us with anything that might strike you later. Sometimes it's the smallest, most inconsequential fact that can open a door.'

'I've witnessed countless cases where even a casual remark has led to someone's downfall or indeed proof of innocence,' Shirley agreed.

'Quite right.' Jarvis nodded, then glanced at his watch. 'Well, it's been a pleasure, thank you. DS Jones, if you would like to follow me, we can set up a time now.'

Sarah nodded at Jack. 'See you back at the office, sir.'

At the Yard, Jack and Kate were chewing over progress. Their earlier spat had been relegated to unimportant, given the gravity of Kate's finding.

'Well, we have to find this Bernard Beaton,' Jack said. 'He's now a priority.'

'I'm on it,' Kate said. 'I'm waiting for a phone call from the Whittington. There's a nurse from the drug dependency ward who seems to be in the know.'

'How could they overlook this?' he said, sounding frustrated.

She sighed. 'Easy. I don't think Hornsey's a lot different from most other stations. It wasn't an oversight or even laziness, so much as a considered opinion. Mr Beaton's track record would certainly suggest he was delusional . . . and he still could be, Jack, let's not ignore that.'

His instincts screamed the opposite, that this might be a glimmer on the horizon for them. 'No. You said his statement mentioned a syringe that was left in the right side of her neck?'

Kate nodded.

'I don't believe that detail was mentioned in the media, do you?'

She frowned. 'Hmm, you're right.'

'No, Kate, this Beaton fellow was there. I reckon he's telling the truth.'

'Well, if he was there, then how he wasn't seen is going to be very interesting to learn. I visited the spot today and it's all open. He'd have to have been hiding in plain sight − the killer too intent on what he was doing to notice, which is hard to believe, right?'

Jack had no choice but to agree.

'So that's where I think those officers could be forgiven for perhaps not taking him seriously enough . . . although, to her credit, DC Farrow made good notes.'

'I want to talk with Bernard Beaton.'

Kate's mobile rang and she glanced at it. 'This could be her now,' she said, eyes lighting up. 'Kate Carter,' she answered and listened, finally nodding at Jack. 'Ah, DC Farrow, thank you for contacting me.' She stood and walked over to the window.

Joan buzzed him and Jack picked up his phone to answer.

'There's a Nurse Jenny Hampton on line one . . . from the Whittington.'

'Ah, great,' Jack said. 'Thanks.'

Kate's conversation with Farrow dimmed to the background when he heard the connection open. 'Is this Jenny?'

'Yes, oh hello, I thought I had to speak with Detective Inspector Kate Carter.'

'Apologies, DI Carter is just on the phone. This is Detective Superintendent Jack Hawksworth and we're grateful for you returning our call. Are you happy to speak with me?'

'Yes, of course. This is about Bernie, right?'

'Yes. We're trying to track him down.'

'About the lady he saw die, I'm guessing.'

Jack blinked. 'It's in connection with that case, yes. We would appreciate any help, but also your discretion . . .'

He heard her sigh. 'I've got no one to talk to about this anyway, but I liked Bernie a lot; he was always so very polite to us nurses, and one of those people you felt especially sorry for. Few believed his story, but I always did.'

'I gather you helped to get him a permanent home?'

'I helped him to apply and I put in a good word for him through my contacts. He's in Hastings now, as far as I know. I can't tell you if he fell off the wagon again, but he seemed pretty determined to make a go of it on the south coast.'

'And I don't suppose you have an address, do you?'

'Well, I don't, but I know who might. Do you have a pen handy?'

'Fire away,' Jack said, feeling a creep of excitement straighten his shoulders as he wrote down *Cassiobury Court*.

'He went to drug rehab there and I think their team helped him to find permanent housing in Hastings. I'm sorry that I don't know where,' Jenny was saying.

'No, that's okay. You've been very helpful, thank you.'

'Oh, you're welcome. Let's hope he's one who got away and beat the drug habit.'

'Bye, Jenny.' He rang off and looked up expectantly as Kate returned.

'Have we got him?' she asked.

'Nearly. I have to make a phone call.' She nodded and motioned that she'd be back shortly.

It took Jack ten minutes of being passed around to various people before he finally got through to someone who was prepared to look up Beaton.

'Okay, Detective Superintendent, it looks as though Mr Beaton found sheltered housing at St Leonard's-on-Sea near Hastings at a place called Beaufort House; it's run by a group called Orbit South. That's the best I can do this evening.'

'That's great, thanks so much.' He put the receiver down and, as Kate arrived, he said, 'I think we have him.' Kate formed a fist of triumph. 'Now, let me ask Joan to hunt down the flat he's in.'

He stepped out and set Joan the task, returning to his desk. 'We have to hope Beaton is still at the same place. Fancy a trip down to Hastings with me?'

'Oh gosh, Jack, you show a girl the very best time.' She grinned and he returned it; this felt more like the Kate he enjoyed having around him.

He buzzed through to Joan to organise train tickets and listened to what she had to say before looking back at Kate. 'Joan reckons the train all the way and a taxi at the other end. Meet you at six-thirty at Charing Cross?'

She groaned. 'That's hideously early.'

'It will take us a couple of hours direct, and I don't want to miss him if he's there.'

'Why don't we ring ahead? I'm sure we can track him down. And it might save us the hassle if he's no longer there.'

'I don't want to spook him. Bernie sounds fragile, and if he's used to the police treating him with disdain, he may just want to give us the flick by not being available, or worse – taking off. Right now, he's our single bright light, isn't he?'

'Okay, right. Tomorrow at nasty six-thirty, it is . . . I'll be at the Marks & Spencer buying goodies for the journey.'

He frowned at her in question.

'Never fully grown out of the childhood palaver of a day trip,' she said self-deprecatingly. 'Moving on, I just spoke with DC Lisa Farrow and she remembers that interview very well, which is fortunate. According to her, Beaton was sleeping rough, smelled awful, but had excellent manners. He was treated with condescension by her fellow officers and they specifically asked her to do the interview because it amused them to see if she could stand the smell of him in the interview room long enough to take a statement.' Jack gave a look of embarrassment as Kate continued. 'Anyway, she thumbed her nose at them by offering to make Bernie a cuppa, which he graciously accepted, and then he told her his story, which she dutifully copied down.'

'I sense there's a *but* coming.' He sighed.

'There is. As we learned, Beaton chose to come into Hornsey in the evening. Right in the middle of his statement, before she could ask any questions, they were interrupted by Detective Sergeant Coombs, who was the night duty CID on shift with her. According to Farrow, there had been a rape and they were being sent to take statements; he gave her the hurry-on. She saw Beaton on his way and only then learned that the rape victim had been taken to hospital and the presumed urgency had been a ruse to wrap up the interview.'

'Saving her from Beaton, you mean?' Jack asked, his tone tight.

'Yes, I believe that's exactly what she meant. She wasn't happy about it but by then it was too late. In their defence, they did leave soon after for the hospital. Before she did, however, she checked with the reception officer . . . the one I met called Phil

Brown, and he assured her he would file her notes, which he did . . . but they were never transcribed and thus overlooked, never taken into account – or indeed taken seriously – when the case was being investigated.'

'Buggery bollocks!'

'I heard that,' Joan said from the other room.

Kate grinned. 'Better dig out your fifty pence; you know how wrathful Joan can be.'

'I heard that too, Kate,' Joan said, arriving at the doorway. 'Fifty pence, Jack . . . pop it in before you leave. Right, here's the address for Mr Beaton, who is still at that property.'

Both Jack and Kate gave sounds of relief.

'Well, my lovelies, I'm off, unless there's anything else you need?' They both shook their heads. 'Don't be late for that direct train; you'll regret it because you'll take all day to get there otherwise on the pretty route,' she said, looking at them over the top of her half glasses. 'Show your warrant cards on the train and you'll be fine.'

'Okay, thanks, Joan.'

'Enjoy the seaside, you two.' She lifted a hand in farewell and left them.

'I didn't ask how it went at the courts today,' Kate said.

'Nothing much came out of it immediately, although one of the clerks said he could cite a couple of regulars who might be worth looking into. Sarah's gathering that info. I'm yet to hear how Mal got on and—'

Sarah interrupted them by bustling in.

'Hi . . . any news?' Jack asked,

She leaned in his office doorway, which was fast becoming a favourite spot for all. 'Yes, actually. Mr Jarvis is good value. He suggested that we ask the court security to supply CCTV footage of all the regulars from the public gallery that any of the clerks consider "off", as you put it, sir, and then they can point out the various people.'

'Excellent. When can we begin?'

'I spoke to the security team and we need to narrow it down a bit. I thought we'd bring Mr Jarvis into one of our meeting rooms here tomorrow – he's happy to come in after work. Meanwhile, Mal and Ali are doing the same with the clerks they've interviewed. Okay, sir?'

'Excellent. Kate and I are heading down to Hastings tomorrow to see Bernard Beaton. Kate found out today that his witness statement has credence.'

'Ahh, for Peggy Markham? Let's hope his memory holds, then. Mal said they'd head off directly from the courts, unless you need them?'

He shook his head. 'Tell the others to go, Sarah. I'd rather they got in early and fresh.'

'Will do.'

'And why haven't you gone home too?'

Sarah pulled a frown. 'Something's nagging me. I'm not sure what it is, and I think better at my desk.'

Jack knew exactly what Kate was thinking when she cut him a sly look. Better at your desk *with your anorak on* was what came to mind, as though she were planting thoughts for him. He dismissed it with a soft glare only she could catch. 'Okay, then. I'll leave you to that pondering and hope it yields something. I'm off. Kate, no need to hang around.'

'Well, not with your hideously early start. Bring coffee, Jack, or I'm not going to be very pleasant.'

19

Jack should have gone home. But he was giving the taxi driver instructions to take him to an address in Bayswater, not far from Paddington Station, before he'd really thought it through. He glanced at the scrap of paper in his hand as he looked up at the terraced houses. Nothing too shabby about this address, he thought, frowning. Had she been lying?

He dialled a number.

'Hello?'

'Lauren, it's Jack.' There was a pause. He had used her personal number so maybe she was trying to work out who it was. 'Jack Hawksworth.'

'Oh, hello,' she said, sounding shocked. 'It's nice to hear from you. I was just having a glass of wine on my rooftop.'

'Sounds glamorous.'

'It's not.' She laughed. 'I only say it to impress people but it's our first lovely evening for spring – I didn't want to waste it and it will help my mood.'

'Not good?'

He heard a sigh. 'I think I hate my life, Jack.'

'Well, let me brighten it for you with some news. You're on your rooftop, you say?'

'Yes, why?'

'Do you face Gloucester Terrace?'

'I do,' she said, sounding intrigued.

'Then look down.' He heard rustling and movement, and kept his gaze focused on the top of her building until he saw her head poke over the railing. He lifted a hand in greeting and heard her laugh. 'You're here.'

'Indeed,' he said.

There was now a pause as they both weighed up what that might mean. Jack decided he would ask her to come down if she asked him why he was standing in her street; they would talk at her building's doorway and then he would be gone as swiftly as he'd arrived. He waited.

'Fancy a wine on my rooftop?' she finally said.

He knew she was watching him from her vantage point, and he looked at his watch. 'Quick one, sure.'

'Great. I'll buzz you in. It's the very top flat, as you can guess. Be warned, there's lots of stairs.'

As she disappeared, he moved to the main door and waited. The tinny buzzer sounded, cueing him to push on the shiny black door to enter the vestibule of chessboard-tiled floor and parchment-painted walls. There was no lift so he had no choice but to heed her warning. Fortunately, the stairs were broad and shallow, and he wound his way up four floors until, greeted by insufferable laughter, he arrived on her landing.

She still had hold of her wineglass. 'That was actually rather fast, Detective Superintendent. I think you're in very good shape.'

He grinned; he was not out of breath but could feel the exertion. Little wonder she kept trim.

'Come in.' She gestured to her door and let him go first.

He arrived in a studio flat with tall stairs that led to a narrow mezzanine, which he presumed acted as her bedroom. It was a tidy space; lots of books and a pair of shuttered floor-to-ceiling windows added to its charm. 'Very French,' he said. 'A pied-à-terre.'

She nodded. 'This was my one tiny stroke of luck in recent memory. My cousin was posted overseas and he's letting me rent this from him cheaply. He knows I'm obsessively neat and reliable.' She pointed towards the second room. 'Here, take a look. Small galley kitchen, tiny bathroom . . . but so nicely done that I have to count this single blessing in my life, because I do enjoy coming home to my space.'

'It's lovely,' Jack agreed, walking around as she fetched a second glass and filled it to just over one-third. 'Does the mezzanine lead to the roof?'

'No, the rooftop garden − and I use the word "garden" with care − is communal, but I don't think anyone else uses it.'

'Too many stairs?' He grinned.

'Exactly,' she agreed, 'so I win.'

'Those are quite steep to the mezzanine,' he said, taking the offered glass of wine.

'Yes, I have to be very careful if I have one too many.' She smiled, bringing her gaze away from her bedroom to him. 'That's not very often though. I'm no big drinker.'

'Well, that doesn't fit the journo stereotype.'

'No, not much of me does. Anyway, cheers.' They clinked glasses over a smile. 'Come on, I promised you a rooftop.'

He followed her onto her landing, then out onto the roof.

'And here we are.'

He looked out across Paddington Station's roof line and beyond. Darkness was still to claim the night and it definitely felt like winter had handed over to spring. They weren't exposed here, and Lauren was right, it was mild enough to enjoy the evening as the moon brightened.

'How was your day, Jack?'

'Well, I enraged my boss by telling him about you.'

Her eyes widened and her expression turned wicked.

'Then, even though it seemed impossible, I incensed him even further by telling him something else I'd done that had broken the rules.'

'Such a rebel.'

He liked that she didn't ask further. He sipped. 'This is lovely . . . a riesling?'

She nodded. 'I can only afford one bottle a week because I only want to drink quality wine. That's my rule. Drink less, drink best. This is from Australia, the south. From a small place called the Clare Valley . . . you may not—'

'I've drunk many a good Aussie riesling, and that's the region that produces the finest . . . especially Taylor's.' He shrugged at her surprise. 'My sister lives in Australia.'

'You've been?'

He nodded. 'And to this winery.'

'Get out!' Lauren looked wildly impressed as they sipped again. 'So, Jack, why the visit? Don't get me wrong, I'm flattered, truly. But there must be a reason – I doubt it's my irresistible personality that's dragged you across London tonight.'

He swirled the wine in his glass. 'I have a proposal.' He levelled his gaze to meet hers.

'Yes, I will marry you,' she said, injecting great amusement into her tone, but it missed the mark; he could sense she was slightly edgy. Perhaps it had been a mistake to deliver his message personally. 'Sorry,' she said, realising the jest wasn't quite as hilarious as it might have sounded in her mind. 'I'm a bit nervous,' she admitted.

'Why?'

'A senior Scotland Yard detective in my home? And potentially a shot at the story I've been cradling for so long?'

His eyes crinkled as he smiled slightly. 'No, that's not it. I don't know you well, Lauren, but I'm guessing a detective in your house who might be opening up a door on that story you want is just the sort of thing that lights you up – it would make you more keen. My instincts say it wouldn't make you twitchy.' He paused but knew it was time to leave. 'Anyway, that's none of my bus—'

'It's you,' she cut across.

'Me?'

She smiled sadly. 'Oh, come on, Jack. Don't be obtuse.'

He looked back at her slightly vacantly. 'I don't mean to make you feel awkward.'

'But still I do. Let's be honest, you are not what most would expect from a police detective.'

'Oh? How should I look?'

'Crumpled, crusty, shiny suit, overweight, unintentional beard stubble . . . egg on your tie, prefer beer to wine . . . bad jokes, bad breath.'

'You watch too much television.' He grinned.

'I hardly watch any. But in all truth, I'd rather you looked more like one of those old fellas on *New Tricks* than . . . well, than you.'

'Sorry,' he said, as if to say, *this is what you're stuck with.*

They both grinned into an awkward silence.

'Don't be. My mother has always said I lack a filter sometimes. I'm probably making *you* feel uncomfortable. Sorry. Tell me your proposition.'

He explained his plan, relieved to be moving on.

'An exclusive?' she said, her tone suggesting she hardly dared believe it.

He nodded.

'My editor will black out at—'

'Wait, you haven't heard it all,' he warned, setting his glass down on the rickety table nearby. 'We'd control the information and its flow.'

'But no one else gets it,' she qualified.

'Only you, and direct from our press office. I will introduce you to our bureau head.'

'Jack, I—'

'There's more.'

She put her glass down by his, her brow knitting. 'I'm guessing this is where you make it really difficult for me.'

'Lauren, I want to try and make sure this emerges in the right way with the right media. It's a highly sensitive situation that undoubtedly polarises people and, handled the wrong way, it could create a circus. I want to avoid that. *My Day* is the circus ringmaster and certainly not the right outlet . . . but you know that.'

She shrugged with grudging acceptance. 'How, then?'

'We're going to talk to the right people to elevate you into one of the other publications in your group, and you would prepare this as an exclusive investigative feature for their weekend magazine, something like that.' He stopped talking then because she was staring at him with obvious shock, her lips slightly parted as though she wanted to speak but couldn't.

Finally she found her voice. 'You're serious, aren't you?'

'Deadly,' he confirmed. 'It's not my intention to tell you how to live your life, but there is absolutely no way you're getting this story if you don't agree to leave *My Day* and allow me to help you reshuffle your working life a bit.'

'Is this normal?'

He shook his head. 'The opposite. That's why my boss took blood pressure pills in front of me today.'

'Your idea?'

He gave a crooked smile with a shrug.

She watched him for longer than felt comfortable before she spoke again. 'I think you're killing two birds with one stone.'

He looked at her, immediately defensive. 'Look, Lauren, I don't want to—'

'No, don't get me wrong. I know by helping me in this way you'll fix the situation of having *My Day* report what I've stumbled onto, but I don't believe you'd bother with me if I hadn't told you my life's story. I feel a bit guilty now . . . I've put you in a difficult situation.'

'Journos don't normally care about that.'

'Yes, but you *do* care, which is a surprise.'

'I just think you deserve better. You might be able to fast-track back to where you want to be – should be. I know you'll impress them; they're not going to send you back to *My Day* after this. If opening a few doors helps your career, then I'm all for it, especially if you cooperate with us on this very tricky operation.'

'So it is an operation,' she qualified.

He nodded. 'We can't risk blowing the very little we have on our side if you go off reporting what you have.'

'A vigilante serial killer?'

He hesitated only for a heartbeat. 'Serial murderer, yes; I am reserving judgement on the vigilante bit.'

'Bloody fucking hell. I knew it!'

'That would cost you a pound coin in our office.'

She laughed. 'No swearing?'

'Not in front of our receptionist, no.'

'How much does she collect?'

'Enough to take us all out at the end of it,' he said, grinning. He stood; knew he should go. He'd achieved what he'd set out to do and felt certain that with a night to sleep on it, Lauren would see the sense of what he was proposing. 'I must go, Lauren. Thanks for sharing your quota of very good wine.'

She stood, reaching to squeeze his arm. 'I'll do it,' she said. 'I'm grateful, even if I don't sound it.'

'Really?'

'Yes. I'm convinced that most people find you hard to say no to.'

'My boss says no to me all the time.'

'And still you defy him.'

'He shouldn't promote me to this position if he doesn't want me taking matters into my hands.'

'Am I a matter in your hands, Jack?'

She was standing too close now. *Damn!* Kate was right. How did women instinctively know these things? How could she know before he did?

'I don't think . . .' he began, but it was already too late. They were both helplessly leaning in, him bending as though an invisible hand was pressing on his shoulders. Before he could stop himself, their lips had gently met. The kiss never deepened but it didn't end quickly either. They released each other with care and in concert, neither wishing to break the spell for the other.

Lauren let out a small sigh. 'It's been a long time since I've felt affection, or even wanted it, from a man.'

They were still close enough to kiss again.

'Me too.'

'From a man?' she asked, making him smile.

'I didn't mean for this to happen.'

'I'm afraid to say I did . . . from the moment I saw you standing in the street.'

'Your mother is right about the filter.'

She gurgled a laugh. 'I blame you!'

He grinned, searching out another slow, gentle kiss during which they could taste the elegantly citrussy scents on each other's breath from the glorious riesling.

'Will you stay?' she asked, sounding hesitant.

'That's a very enticing offer but I have a very early start, driving down to the coast.'

'Which coast?'

He smiled. 'Not yet. But you will hear it all, I promise, when the time is right. In the meantime, I want you to give Mike a call.' He pulled out a card and gave it to her. 'He'll start the ball rolling, and you need not fear your editor at *My Day*. She'll be fine.'

'I think she will be; she's baffled as to why I'm there anyway, and she's a corporate animal – she'll want what's best for the group.'

'Well, this move of yours is definitely best for everyone.'

'Thank you,' she said, and conveyed it with enough emotion that he felt the unexpected kiss, while wholly unprofessional, was important to both of them. It gave them both a sense of trust. Besides, he thought as he disentangled himself from Lauren, only now realising his arms were entwined with hers behind his back, they were simply two people in search of affection.

'You're welcome. I'd rather have you on my side.'

'Oh, would you . . .? How about on top?'

He shook a finger at her.

She smiled. 'When can we meet again?'

'Later this week?'

Lauren's face showed delight, and he sensed she'd imagined he might have been blowing her off with the early morning excuse. He could forgive her that, given she'd been hurt so badly in the past. He needed to show his sincerity. 'Can I text you?'

'Sure, sounds good. I'll call Mike as you ask.'

'He's expecting you, so don't feel bashful.'

Lauren nodded. 'Well, off you go. I'll sit here and finish my wine on my own.'

He grinned. 'I promise more wine and not from your puny stocks.' He leaned in and gave her a brief, soft peck. 'See you soon.' He moved for the door.

'Jack?'

He turned back.

'Thank you for giving me back my faith in men.'

Oh, Jack, he thought as he walked towards Paddington Station, where he was sure it would be easier to find a taxi or, at worst, jump onto the Tube. *Is your heart ready?*

It wasn't yet seven. But he had a long night of reading ahead.

In the small lounge of his Enfield terrace home, the man who was dying slowly took stock of his situation. Davey Robbins had been found, as intended, but the investigators were moving quicker than he'd imagined. He'd anticipated a little more confusion; perhaps they'd discovered more corpses of criminals from a couple of years back? He kept no physical record of his murders, no trophies, nothing connected with his killing spree that could be traced back to him. He knew too much about the policing system to make such elementary errors.

Although he fully expected to be caught – he was not troubled by this – he had no intention of going on trial or seeing out his limited days from a prison cell. Hopefully the disease would catch him first so he could die in his home, a free man and at peace that he'd rid the world of those who preyed on the vulnerable with no regard for the damage they did. Davey Robbins should have done more time. He should have suffered similar fears to those poor Amy had . . . Davey needed to pay a debt to her and to society.

He had meant to write to her – would do so now. He moved
to the drawer beneath the bookcase in his sitting room and found
some plain white A4 paper and a common-style biro with blue
ink. At school he'd been forced to write with his right hand even
though he'd naturally been a left-hander. He still could write left-
handed – not well, but well enough to be legible. If the police
ever viewed this letter, he would waste more of their time trying
to match the words, the slant of his handwriting, its loops and
quirks, the postcode he'd send it from. It would be wholly different to his own.

He began.

Hello Amy

*You don't know me, although I do know you and the terrible
experience you and your family has suffered through. I personally
feel nothing but horror and deep sympathy. The sentences regularly
handed down to perpetrators of similar crimes are insufferably lenient.*

*You may have read in the newspaper, or heard on the news, that
Davey Robbins was found dead recently. That's a polite way of
putting that Davey was killed . . . murdered, in fact. I didn't feel an
ounce of pleasure in ending his life, only relief on your behalf.*

*Let the nightmares go, Amy. Both of the men who changed the
course of your life are now gone. And your dear grandmother's death
and the terrible sin against you have been paid for in blood, which
is only right. Victims' families left behind after manslaughter or
murder, or any sort of violence against those they love, never feel the
sentence suits the crime, and the truth is it rarely does. Judges are
confined by the letter of the law, which is why I have stepped in to
see you enjoy true justice.*

*Please don't show this letter to anyone, but if you have to, don't
feel guilty. I have no fear of being caught before my own life catches
up with me.*

More importantly, Amy, begin to live a life that your grandmother would want for you and one that will bring laughter and happiness again. You deserve it. You were on a wonderful path. Find it again . . . go to university and fulfil those dreams you had.

Sincerely, a friend.

He would post that tomorrow and do some digging into Detective Superintendent Jack Hawksworth, who he'd now discovered was spearheading the investigation into the two most recent murders. Links would be made, of that he had little doubt, but he was not frightened by how much the police learned or how they connected the dots . . . it was about time. How long he could hang on to his health and how many more of these cruel bastards he could rid Britain of because the justice system couldn't.

To that end, tonight was going to be dedicated to the final stages of planning the death of another one of the bastard tribe – a Geoffrey Paxton, who he'd just learned was about to be released from prison far too early. He smiled to himself; Paxton was presently living in quiet ignorance that his debt to society was going to be paid in full in a few days.

20

In the carriage Kate yawned. 'I bought us a toastie each.'

Jack shrugged, as if to say *what are you waiting for?* 'Get them out, then. Our coffee's getting cold.'

'Good. I wasn't sure if you even took breakfast.'

'Always.'

'Really? What's your poison, then?'

'I like an egg in the morning.'

She laughed, enjoying the notion of spending the day together, even though it was all work and no play. 'How proper. How on earth do you find time?'

'I make time. I've always been an early riser. Love a boiled egg and soldiers. Who doesn't?'

They'd make a horrible couple, then. 'You disgust me with your civility,' she said, yawning again and poking around in her backpack. 'Well, this isn't exactly healthy, but it's healthier than stopping at a greasy spoon in Hastings. At least this way you get wholegrain bread.'

'A toastie with healthy bread?' He sounded appalled.

'Followed by . . . ta-da!' She pushed back a buttery paper bag from which the unmistakable belly-grinding temptation of melted cheese wafted towards him, but in her hands was a bag of Revels. 'Dessert.'

He smiled. 'Dessert for breakfast. That's not proper. I don't like the orange ones, let me say.'

'Neither do I, so I'll fight you for the peanuts and toffees. The orange ones are just plain nasty, aren't they?' she said conversationally, but she could tell Jack's mind was already reaching away from the banter towards the business at hand.

'Yes, they make about as much sense as we're making of this case,' he said, suddenly gloomy.

'Jack, give us a chance. I think we're making some headway.'

'Do you? I've got nothing to give the chief.'

She knew she shouldn't but even so, she took this as personal criticism. She worked hard, didn't deserve this. 'What about your friend the journo?'

'Nothing to give her but a smile right now.'

'I looked her up. I reckon she'd settle for your smile.'

'You know nothing about her.'

'How much do you know?'

He shrugged. 'That I trust her to be solid.'

'And you base this on what?'

He stared back at her. 'Don't start.'

She gave a look of bafflement. 'What? I'm a detective – I'm naturally suspicious.'

'I'll handle Lauren. You don't have to turn your attention her way.'

He sounded defensive and, having looked Lauren Starling up, Kate could see that the journalist had everything going for her. They needed to get off this topic.

'Jack, I want you to know I hate going backwards,' she remarked.

It brought the twitch of a smile she desperately needed from him. 'I'll swap,' he offered.

'Chivalrous, thank you.'

'Least I can do in repayment for this toastie.'

'Eat up,' she encouraged him, but privately she sighed and inwardly she knew something had happened between this Starling woman and Jack. He was too protective . . . but then Jack always was towards women; it was his Achilles heel.

'I am not going to view some Norman ruin, by the way; we're not squeezing in a quick side trip for a history lecture,' Kate warned as they clambered into the taxi and gave the driver the address in St Leonard's.

Jack gave her a look of soft despair. 'Not interested in the Battle of 1066? Or the home of William the Conqueror?' He gave a tsking sound. 'Your history teacher would be disappointed.'

'She hated me anyway . . . and the feeling was mutual. Awful woman who smelled of medicated lozenges.'

He laughed. 'Shipwreck Museum, then?' Now her expression showed only disgust. 'That's the old town up there,' he said, pointing.

'Jack, please.'

'Let me educate you, Kate,' he tried in mock pleading. 'You never know when you might need to come back here.'

She mouthed *never* in his direction before speaking aloud. 'These are lovely homes around here,' loud enough for the taxi driver to feel welcome to comment.

'Oh yes, highly desirable around here,' he replied, taking the cue. 'Getting expensive, too. Lots of you London folk buying flats for a song and renovating them.'

'You mean as weekenders?'

'Yes, and to rent out as an investment. They're a good buy around here. Not so much at Beaufort, where you're headed, of course. That's social housing, you know that, right?'

'We do,' Jack said.

'Are you coppers?' he asked, his London accent pushing through. Jack sighed. 'Smell you lot a mile off. Someone been a naughty boy?'

'No, the opposite,' Kate replied. 'Someone helping police with enquiries, although we'd be grateful if you'd not broadcast that, please.'

'My lips are sealed. I don't mind helping the boys and girls in blue . . . or even you suits.'

'Pleased to hear it,' Jack said. He leaned to look out from the window. 'I'm guessing this is it?'

'Yes, sir. Six pounds fifty-five, please.'

Jack gave him a ten-pound note. 'Keep it.'

'Thank you,' the driver said and winked at Kate as she looked back.

'Let's find the caretaker,' Jack said, glancing across the hulking block of functional, sixties, brown brick accommodation, without any elegance or taste. They found the building manager smoking on a bench outside a tiny office on one of the wings.

'Bernie Beaton? Yeah, flat sixty-three. Third level, towards that end.' He pointed.

'Thanks,' Kate said. She'd not had to show her warrant card or explain herself – so much for security if the killer came hunting Bernie.

The lift was out of order on this wing, so they took the stairs via stairwells that smelled like cooked cabbage. Arriving onto the third level, each door looked the same, once painted white but now quite shabbily off-white with cracked paint. Outside number 63 they paused and looked at each other before Jack knocked. He was sure they were sharing the same good-luck thought. They waited. He knocked again after a reasonable pause.

'Coming, coming,' said a man's voice. Both blinked with relief. The door opened and in front of them stood a slightly stooped gentleman in corduroy trousers, a jumper with patches at the elbows, polished shoes and a beanie over hair in need of a trim. He was shaved though. Jack had expected someone less groomed.

'Mr Beaton?'

'It is,' he said, his gaze sliding between them. 'Good morning.'

They both showed their warrant cards.

He squinted at them. 'Detective Inspector Carter and . . .' He looked taken aback. 'Detective Superintendent? Good gracious.'

'Jack Hawksworth,' he said, offering a handshake. 'Sorry for the overkill.'

Bernie laughed, shook Jack's outstretched hand and nodded at Kate. 'No, no, I'm honoured. Come on in. I've been hoping one day to hear from the police again.'

They stepped into a home that didn't smell of the alcohol or slothful living they'd braced for. His appearance was the clue to his small, extremely modest but tidy abode, which gave off the faint hum of a pleasant fragrance.

'Your roses are lovely, Mr Beaton,' Kate noted, finding the source.

'You're most welcome to call me Bernie, Inspector Carter. In a different life I used to have roses delivered to my mother every week. She passed away many years ago, so now I give myself roses each week . . . except they're not long, perfect stems with impossibly beautiful blooms imported from the Netherlands,' he said with a grin. 'No, these days I grab them from Tesco and I take whatever they have. But they make me happy.' He gestured to a small sofa, and they sat. 'Anyway, I imagine you're finally here to talk to me about Peggy Markham, am I right?'

Jack was impressed by his directness. 'Yes, if you wouldn't mind.'

He gave a cheerful shrug. 'Not at all. Can I offer you both a drink?' He laughed. 'And I don't mean scotch. I guess you've heard plenty about me and no one would blame either of you for leaping to that conclusion.'

'We're fine actually,' Kate said, answering for both of them, 'but it's great that you've turned your life around, Bernie.'

'Coming here was like . . .' He smiled. 'I don't know, really it was like leaving one planet and entering another. I would probably be dead by now if those lovely nurses at the Whittington hadn't put in a good word for me.'

'And before I forget, Bernie, those same nurses send their love and best wishes to you,' Jack said. 'There was one, Jenny—'

'Jenny's a sweetheart,' he said.

'She said much the same about you,' Jack said gently. 'And DI Carter and I are here to apologise, too, for the somewhat careless way in which you were treated when you made your witness statement at Hornsey a while back.'

Bernie gave a sympathetic shrug. 'A very nice young detective constable – Lisa Farrow, I recall – served me a most welcome hot drink on a wintry night and she listened. She was kind and diligent. I don't blame them. I was a homeless addict who suffered hallucinations when I was using.'

Kate leaned forward. 'To remember her name, your memory is exceptional. We've read your statement and we'd really appreciate it if you'd let us ask a few questions.'

He glanced at his watch. 'Yes, of course. I'll tell you what I remember – I'm surprised my memory has stuck with me, given the abuse I gave it,' he said. 'I do have an appointment to call bingo at the local senior citizens hall in about an hour and a half, so . . .'

'We'll keep this brief,' Jack assured him.

Bernie didn't wait for them to start in with their questions. 'Peggy's death was considered suicide . . . has something changed?'

He might have been a drug addict, delusional, psychotic, a tramp even . . . but Bernie Beaton's mind was sound, and his question cut right to the heart of their visit. Only honesty would serve them now. 'It has, Bernie,' Jack confirmed. 'There is an investigation into a series of inexplicable deaths of mostly convicted criminals, although to date Peggy is the exception.'

'Why count her in, then?'

'Because the suicide explanation doesn't sit comfortably with us,' Kate answered.

'Not with me either, because I watched her murderer end her life, that's why. She was a character, that one. And putting it down to suicide was easy, I imagine; who cared about a crim getting her deserts that the police thought were just, anyway?'

Jack frowned. 'So you knew her?'

'Oh yes, Peggy and I went way back. I was having a wonderful time in the eighties and made very good use of her services.'

'So what was she doing in Finsbury Park that night?'

'Who can say? She and I had lost touch, and I was in no position or headspace to afford Peggy's special kind of service. My feeling is that she was drugged before being brought to that place and killed. It was swift. It was ruthless. There was little conversation, and I doubt Peggy had any idea what was happening. And he didn't look back . . . just stuck her and walked away.'

'You're sure it was a he?' Kate checked.

'No doubt at all.'

'Now, Bernie, I'm not calling into question anything you're saying, but I do have to ask how you had such a clear view of this scene. How come you weren't noticed?' Jack asked.

He nodded. 'Do you know the area where Peggy was found?'

'I do,' Kate confirmed. 'I was there only yesterday.'

'Okay, well, did you notice a timber shelter nearby?'

'I did. But Bernie, you couldn't be seated in that shelter and not be—'

'I wasn't seated. I wasn't even intentionally hiding. I was living in it,' he said, sounding faintly amused by his ingeniousness.

They frowned back at him. 'Can you explain how?' Kate asked. 'Here, let me draw it so the Super knows what we're both talking about here.' She turned to a fresh page in her pad and made a good effort of sketching the structure. 'It's wonky, but do you agree it looked like this, Bernie?'

Bernie glanced at it. 'May I?'

She nodded, handed over the pad.

'The roof is taller, sloping higher like this,' he said, adjusting her drawing with his own rendition, 'but it had a proper ceiling. Like this, with timber slats . . . imagine narrow floorboards.'

'Okay,' Jack said, waiting, watching Kate nod along.

Bernie grinned. 'A few months before Peggy was killed, I knew I had to find somewhere safe to sleep through the winter months. If people bothered me, as they invariably did in that area, I could move on in summer, but in winter and at my age, I needed something less transient.'

'Of course,' Kate agreed.

'So when I came across this shelter and slept on its bench, I worked out that perhaps I could remove a few of those ceiling slats.'

Dawning hit Jack. 'Aaah,' he said, looking back at the sketch and then again to Bernie. 'Clever you.'

'It was rather inspired.' Bernie smiled.

'Hang on,' Kate said, frowning. 'So you took some of the ceiling boards out . . .?'

'They were easy to remove. I think I could squeeze through once four were gone.'

'And then you'd put them back?' she said.

'That's right,' he said, sounding chuffed. 'It became a private crawl space. No one knew I was there. I was silent. Had to be or the council workers would have found me. I kept it tidy. And there were vents cut into the side, but they had mesh on them to keep birds and rats out, I suppose. It was a handsome structure and really well made. I was happy in there and warm as toast.' He grinned. 'It also gave me a great vantage point – I could see all the way up and down the path, although my view north was better.'

'And this is how you saw Peggy and her killer arrive?'

He nodded. 'It was a very cold night. The park was deserted. Not even the usual gang of ratbag teens out and making mischief. I was asleep but was woken by voices that didn't sound like the usual hoodlums. I moved silently to peep out and saw them.'

'Did he have a torch?'

'No, and there were no park lamps around. But it was a full moon and my eyes were already well adjusted to the dark, so it made the scene relatively clear. Took me a few moments to make out that it was Peggy and, to be honest, it was her voice that convinced me; she had a uniquely deep, scratchy tone that was unmistakable and she always wore fur . . . prided herself on it. She was in a fur coat I recognised.'

'How? Furs tend to look the same.'

'Not this one. It was red, dyed to her colour of choice. She used to boast about it. No doubting who it was.'

'How did she appear?'

'She sounded drunk, needed help staying steady, but she kept asking questions. I heard fear in her voice as she kept asking him why.'

'It says in your report that Peggy asked *why* four times?'

He nodded. 'From memory, yes. But she also said *I didn't do anything*, and *it wasn't my fault. You were there, you knew.*'

'*You were there*?' Kate frowned. 'I have a copy here of your statement; it's not noted.'

Bernie shrugged. 'We were interrupted. DC Farrow was taking me seriously, but the others weren't. Coombs and Phil Brown, they already had their minds made up that I was a looney coming in from the cold.'

Jack and Kate glanced at each other with collective guilt on behalf of those officers.

'But Peggy was trying to explain through her slurring – that's the only way I can describe it – that the girl's death was not her fault. She had no idea – her words – that the Turk was going to give her cocaine or act as depraved as he did.'

Jack gave a low whistle. 'All right. What do you think "you were there" might mean?'

'Ah, I took it to mean that the man who killed her was one of the men involved with the girl who died.'

Jack frowned. 'There was only one man mentioned. A Turkish gentleman.'

Bernie shrugged. 'The man who killed Peggy was not foreign, from what I could tell.'

'What else can you recall about him?'

'He was ordinary . . . what else can I say? He wore a parka – could have been grey – and trousers, an old-fashioned flat cap . . . you know, the sort of chequered thing a country gent might wear.'

They nodded.

'He had a scarf that was pulled up high around his mouth, but I could still hear him well enough, even when he made a call. I think he was cold, to be honest. He didn't waste time. He put her against the tree, made her sit down.'

'Was he rough?'

'No. Gentle, polite even. He eased her back against the trunk, shooshing her anxiety until she sat in a terrified silence. He actually helped her into a seated position.

'I heard her say, "Please Mr . . ." but she never finished, and then it was a quick movement I barely caught, and he was walking away. "Bye, Peggy" was all he said to her and he was gone, disappearing up the pathway into the darkness. I watched him leave before I looked back and realised there was a syringe in her neck.'

'She called him Mr . . . as though she knew him?'

Bernie nodded. 'I believe so.'

'Did she say anything after he'd gone?' Jack asked.

He shook his head. 'She cried out once, at the shock of the needle perhaps, and then dissolved into tears, but they only lasted a moment because she choked a little and then she fell silent and still. I waited about five minutes – it felt like a lifetime. By the time I'd climbed down, she was already dead.'

'How do you know? Did you check for a pulse?'

'No,' he said abruptly. 'I didn't have to. I also didn't want to leave my prints or any clue that I had been there. Her eyes were staring open, her mouth was slack and she'd vomited. The syringe was still stuck into her neck and, as a user, I didn't need a lot more information to know that heroin had been pumped into her. I took the risk of lighting a match and I was looking for that blueish colour to her skin.'

They nodded.

'Hard to tell, but I gauged that she was pale and blueish.'

'Heroine and morphine,' she qualified for him. 'So then what happened?'

'I was careful to put the match into my pocket and retreated to my hiding spot; I was terrified, so I waited it out until she was found and your people arrived. They put a tent around her as all the voyeurs were onto it quickly – and the media, of course. I watched them lift her body into a bag.'

'And you waited a few days to report it, I see from the witness statement.'

'Yes. I was scared. But my conscience got the better of me, especially when talk of suicide erupted. I heard it on the radio in the local café, so I chose a night when I wouldn't be seen by many and decided I'd make a proper statement to the police, but . . .' He shrugged.

'Back to the killer, Bernie – is there anything else you can remember about him?'

'Well, I suppose the only oddity was his shoes.'

'What about them?' Kate asked.

'He was neatly enough dressed, typical for a middle-aged man, but he wore these strange trainers. I couldn't be sure but they weren't white . . . more a greenish colour in the moonlight. And he seemed to move oddly in them.'

'Oddly? As in not used to walking in them?' Jack wondered.

'Er, no, more that he was uncomfortable.'

'How could you tell?'

'Well, it's just a feeling I got,' Bernie said, dismissing his thought. 'I was worried they'd find my footprints and accuse me.'

'How did he sound?' Jack began the questions burning in the back of his mind, which would build a picture of the killer they hunted.

'Almost friendly, I'm embarrassed to admit. He wasn't rough, as I said. He wasn't aggressive, he didn't shout, he spoke in an even tone when he made the call.'

'Deep voice?'

'Not especially, no.'

'Language?'

'Educated, I'd say. He was polite.'

'Hair colour?'

'I couldn't tell you other than not dark. His cap covered most of it – certainly fairish.'

'Height?'

Bernie shrugged an apology. 'Average. Not tall, not small. He wore gloves.' He suddenly fell silent, looking into space with an expression of puzzlement.

'Bernie?' Kate asked. They waited but he just sat there, frowning. 'Mr Beaton, are you all right?'

'Wow,' he breathed. 'Something just flashed into my mind; I'd completely forgotten it. I failed to mention it at Hornsey and this is the first time I've recalled more. Extraordinary! I've thought on that scene so many times, feeling guilty, wishing I could have done more.'

'Bernie?' Jack prodded gently, trying to bring him back to them.

He refocused. 'I'm sorry, it's something but I don't know if it's important.'

'Share it with us,' Jack urged.

'It's because you got me talking about the shoes, but I'd completely lost this fact until now.'

'Which is?' Kate asked, her expression all but pleading.

'He . . . er, the killer stepped quite deliberately away from Peggy, across the patch of grass. Just at the edge before he rejoined the path, he changed out of his trainers.'

Jack did a double take. 'Into what?'

'Normal shoes, I suppose. I couldn't describe them for you – they looked so ordinary from the distance I was watching from. I couldn't tell you if they were black or brown either . . . but certainly dark.'

'Normal shoes?'

'Yes, leather, I presume, with a proper heel, rather than trainers.'

Kate looked at Jack. 'Covering his tracks?' she murmured.

'His Sulemein tracks.' he replied.

She wanted to smile, but schooled her features to remain grave.

'It struck me as odd because he didn't seem to bother about arriving in his trainers and moving about the tree, but he obviously planned to leave in his proper shoes.'

'Which presumably he brought with him in what . . . a back-pack?'

Bernie considered. 'A sort of holdall, I think.'

'Anything distinguishing about it?'

'It was a Tottenham Hotspur holdall; greyish blue material with a distinct cockerel logo, which struck me as odd.'

'Why?'

Bernie gave a snort. 'You don't walk around the Arsenal stronghold of Finsbury Park wearing anything to do with Spurs.'

Jack grinned. 'I'm a Chelsea man myself.'

'I'd never declare that, because it's just as bad to Arsenal folks. I'm Spurs, but I used to wear the red and white on game day just to prevent getting my head kicked in. Yobbos everywhere like to pick on the rough sleepers . . . especially if their team just lost. The Spurs bag wasn't the usual one, though.'

'Not usual, how?' Kate asked.

'It was a limited edition and I recognised it because I had one once too, but it was stolen.'

Jack nodded. 'Okay, Bernie, thank you,' he said, sounding as impressed by the man's clarity and eloquence as Kate felt. She had anticipated neither. 'If you think of anything new, anything at all, you must call us,' Jack said, reaching into his pocket, even though Kate was already handing Bernie her card.

'I will. Anyway, folks, I'd better get a move on. The senior citizens of Hastings cut me no slack on bingo day.'

They shared a chuckle as they stood and prepared to leave. 'Thanks for your help, Bernie,' Jack said, 'and I really am glad that you've turned your life around.'

Bernie nodded. 'What a life I've led. From the heights of riches and fame to rolling around a gutter in soiled trousers. The extremes I can do without. I find myself in a good place now, a good headspace, recovered from my addiction and fortunate to be able to say that.'

'Pleased for you, Bernie.' Kate nodded. 'You'd better not keep the bingo gang waiting – thanks again for your time.'

He gave them a little salute and Kate realised they were both smiling as they walked away.

21

The family-sized bag of Revels yawned open between Jack and Kate as they helped themselves on the journey home; from time to time one of them would make a face of disgust as they bit into an orange one.

He didn't want to admit that his favourites were not the coffee ones because that would be inconsistent with his passion for the flavour. He moved on to the case. 'So, what do we derive from Bernie's revelation?'

She chewed as she considered – lucky thing, it had to be a toffee, Jack decided. 'Well, the man we're after increasingly sounds like someone who knows his way around policing, wouldn't you say?'

'Exactly. He's left no forensic evidence other than some obvious things like footprints, and after what Bernie said today, I think he wanted us to find them.'

'Red herring?'

He nodded. 'Smart enough to throw us off looking for Solihull shoes . . .'

'Saloman,' she corrected, trying not to laugh.

'. . . that are size nine and a half.'

'Which he removed straight after the murder of Peggy.'

'Alan Chingford categorically remembers the shoes his mugger wore. They're smart enough for work and, I suppose from a distance, could be described as formal. I don't think Bernie meant formal as in dress shoes, do you?'

She shook her head. 'Just shoes, as opposed to sneakers.'

'Good, well, our killer favours Hush Puppies and I have the style number, so we need to get a photo of that type circulated.'

'Bernie mentioned that he walked as though uncomfortable in those sneakers, too.'

'Yes, so maybe our hunch that he's not size nine and a half is on the money. What if that's smaller than his shoe size? That might explain the discomfort. And the change into proper fitting shoes means he can walk properly.'

'So he's left footprints deliberately in the wrong size for us to find.'

Jack gave a sniff. 'Forensics would have told us as much any minute. Even so, I reckon he thinks he's a smart bastard.'

'Yes, I agree and I'm wondering where else he's toying with us.'

'We've got to get ahead of him.'

'How?'

'Get onto Mal. Let's find out which prisoners who originally committed crimes in Enfield are about to get an early release.'

While Kate did that, he called the eager Constable Johnson.

'And you want me to find out how these limited edition holdalls were purchased?'

'Yes, Ali. Anything you can learn. Brief me when you know more, if at all.'

'I'm on it, sir.'

Jack smiled and rang off, then pondered absently, listening while Kate gave instructions to their colleagues.

He rang Sarah. 'Hi, it's me. Did anything erupt from that itch you couldn't scratch last night?'

'It did, sir,' she said with no amusement. 'I didn't want to interrupt you while you were interviewing Mr Beaton, but we've got a break.'

He sat forward. 'Tell me.'

'All it will do is narrow things down, but it will put us in a better position than we were yesterday.'

Jack knew to remain patient.

'Not just a couple, as we originally surmised, but every one of the original crimes committed by the people who have been picked off – and I must qualify that these are the people that we know about – was tried by Judge Leland.'

'Fuck me!' he breathed. 'Don't tell Joan I said that.'

'I won't.'

'Does Judge Leland work one courtroom?'

'Well, I'm pretty certain the judges like to settle into one they consider their own but if they have to, they'll move for reasons of the case. She is normally in Courtroom Eleven.'

'So we need to tap into the regulars of that courtroom.'

'Mal's already onto it. He's gone down there.'

'Good.'

'Also, I saw Mr Jarvis last night and he gave me a pretty good description of a couple of men who are regulars who, in his opinion, had that whiff of something not quite right that you asked for. But he's also got some others in mind who are a bit righteous, from other courtrooms.'

'And?'

'He's got a good memory, sir, so he'll be in to look at CCTV with me to fast-track. He's arriving shortly.'

'Good work, Sarah. We'll be back soon – we should be pulling into Charing Cross in about . . .?'

Kate, keen to hear what he'd discovered, murmured, 'Fifteen minutes.'

'In about fifteen. We'll jump in a taxi and hope to miss the evening crush.' Jack hung up as Sarah said she'd see them soon. He'd remembered something. 'Kate, about the call Bernie mentioned the killer made.'

She looked back at him as if waiting for more clues.

'When he was describing the killer, he mentioned a mellow, educated voice.'

'Yes, and that he could hear him clearly, even though his scarf was pulled up close to his mouth . . .'

'. . . *when he made the call*, is what Bernie said,' Jack reminded her.

She gaped back at him now as its importance hit. 'He called someone.'

'Go back to Bernie. Find out everything you can about that phone call.'

She tried. 'No answer. Not even voicemail. He'll still be calling bingo.'

They stood to gather up their stuff as the train began slowing into the station. With summer not far off it was still so light, but it felt like a long day. 'Stay on him,' Jack insisted.

They arrived back at the op room and Jack immediately went to the visitor area where he knew Sarah would have taken the clerk of Courtroom Seven.

He didn't bother knocking. 'Hello again, Mr Jarvis . . . Sarah. Sorry to keep you both so late.'

'Evening, sir,' Sarah said.

Jarvis beamed and stood. 'Good evening, Detective Super-intendent Hawksworth. It's only six-thirty . . . not too bad. We've found one of them but also a couple of others that I know lurk around the courthouse itself. I don't know if they're relevant, but I'll point them out to Sarah. I've just realised I'm the clerk who has been there the longest by at least five years, so I probably do have a reasonable handle on those regulars.'

'Excellent,' Jack murmured. 'My apologies to have you cramped in here, but we don't normally have visitors—'

'Don't mention it. I'm pleased to help. I know how it goes. I have no desire to look upon details in the incident room – it's bad enough in court when we have to look at pathology photos.'

Jack nodded. 'Can we get you anything?' he said, noticing the empty table. 'We do reasonable coffee here.'

'Oh, well, I'm all in then.'

'I'll get it, sir,' Sarah said, looking appalled that she'd over-looked fundamental hospitality.

'No, no. I'd be happy to.' Jack smiled. 'You've got work to do, Mr Jarvis.'

'Brian,' he insisted.

'Want one, Sarah?'

'No, thanks, sir.'

Jack pondered while the small machine whirred and groaned, spurted and clicked, finally delivering two good-looking lattes. He delivered the clerk his coffee with tiny packets of sugar, remembering Jarvis had taken sugar with his tea the other day. Old-school . . . a child of the sixties. 'Sarah, I've got a call to make,' he said, mimicking holding a phone to his ear. 'See you with the others shortly.'

'Yes, sir.'

He shook the clerk's hand. 'This is really good of you, thank you. Has Sarah mentioned that all the murders we know about were originally tried in Court Eleven?'

Jarvis blanched. 'That's Judge Leland.' His voice was tight, almost choked.

'How long have you clerked at North London Crown Courts?' Jack asked, reaching for any lead.

'Fifteen years in number seven.'

He nodded. 'And Judge Leland?'

'Um, let me see. Judge Leland arrived in winter 1994. It was the end of January, I can recall, as Terry Venables became the new coach for our English football team.'

'What's he like, this Judge Leland?'

'She,' Brian corrected with a smile. 'Clinical. By that I mean she's a real professional. But she has heart.'

'What does that actually mean?' Jack asked, his head tipping to one side in query.

'Well, as Shirley and I remarked, she's lenient. She sentences within the full range of the law, but she errs on the side of caution because she takes the more liberal view that doesn't believe prison equals rehabilitation.'

'And the other judges?'

'A mix. We have those who always hand out a maximum sentence. We have those who, in my opinion, are too lenient, and then we have judges who are troubled.'

'Troubled?'

He nodded. 'I shouldn't be speaking out of school, but I suspect that Moira Leland struggles to reach her decisions. She certainly takes her time weighing everything up.'

Jack frowned. 'And how do you feel about that?'

'Me?' Jarvis looked surprised to be asked. 'I am not a political animal, Detective Superintendent. I learned a long time ago in my career to remain in a neutral gear. No sentence is ever harsh enough for the victim or their families. No sentence is lenient enough for the perpetrator or *their* families. I don't envy the role of a judge, but I do admire someone like Moira, who does a lot of hard yards to reach her decisions.'

'Because it means she's considered everything, you mean?'

'Yes. Moira Leland is able to step away from all the emotion, the personalities of the people involved, the accusations and the hurt. She scrutinises which laws have been broken and pays long consideration to how best to interpret our laws against the crimes committed. Her sentencing is always measured.'

'But still, in your opinion, too lenient?'

Jarvis nodded unhappily. 'Yes. But then that's the opinion of all the clerks I know. Judge Leland and I have had this conversation. We're about the same age, and I filled in for her clerk on a major case, so she knows me. I accept her argument that if she metes out the toughest sentences, then all that's going to happen within our overcrowded prison system is that those people will get early parole. They will be considered quickly because their sentences are especially harsh, and they will have their time reduced.'

'Why? You can see how much goes into putting those people behind bars.'

'But to what end?' Jarvis queried. 'I mean, don't get me wrong, I agree with you and even your despair that police are giving every waking hour to catching these people. It is surely soul-destroying to see them walk out of prison having only done a few years. But all the research does confirm Leland's view that prison is not a deterrent. All it does is take those people off the streets for a while.'

'I'd settle for that,' Sarah remarked, and then looked instantly embarrassed for having joined the conversation.

Brian smiled sympathetically. 'You and the rest of us who live within the law. But you surely know that the Blair government is looking to release thousands of prisoners prematurely in order to ease overcrowding and the massive drain of the prison system on the public purse?'

'So we hear.'

'There's rumours of numbers as high as twenty thousand or more . . . this year alone.'

Jack was stunned. It must have reflected in his expression because Jarvis nodded and gave a helpless shrug. 'You catch them, we convict them, Leland puts them away briefly, and the government releases them even earlier. That's the cycle. No one to blame, but caught in the middle are the victims and their families, who serve their full sentences with no reprieve.'

'The Clarke family will be relieved, then,' Jack remarked.

'What do you mean?'

'Davey Robbins is dead. Killed last week.'

Shock wrinkled the clerk's face. 'I've been so busy this last week I haven't read the newspaper, haven't watched the news; I knew there'd been a death though. Up north, wasn't it?'

Both nodded.

'Heavens. I had no idea it was him.'

Jack shrugged. 'It's part of our inquiry.'

'Davey Robbins dead,' he repeated, as though still trying to process it. 'I can't say I feel sad. It's a young life, but he struck me as a bad sort who would only go on to worse things. He was impressionable and, even though he displayed arrogance and confidence in our court, I suspect that lad was a follower and would be easily led into more crime. That poor Clarke girl was in court every day of his trial, as I understand it. Takes courage.'

Jack sighed. 'Anyway, that's why what you're doing here with Sarah is a great help.'

'I'm very glad to, and I know Hugh Pettigrew from eleven will do all he can. One more thing that occurs now you talk about a specific judge . . .'

'Yes?'

'Is Moira Leland a target, do you think?'

Jack blinked.

'I mean, will you be putting any protection in place?'

'Potentially,' Jack replied, making a mental note to check the judge's security measures.

Jarvis nodded. 'Maybe all of us from North London Crown Court need protecting,' he quipped and then chuckled at his own jest.

'I think you're safe.' Jack grinned. 'Thanks again for your help. I'll leave you to it.' He nodded at Sarah and left, finding Kate.

'Are they making any headway?' she asked.

'Some. Listen, have we contacted Amy Clarke?'

'The rape victim?'

'Yes. Apparently she came to the courtroom every day. She may remember something others haven't, or just open us up to something fresh. We need to find out everyone who worked that trial as well.'

'Will do. Now, Bernie . . .'

'Yes?'

'I got him. All he could give us is that as the killer turned away, he paused briefly to dial a number on his mobile phone. Bernie didn't hear the conversation but he could just make out the words "It's done" before the man got out of earshot.'

'*It's done?*' Jack asked. 'Like a hit?'

Kate shrugged.

'So . . . had he been ordered to kill Markham? Paid to kill Markham?'

'The plot thickens,' she remarked unhelpfully.

His gaze narrowed. 'But does that mean he was ordered or paid to kill the others too? We need motive! And if it is a paid hit, then we need to get behind the killer to his boss . . . and why? I need to think. Thanks, Kate.'

'Sorry I had nothing more helpful.'

He shook his head absent-mindedly and wandered off towards Mal. 'Anything?'

'Two early passes from jail.'

'Go on?'

'Jimmy "The Lad" Parsons,' Mal began, 'is a career criminal but mostly for petty thieving. The other, Geoffrey Paxton, has made a career of rape and attempted rape. Nine victims. Served eleven years of a twenty-year sentence.'

Jack could see Mal was filled with an excitement he couldn't contain; his eyes were glinting. 'I just know you have more to tell us.'

'Sent down from North London Crown Court.'

'Judge?'

Mal frowned; he hadn't expected that. 'Er . . . just a mo. It's in this file.' He reached over and shuffled some folders, selecting one. 'Sorry, guv. Er . . . yeah. Judge Moira Leland.'

To Jack it felt like someone had just lit a rocket firework in his belly; he was sure he flinched as the news zoomed around, exploding in his thoughts. Who was targeting Judge Leland's cases? 'When is he being released?'

'Day after tomorrow. He's worth a look, right?'

'Hang on.' Jack walked back to where Sarah and Jarvis were still poring over a computer. 'Mr Jarvis?'

'Yes?'

'Do you recall the case of Geoffrey Paxton?'

'Yes, of course,' he said, pulling off his glasses to give them a polish. 'Not my courtroom, though. Maybe Hugh's, from memory.' He put his glasses back on. 'Don't tell me,' he suddenly said, his voice tight.

'No.' Jarvis gave a sound of relief. 'But apparently he's on an early release.'

'That was Leland too. A twenty-year sentence, as I recall. A lot of broken victims and certainly not long enough, in most people's opinion.'

Jack nodded. 'Well, he's out in a day or so.'

'So will you watch over him?'

'A logical move,' Jack replied. 'Keep up the good work, you two, thanks again.'

'Just finished up, sir,' Sarah said. 'I'll show you out, Mr Jarvis.'

As they stood to leave, Mal appeared at Jack's side. 'Shall I alert the Thames Valley Police in Reading and ask them to assist?'

'That's home for Paxton, is it?'

Mal nodded. 'He's returning to his father's place in Reading.'

'Yes. Have them there from first thing, day after tomorrow. I don't know what time he'll be let out but our people will do round-the-clock surveillance at his father's house.'

'Will do.' They saw Sarah and Jarvis waiting as they blocked the corridor. 'Oops, sorry,' Mal said. 'Goodnight, sir,' he said to Jarvis as the clerk and Sarah moved past.

Jack returned to pick up his phone and Kate caught his attention. 'Paxton might be our chance.'

'It's a good shot,' Jack agreed.

'Right. Shall we summarise for everyone? Keep us all up to speed?'

He let Kate take the floor and give the team a run-down on everything discovered in Hastings with Bernie and then an update on Mal's findings about Paxton heading to his father's home in Reading. 'We'll be bringing in a special undercover team for that. And they'll report back through Mal.'

Judge Leland's name came up.

'Well, we can't deny that the killer is preying on convicted criminals – plus Peggy Markham – who have had Moira Leland sit in judgement at their trials,' Kate observed for the group. 'We can't say there aren't other corpses, yet to be discovered, who were not on trial under Judge Leland, but the deaths that this operation has come together to scrutinise were all from her court.'

Jack stood, deciding to share his thoughts with the team. He'd been prodding at them for a couple of days, concerned that by

MIRROR MAN   267

airing them he'd take everyone's thinking down a particular path. Now he was convinced he was right.

'Before we head off, I have something I'd like you to ponder overnight.'

Everyone waited, expectantly.

'I'm now convinced we're dealing with a vigilante.'

There were sighs of surprise, some wry smiles; Kate lifted an eyebrow.

'While I agree that we can now link the crimes through the use of the drug propofol, through North London Crown Court, and now Judge Leland . . . I'm convinced there's more commonality.'

A hush gripped the ops team.

'I drew up two sheets. Original crimes against the perpetrators' deaths. And the name of our op is, for a rare time, highly appropriate. I believe our killer is, to a point, mirroring his murders with the original crimes.'

That sent a buzz around the room.

'Peggy Markham was never convicted.' Kate frowned.

Jack didn't falter. 'I did some digging. The man who fathered her child and shared her life for many years was one of the drug lords who gave cocaine and its sister, crack cocaine, their rise in popularity in this country. Did you know that we snort more than any other country in Europe?' The question was rhetorical and he didn't wait for an answer. 'I believe her death via the drug overdose was simple, effective but also symbolic.'

Kate pressed. 'Subtle, I'd say, given she was on trial for procuring.'

'All right,' he accepted. 'Try this. Brownlow was dragged behind a car – you know two of the children he killed were dragged beneath his father's four-wheel drive.'

The group was nodding as one.

'The district nurse we learned about through journalist Lauren Starling? She was killed by smothering.'

Sarah gave a sound: her understanding dawning.

'I thought she was killed by an overdose?' Mal said on behalf of everyone.

'Pathology showed there was plenty of propofol in her system. Either he was making sure she wasn't going to do anything surprising like regain consciousness or he was hoping for sloppy pathology to focus on the drug.'

'It worked,' Kate remarked.

'Exactly,' Jack said, eagerly leaning forward. 'She was added to the suicide statistics. But Lauren Starling actually interviewed the pathologist years ago. He said his report showed this woman had stopped breathing through suffocation. The police team, meanwhile, latched onto the lethally high dose of the drug in her blood.'

'I suppose we can't blame them. It is logical,' Mal said.

Jack nodded. 'And that's why this op has never been about a witch-hunt of our own, or we'd be hauling in the Hornsey team as well for ignoring Beaton. Mistakes are made, but they say the devil's in the detail. And I've now given you three murders of criminals that match their criminal ways.'

'All right – Smythe? The wife basher who had litres of boiling water poured on him?' Kate challenged his theory.

'Ah, that toad. Clearly symbolic. I know there was propofol in his system, probably to sedate him. But we've all now read every-thing about the original crime. Buried in the back of the original file notes are interviews with the hospital nurses who cared for his wife when she'd come in bruised or broken, making excuses. I rang that hospital a few minutes ago to talk with the most senior nurse and she confirmed, although it wasn't specified in the report but came out in the trial, that Smythe's favourite torture was to burn her with his cigarettes or splashes of freshly boiled water, but only in places it didn't show.'

Kate's mouth opened in silent surprise.

He nodded. 'I am certain now this is the work of one person, and he is killing his victims with references to their previous crimes.'

'So where does this take us, sir?' Sarah asked, looking owlish and determined through those round glasses of hers.

'I do think this is someone on the inside.' At the sound of their surprise, he held up a hand. 'I don't mean the police, but I do mean someone with access to police files . . . it could be from hospitals or morgues, or anyone connected with the courts, especially. We need to scrutinise Leland's cases and find any more suspicious or inexplicable deaths of crims she's sent down.' He gazed around at their thoughtful faces. 'Okay, let that percolate and we'll regroup. Goodnight, everyone.'

'Jack?' He looked over as everyone was moving to leave. It was Joan. 'Lauren Starling just rang. Said she tried your phone but couldn't get through. I said you'd call back. It's about the press office . . . apparently.'

Apparently. Bloody hell, now Joan was onto him. 'Thanks, Joan. I will. Good work today, everyone.'

Jack was seated again in front of Anne McEvoy, in a different room this time; it was small and airless, with only a high oblong window. Their knees almost touched beneath the desk they sat across, nursing chipped mugs of tea.

'It's good to see you again so soon,' she began, once the prison officer had departed. They'd been left alone this time with the officer outside the door.

To avoid any more awkward moments, Jack launched straight into an explanation of how the original crimes had occurred in and around the Borough of Enfield, and he also gave her the information on North London Crown Court.

'Oh, that's gold, Jack,' she said. 'That has surely narrowed things down.'

'You'd think so,' he said, not sounding overly positive. 'We still feel like we're blundering around in the dark.'

'I've been thinking on your prey.'

'And?'

'It's my opinion that he's a person in a position of power.'

'Why do you say that?'

'Well, I already believe him to be educated, of higher than average intelligence, plus I reckon he maybe doesn't have a family.'

'Because?'

'From what you've told me, he's getting around, isn't he? Yorkshire, Portsmouth, Eastbourne, Hastings . . . he's got the money to move around at ease and presumably to use whatever transport is required, from trains to hire cars. Or even his own car, potentially . . . and none of that comes cheaply. He'd need to be earning and have flexibility at home. If he's answerable to a wife or children, he wouldn't be able to respond to his needs or the timing of the victim's release dates.'

She was making sense. 'So he lives alone, you think?'

She sighed. 'Well, without anything to study, I'm poking into thin air but, yes, I would say that this fellow lives alone and quietly. Doesn't draw attention to himself.'

'A loner?'

'Not necessarily.' She shook her head. 'I wouldn't jump to that conclusion.'

'But you said in a position of power.'

'Let me clarify: by power, I don't mean he intimidates people. I mean I believe he has status.'

Jack frowned, listening intently.

'I'm probably reaching, but he has access to information, right?

Either that or he's seriously well connected. He can't be relying on the news headlines alone.'

'I've been thinking on that. What about prisons?'

'Prisons would make their internal recommendations for early release well before they become public knowledge. I know that for a fact.'

'That's good to know.'

'The courts – any luck?'

'We've narrowed it down to one judge, whose lenient sentencing is where our killer's attention is focused. I'm wondering whether we need to throw a ring of protection around the judge in question.'

Anne nodded, but finally shook her head. 'If the judge was my target, he'd have been the first person dealt with.'

Jack didn't correct her on the gender of the judge but agreed with her sentiment. 'I think his wrath is reserved for the system that he feels is letting victims down.'

'Yes. Judges, defence lawyers, barristers and everyone connected with the cases that catch his attention. He can't kill them all – much as he'd probably like to – so he targets the perpetrators. I suspect he'd win sympathy from the public at large.'

Jack nodded. 'At times from us too, if we're honest.'

'Mirror Man doesn't just get angry and appear out of nowhere. This is likely an old grudge.'

'I'm thinking someone who has lost someone he's loved to a crime and the system has let him down. If the system can't look after the victims and award justice, he will.'

She smiled. 'You don't need me. You never did.'

He wasn't sure whether she was talking about the present investigation or including the past. He didn't overreact. 'Helps to talk it through, though.'

'Good.' She looked at him and he knew what she needed.

'Er, listen, I don't have any information yet on the other business, Anne, but I'm working on it.'

'No rush, Jack. I'm not going anywhere.'

He pulled a wrapped box of chocolates he'd been allowed to bring in that had been X-rayed, opened, rummaged through and pressed all over. 'They let me bring these for you. I'm sorry the seal is broken but . . . well, you know.'

'Thorntons,' she murmured with shock, as though he'd just handed her a key to Holloway's gates. 'You remembered.'

'You used to have a thing for the chocolate-smothered licorice toffees, didn't you? I got some of those but also a box of assorted . . . their premium. They look delicious.'

He could swear her eyes looked damp as she laughed and lifted the two chocolate boxes from the bag. 'I did . . . I mean, I do still have a thing for their chocolate-coated licorice chunks. Thank you. I'll have to find a hiding place for these in my cell with the same care that someone else would hide a shiv.'

That switched off the smile he'd been beaming. It was easy to forget that she was living around dangerous people every hour of every day.

She noted his anxious gaze and laughed. 'Don't worry, Jack. I told you, I have respect in here. No one would knife me for my chocolates. Besides, I'll probably share them. What a treat.'

Now he felt embarrassed that a spend of less than twenty pounds could generate so much gratitude. 'Is there anything else I can bring in for you?'

'Don't offer that — there's a million and one things I could want but I have already learned to live without. You know what I need . . . just the confirmation that you have the information.'

He nodded sadly. 'If I can get it, then I'll tell you I have it.' He stood to leave; wanted to shake her hand at least but dared not risk breaking any rules, knowing they were being watched over by cameras. He made a silent promise to himself that seeing Anne was too hard on his heart and so until he discovered – if he could – what she wanted in return, he would not be back. Besides, without allowing her access to the files, he couldn't imagine she could do much more for the investigation . . . and then she did.

'One more thing.'

'Yes?' He turned.

'Don't for a moment believe he doesn't know you're onto him.'

Jack blinked. 'But we haven't gone public with any of this.' He thought about Lauren. 'We may soon, but as yet it's all under the radar.'

She gave a tight smile. 'You may think so. But don't forget that I stayed ahead of all of you. This guy is every bit as cunning.'

'We're all hand-picked. My unit would tell me if any stranger had suddenly entered their lives.'

Anne cut him a patient look. 'Well, he's not obvious . . . Always watch those who watch. And Jack?'

He waited.

'If he's escalating, that means slightly more desperate actions. If he knows you're onto his scent, he might turn on you, and by you I mean your people. Nothing more desperate than a trapped animal.'

She lifted a hand in farewell in a way that suggested she understood this was likely his final visit. With her sharp perceptions and insight, Jack could imagine the good that Anne McEvoy could have done in the world if only she'd been allowed to grow into herself, without that blight in her teenage years that split her into two people.

'Bye, Anne.'

'Goodbye, Jack.'

22

The killer had waited. He was in no hurry but he had been surprised to follow Jack Hawksworth to Holloway. What on earth was the detective superintendent doing here . . . at a women's prison? He realised quickly that there were potentially several reasons – including that Hawksworth had recently put one of its inmates behind bars. The chocolates were intriguing though; one could hardly miss that big bag containing Thorntons. Even so, he let go of the intrigue as he was here purely for self-interest, especially now that Hawksworth's team were inching closer; he needed to move faster and put some distance between them and him so he could finish the task he'd set himself.

It was a mild enough early evening, and he was dressed for the eventuality that it would begin to drop in temperature shortly. It was necessary to remain unobtrusive, but he'd always held to the belief that people could be fooled into not recognising someone if they didn't expect to see them out of context. He nevertheless showed caution, reminding himself that this was an individual of equal intelligence he was pitching himself against . . . a bit of a sharp one, if his instincts served him right, and he shouldn't consider himself superior. Hawksworth hadn't got to his senior status without impressing all the right people and being exceptionally good in his role as detective. He would likely have a sixth sense for noticing someone who was loitering or somewhere they shouldn't be.

Holloway stretched like a sleeping beast down the main artery, where cars and bikes dodged and weaved while London buses lurched and groaned on their way, creating obstacles for other drivers each time they hauled into a bus stop. The prison's main doors could be seen if he sipped a takeaway coffee, pretending to talk on his phone, just at the tip of the triangle where Camden Road met Parkhurst. Roadworks created a jumble of untidiness to frustrate drivers further, but the slightly chaotic conditions meant he could stand just behind a bus shelter unnoticed and still have a reasonable view.

He'd turned his reversible parka from his favoured tea-coloured beige into its hidden gunboat grey and had changed his flat cap for a charcoal-coloured woollen beanie. He removed his glasses. His vision was still reliable; it would do. He felt confident that he was not only unrecognisable from a skimming glance, but his garments meant he would all but disappear into the background colour and turmoil of traffic if Hawksworth happened to look his way.

He'd expected the visit to take longer – at least an hour or so – but the senior detective was making his long strides away from the prison, without his bag of chocolates, within a half hour of arriving. Hawksworth looked lost in his thoughts, reaching for his phone while craning his neck to search out a taxi. Perfect. He would use his prey's distraction to get closer. He moved swiftly, but without rushing, so as not to draw any undue attention. He turned away from Hawksworth's preoccupied gaze and signalled to the taxi down the road that he could tell Hawksworth had his sights fixed on. He risked a glance, along with a small ping of helpless schadenfreude as he noted the policeman sigh with frustration to see someone else flag the taxi. The taxi fortunately found a nook in the traffic to pull into and he clambered in.

'Where to, sir?'

'Er, I know this is going to sound odd, but do you see the gentleman standing there outside the prison?'

'Yep.'

'He's flagging a taxi too.'

'Excellent, so two cabbies are happy.'

The gentle sarcasm was not lost on him. 'I want to follow him.'

The taxi driver laughed. 'This isn't Hollywood, mate.'

'No, I realise it's unusual but I just need to know where he's going.'

Now the driver shook his head. 'Not liking the sound of this, sir. I don't want to get involved in anything—'

'You wouldn't be. He hurt my daughter . . . left her standing at the altar.'

'Ah, sad. Going to beat him up or something?'

'No.' The killer chuckled. 'Do I look the type?'

'You don't actually, sir. With respect, you look more like a librarian.'

'Ha . . . close. No, I just want to follow him.'

'Ah, you see, I'm still not sure I feel comfy doing that.'

'Not for any other purpose than to know where he lives these days.' He squinted at the driver's name on his identification tag. 'You see, Paul, he took all of my daughter's savings as well the money that we'd given her for her wedding, and he used it for himself.'

'Bit of a bastard, then.'

'You could put it that way.' They both looked over at Jack, who had just flagged another black taxi. 'I think he used our money towards a new flat and his bit on the side, if you get my drift?' He smiled sadly. 'Do you have daughters, Paul?'

'Two of them. And whoever wants to marry them has to get past me first.'

'There you are. I'm just a regular father and I just want to prove to my daughter that she picked a no-good rogue so she can get over him. Two years on and she's still at home, broken-hearted, unable to get on with her life.' His lie was spectacular even to his ears.

'All right, sir. I'll take you to his street but that's all . . . as soon as I see his taxi indicating to pull in, you get out wherever we are. You can do the rest of your spy stuff on foot.'

'Fair enough. Thanks.' He sat back and watched the black cab in front as they followed, two cars behind.

'I think he's headed for Paddington Station,' the cabbie observed.

Right enough, the killer found himself alighting and paying for his taxi before following the detective through the station complex. Why here? Evening was closing in; surely Hawksworth wasn't about to take a train somewhere? His hopes fell – this would be a waste of time if the detective was making a journey, but his hopes rose as he realised Hawksworth was avoiding the platforms, walking swiftly on those long legs. The killer had to break into a slight trot to keep among the river of people that seemed to be flowing towards the platforms against the direction he was heading in. Luckily Hawksworth was tall and he could keep him mostly in view, but there was a danger of losing him to these crowds so he risked a running catch-up. The detective was angling for a particular exit, it seemed, pausing to grab a couple of bunches of bright daffodils. And then he was moving again, through the bustle of the Paddington neighbourhood and into the quieter outskirts of Bayswater.

He held back, stepping into the courtyard of a mews to watch as the policeman skipped up some stairs at a residence and pressed an entry buzzer. The killer waited, saw his prey say something into the speaker and grin before pushing in through the door. He sighed; the policeman was likely visiting a woman. Had to be. That could be handy.

Pulling his beanie down further and hunching deeper into his parka, he walked casually down the street, mobile phone to his ear again as though engaged in a conversation. He forced himself to keep a normal walking speed – a person hurrying would attract attention. As he drew level with the terraced house that Hawksworth had entered, he moved up its stairs to study the five names on the various buzzers: Didcott, Farmer, Joffe, Starling and Rose. He surprised himself by smiling as he calculated the risk. He looked down the street: it really wasn't that far to the corner, and once he'd made it round there, he could get lost in the shops or any of the buildings, plus there were mews, taxis, if he could get one, and, if he really legged it, he could make a dash for Paddington and get lost there.

The risk was worth it. He pressed the buzzer for Didcott. Waited. Tried again. No response. Well, presumably that person was not in and so Hawskworth was with one of the other four. He pressed Farmer.

'Hello?'

'Er, yes, sorry to disturb you, I'm looking for a Mr Jack Hawskworth, please?'

'No one of that name here, sorry.' The connection was cut.

He tried Joffe.

'Hi. Tracey?' Joffe was expecting someone.

'Er, no. Forgive me, I'm actually looking for a Mr Hawksworth, please?'

'Wrong flat – sorry, mate.' Again, the connection went dead on him.

'And so, Jack, you are with a Starling or a Rose. What feminine surnames. Which of them might you be wooing with those daffodils, I wonder?'

The odds of being caught had increased and, as he contemplated this, he heard laughter. There was no one in the street, and at the second burst of laughter he risked tiptoeing back onto the pavement and looking up. The voices were coming from the roof, it seemed. He listened carefully and was convinced he could hear a man's voice that was not unlike Hawksworth's. Okay, it was too dangerous to risk those overwhelming odds and press one of the two remaining buzzers. If Hawksworth was a guest, suddenly alarmed by someone asking for him, then he would remain on the roof and have that bird's-eye view to watch his pursuer rush away.

Instead, the killer stored away the names Starling and Rose. He would find her and, if need be, he could potentially use her; it always paid to do one's homework.

With the sound of their laughter echoing, he pulled up the hood of the parka again and walked away, again with no urgency, back towards Paddington to catch the tube to his Underground station. He'd have the next day after work and the whole of Saturday to get organised, and then he would arrive under cover of dark to where Paxton was ticking off his final days of incarceration. But his freedom, scheduled for Monday morning, would be fleeting . . . cut short when Justice would find him.

Jack hoped their laughter hadn't disturbed anyone. He glanced down onto the street and saw there were not many people about. The one fellow in the grey parka walking in the direction of Paddington hadn't even looked up. Perhaps he couldn't hear with his hood up like that.

'I didn't think I'd see you so soon,' Lauren admitted, leaning into him.

Anne had said much the same earlier. 'Well, I didn't want you to think I was a kiss-and-run guy.'

'I don't think that. And I haven't had flowers that I haven't bought for myself for such a long time that . . .' She didn't finish.

'They're just a bunch of daffodils – cheerful in anyone's life.'

'But it's sweet. Thank you.' She reached up and stole another kiss. 'Jack, you don't have to be my knight in shining armour, all right? You've already done enough. Mike's being brilliant, too. That's all progressing faster than I'd imagined.'

He nodded. 'The chivalry is a helpless reaction to all sorts of things, but particularly connected with work and the crap all police deal with on a daily basis. But you're a strong and independent woman, I get it. And if we're on this topic, I need to be honest with you and say that I'm not in a position to be looking for a serious relationship . . . not emotionally, not professionally, not physically. I hope you'll forgive me for being candid.'

She shook her head with a sort of shrug.

'I need some time living alone, finding my way back to fun.' He hesitated and then figured if he was being this open, he might as well continue. 'Lauren, there's a woman I see casually from time to time. She lives abroad. And she sees lots of other people,' he said.

She frowned, but said nothing.

'The thing is, I'm not long out of something . . . an affair, I suppose.'

She stepped back to lean against the balustrade. 'Married?'

'No, no. But she was in a long engagement towards an arranged marriage that she feared. She was a modern woman, in a modern city, being coerced in very traditional ways. Culturally we would never have been allowed to turn it into anything more than a secret longing.'

Lauren gave a tsking sound of amused admonishment. 'Complicated. What happened? Tell me you were a guest at the wedding, stealing looks of yearning at each other.'

'No. She died before she could marry or I could save her from the man who killed her.' It was out before he could stop sharing the pain. He didn't enjoy the shock that marched across Lauren's face, collapsing her smile, hooding her eyes as she opened her mouth in horror. She began to stammer an apology. 'I could have handled that better,' he admitted. 'Sorry.'

'Fuck! Jack!'

'It was the last big public case I worked on. It makes me reluctant to get involved with anyone while I work on something so intense, especially anyone I meet through work.' He gave a sad smile. 'It will change in time, but at the present, I'm concerned that someone I care about might become a target because of my work.' Anne's warning thrashed about in his mind.

'I don't know what to say.'

'Say that you can enjoy this for what it is and not get in too deep. If you do, I'll almost certainly let you down. And you don't need two losers in a row.'

She gazed at him sadly as she touched his face affectionately. 'You're no loser, Jack. But if it helps, I'm in no headspace to get in too deep either. But I am enjoying this . . . whatever it is. It's walking me back into the sunshine, you could say.'

'Good.' He hugged her. 'So, dinner tomorrow, perhaps? For now I must run.'

'So soon,' she said, sighing.

'Just wanted to bring you some flowers, let you know that you're a special person and you deserve more than you've had.'

'Would you like to know just how special and clever your non–girlfriend friend is?'

'Go on, impress me.'

'North London Crown Court.' He grinned. He'd known she'd catch up. 'It gets better though, right?'

'Does it?'

She nodded. 'Judge Moira Leland is the connection. I nearly blacked out when I discovered that.'

'And you think working for *My Day* can fulfil you?'

'No, working for *My Day* has been paying the rent, but without it I wouldn't be getting my shot at the big stage, so in a way I'm grateful for the shit job.'

'True.'

'I should add . . . and thanks to you.'

Jack gave a little bow of acceptance.

'But I'm thinking I haven't told you anything you haven't discovered already?'

He shook his head.

'All right. I'll try to surprise you next time.'

'You do that.' He kissed her softly, briefly. 'I have to go.'

'Call me,' she said. 'And Jack?'

He turned.

'If I was of a mind to fall for someone . . . I'm sorry to tell you that it would be you.'

'Stay strong and single, Lauren. I'm not your guy, but I'm enjoying it too.'

'It's called friendship.'

He nodded with a smile.

'With a little extra,' she added, beginning to unbutton her blouse.

He fled and, as he began down the stairs, his laughter was genuine. It felt good. As he was flagging a taxi, his phone rang.

'It's Constable Johnson, sir.'

'Bit late for you, Ali.'

'I was waiting to get hold of the information re that holdall, sir.'

'Go on.'

'I tried tracking it through the Spurs website but no luck; it's not on the site. So I contacted the police liaison at Spurs.'

Jack wanted to congratulate her on such broad thinking, but she sounded enthusiastic and he didn't wish to interrupt.

'. . . so now I'm in touch with the manager of the shop. She has explained that this particular bag was a special edition from a few years back, which only season ticket holders had access to. I'm hoping to get a list of ticket holders who purchased the bag by tomorrow.'

'Very good, Ali. I'm impressed.'

'Thank you, sir. Goodnight.'

That one will go far, he thought, as he slipped the phone back into his pocket.

Brian Jarvis had only recently arrived home when his doorbell rang. He frowned, walking back towards the front door, anticipating members from the Jehovah's Witnesses, perhaps. He was already formulating his response.

He opened the door to see DS Sarah Jones, shrugging with slight embarrassment. 'Mr Jarvis, I'm so sorry to disturb you.'

'Good grief, DS Jones. Is everything all right?'

'Um, you look like you're going out. Am I—?'

He laughed. 'No, come in, come in. I've just arrived home, actually. Haven't had a chance to get my coat off.'

'Oh, is it dreaded supermarket time?' She smiled, stepping inside the doorway and pulling off the hood of her anorak.

'No, after I saw you, I called in to see a friend.'

'Oh, right. Me too, I'm off to see a friend not far from here so I hope you don't mind me interrupting your evening. I'll just be a few minutes.'

He showed her into his sitting room. 'Are you cold?'

'I'm fine, thank you.'

'Well, I was about to put the kettle on, so I hope you'll join me.'

She looked unsure.

'It's no trouble,' he encouraged her.

'All right, thank you.'

'Make yourself at home. I'll be back in a jiffy.' He was as good as his word, only leaving her briefly while he filled the kettle and flicked its switch. 'Is English Breakfast all right for you?' he called, then looked at his watch in the kitchen. 'At nearing seven in the evening?'

He heard her laugh from the other room. 'It's perfect,' she said. 'I like this tiny enclave of Conical Corner, and what a lovely house this is, Mr Jarvis.'

'Thank you. It is, isn't it?' he said, arriving back. 'I cycle to work most days, you know. It's such an easy location and there are parks all around. There goes the kettle.' He pointed back to the kitchen. 'I'll just get our tea things together.'

'Thank you. May I look at your paintings? I've just started an art course.'

'Be my guest,' he said, and returned a few minutes later balancing a small tray with the tea things. He found Sarah peering closely at one of the hangings.

'What do you think?' he asked, setting down the tray on a coffee table between them.

'Well, my art teacher has just got us working on a still life. I had never imagined how hard it would be to draw and paint an empty ceramic jug, a glass and an apple! But this is lovely. The perspective is perfect and the way the artist has captured the glass of the goblet is amazing. I'm really struggling with how the light moves around glass.'

'That's pastel, of course.'

She nodded. 'Yes, love all that smudging.'

'My wife did that.'

Sarah looked back at him with wide eyes. 'My gosh, I'd be so proud if I did that. No wonder you've hung it for her.'

'Milk and sugar?'

'Both, please.'

He obliged as Sarah took a seat opposite him. 'Yes, I'm very happy living here,' he said, returning them to the previous conversation. 'Although there's a school complex down the road with vast sports fields, there's also a small river behind here, with a couple of lovely old pubs that overlook it. Summer with the ducks on the water and woodland around – it's very pretty. I've lived here since we were married.'

'And Mrs Jarvis is . . .?'

'Oh, my apologies . . . She died.'

Sarah looked mortified. 'Oh. I didn't . . . I'm sorry . . . foot in mouth. I always do this!'

He smiled genially, handed her a china mug of tea. 'It was fifteen years ago. No, it's fine, Sarah. I've become used to living alone. I'm quite good at it now. Anyway, tell me how I can help you?'

'Thank you.' She dug into a small satchel and withdrew a file that had two A4-sized mugshots in them. 'I'm just wondering if you might recognise either of these men, Mr Jarvis?'

He took the photos, digging in a pocket to pull out his glasses case. He studied the photos, taking his time. Finally he sighed. 'I'm sorry, but I can't say that I do. Should I know them?'

'Both convicted out of the North London Crown Court.'

He frowned. 'Which judges presiding?'

'Kenwood and Pascoe.'

Jarvis put the photos down, then sipped his tea and shrugged. 'I don't recognise them. But tell me how I can help with regard to these men?'

'Well, those two are coming up for early release and I just wondered if you knew of them. If anyone was watching them during their court cases, or if you noticed anyone from the public gallery who seemed particularly agitated by these cases.'

'I can only really shed useful light on court seven – my regular courtroom – for the most part. I do relief from time to time, you know, filling in for others and, of course, we're all plugged into the big cases, which is why I can talk to you about the Robbins fellow or Rupert Brownlow, but general cases . . .' He looked confused. 'I really don't know how to be of any useful assistance.'

'I do understand, and I've sent these mugshots to all the clerks of the courts at North London Crown Court, but you have an excellent memory and I thought I'd just ask you first as you've been so helpful. I'll be checking in with the other clerks tomorrow and I really didn't wish to bother you again then. You've been generous with your time, so if you see me or any of our people around the courts tomorrow, I promise we won't be hunting you down.' She gave a smile, which he returned.

'Er, well . . . Look, I did say I want to help and you're to ask me anything, so I'm glad you did, but I'm sorry – I can't offer up anything on these two fellows. Perhaps they were before my time.'

'Fourteen years, you said?'

He nodded.

'This man was convicted thirteen years ago, but this one, about eleven.'

He shook his head. 'Perhaps I wasn't as old and jaded as I am now. Back then, when I was new, it was all about just trying to do a good job.' He gave a twist of the mouth in regret. 'I'm more experienced now, I suppose; I watch everyone in my courtroom. I did write down some thoughts on that other man we discussed. I'll email those to you tonight. Is that okay?'

'That would be great, thank you.'

He pointed at the mugshots. 'Is this as far as you've got?'

'No, we do have some leads, but I'm a stickler for detail, Mr Jarvis, and I believe in following up every thread and tying it off.' She took a big swig of her tea, obviously preparing to leave and trying to be polite about it. It was fine. He was tired and certainly didn't need company.

'Well, I applaud that. Is there anything else?'

'No, that was it, although I hope you won't mind if we stay in touch?'

'I want you to. Shirley, me, all the clerks are keen to help. This is a terrible business and an awful spotlight on our courts.'

She nodded, swallowed another long swig and sighed, putting her quarter-filled mug down. 'That was delicious, thank you.'

'Where to now?'

'A long walk up the hill.'

'Ah. Well, you have a lovely evening with your friend. Here, let me get your coat.'

He helped her on with her anorak.

'I'll just get my music organised for the walk or I'll never make it up the hill.' She pulled out her iPod from her pocket and threaded the loop of white cord attached to the tiny headphones to come out at the top of the anorak's zip.

'Gosh, how clever,' he noted as they entered the hall. 'All these newfangled things.'

'But don't you do this with your iPod, Mr Jarvis?' She nodded at the basket on the sideboard in the hallway, which contained a small bunch of keys, a separate car key, some gloves and a blue iPod.

He picked up the revolutionary piece of technology and the action woke it up, the tiny window illuminating with the name of a song. They both stared at momentarily. 'This?' He put it back, gave a long sigh and considered. 'It was a gift but I rarely use it. I've never thought to be so cunning with the head-phones though. You've taught me something,' he said, watching her put in one earbud, leaving the other hanging so she could hear him.

'Well, there you go. Now they won't flap about when you ride or walk.' She smiled and he thought she looked embar-rassed . . . or was that nervousness? He couldn't tell with DS Jones. She was charming, with an unnervingly focused gaze, but often awkward, especially now.

'Again, sorry to disturb and . . . and thanks for the cuppa.'

There it was again – suddenly a strange atmosphere around her. 'Night, Sarah.'

He waited until she'd closed the gate on his small front garden and lifted a hand in farewell before he shut the door.

Behind it, he frowned with an increasing sense that DS Sarah Jones had just made a strategic visit, which had nothing to do with the two mugshots she'd asked him to look at.

Sarah walked up the hill a short way before swiftly turning down a street and doubling back on herself to head for the Enfield Chase Station. Every ounce of her was on alert. She knew that to keep teasing at a problem rarely delivered more than frustration; experience had taught her that distraction was a more nourishing mindset for creative thought when *you can't see the wood for the trees*, as her dad often liked to say.

She was certainly stumbling around trees; she couldn't get the whole picture of a forest, but there were daubs of paint on those trees – like signs – leading her somewhere. She needed to let go of the rush of nervous energy so her thoughts could move systematically in the orderly fashion they preferred.

'Sleep on it,' she muttered beneath her breath.

23

Geoffrey Paxton didn't expect it all to happen quite as fast as it did. One moment he was eating rubbery scrambled eggs and baked beans for breakfast and the next he was standing outside the main entrance to HM Prison Pentonville. Everything between those few mouthfuls of egg and now, staring back at the stone edifice that encased what had been his home for more than a decade, was a blur.

Clutched in his grip was a polythene bag with the few possessions he'd arrived with all those years earlier. They were somehow familiar but strange at the same time: a wallet, a cap, a scarf, a windcheater, smokes – they'd be stale – and a cheap lighter. He was wearing his zip-up hoodie, which felt a lot looser than he recalled, and his watch was back on his wrist. It wasn't worth much, but it spoke of his life before prison. Now tossed in the bag were a couple of books, his pastel crayons that he'd acquired through art classes, as well as his favourite drawings, which he'd rolled up carefully. He'd also tossed in the photos of his sister's kids and one of himself with his best pal from school in happier days.

He'd not planned properly, had told his father he'd call from the prison as soon as he knew the arrangements, but there hadn't been time. The processing had been swift, unceremonious and the kindest words spoken were: 'Good luck on the outside, Mr Paxton.' To him it felt like only hatred was holding that farewell wish together . . . certainly a cool threat that the outside would beat him.

There was another threat too, apparently. A foreign-looking bloke called Malek Khan had been to see him the previous afternoon, to warn him that there was a killer selecting criminals for a special sort of justice if they were given an early pass.

'What's this got to do with me?' he'd grumbled at the clean-cut, well-dressed detective with a London accent and a cocky bearing.

Khan had given a light shrug. 'We're just taking some precautions, Mr Paxton.' *Mr Paxton.* What a joke. So polite now. He knew they all thought him scum and would sooner see him dealt with by a lynch mob than enjoy early release or any other government handouts. 'We feel you are a potential target.'

'Me?' He laughed. 'Why?'

'I'll give you some bullet points, sir. You were convicted and sent down for the rape of four women and the attempted rape of a further five women. You have not served your full time.'

'So what?'

The detective with the precisely contoured beard didn't show offence at his tone. 'We believe there is a person targeting prison inmates on early release.'

'There must be dozens,' Geoffrey reasoned.

'And we shall be giving this same advice to anyone in a similar position as yourself, sir,' the detective said in an even tone. 'It's a precaution.'

'Can you protect us all, Mr Malek? Not that I give a toss about the others.' Geoffrey smirked.

'It's Detective Inspector Khan, Mr Paxton. And to answer your question, there will be surveillance on your father's home in Reading when you return.'

'I don't want to be watched. I've spent the last eleven years being stared at by you lot.'

'I'm not a prison officer, Mr Paxton.'

'Same deal . . . all pigs.'

'I'm sorry you see it that way, sir.'

'I couldn't give a rat's arse. No one cares about me and no one's targeting me. I'll be damned if you think I'm going to look over my shoulder from the moment I step out of here. Call your pigs off.'

The detective stood. 'Well, I would urge that you stay alert and contact us if anything doesn't feel right.' He pushed a card across the table. 'That's my direct number. You can call it any time.'

'Like I want to call the fucking police back into my life,' Geoffrey sneered, flicking at the card so it fell on the floor.

'Keep it on hand, Mr Paxton. We're trying to keep you safe.'

'Oh, fuck off, would you?'

'I shall, sir. Is anyone meeting you on your release?'

'My father's eighty – what do you think? I can make my way back to his place easily enough.'

Khan nodded. 'I recommend you head straight back to Reading once you're released.'

'Shove your polite recommendation up your Lebanese arse.'

'I'm Pakistani,' the detective said, and gave Paxton a look that said, *you're too uneducated to know the difference*. 'Enjoy your freedom, Mr Paxton.'

He had left before Paxton could make a smart response. What a load of bollocks. A killer on the loose. Well, no one was interested in him. He was going to enjoy the years he had left as a free man.

One officer had stepped out with him through the small man-gate in the main gates. 'All right then, Paxton. Straight home now. Your best bet, mate, is Caledonian Road and hailing a cab. There's plenty of them.' He had pointed in the right direction. 'You're sure you don't want me to have one called?'

'I'm fine,' Paxton said with a nod. 'See you, Mr Bright.'

'I hope I don't, Geoffrey. I hope I never see you again. Good luck.'

The officer had headed back into the prison as Paxton took his first tentative steps of freedom. Although Mr Bright had told him which way to go, he felt torn between getting to Reading as fast as he could with the little money he'd been given . . . or blowing half of it at the pub, having an ale for the first time in so many years he could believe he'd forgotten the taste. He was feeling optimistic and still defiant that any foreigner should be telling him how to live his life. He chose the pub, promising himself a quick half and maybe some tins to carry home to share with his dad. With no idea where the closest pub was, he decided to just walk for a while in the smug deliciousness of freedom until he found one.

He set off, refusing to look back; he would never return to this place or any jail. He'd seen the therapist regularly – was as convinced as the psychologist that his urges were now under control. And if, for any reason, the devil took over in the driver's seat, he'd seek immediate help. Part of the deal of this early release was his involvement in a new trial for a drug to chemically castrate him. The government was supportive of the scheme and although it was headquartered out of Newcastle University, he had pleaded to be allowed in on the lengthy trial when it was brought to his attention a year ago. His enthusiasm to sign any waiver on side effects, as well as continue regular visits with a psychologist and attend a weekly outpatient clinic for testing of his

testosterone levels, had won through. Paxton genuinely wanted
to rid himself of the formidable desire for violent sex, which from
time to time overwhelmed him.

He held no delusions that he might one day have a regular girlfriend; he was prepared to sacrifice that dream for freedom from
the shadowy twin that had walked by his side during his adult life,
and from the prison doors that incarcerated him. He preferred
the solution of drugs and therapy for his illness. The constant
monitoring by the trial made him feel safe from himself too. It
was their responsibility to keep women secure from his devil, not
his alone.

As far as he was concerned, this was a day to celebrate for
several reasons. He admitted to himself with a rueful smile that
you actually never forget the taste of beer – he could taste it now
in his imagination – and was glad he had opted for the pub first.
He was wholly distracted when he realised someone was calling to
him as he was about to round the corner.

'Mr Paxton . . . Mr Paxton?'

He frowned, looking across the road to where an unremarkable
bespectacled man in a grey parka was waving at him. Should he
know him? He nodded.

The man beckoned. 'Sorry, I didn't want to come into the
main yard,' he said, approaching a few steps and then flashing
some sort of card that said *PRESS* on it. 'Prison guards don't like
us lurking.' He grinned.

Paxton shied. 'How did you know I was getting out now?'

'Oh, ear to the ground, Geoffrey – may I call you Geoff?' He
didn't wait for an answer. 'I've been waiting for you since dawn.
I didn't want to miss you.'

'Well, I've got no business with you or anyone from the press.
Bugger off!' Geoffrey strode away.

'Hear me out, Geoff.'

'Fuck off! Anyone who knows me doesn't call me Geoff. I was warned against strangers.'

The journalist laughed. 'What are you, a child now? Is that what prison has done to you?'

Paxton turned briefly to glare down at the smaller man but kept walking.

'Listen,' the fellow said, hurrying to catch up. 'We will pay very good money to interview you.'

Paxton slowed.

'A big sum,' the journalist reiterated.

Paxton stopped. 'Why would you want to?' he growled.

'There's a side to everyone's story, but moreso, sir, because the general public has a morbid interest in serial criminals. No offence – I know you've done your time.'

Paxton noted that the creepy journalist didn't seem to share the view he'd heard from others that the key to his cell should have been thrown away. 'We're doing a series of feature articles on the criminal mind, but we'll also focus on the rehabilitation of offenders. A little birdie whispered to us that you're on a revolutionary drug trial combined with constant therapy and testing. Well, that alone will earn you some interest. Plus, there are families out there who would like to hear of your remorse, for instance. And we'll pay you plenty to express that.'

'Saying sorry isn't going to turn time back.' Even Paxton thought he sounded more philosophical than most probably thought he could ever be.

'No, and I'm not suggesting you necessarily apologise directly. Perhaps people will leave you alone if you show them who you are . . . that the justice system has made you pay your dues, that you're taking real responsibility for yourself and your illness. That will say a lot about your desire for penance, if not atonement.'

'All those big words.' Paxton shook his head.

The journo gripped his elbow to stop him moving away. 'It might just mean you can live out your days in peace. No one will hound you.'

'Except you, you mean?'

The man chuckled self-consciously. 'Er, so no one's meeting you?'

'Why would they? My dad's an invalid and lives in Reading. I haven't got anyone else.'

'Is that where you're headed?'

'When I feel like it.'

'Want a lift?' The man, who stood a full head smaller than him in his flat chequered cap, lifted his hands in deference. 'No obligation, Mr Paxton. But we can talk on the way. It's a chilly morning and I'm happy to drive you door to door.'

'To Reading?'

The man gave a sound of dismissal. 'What's that? Forty miles? Nothing.'

Would save him a lot of hassle and he could still have his beer locally before he knocked on the old man's door. 'How much?' he demanded and was glad the fellow caught on fast.

'Well, I'm supposed to start at three thousand pounds, but I'm actually permitted to go as high as four and a half. Push me all the way. I'll gladly pay it if you'll give me the exclusive.'

'What's your name?'

'It's Peter Shepherd.' He gestured across the way. 'My car is just over there. I'll take you straight to your father's home in Reading and you can still say no to me, and I promise to leave you alone. Look, here's a hundred quid, all yours, to keep one way or the other . . . even if you say no by the end of this journey.'

Paxton stared with hunger at the two fifty-pound notes, Her Majesty staring benignly back at him from the side of one and a man in a curly wig with pinched lips giving him a look of challenge from the other. That was plenty of beer money right there. 'When do I get the dosh for this story thing?'

'Half up front as soon as you agree . . . so, two thousand, two hundred and fifty pounds as you sign the contract, which we can do at your father's home this morning – I've got all the paperwork in the car. The other half will be paid after the interview and we can do that from the quiet of your father's place as well – I'll come to you at a time that suits.'

Paxton dared himself to negotiate big. 'I'll do it for five big ones.' He lifted the fingers of one hand to ensure the guy understood. 'Or no story.'

The man who intended on killing him gave a crooked smile and took off his glasses to polish them with a clean white handkerchief from his pocket. 'Well, you drive quite the hard bargain. I'm sure I can lean on my management to get that extra, but you have to say yes now – I mean right now – so I can call them and confirm we're on. Then we can organise the fee. We can withdraw five hundred from a local ATM in Reading, but you have to sign the contract before I hand that over.'

'Where's your car?'

'You can't see it from here, but it's parked just over there.' He pointed. 'About two minutes' walk and it's got good heating. Pretty cold spring morning, eh?' He mimed shivering. 'Shall we?'

'I want the first payment immediately; we go straight to the bank,' Paxton demanded. He'd never held that much money in his life. *Five thousand pounds!*

'Done! If you don't have a preference, I can go to any ATM we see once we hit Reading. Actually, if you're going to do it, I'm happy to grab the money in the next few minutes if you wish?'

Paxton hesitated only for a heartbeat, remembering the Paki policeman. Stuff him and his warnings. He gave a nod.

'Come on, then. Let's walk and talk.'

The car was further than he'd anticipated, down a quiet residential street. The guy had lied about the distance, but he was a smiley sort of fellow who kept up a stream of chatter. Plus, he looked harmless with those owl glasses. Paxton decided he could still say no if he chose, although the money was irresistible.

'Seatbelt on, please,' the killer said brightly as he held open the door for his passenger. 'Don't want to be picked up by the police, do we?' He chuckled. 'Right, I think there's an ATM down Caledonian Road . . . okay for you?'

Paxton sneered, landing in the seat and snapping on his seatbelt. 'Yeah. Put two and half thousand quid in my hand and take me straight to Reading, and I'll sign whatever you want,' he said.

'Righto, that's all fine with me.' The man who called himself Peter walked around to the other side and began fussing with getting his parka off, opening the back door and placing it on the seat. Paxton looked away, trying to get his bearings after so long on the inside. He didn't see his driving companion suddenly reach over from the back and stab something into him. It took Paxton a moment to feel the sting of the wound. He watched, confused, as the journalist closed the back door, stood outside staring at him and then deliberately held up the key to show he was locking him alone inside the car. He heard a solid clicking sound as all the doors obeyed the command.

'Not the bank or Reading, actually. Straight to hell, Geoffrey Paxton, for you,' Peter said through the closed window.

'What the f—' His hand flew to the site of the sting. 'What was that?'

'Propofol,' the journalist said through the glass. 'Don't fight. Just relax.' He grinned. 'I'm sure that's something you whispered to all your victims. Well, this is for them but especially for the mother of four you abused so heinously that she needed several surgeries after you'd finished with her.'

Geoffrey Paxton's last sensible thought was strangely abstract . . . that he'd forgotten to ask the journalist where he worked. The face of the smart-arse detective loomed large in his mind, waggling an admonishing finger. *I tried to warn you.*

'Bye-bye, Geoff,' he heard before he lost consciousness.

Later, with the body dumped down by the canal, no longer dreaming of beer . . . no longer dreaming at all, the killer made a call.

'It's done' was all he said before he rang off and slipped the Mazda into first, pulling back out into traffic to make for the garage where he hid the car.

Lauren was thrilled to have an appointment with Judge Moira Leland, especially in her new capacity as a feature writer for a weekend magazine that had clout. Jack had been as good as his promise and all the arrangements had moved fast and slick to transfer her within the publishing group. Rowena had wished her well, giving her a nod of approval that implied she wasn't surprised.

She had arrived at the St John's Wood apartment promptly at eight-thirty as the judge had requested. Judge Leland opened the door, glancing at her watch and speaking into a phone. 'Right, thanks for that,' she said, and her smile lifted to see Lauren. 'On time. I'm impressed.'

'I wouldn't dare do otherwise. Thank you so much for seeing me.'

'Come in. I'm sorry I don't have very long.'

'No, that's fine. This was always just an introductory meeting so you could assess what I hope to achieve with the feature.'

Lauren entered the elegant reception hall of the judge's apartment, where parquet flooring sprawled in all directions.

'This way, Ms Starling.'

'Please, call me Lauren.'

'Can I offer you anything?' the judge asked, showing Lauren into a large drawing room flooded with sunlight from two tall windows. Books lined three of the walls and the fourth was a gallery of artworks, she noted as she lowered herself onto a huge, plump sofa in a muddy chalk colour, littered with sumptuous cushions. 'I was just having a peppermint tea,' the judge said, reaching for a Japanese porcelain cup that had no handle.

'No, but thank you. These are beautiful; colours like jewels,' Lauren remarked, gesturing at the cushions while she dug into her bag for a notebook and her pen.

'A traditionalist,' Moira Leland said, nodding at the notebook.

Lauren smiled. 'I find a lot of people won't open up if I switch a recorder on.'

'And you're sure I will?'

'No, I'm not. I'd like to try, though, because I know that you are someone who has an opinion on lenient sentences.'

'Oh? Who tells you that?'

Lauren held the gimlet stare that matched the scarily sharp haircut, which had greyed to steely perfection for this statuesque woman. *She must have her hair trimmed each week for that exquisite line to be kept*, she mused, then realised the judge was waiting for her to reply.

'No one. I have looked at your cases and all of them seem to favour leniency.'

'And this is what your feature is about?'

'Yes, Your Honour.'

'Well, I have respect for *Britain's Voice*.'

Lauren felt a soft thrill to hear someone else refer to the top publication she was now writing for. 'I promise it will be balanced and thoroughly researched.'

'And you wish to talk to me about why so many of our worst criminals seem to do so little jail time in the eyes of the general public . . . does that sum it up?'

'Perfectly.'

Judge Leland nodded, sipped. 'Do you know how many people are in jail across Britain right now?'

'Around seventy-five thousand?'

'A little higher, actually.'

'Near enough double from ten years ago, as I understand it.'

The judge nodded. 'And the average annual cost to keep a prisoner?'

'Er . . . nearly forty thousand pounds per prisoner.'

Moira Leland sighed. 'Does that trouble you?'

'In what way?'

'That all that money might be spent more wisely in our health or education system.'

'Does it matter what I think?'

'You're one of the public.'

'To be honest, Judge Leland, I think I'd rather know I was safe from a rapist. My research shows that more than forty per cent of adult men in prison are there for sexual offences.'

'Exactly! And do you think that when they are released they magically stop being sexual offenders? Some maybe, because they've got old. But generally it's unlikely that those urges and motivators change — not without some intervention. The statistics show that long-term prison sentences do not achieve rehabilitation, and it's my belief that we have to find ways to make serial sexual offenders, for instance, more accountable, by combining their prison sentences with both physical and mental therapies.'

Lauren nodded. 'May I ask, are you and your fellow judges under pressure to not jail people?'

Judge Leland gave a slightly cynical laugh. 'No. But we're certainly encouraged to be aware of the crush in our prison system. Locking people away is all very well but there's an enormous toll on the public purse, and recidivism rates are real.'

'I can hear your frustration.'

The judge shrugged. 'Absolutely. I and every other judge has to weigh up sending a man down for his second or third rape, for instance, knowing he'll likely be back at it. And even if we do jail him for the maximum term, it will be reduced . . . it's just a nasty cycle. I find it easier to campaign for therapies that cut that vicious cycle. Less time in jail, more money to spend on finding solutions to sexual offenders. And that's just one area – there's the thieves, the hardened criminals, the drug suppliers and sellers, the murderers . . . on and on it goes. Once we send them down, half of them start to suffer from depression and anxiety – and how do you think that plays out within the prison system? And then when they're released?'

'It's a question with no answer, really, isn't it?'

Moira Leland held up her cup as though making a toast. 'Welcome to my world, Ms Starling. I know the public want harsher sentences – put them away, castrate them . . . some might even argue for capital punishment in some instances. I respect that view, but my role unfortunately is less black and white. Courts wrestle with this dilemma every day, every trial.'

Lauren nodded slowly, thinking on what the judge had said. 'With your permission, I'd like to schedule an appointment to talk to you at length.'

'Who else are you speaking with?'

'Well, I guess to keep it balanced I would need to speak with a judge who believes in dishing out the maximum sentence.'

'You should. I would recommend Judge Edwin Fenshaw. Old-school, and will argue his position eloquently.'

Lauren smiled. 'Thank you. Is he at North London Crown Court?'

'No, the Old Bailey. And if I were you, I'd organise to speak with Justice Laurence Brimfield; he's at Blackfriars these days. He takes a sort of midline view, you could say.'

'What about the clerks of the court? Are they worth talking to?'

Judge Leland shrugged. 'The more the merrier, I suppose, if you want to take the temperature of the legal system. But they run the courts, as you know; they have no say in what actually happens.'

'Do you talk cases over with your clerk, Your Honour?'

'Yes. Often.'

'Then I probably will follow through on a meeting I've arranged with one of the clerks from North London Crown Court.'

'Who's that?'

'Brian Jarvis; he's being very helpful.'

The judge nodded with a soft smile. 'He's a lovely man, that's why. He's also been around the longest, so you'll get a solid snapshot of the courts I work from.'

'You don't work with him, though?'

'Only once,' she said, glancing at her watch and managing to stand up in a way that Lauren felt sure she should practise at home for its grace. She understood it was time to gather up her things. 'It was a terrible case and I was glad for Mr Jarvis and his calm, very reliable and pedantic running of the engine room, so to speak. He kept all parties very clearly on track.'

'Was this the Davey Robbins case?'

'You have done your homework, Ms Starling. I'm impressed. I agree to see you again. Call my clerk – her name's Andrea – and let's set something up for next week. You can come to my chambers if you wish.'

Lauren shook the judge's hand, noting well-kept fingernails polished with clear varnish.

'That would be perfect, thank you. This is a lovely apartment, if you don't mind me saying. Do you live here alone?'

'I do, since my husband died. This was his choice though. I'm sure you didn't fail to notice Lord's Cricket Ground all but next door.' The judge grinned.

Lauren stepped back across the threshold and turned. 'My dad's a big cricket fan.'

'Oh, Gerald was just crazy for the MCC and I'd lose him for days. He could stroll there – he loved it.'

'I can hear in your voice you miss him.'

'Do you have someone in your life?'

Lauren smiled coyly. 'There's someone new who would be so very easy to fall in love with, but I suspect pain only awaits me.'

The judge frowned. 'Gorgeous, confident career woman like you . . . why do you say that?'

'I think he'll break my heart. Not deliberately; his line of work doesn't make for an easy lifestyle if you're the partner.'

'Oh, what does he do?'

'He's in the police force. A senior detective.'

Moira Leland nodded. 'Well, don't be alone too long. I do it well enough, but I'm decades older and it's not a state to envy.' She smiled.

'Oh, forgive me, I haven't had a chance to ask you about your feelings on the criminals you'd tried and sent down who have been murdered. I hope you won't mind if we touch on that next week?'

The judge looked pained. 'What a conundrum that is. Yes, no problem – we can discuss it next week. I've been contacted by a detective from Scotland Yard, no less, who has made it clear to me, despite my protestations, that his boss has ordered a security detail.'

'I think you should.'

'It's preposterous. More waste that could be spent where it's better needed.'

'You're not frightened?'

'Why should I be? I agree it's bizarre that my cases are the target, but whoever is killing these people is killing criminals. The grudge is obviously with them rather than the court system that put them away. I'd like to wring the neck of the person who got it into their head that I need protection.'

Lauren decided not to tell her it was the same man she was not going to fall in love with.

'Goodbye, Lauren. Good luck with your research.'

Lauren left the leafy, quiet neighbourhood. It was hard to believe it was barely a couple of miles from this affluent street to busy Charing Cross. She walked to St John's Wood Underground station and caught the Jubilee Line to Green Park, changing onto the Piccadilly line north to Wood Green and the criminal courts in North London to meet with Brian Jarvis.

As she hurtled through the dark tunnels, she decided that one day she was going to live in an apartment not dissimilar to Judge Leland's and have that totally powerful approach to life that she seemed to possess.

24

Mal Khan arrived at Jack's office. 'Sir? Sorry to interrupt.'

'Yep?' Jack said distractedly. He had been listening to the audio file of the emergency call made by Brownlow's killer but switched it off. 'This guy is brazen,' he said, something nagging at him to take notice, but Mal was waiting. 'What's up?'

'Paxton was released at eight this morning.'

'Yes. You said we've got Thames Valley police in position around the father's place in Reading.'

'They've been there since the dawn chorus.'

'So?'

His DI looked doubtful. 'So . . . he never arrived at his father's.'

Jack's attention snapped to the moment in sharp focus as he frowned. 'He was wearing a cuff, right?'

'That's what they told me yesterday, but I've got one of ours confirming with Pentonville now.'

'Okay. But definitely released at zero eight hundred?'

Mal nodded. 'The doors closed behind him at less than a minute past. An officer called John Bright walked him out and made sure no one was lurking around. Paxton was given information about catching a cab, but the CCTV shows he left alone. The cameras followed him halfway down the road safely.'

'Right,' Jack said, thoughtfully. 'I probably wouldn't blame him if he headed for the nearest pub. In fact, what is the nearest pub?'

Mal frowned. 'Er . . . I think it might be that three-storey place called Balmoral Castle, is it?'

'McLaughlins, I think, sir,' one of the constables said, arriving with a note for Mal. 'Paxton is definitely wearing an ankle cuff. Part of his release rules. Here's who to call.' She left with a nod.

Jack sighed. 'Get onto it.'

'Righto!' Mal said, ducking out of the office.

He was in the midst of standing up when it hit Jack like a punch. *Righto* . . . that was it! He looked up to see Kate arriving.

'Inspiration or horror?' she asked, noting his expression.

'The former.'

'Good. Tell me,' she said, placing a small cup of coffee on his desk for him. 'That's the one you like . . . purple.'

'Do I?' He smiled, took the cup and sipped. He scratched his head, frowning, as though reaching for something.

'Well, don't keep me in suspense,' she said.

'The killer has an expression. He says *righto*. I mean, it's common enough, though not a word I use – but Mal did just now.'

'And?'

'Our killer said *righto* on his emergency call. He might have disguised his voice and probably disguised his shoe size, but, perhaps, in his excitement, his regular vocabulary remained intact.'

'You're basing this on one phone call?' She didn't sound convinced.

'No. He used the identical expression when he attacked and tied up Chingford. But here's the thing, Kate.'

She sat forward.

'I've heard it recently.'

'You just said Mal uttered it.'

Jack shook his head, his gaze turning distant. 'Someone else . . .'

'Well,' she said, looking bemused, 'that little knot is best waited for . . . it will loosen itself.'

He accepted her rationale with a sigh. 'Have you heard about Paxton?'

'Don't tell me,' she said, as if warding off bad news.

He looked back at her steadily.

'I thought we were watching him.' Her voice was filled with disbelieving despair.

He explained. 'Either he's having a long and understandable early-morning walk around London waiting for pubs to open . . .' He expressed a look of worry. 'Or he's been snatched somewhere near the prison.'

'Fuck!'

'That's a pound coin from you, please, Kate,' Joan said, striding in, no smile this time. 'Jack, very bad news, I'm afraid.'

'Please don't say Geoffrey Paxton, Joan,' he warned.

'All right, I won't. I'll say instead that a newly released inmate from Pentonville Prison has turned up at the Whittington emergency unit having been dragged from the Regent's Canal. I'm very sorry, both of you, but although he arrived breathing – just – he has died.'

She watched both of them sigh out despair and hang their heads.

'Sir.' It was Mal.

'We've heard,' Jack said, standing and flinging a stapler across the room.

'I don't have a penalty for stapler flinging,' Joan admitted, 'but I do have a glimmer of good news for you.'

Jack took a breath and joined all the other gazes staring at Joan. 'We may have a witness. One of those yummy-mummy joggers. Here's her address.'

'Let's go,' Jack said, and Joan held up some car keys. 'Thanks. Mal, I want that CCTV scrutinised. Anything yet on the footprint?'

'Yes, sir. Definitely not a size nine. The weight distribution wasn't right. He deliberately wore bigger sneakers, as we guessed.'

Sarah was arriving as Jack and Kate were moving with haste.

'Er, sir . . .'

'Not now, Sarah.'

'Please, it's—'

'Back soon. Get the others to bring you up to speed.'

They left her in the corridor, not waiting for the lift but using the fire stairs.

Lauren was seated in North London Crown Court's cafeteria, waiting for the clerk of the court. Her phone lit and hummed quietly against the table.

She recognised the number she'd dialled earlier. 'Is this Amy?' she asked, excitement trilling through her but not showing in her voice.

'It is. You're Lauren Starling?'

'I am. Thank you for calling back.' She listened for more but only heard silence. 'Amy, I'm a journalist.'

'I see.'

'I was hoping I might come and see you, please?'

'Why?'

'It's about the death of David Robbins.'

'No, I'm sorry.'

'I won't be asking you about—'

'I don't want to recall that time.'

Lauren took a low breath, glancing at the clock. Her clerk was three minutes late. 'I understand.'

'I don't think you can, or you wouldn't have asked.'

'May I at least brief you on what I'm doing? It's not what you might think.' Silence again. She'd take that as permission. 'I'm preparing an in-depth feature article for a serious publication called *Britain's Voice* about the public's despair at lenient sentencing for serious criminals. Even Judge Moira Leland, who you'll recall from the trial, has agreed to go on record and be interviewed.'

'He served a few years of an already short sentence. Don't expect me to feel an iota of sympathy for him.'

'I don't expect you to . . . and, frankly, I have no qualms about saying to you that Robbins got what he deserved. But that's between us. As an investigative journalist, I must take a neutral position; my role is to lay out facts. It's up to readers to weigh up the evidence and make a decision, but if enough people have those facts and can make an informed opinion, then maybe the lawmakers will have to listen. My point is that this article is not about the terrible crime against you and your family. Instead, I want to shine a spotlight on why serious and violent criminals are being given light sentences, while the victims and their families suffer the life sentence, come what may. It's not sensationalist or lurid, that's a promise. I will present the generalised details of your case, but be assured it isn't the focus, nor are any of the other cases I'll refer to. It's about sentencing and the judicial system, not the crimes themselves.'

'Then I will talk to you, but I don't want to see you,' Amy said defiantly. I'm sorry. I'm not very good with strangers any more. I'm returning your call and the one from the police and that's it. I won't be discussing this again.'

So, Jack's team were onto Amy. Hardly a surprise. 'That's fine. Frankly, I'm just grateful you'll talk to me—'

'When is this article coming out?'

'Well, I suspect it will be three months in the making, at least by the time I do all the due diligence that the managing editor will demand.'

'All right. When do you want to do the interview?'

'How about . . . oh, hang on, Amy, someone's brought me a message.' She looked up at a young woman.

'Are you Lauren?' She nodded. 'Mr Jarvis asked me to let you know that he's running very late and will understand if you can't wait.'

'How long will he be?'

'I'm afraid I can't confirm but I would say about an hour.'

'That's fine. I'll wait.'

The young woman smiled. 'I'll tell him.'

Lauren returned to her call. 'Amy, sorry about that. Actually, we don't have to make another time. We can talk right now if you're up to it?' She waited, her breath all but held.

'What I'd like to say is that while victims like me obviously feel very strongly about the lenient sentencing, there are people out there who were not connected to me or my family and still they feel so angry and betrayed by the judicial system. There is no justice . . . that's how I feel anyway.'

'Your attackers—'

'They weren't just attackers. They murdered my grandmother in front of me and they laughed about it. The men who raped me got just a few years, yet they changed my life forever . . . Davey Robbins got out in less than four years. He changed the trajectory of my life. He changed my whole outlook. Now I suffer panic attacks even when I'm in the garden. I can't meet my friends outside of my home, and attending a party is impossible for me. I can't go on holiday with my family. I can't go to university. But the justice system wanted to forgive Davey Robbins and give him another chance. What about me? What about my grand-mother? What about our family? We've all suffered at losing Granny . . . my poor brother is too scared to leave us and pursue his life, just in case I top myself or something. Where's *our* second chance? I'm glad Davey Robbins is dead.'

Lauren swallowed but let Amy talk on. This was gold. She had simply unscrewed the lid on a bottle of fizzy drink that had been shaken up, just waiting to explode. 'I hope he was as frightened as I was when that man found him and killed him. I feel no shame in saying that. I wish I could thank him properly for his—' She suddenly stopped.

Lauren blinked. 'Amy?'

'I've said too much. I shouldn't have mentioned him.'

'Who? Davey Robbins?' she asked gently.

'No, the man who killed him.'

Lauren paused, feeling an instinctive twist in her stomach begin to knot. She opened her mouth and hesitated, then let the thought out. 'Amy . . . do you know him?' Her tone was soft.

'I don't know him, no.'

'But you know of him . . . how?' She could almost see Amy shrugging, not wanting to answer.

'I don't want to say any more.'

'It will not appear in the article if you instruct me not to include something that you want to share.'

'I've said too much. He said it wouldn't matter, but I owe him.'

'Amy, have you spoken with the man who killed Davey Robbins?'

'No. He sent me a letter, that's all.'

Fuck, she mouthed silently, wishing she could tell Jack immediately. Instead she schooled her voice to sound calm. 'You sound relieved.'

There was a long pause. Lauren held her nerve.

'I am. I'm not ashamed to be happy he's dead, but I haven't been sleeping, thinking that now a different sort of killer knows where I live and . . .'

'Amy, you have to let the police know.'

'I suppose. But I also want him to get away with it, you know. He's the one giving us justice. Now Davey Robbins won't hurt anyone else.'

'Can I tell you something?'

'What?'

'I think you should know that the man who killed Davey Robbins has almost certainly killed others.'

'You mean in your opinion?'

'No. Fact. The police have whispered to me that there are a number of unexplained deaths that they believe can be attributed to this same killer.' That won another silence. 'I know you're wrestling with this, but murder is murder, Amy. And while one killer seems somehow much worse than the other, they are both taking lives. It really does amount to the same thing and the police can't treat him differently.'

'Why is that my problem?'

'It's not, but . . . I can hear it's on your conscience, and now unfortunately it's on mine.'

'You mean you'll have to tell the police?'

'If I don't, I'm perverting the course of justice . . . even if for you, such a thing doesn't exist.'

'Go ahead. Do what you like,' Amy sneered but there was something contrived in her tone. It occurred to Lauren that this was precisely what Amy wanted: to avoid being the one to turn him in, even though she knew the police had to be informed.

'And if the police visit?'

'They want to talk to me anyway . . . some Hawksworth bloke.'

'I know him. He's a top guy.'

'I don't care. I won't give them anything . . . unless they force me to.'

Again she heard the little gate that Amy left open for herself. Clearly she did have a conscience; she knew what the killer had done was not right.

'Amy, he's killed at least seven people that I know about, though Robbins was perhaps the most brutal.'

She heard the soft gasp even though Amy tried to cover it.

'I'm going to call you back. Is that all right?'

'It's fine. I'm tired anyway.'

'Okay, Amy, thank you. Talk later.' Lauren hung up and immediately dialled Jack.

'Hawksworth.'

'Where are you?'

'On the way to see Amy Clarke after a yummy mummy drew a bit of a blank.'

'Pardon?'

'Doesn't matter. Amy is next.'

'Good. Ask her to tell you about the letter.'

'What letter?'

'Allow her to tell you.'

'Cryptic. Are you trying to stay one step ahead?'

'Hardly. If I was, I'd already know what your middle name is, or your favourite food.'

She could imagine that grin of his . . . could wish it belonged only to her, but that was the stuff of teenage daydreams and Lauren had become a realist. And that new pragmatic side reminded her, as she gave him a smiling goodbye, that Jack Hawksworth was not for keeps.

25

Jack decided to take the Underground followed by another train, preferring not to get stuck in mid-morning traffic. As he alighted at Winchmore Hill, still thinking about the letter Lauren had warned him about, his phone rang.

'Hawskworth?'

'It's me,' Kate said. 'I got the team to study all the cars in the surrounding streets around Southsea, and we were able to watch the residents coming and going. Three cars arrived into various parking spots in the early hours on the night that Brownlow was murdered. Pathology tells us he died not long after nine-thirty. The closest in time was a Mazda hatchback parked at nine fifty-four in a nearby street, number plate illegible.'

'Okay. Did we get a look at who was driving?'

'No, it's murky. It's a bloke, though. He walks down the street and we lose him for a while but pick him back up at Fratton Railway Station. He catches the last train to London, which left just before ten-thirty.'

'Is it just the timing that has your radar up?'

'Yes. The car remains untouched and in the early hours of the next morning, a different person picks it up. A woman. Again, still very dark when she departs.'

'Why is that suspicious?'

'I'm clutching at straws. The street is not resident-only parking so it would be a good spot if the killer needed to hide the car.'

'In plain sight, you mean?'

'Mmm, yes. I suppose the timing could be a coincidence. It could be his wife picking it up and driving back to London.'

'Do we know which house?'

'No. She arrived in the CCTV shot as she walked down the street.'

Jack felt a flutter of hope. 'Did we get a visual?'

'This is the thing, Jack, and why it's caught my interest. It's like they know. She was wearing a beanie and a scarf curled up high, dressed all in black with a big overcoat so we can't really distinguish her shape. She's tall. In any other situation I'd think I was imagining it, but when I watch the footage I'm convinced she's deliberately dipping her head when the camera can get its best view. He did the same. He had on a parka, a flat cap and a scarf pulled up high around his mouth. He's short.'

'Slightly mismatched?'

'If they're a couple, then yes, on the surface.'

'They could have been down for a few days by the seaside.'

'In winter?'

'Well, they may have family in Portsmouth they were visiting. It's too loose. That said, he has similarities with the guy who killed Peggy Markham. He wore a parka and a flat cap, if I'm not mistaken.'

'You're not.'

'Keep the team at it, then. How's Mal going?'

'Going through everything he can with Hugh Pettigrew, the

clerk for courtroom eleven. I'm hoping to speak with Judge Leland shortly, but she is hard to pin down. Forensics is back with details of the caravan. Lots of different DNA, as you can imagine. None that matches Davey Robbins, so he never took him inside.'

An idea broke through his mind like a slash of sunlight. 'Can you find out who rented it after the Polish musician moved out? Awfully convenient for the killer to have that isolated caravan, emptied of the previous tenant, and so easy for him to work in a quiet place near the roadside bend where he snatched Robbins and he could guarantee he wouldn't be interrupted.'

'Right, that makes sense. Ali wants a word.'

'Okay, put her on.'

'Sir?'

'What have you got, Ali?'

'I should have the list later today of all the Spurs members and the owner said it will show their purchases.'

'Excellent. We'll talk later then.'

Kate took back her phone. 'Where are you?'

'I'm with Amy Clarke if anyone needs me.' Jack hung up, feeling the first glimmer of optimism he'd experienced in days.

Now off the train, he made his way to Amy Clarke's house. An older woman with a pinched expression answered the door.

'Mrs Clarke?' She nodded. 'I'm Detective Superintendent Jack Hawksworth.'

'Good morning. We've been expecting you. Please come in.'

Behind her in the hallway he was met by a man. 'Jack Hawksworth,' he said, extending a hand.

The man shook it. 'Jim Clarke. Amy's through here.'

Jack paused. 'Would it be all right with you both if I spoke with Amy alone? I am not going to be referring to the rape – that's a promise.'

They regarded each other. Mrs Clarke nodded. 'Come on, Jim.' She looked at Jack. 'There's filter coffee just made.'

'Thank you. I won't need long and I promise to tiptoe through all my questions.'

Amy's father walked him down and introduced him to a young woman who was curled up in an armchair, looking out across the garden through the long café-style doors. She appeared sullen; that didn't bode well.

'Morning, Amy. I'm Jack.'

She looked up and he realised his initial assessment was wrong. She was simply melancholy, he deduced, as she welcomed him with a solid attempt at a smile. 'I've been speaking to someone I think you know. She's a journalist.'

'Lauren Starling?'

'Yes. She's nice.'

'May I?' he said, pointing to a nearby sofa and winning a nod. He lowered himself to sit. 'Lauren's solid. You can rely on her.'

'So you don't mind me talking to the media?'

Jack shrugged. 'That's your business, Amy. I just want to ask you a few simple questions. This is not about the crimes committed and not about the trial either, but simply about the courtroom itself, actually.'

'Okay,' she said, sounding relieved. 'What do you need to know?'

'I know you attended every day of the trial. Were there any other regular attendees that you perhaps didn't know before the trial began?'

She thought about this. 'Dad came with me every day. Mum couldn't stomach it, but she was there when I took the stand.' She paused for a moment, then shook her head. 'There were several people who came now and then. I began to recognise them. Some journalists, a couple of the police were very supportive and turned up, but no . . . you mean, can I recall someone who could potentially be the person who killed Davey Robbins?'

He lifted a shoulder in a half shrug of encouragement. 'Not really but I'll think on it.'

'How do you feel about his death?'

She gave him a look that he was sure could stop traffic. 'How do you think I feel?'

'I'm asking,' he said, equally direct but not firm; he kept his tone even and gentle.

She blinked. 'I'm ecstatic is how I feel.'

He nodded. 'That's understandable. Did you know that Don Pratchett died in prison?'

'Hooray.' Her voice had no joy in it. Jack waited a beat and she filled it, switching topics. 'How well do you know Lauren, the journalist?'

'Well enough.' He smiled.

'Do you like her?'

'I do.' He kept his expression neutral.

'Did she tell you?' No need to play ignorant. He nodded. 'Then she must like you.'

'Will you show me?'

'I don't especially want to betray the one person who has done more for our family than the justice system.'

He held his tongue; she didn't need a lecture. She wouldn't have mentioned it if she didn't have every intention of showing him.

'But I also don't want to be an accessory or anything.'

'You won't. But I would like to see that letter, Amy.'

She reluctantly put her hand down the side of the armchair and pulled out an envelope. She'd obviously expected him to ask. Jack immediately reached into the messenger bag he'd put on the floor beside him and withdrew some thin gloves, which he quickly stretched over his hands. 'May I?' She handed it to him with a scowl, although he sensed relief. 'Have your parents seen this?'

'Mum has. She said not to tell anyone. She agrees with me that whoever sent this has done us a favour.'

'I can imagine,' he said without sounding judgemental. He scanned the letter, feeling excitement quicken. This was him. The killer was here in the room with them and he had even antici-pated that Amy would likely give him up; didn't hold it against her. 'Listen, Amy, I have to take this. It's crucial evidence of guilt. It might also deliver us some clues.'

She nodded with reluctance. 'I hope you don't catch him.'

'Thanks for not standing in my way, though.'

'I thought I liked Judge Leland but she turned out to be the most treacherous.'

'What do you mean?'

'She gave Davey Robbins just a few years. If she'd had to go through what we went through that day . . . or if it was her daughter who was raped and her mother who was murdered in cold blood, she might not have been as lenient.'

'It never seems fair, but she and all judges are constrained by the law.'

'That's crap.'

'Amy, I'm the last person to debate this with because I'm on your side,' he said, trying to lower the passion in the room. 'People like me and my team spend every waking minute of our working lives trying to hunt the bad guys down, and when we do, they get off, or they get a light sentence, or they're let out early.'

'Well, do something!' she bleated. 'Show them how little respect you have for the judicial system. Protest, at least! It's like they're being paid off.'

'Paid off? Judges? No. I doubt that.'

'Why does it feel like it, then? If you were Judge Leland – a woman who should sympathise with the terror of the crime – why wouldn't you give Davey Robbins the harshest sentence that you possibly could? We all knew he was lying. Even the judge knew it – I might be young but I'm hardly stupid and I could read the judge's disgust as much as the next person. The clerk of the court even apologised for the way the trial was going. He suggested that I didn't come in any more but nothing was going to keep me away.'

'This was Hugh Pettigrew, right?'

She shook her head. 'No, I think his name was Brian, but he was a really nice gentleman. He was always so polite and kind to my family.'

Jack frowned. So Brian Jarvis had shifted courtrooms?

'Anyway, at least now I feel we got our justice with both of those evil men dead . . . But we don't have Granny, and I don't have my life, and don't tell me it will get easier, because I'm not interested any more.' She turned to look out the window again.

He nodded. 'You know, I felt like that a couple of years ago when the woman I was seeing was murdered.'

Amy's head whipped around in shock. 'Murdered? Really?'

'Yes. I felt like giving up on everything because I felt like I'd failed somehow.'

'But you didn't give up?'

'No, I absolutely did for a while, and it was probably the best thing. I stopped work, I gave up my house, I put my life on hold. And I fled.'

She gave him a soft smile of shared understanding.

'I travelled, I took time away from everything familiar so that when I did return – as I knew I must – it would feel different and also distant.'

'Is it easier?'

'The pain is easier to bear,' he admitted. 'And I'm glad I've picked up the threads of my life again. But the memories travel with me. You can't escape what you know. Time simply makes the wound scar over and makes it easier to look at. Just take the time you need, Amy, to get that distance, but never give up on yourself. Your granny wouldn't like that.'

She chewed her lip. 'Yeah, that's what Dad says.'

'He's right. You've been incredible to get this far. Don't stop.' He stood. 'Thank you for seeing me and for this,' he said, holding up the letter.

Amy shrugged. 'I wonder if you'll catch him.'

Jack gave a sad smile. 'I know I will.'

Jack was waiting in the reception of Martin Sharpe's office; his boss was running late but Jack was enjoying the view, looking out across London, which for the most part had nothing to fear from the man he was stalking. He was thinking about what Amy had snarled about Judge Leland. Why hadn't she thrown as many years as she could at Robbins? At least he would have gone to prison feeling the horror of knowing he had a long sentence to serve.

Jack's thoughts were disturbed when his mobile jangled softly in his pocket. He grimaced. 'Sorry,' he murmured in the direction of Sharpe's secretary.

She waved away the interruption. 'Happens all day with everyone . . . these mobile phones will be the death of us.'

He grinned at her while answering the call. 'Hawksworth?'

'Boss, it's Sarah.'

'Hello. I'm sorry I had to rush away earlier.'

'Er, are you still too busy?'

She heard him gust a low laugh. 'Not if you need me.'

'I do, sir.'

'Now?'

'If that would be possible, yes.'

'Of course. Do we need Kate in on this?'

'I'd like to just run some thoughts by you.'

He got the message. 'That's fine. Hang on.' He looked up. 'Marjorie?'

She smiled over her glasses at him. 'Is it Mirror? Do you need to go?'

He pointed at the phone. 'It's urgent, yes.'

'Go. I'll explain. He's running late anyway.'

The lift looked as though it was inching its way up the various levels. Sensing Sarah's excitement – if he could put it that way – he didn't wish to stand around waiting for the lift to haul itself up each floor, so he took the fire stairs, quickly. He arrived into Mirror's suite and nodded at Joan, who was busy on a call and lifted a hand in greeting. Scanning for Sarah, he saw she was already seated in his office, in her brown anorak. It wasn't cold today. She pushed her glasses up her nose as he arrived and stood.

'Hello, sir. Thank you for coming so quickly.'

'Sounds as though something's about to burst out of you.'

She gave an embarrassed half smile. 'I think it might be. It's been threatening since last night.'

'I'm all yours,' he said, opening his palms. 'Impress me.'

'Yes, sir,' she said, sitting forward. 'I have some odd observations I'd like to run through. In isolation they are easy to ignore, but I feel there're enough of them to make my skin prickle.'

He nodded. 'And skin prickles are gravely important in our business. Never feel reluctant to share them.' He smiled to reassure her.

'Okay.' She took a deep breath. 'It's about Brian Jarvis.'

Jack frowned as the man's name came up for the second time that day.

'I don't believe the big glasses he wears are real.'

It was such an unexpected remark that Jack sat back, but he knew to school his body language to remain encouraging.

She continued. 'I could be mistaken, but you know the other night when we were going through the CCTV footage?'

He nodded.

'He turned to speak to you, and I was to his side but sort of at an angle.' She made an attempt to gesture her position using her hands. 'Anyway, because his glasses are so large, I could just see through them.'

He caught on fast. 'And there's no magnification?'

'Not that I could tell, sir. To me they looked like clear glass.'

'But you're not one hundred per cent certain?'

'No, I'm not. He probably does need glasses for reading. As I suggested, on its own this idea seems inconsequential, but there is something else that's nagging at me about him.'

'Go on, Sarah,' he encouraged her, as a thought began to nibble on the edge of his mind too.

'I went to his house yesterday.'

'Whatever for?'

'I shouldn't have, but I couldn't stop the nag.'

'I know that feeling, but Sarah—'

'Sir, I'm aware it was unwise. But I felt I needed to catch Mr Jarvis slightly off balance. So far he's . . . well, he's sort of always been in control of the situation whenever we've been with him.' She shrugged. 'At North London Crown Court, in here showing us the CCTV footage. We trust him – why wouldn't we?'

'Okay?' She was leading him and he needed to go with her.

'So I thought if I took him slightly by surprise and thus unprepared, I might be able to rattle his almost constantly cheerful and genial composure. I can't ever imagine him raising his voice, let alone a hand.'

'True.'

'I used the pretext of urgently needing to show him mugshots of two prisoners about to be released early. Don't worry, they were fakes, and I am confident he accepted my excuse of turning up on his doorstep en route to a friend's for the evening.'

'Wow, Sarah. We'll make a detective inspector of you yet.'

'I hope so,' she said, and for the first time since knowing her, he glimpsed her ambition. The fact that she didn't encourage others to call her Sarge, or even refer to her status, didn't mean she didn't want to move up the ranks. Plus, he'd always trusted her judgement as he trusted it now; she was an asset to any team.

'So what happened?'

'Well, nothing. He responded with calm confusion that he had no idea who these men were – obviously – but he didn't give any sign of the sort of reaction that I was looking for.'

'What were you looking for?'

'I thought he might be interested in these two men – perhaps ask some questions about their crimes, their sentences. But he said nothing. He didn't even ask their names. Him being a Crown Court official, I suppose I anticipated more.'

'Absolutely no interest?'

'None, sir. No body language suggesting otherwise.'

'Do you think he sensed a trap?'

She shook her head. 'Not at that stage, no.'

Now Jack was confused. Was she lining the mild-mannered Brian Jarvis up as a potential suspect or not? 'Forgive me, but—'

She held up a finger. 'Just a couple more oddities, sir. Mr Jarvis speaks warmly of his family, would you agree?'

'I would.'

'His wife passed away about fifteen years ago but he didn't say why or how. He also mentioned a daughter with daughters of her own.'

'Okay?'

'I was in his family sitting room and there wasn't a single photograph of them anywhere at all that I noted.'

'I don't have family photos around my home. Doesn't mean I'm hiding something.'

'You're not married, sir. You don't have children, if I'm not mistaken, and a grandparent tends to be even more adoring than a parent. Would you agree?'

'In general, yes. I do have a nephew and niece.'

'Do you have a photo of them anywhere in your home?'

'No.'

She looked crestfallen.

'But I used to. In the last house I did, but then I sold it and put a lot of my gear into storage, including photos. Where I live now is temporary . . . it's not worth, er, well, unpacking my life until I have somewhere to put my own belongings.'

'His house is not temporary, sir. He's lived there all of his married life, raised his family there. Maybe twenty-five or more years in that house and not a photo to speak of the happy times, of childhood, of weddings and births? Please say you agree with me that this is strange, sir?'

They paused and regarded one another as the curiosity percolated.

'Is there more?' he pressed.

She nodded. 'This is the one that did it for me, sir. As I was leaving, I was putting on my headphones in his hallway and I noticed he had an iPod in a basket on a small sideboard where he leaves his keys, et cetera.'

'So?'

'I got the distinct impression that Brian Jarvis doesn't know how to use an iPod. There was something about his manner, and I definitely don't buy that he would be listening to the song I saw flash up on the screen when I mentioned his iPod and he picked it up.'

Jack felt the second prick of something he liked to call
The Tingler since he saw the terrible 1950s horror movie as a
child. The dreadful B-grade movie starring Vincent Price explored
the fictional discovery that the tingling of the spine in states of
extreme anxiety is actually a parasitic creature that thrives on human
fear and can crush humans when it curls up for long enough. As a
child, he had worried that his tingler was going to kill him. Now
he referred to moments of extreme dawning in his work as 'tingler
moments' because they usually combined a new understanding of a
crime with a sense of horror.

Sarah was still talking.

'Pardon?'

'The song that flashed up was by a band called My Chemical
Romance, sir. I didn't recognise it because I don't listen to
much contemporary music, but I looked it up and I am wholly
convinced that Brian Jarvis is unlikely to be listening to what is
described as pop punk and post hardcore.'

'Whatever that means,' Jack replied, frowning at where his own
thoughts were travelling.

'Exactly, sir. Now, I did note a CD player in his sitting room,
and while he made me a pot of tea I glanced at a couple of
the discs.'

'Perry Como?'

'Who's that?'

He shook his head with an ironic smile.

'No, it was, er . . .' She checked her notes. 'Van Morrison's
Greatest Hits, the best of some band called The Carpenters, and a
boxed set of Simon and Garfunkel. They looked like easy listening, going by the album covers. There were others but I didn't
have time to rummage.'

His gaze narrowed. 'Sarah, are you asking me to formally put
up the clerk of the court, Brian Jarvis, as a suspect? Because right

now, while I do share your bafflement at the photos and even the music, I'm not sure . . .' His words petered out as he watched her expression struggle to disguise that she still had her main point yet to make. Apparently everything so far had been the warm-up. 'Oh, Sarah,' he said, with fresh understanding. 'So now tell me something that's going to make my hair stand on end.'

She took a low breath. 'I spent a lot of last night looking back through all the details we've assembled on the recent murders and I landed on Davey Robbins. Do you recall that the statements from the fellow residents at the sexual offenders' home in Yorkshire all had one common component?' She pressed. 'Every single person we spoke to made a similar comment about Robbins.'

Jack frowned as he reached for where Sarah was leading him; he mentally flipped back through the file that he stored in his mind. 'Fuck!'

Sarah risked a twitch of a smile. 'I imagine that's going to cost you, sir.'

'His blue iPod,' he murmured.

She grinned hesitantly, looking like she had thoroughly enjoyed leading him to her reveal. 'It was never found in his backpack or at the crime scene, and everyone we spoke to confirmed that he wore it to, from and during his day. He was never without it. One of the adults in charge recalled that Robbins had once claimed the blue iPod was the only thing he'd owned in his life; that he guarded it like a precious jewel and even kept it under his pillow at night. I made another call to the residents this morning to ask about his playlist.'

'Make my day, Sarah,' Jack pleaded.

She smiled slightly wider. 'All agreed – his favourite band was My Chemical Romance.'

Jack stood, his chair rolling back to hit the wall as he punched the air. 'Oh my fucking hell.'

Joan arrived jangling a tin. 'And don't think for a moment I didn't hear the first one, Detective Superintendent Hawksworth. What sort of an example are you setting?'

As he dug into his pockets for pound coins, he shook his head with awe at Sarah. 'Get everyone together, Sarah. You'll be doing the briefing.' He pushed past, dropped coins into the tin and kissed Joan on the lips with a big smooching sound before casting Sarah a beaming grin. 'Amazing work, Sarah. Just brilliant!'

As he left his office, Joan recovered from the kiss and grinned at Sarah, giving her a wink. 'Oh, that's a promotion for you right there.'

26

There was a stunned silence after Sarah had presented her 'oddities'.

Jack gave an audible low whistle. 'Anyone else feeling goose-bumps?'

It burst the bubble of quiet and everyone began murmuring. He let it roar for a while, knowing it was like a valve that needed the release. Kate was shaking her head in quiet shock and he knew she would be beating herself up over what she might have missed.

'Okay, let's settle down, everyone. As shattering and indeed enlightening as Sarah's observations are, there is no hard evidence yet to suggest that we have our man . . . unless we can get hold of that iPod, which I suspect is now highly unlikely.' Jack nodded as though reaching a decision. 'One more detail, referring back to the fake photos that our intrepid sergeant here showed Mr Jarvis; his lack of questions perhaps confirms that he's only interested in cases he has worked. We'll triple-check it but I believe every death we're aware of can be attributed back to an original court case that he clerked for at North London Crown Court.' He gave

Sarah a triumphant nod, which she returned with an embarrassed but grateful smile. 'So now we have to work out a battle plan for gathering evidence against Jarvis that holds up.'

'The CCTV we have isn't conclusively Brian Jarvis,' Kate confirmed, appeal in her tone.

'But it could be,' Jack cautioned. 'You said the fellow was short.'

Kate gave him a look that said he was clutching at straws. 'And the woman? He could dress up as one, but he can't make himself thin and tall.'

'He could have paid someone to pick up the car. Have we had any luck tracing where it ended up?' The notion of an accomplice arrived in his mind but he didn't poke at it yet.

One of the PCs shook his head. 'Still looking through it all, guv.'

'We've got three constables on that task alone,' Kate cautioned.

'Keep going,' Jack insisted.

'Perhaps not being able to pick him up easily via CCTV reinforces the speculation, though,' Kate relented. 'We know whoever Mirror Man is, he's somehow well versed with police procedures and the sort of errors crims make that get them caught. His caution feels like second nature and his risks feel calculated . . . because he certainly does take risks. Jarvis would have professional knowledge of police operations and even the forensics experience to try and trick us with his shoe size.'

'But there's something about his daring, isn't there?' Mal remarked. 'I agree with you,' he said to Kate. 'I mean, even with all his caution he's taking huge risks. I've met Jarvis – he doesn't strike me as someone with that edge to him.'

'Could be faking?' Jack offered.

'Do you think he is?' Kate asked. 'How does a little beige bloke like him kill all these people?'

'Flip it,' Jack said, frowning as he talked it through. 'It's the little beige bloke who can fly under the radar. It's why he's not obvious. What Mirror Man has done has not once required much strength. He uses sedatives or hardcore hallucinogens to make his victims compliant before he does his deed. And each of those punishments seems to echo the original crime in some form or another. That's his satisfaction – their final comeuppance . . . the justice that he and the rest of the public want.

'What's more, he's in plain sight,' he said, thinking aloud as his team waited, listening. 'I've spoken with a criminal psychologist – an acquaintance,' he said, avoiding glancing at Kate. 'The advice that came back, based on nothing more than a few generalised remarks about our killer, is that whoever our guy is, he knows we don't notice him. The five-minute profile I was given suggests he's friendly, betrays no obvious signs of guilt or anxiety over the criminals he hunts. He's confident in his disguise, which is right in front of us . . . so said the psych.' Now he glanced at Kate and she gave him a knowing nod. 'Brian Jarvis does fit the picture we're building but I have to caution you that so does Martin Sharpe.' That won a burst of gentle laughter. 'Please don't repeat that.'

'What's it worth?' Joan asked; he hadn't seen her arrive. 'Has to be afternoon tea all round, right?' Claps and whistles of appreciation followed. She grinned at Jack. 'Leave that with me. You all need some sugar.'

'All right, so while I am saying our killer could be the guy in the seat next to you on the bus or on the tube, I have to agree, he could also be Brian Jarvis . . . with the blue iPod being our most damning clue.'

'Why don't we get a search warrant?' Ali asked.

'He'll have already got rid of it,' Kate said, taking the words out of Jack's mouth. 'And we don't want to give him any notice of our suspicions before we strike. If it is Jarvis, then we know this guy has rat cunning. Sarah, how did he react around the iPod thing?'

Sarah blew out a breath, deliberately taking time to recall the exact moment in detail. 'Casually dismissive. No overreaction at all. But I don't know why people presume that those of us who wear glasses can't see. I clearly saw the song on the screen, but I suspect he assumed that I'm somehow incapable of seeing anything small or distant. In terms of behaviour, he was his usual friendly self, entirely neutral in his tone, expressionless, relaxed. If it is him, he's super controlled. He told me he'd just come in from seeing a friend but he could just as easily have been going out . . . he had his parka on.'

'What colour?' Kate asked.

'Er . . . grey.'

Jack frowned, a thought reaching towards him but remaining just out of range. '. . . might also be presuming that we don't know about Brownlow's iPod,' Jack heard Mal remark, and it snapped him back to the conversation.

'Doubtful,' Jack said, softly. 'No. Brian is wise enough to know that we will have done our homework, that we know about the missing iPod.' He frowned into the distance.

'Then why leave it out in the open?' Kate asked, sounding lost.

It was Sarah who made the best sense of it. 'Because he wasn't expecting me and so didn't have to take that sort of precaution at home.'

Jack pointed a finger of agreement her way. 'It could be as simple as that. He planned to deal with it but there was no immediate rush.'

'But he's cautious – why would he hang on to it?' Kate debated.

Jack had no ready answer; it was Sarah who navigated the waters again.

'Sir, if Brian Jarvis is Mirror Man, then presumably he's used a car that he's got in hiding to drive up to Yorkshire; he certainly had to transport Robbins to the field where the caravan was, and of course to travel to and from Portsmouth to kill Brownlow.'

'Absolutely,' Jack agreed. 'We believe it's a Mazda hatchback.'

'What if it's simply that Robbins left his iPod in the car . . . it could have been dropped or slipped out of his pocket or his lap?' Everyone was paying attention. 'The killer isn't aware that the iPod is so important to Robbins, so he didn't know to look for it. He's also not an iPod user, so he wouldn't know that you can have the headphones without the iPod itself. The headphones were there in the backpack . . . I'm sure I'm not imagining that?'

Kate flicked back through a notebook. 'Yes, they were wound up neatly in a side zipper.'

Jack smiled. 'I doubt Davey Robbins was that neat. If this is Jarvis, then it does sound like something he'd do – that is, neatly wind up the messy headphones.'

Sarah nodded. 'He's a very tidy man. In his haste at the scene, perhaps he presumed the player that they attach to was already in the backpack. Then he finds the iPod in his car, removes it, takes it home, knowing he must get rid of it properly. He flings it into the basket with his car keys to be dealt with in the next day or so.'

'Not for a moment imagining that a sharp-eyed young detective might arrive unannounced so soon after,' Jack said. 'Yes, it works . . .'

'How would he know about Paxton?' Kate asked.

Jack sighed. 'If it is Jarvis, then we have Geoffrey Paxton's death on our conscience because we spoke about him openly while Jarvis was here in our incident room a couple of days ago.'

Sarah and Mal in particular looked shocked as they recalled the sequence of events.

'I'm to blame,' Jack assured them. 'I even asked him about Paxton, you may remember.'

'He recalled the courtroom, as well as Paxton's offences and victims,' Sarah said, sounding horrified.

'He did,' Jack said. 'But as an official of the courts, he also has other means to find these details out – perhaps he's regularly in touch with the prisons. This is circumstantial. We need evidence, everyone. We need any proof that puts Brian Jarvis in connection with any of our other suspicious deaths. With all the focus on Brownlow at present through the police network, lean on that one, as I imagine information is flowing fast.

'One last thing. Having spoken with Amy Clarke, I've learned that Hugh Pettigrew was not available to clerk in Courtroom Eleven for the Davey Robbins trial. I'll give you all one guess who did.' There was a stunned silence. He didn't wait for it to end. 'So get to it, everyone. We now have a genuine suspect. I want to know where that car is, who rented that caravan in Yorkshire; I want CCTV of Brian Jarvis in Yorkshire if possible; I want to know whether he is a Spurs member and had access to the special edition holdall. If someone can get me a sample of his handwriting, I could compare it with a letter that Amy Clarke provided today, which I suspect was written by the killer of Davey Robbins. Then we'd have a very large piece of our jigsaw in place. We'll reconvene at four today.'

Everyone got busy. Kate followed Jack to the lift.

'You're headed out?' he asked.

'You asked me see Judge Leland,' she said. 'She's a good place to start and I think I'd prefer a face-to-face.'

'Jarvis made it clear to Sarah and me that the courtroom officials have nothing to do with the people in the gallery. They operate within a sort of bubble and the gallery is the fourth wall, which they never break. And yet, he all but gave us a small lecture on how Amy's life has changed. Now I know that he was the clerk for that trial, it gives him even more cred as Mirror Man.'

The lift sounded its arrival and the doors opened. The Deputy Assistant Commissioner was inside with a woman they didn't recognise.

'Morning, sir,' they said together.

'Hawksworth, good to see you. DI Carter.'

'Ask her about Jarvis,' he murmured to Kate. 'Prod gently. We now know for a fact that he clerked in courtoom eleven with her at least once. She may paint us a picture of him.'

She nodded as more people got in on the lower levels and they remained silent for the rest of the descent. As they parted at the main doors, she asked the question he knew she wouldn't be able to resist. 'Will you be gone long?'

That was female code for *where are you going*, he was sure of it. 'I'll be back in a couple of hours. Our criminal psychologist might offer some fresh insight.'

She nodded. 'Good luck.'

Mal called while Jack was in the taxi heading to Holloway.

'News?'

'Boss, I've just been speaking with the person who I believe might be supplying the propofol.'

'Excellent. Tell me.'

'Describes the punter as *unlikely*. From what he would tell me, he thinks this guy used to buy heroin from some dealer around Barrowell Green.'

'Barrowell Green?' Jack couldn't place it.

'That's not far from the North London Crown Court. It's a residential street, sir, some shops nearby in a place called Firs Lane and a café. Perfect for our roadside chemist.'

'Okay, go on.'

'The punter apparently found using heroin cumbersome and

when his dealer got banged up, he went looking for another. He found this guy, who suggested he could get him propofol and, as he put it, he made a killing from him.'

'Prophetic choice of words.'

'Yep. He reckons the punter bought his whole stash. Five hundred milligrams.'

'How much is needed?' Jack frowned.

'We're getting onto that now. Kate said she'd find out quickly.'

'Okay, and did you get a description?'

'Yes. Describes him as middle-aged, not at all the usual smack-head he deals with. Nervous, well spoken, cashed up. Refused to exchange on the street. Insisted he buy him a coffee in a local café and do it there like old friends. The dealer understandably thought he was being set up, but when the buyer offered to pay triple rate for what he was selling, he couldn't resist. Never saw the guy again. Apparently, this man said he needed it to reset a poor sleep pattern after a shock bereavement.'

'Okay, Mal, that sounds like Jarvis . . .'

'Could be Mr Sharpe,' Mal added.

Jack gave a wry chuckle. 'We really must never repeat that. I think you need to get a photo of Jarvis to this guy. In the meantime, let's find out about the toxicity of this drug.'

'One more thing, boss. The dealer said the guy's likely a Spurs fan; was carrying a bag with an emblem on it.'

Bingo! 'Good work, Mal. We'll talk later. Tell Ali to push hard on that Spurs list. I want to know as soon as she does whether Jarvis is on it.'

'Will do.'

Jack rang off. 'Brian Jarvis,' he whispered to himself with a low whistle. He wasn't sure whether to feel impressed or consider the man a snake. Either way, with luck they'd have sufficient evidence to arrest the clerk of the court by tomorrow evening.

27

They were back in the open, airy room that doubled as a small library, and the conversation immediately felt easier for the space.

'How are you?'

'I'm the same every day, Jack.' Anne grinned, covering the truth, desperate to tell him how each time he visited it took all her willpower in this sad and dread place not to contemplate suicide. She was going to have to ask him to stop visiting. It felt counterintuitive because she loved looking at him, hearing his voice, reminding herself for the time he was with her that this man had once loved her so deeply; had wanted to spend a lifetime with her. Jack Hawksworth represented the future she could have had and yet she had ruthlessly turned away from him in order to pursue her dark revenge. 'No complaints,' she lied.

The warmth in his smile hurt like a burn. He pushed over a small paper bag. 'For your stocks. Everyone needs Munchies and KitKat at the ready,' he said, like a conspirator. 'But I do promise to get some more Thorntons coming your way.'

'Oooh,' she said, feigning excitement. 'Thanks. You may need to get permission.'

He waved away the caution. 'They know me now and they know I will either bring or send chocolates.' He hesitated only for a heartbeat. 'Anne, on that other business . . . I've made some calls.' He sounded matter-of-fact; she knew he took this professional approach in case anyone was eavesdropping.

Anne nodded in a breezy fashion and that helped to disguise the horse kick of pain that even a reference to Samantha brought. 'Great. Is that what you came to tell me?'

'I wanted you to know I'm trying.'

Try harder, Jack, she thought. *Find her. Watch over her.*

'We've got some suspicions about someone in plain sight.'

She nodded, immediately understanding. She waited.

'Lots of circumstantial stuff, unfortunately, combined with strong instinct.' He sighed.

'Sounds as though he's too clever to leave evidence,' she remarked.

'I believe so. One step ahead.'

'Are you onto someone, Jack?'

'We've got a sniff.'

She grinned. 'I think you're underplaying it.'

'Nothing concrete. Lots of hunches and some very strong circumstantial evidence, but it's not enough to convict.'

'Okay. If you've got your sniff, hunt him and corner him. Mirror Man is not infallible. Remember that. He covers his tracks well, but he's human, with all the same drive, motivation and desire to leave his private mark. He's not doing this for kicks. This person is workmanlike in his endeavour.'

'That's a good way of putting it. He brings lives to an end, lives that he believes were not worth being allowed to run their natural course.'

'There you are. There's arrogance in that alone – that he's somehow judge and executioner – and where there's arrogance, there are cracks that can be exploited.'

He glanced away, exhaling softly as if considering this. *Judge and executioner.* It was a perfect summary. 'How would we have exploited you?'

'I would have been harder, because only I knew my prey.'

'But he's easier because we know them?'

She shrugged. 'Exactly! You know which court, which trials, which prisoners. He waits for any one of them to be given their early release, presumably, and that person becomes his next target. That's what you exploit. You could even set a trap.' Anne gave him a crooked sort of smile and shrugged again. 'Why not?'

Jack regarded her and she found his searching gaze far too confronting.

'Jack, I can't see you again.'

He cocked his head, studying her.

'Can this be the last time, please?'

He looked immediately bruised from the remark, but she knew he would grasp why without her explanation. 'Well . . .' He searched for something to say and then gave a sigh. 'I would probably need to see you once more in order to keep a promise.'

She nodded. One more time to have the sensation of her heart being cut out of her body, carved up and presented to her. 'See you one final time, then.'

'May I still send you chocolates from time to time?'

She nodded with an affectionate smile.

'Anne, how obvious a trap?'

She was grateful his thoughts had returned to his case. 'As invisible as you dare. This is a subtle man, Jack; he's not laughing at you, he's not attempting to lure you, he's not inter-ested in having his name carved in stone or up in lights. I'd go so far as to suggest that if he died without anyone knowing he was the murderer of all these victims, it wouldn't trouble him in the slightest.'

'But why? He doesn't fit the psychopath profile, does he?'

She laughed. 'That's because he isn't one.'

Jack waited.

'Not all psychopaths are killers. The true definition is someone with absolute disregard for others or how their actions affect others. There's usually a pattern of lying and indeed lying to themselves . . . a lack of remorse. These people move around the workplace – they're the office bully, the high-handed surgeon, the arrogant CEO, the cruel teacher who everyone despises. But he may not fit this mould at all. He might just be a man in pain for whatever reason. He is driven by his own mission and rationale – whatever they are. He has a specific target and he feels nothing for them except contempt that they cheated the system, which he perhaps respects. They're making a mockery of justice, and so he's going to judge them and he's going to sentence them his way.' She waited. 'Does your fellow fit this?'

Jack nodded warily. 'I believe he does . . . rather neatly, actually.' He sighed.

'Then go get him, Jack, although I secretly hope the bad guy gets away.'

'I suspect you're not alone in that. I feel slightly ambivalent myself but, as I did with you, I have to do my job.'

Their gazes locked in sad admission.

She held up a finger. 'One more time.'

He nodded and she knew he understood why.

Outside the prison and feeling a sense of surprised release, Jack paused to call Lauren to set up a time for a proper date.

'So where are you now?' he asked, smiling, hoping she'd tease him and say she was taking a long bath or something along those lines.

'I'm at North London Crown Court.'

'Whatever for? I mean, who are you interviewing?'

'Well, if you must know, it's one of the clerks of the court. I had hoped to see a Mr Pettigrew, whose quaint name I rather like, but I'm seeing a Mr Jarvis instead.'

Jack was sure the tingler had moved from his spine into his belly and was curling up tight inside there instead. 'Why?'

'Oh, do you know him?'

'We've spoken to Jarvis a few times,' he said, not revealing any concern.

'Well, I've already met with the judge who presided over the cases I know about.' Jack couldn't help but be impressed by how deep Lauren had travelled alone into the same territory as he and his team. The newspaper group was lucky to have a talented investigative reporter like her coming into its fold. 'What's Jarvis like?'

'You'll find him extremely helpful,' Jack said. 'Um, Lauren,' he added, an idea occurring. 'Can you do me a favour?'

'I'm sure it's the least I can do for you, given you're cooking for me tonight, not to mention all the rest,' she said. He could hear the smile in her voice.

'Listen, I can trust you to do this because I know how perceptive you are.'

'Such high praise, Detective Superintendent – I have many other skills too,' she teased.

He smiled but hesitated just for a moment to test whether he should load this onto her shoulders. He decided in a heartbeat that Lauren would likely be devastated if she ever learned he hadn't relied on her. 'We want to test a theory, but it needs to come from a different source than the police.'

'Go on.'

'Would you be prepared to suggest to the clerk you're seeing that you've become aware of a prisoner about to be released who will likely cause a media frenzy?'

'Is it true?'

'No.'

'Why would I lie?'

He didn't wait for her to make the right connections, needing to throw her off the scent. 'I just want to see if that news travels back through the administrative team.'

'Oh, right. Do you have a suspect?'

'There's someone we've got eyes on. Nothing concrete, though. But I wondered if I could take the opportunity of seeding an idea through one of the clerks. They are in touch with all the admin team but also the security services, doormen, front reception staff.' He deliberately made it sound as though they were the real target.

'Okay. What do you want me to say?'

He hated to lie, but Anne's idea to set a trap was still large in his mind. 'That a child predator and paedophile called John Murphy might be coming up for parole, having served nine years of a fourteen-year sentence. He's agreed to wearing a cuff for the rest of his life, among other invasive requirements.'

'John Murphy?'

He nodded. 'He was sentenced by Judge Leland at North London Crown Court.'

'Okay.'

'One more thing.' This was it; he felt a momentary rush of bile that he might be placing Lauren in danger, but he was sure they could protect her. He also needed to share a nagging notion. 'Can you reveal to him you've heard through your sources that potentially there may be a woman accomplice involved.'

'What?'

'Lauren, just seed it into the conversation.'

'But—'

'I promise I'll explain tonight. Watch for his reaction and we'll watch for how it germinates and spreads.'

'I will want the full story tonight.'

'I'll pick you up at six. Unless the day unravels spectacularly,' he qualified, suspecting it might. 'It might have to be a casual dinner somewhere as I may be working again tonight.'

'That's okay.'

'Lauren, thanks for this. Remember, not too much detail – just throw it in, keep it vague . . . you already know how to do that.'

Lauren was seated opposite the genial clerk of the court for Courtroom Seven, discussing what she knew over a bacon sandwich with plenty of tomato ketchup. It was an indulgence she rarely allowed herself, but Brian Jarvis had made it sound like a sin to deny herself the treat. Besides, he had insisted on paying, given he'd kept her waiting.

'I have to agree, I've never tasted better,' she admitted, easing a dab of ketchup from the corner of her mouth. 'Mmm, really delicious.'

'And you'll still fit your jeans.' He grinned.

'How do you know how a woman's mind works, Mr Jarvis?'

'Wife and daughter . . . and twin granddaughters,' he said, eyes sparkling behind large glasses.

'Ah,' she said. 'I'm betting they all keep you busy.'

He chuckled and sighed. 'Now, Ms Starling – such a lovely name – or may I call you Lauren?'

'You may, of course. Thank you for taking the time.'

'A pleasure. It happens a lot that cases are delayed, pushed back, wrong documents, incomplete documents, juror ill, prisoner problems . . . there's an endless array of pressures on the court's time.'

'And today?'

'Today is incorrect paperwork.' He grinned again. 'But it means I now get a few minutes to share with your good self. It's not great coffee, I'm afraid, but tell me how I can help a journalist?' She gave him a smile that came easily from years of being noticed for her looks and she suspected he knew it. She was convinced the smile he was giving her was practised too. 'I should add,' he said, as she took a breath to explain, 'that we're already doing all we can to help the police with this case. You said this was an exclusive feature?'

She nodded and explained to him how circumstances had given her this opportunity. 'And so with Detective Superintendent Hawksworth's blessing, I have the chance to do this right and present a balanced, informative, well-researched feature piece.'

'My, my . . . that's a big leap for you and how thrilling. I certainly know *Britain's Voice*. I think it's very well read here by the legal community. Good for you. I've actually been consulting with Jack Hawksworth's team too.'

'Is that right?' she said, playing ignorant.

'Mmm, yes. In fact, I had one of his team at my house yesterday collecting my thoughts on some mugshots.'

'There's no suspect yet, as I understand it?' They both knew she was fishing. She shrugged. 'Sorry, I have to try, and I doubt they'll mind me knowing, given the access I now have.'

'No, I don't believe there is a firm suspect.'

'So you were in the incident room? Gosh, I wish they'd let me in,' Lauren said, hoping her admission might play to his vanity and give her more. 'What's your role?'

'Oh, just identifying the regular patrons of the public galleries in our courts. I was helping with CCTV.'

Lauren nodded. 'Smart. Anything?'

'They're looking closely at a couple of lads who have a thing for courtroom seven but, if I'm honest, Ms Starling, they really don't strike me as killers. More that they're fixated.' He chuckled. 'Still, I like Detective Superintendent Hawksworth's attitude to leave no stone unturned.'

'He always gets his guy, I gather,' she baited him.

'Is that so? No disappointing cold cases for Hawksworth?'

'Not as I understand it . . . certainly not on the big cases he's worked. One of his notorious ops was to track a serial murderer who turned out to be a woman. They were friends, even lived in the same apartment block.'

'Truly?'

She nodded. 'Right now she's doing her time at Holloway.'

'Ah,' he said, smiling to himself as if understanding something.

'Is that intriguing?' she asked, wondering why it sounded like a dawning to him.

'No, I've just never participated in a murder trial where it was a woman perpetrator. I wonder if that changes anything for all the participants?'

'If you mean judge or jury, I should hope not,' Lauren said.

'I agree but it's a fascinating thought.'

'Anne McEvoy – you must know the case.'

'McEvoy, of course.' Again he smiled, but to himself, she noted. 'Notorious, as you say. But perhaps I'm jaded – I have been involved in several murder trials in my time.'

'Which is why I'd like to talk to you, Mr Jarvis. As I explained when I rang, there've been a mystifying number of deaths of released inmates who originally faced trial in these courts.'

'You make *me* feel guilty.' He chuckled.

He was such a colourless fellow: smallish, presumably over-looked in life, and if he was always this pleasant, then he was definitely going to be stepped on. Nice people didn't fare well in the dog-eat-dog world of 2007.

'Would it be possible to interview you formally, Mr Jarvis?'

'You mean quote me?' he asked, dabbing at his mouth with a paper serviette.

'Yes, that's what I mean.'

He looked uncertain. 'I'm not sure that's my place.' He shrugged, suddenly coy. 'I don't mind helping the police, Ms Starling; that feels like civic duty. But giving some sort of exposé would go against my conscience. Courts might be open to the public, but lives are being laid bare and it's hard enough for victims and their families anyway – and indeed the perpetrators have rights as well – so I'm not sure I need to be helping a wide audience to poke around in their lives.'

'I applaud that; I do respect your position and theirs. What if I asked you to comment in a more generalised way?'

He shook his head. 'No, because that would then open it up for something more political. I would say it's better to talk to someone higher up the food chain than a clerk of the court. Look, the truth is, we simply make sure that the cases run smoothly, so I have no place making remarks about trials or policing in general.'

She bit her lip, trying to find a way in, and watched as he smiled back benignly.

'I'm sorry to be such a fizzer for you,' he said, clearly sensing her frustration.

'You're not at all. You have the knowledge I need to give the article some weight . . . its credentials, so to speak.'

He gave a light laugh at the compliment.

'What if we made it highly specific, then? Picked out, say, two cases tried in Courtroom Seven and two from another court that you might like to point me towards, where convicted criminals were considered to have received lenient sentences and then early release.'

'Ah.' He nodded. 'That has merit. I don't think there's a clerk of any court who hasn't felt the pain for victims and their families when a sentence feels horribly light compared to the sentence the victims are serving. We'd be lying if we pretended not to experience that despair. But we more than most understand that judges have to work within the constraints of British law. And, I might add, that nods to government pressure to empty out our jails, find new opportunities for rehabilitation, get them out of a system that can potentially only make them worse over time, not better . . . and so it goes.'

'Exactly! Even just what you've said there is marvellous and carries some power in it.'

He gave a soft laugh. 'Really? Well, you need to speak to my colleague, Shirley; she can be quite outspoken on the topic.'

'I will. In fact, I heard through my contacts that the paedophile John Murphy is about to be granted an early release.' She was thrilled with herself for how well that came out; not as a question, just a casual statement. 'I can imagine he's exactly the sort of early-release prisoner who can polarise the population.'

She watched Brian Jarvis reach for the paper serviettes in the middle of the table and carefully dab at his lips again. 'Murphy?' He nodded to himself. 'I . . . er . . . I hadn't heard.'

'Well, I've got my ear to the ground on the bad guys being let out early or being given sentences that the public at large believes are much too lenient for their crimes.'

He frowned. 'Where did you hear this?'

'I have a contact at Wormwood Scrubs. Anyway,' she said, waving that away, 'I have heard something juicy. I don't think I was meant to discover this, but I overheard a phone conversation . . . Apparently Hawksworth's team are toying with the notion that the killer may have an accomplice.' She deliberately didn't look at him directly; instead she began brushing away crumbs from her lap before sneaking a look. He was watching her. 'What? Does that shock you?'

'No, but what makes them say that?'

She shook her head. 'Like you, I'm very much on the fringe, but I got the sense it was a woman. I'm sure I heard that Inspector Carter say "she".' Lauren flipped her hair back. 'I could be wrong. Anyway, about that formal interview, Mr Jarvis?'

He glanced at his watch. 'Not right now, Ms Starling. It is time I returned to my desk.'

Did he look rattled? 'Can we arrange a time to meet?'

'Of course. So long as we understand the boundaries of what I can and can't get involved with regarding your feature.' He sounded composed but eager to be gone.

'We'll lay them out carefully before we begin, I promise, and you can ask me to strike something off the record if you feel our conversation is moving into a territory that makes you uncomfortable.'

'That's fair.'

'Good. When?'

'Tomorrow, perhaps. Just not sure, er . . .'

'Here?'

He shook his head. 'No, er, wait . . .' He lifted a narrow diary from an inside pocket and, holding it up so she couldn't glance at it, he turned to the day in question. 'Oh . . . that may make it awkward.' He sighed. 'A colleague and I have to be at the Central Criminal Court for a meeting tomorrow afternoon.'

'Central Criminal Court?'

He looked over the top of the diary. 'Old Bailey to you.'

She laughed. 'Ah, yes, so in the city. I could—'

'And then I'm meeting a friend for dinner at some Greek place she assures me is the best in London.'

'The best in London is called Halepi,' she remarked, not expecting the response that came.

'Well, that's it! I've written down Halepi for six-thirty.'

Lauren felt her excitement ping like a firework exploding within. 'Mr Jarvis, that restaurant is within walking distance of my flat!'

'Oh, you're joking,' he said, sounding as astonished as she felt. 'You live in Bayswater?'

She nodded and gave him a gleeful grin. 'I'm barely five minutes away from where you'll be.'

'Good grief. Isn't life curious when it does this to you?'

Curious or not, she wasn't going to overlook an opportunity like this. 'We can meet at mine, can't we? I mean, perhaps we can get together for half an hour before your dinner engagement? It's honestly just a short stroll from the restaurant. I promise not to make you late.'

Jarvis scratched his head. 'Well, I don't know what to say . . . It's rather irregular, Ms Starling.'

'Lauren,' she insisted. 'I've invited you to my home.' She shrugged. 'Friends. And the fact that we happen to discuss your work is simply conversation.' She could see he was undecided but she didn't want to wait for him to choose the option that cut her out. Lauren dug in her bag for a card. 'I'm sorry, that says *My Day*. Not for long, I promise. But the mobile number is mine. Can we try for tomorrow any time after five? I'll be at my flat and waiting.' She grinned. 'Kettle on and wine in the fridge or breathing comfortably at room temperature – whatever your preferred poison is.'

'Tea is fine,' he insisted, and she realised just how colourless a man sat before her. Pleasant but so very lacklustre in any aspect of his personality. *Don't judge, Lauren*, she warned herself. *He may have the secrets you need.*

He took the card. 'Righto. I'll call you, provided our meeting won't run long, and I'll mention this to Shirley.'

'That's great. I'll look forward to seeing you early evening. Er, no, I know you offered but please, let me,' she said, waving him away as he reached for the bill. 'It's the least I can do.'

28

Kate sat across from Judge Moira Leland in her chambers. They were surprisingly minimalist. Modern, too . . . if you considered the late seventies modern. Kate had always thought of the seventies as a rather ugly era of furniture, the colour brown everywhere, often teamed with a ghastly burnt orange and teak veneer. Granted, this was a honey-coloured wood veneer, its shelving full of leather-bound volumes of law, but there were touches from the judge that spoke of her elegance: a beautiful vase of fresh spring flowers on her well-ordered desk; a silver-framed photo of the judge leaning back against a handsome, smiling man with hair greying at his temples. They looked effortlessly happy on a yacht. Near the photo was a fountain pen and a squat bottle of Parker Quink in green. She'd never seen anyone write with emerald ink before, so this made Moira Leland even more interesting, if her tall, arrestingly sophisticated presence was insufficient.

Kate was used to feeling like the best-dressed person in the room but the judge would give her more than a competitive race to that finish line. Her outfit was tasteful, modest and yet screamed its expense through its tailored line and quality fabric. The charcoal dress she wore fitted her immaculately and, teamed with neutral nude heels, was perfect. Kate spied the Burberry coat hanging on the stand and that too was a clue to this woman. Taste, money, confidence. The green ink was a lovely extra flourish of arrogance, Kate thought as she watched Judge Leland finish her telephone conversation and place the receiver back onto its cradle. Her long fingers had oval-shaped nails, manicured with a pale French polish; to Kate she was perfection in an older woman.

'I'm sorry about that, Detective Inspector Carter.' Even her voice was schooled elegantly to a mellow pitch, slightly raspy in a way that suggested she liked a drink or a cigarette now and then . . . or both.

'No, that's fine, thank you for seeing me at short notice.'

'I'm sure I can guess what this is all about; the courts are abuzz,' she remarked, her gaze level, a smile crinkling the edges of it.

'Does it trouble you?'

The judge rightly looked back at her as though she were simple. 'Yes, of course. It's baffling and scary at once.'

Kate nodded. She walked the judge through a series of questions that she already knew the answer to, but it was important that the same ground was covered by all their enquiries.

Moira Leland shrugged as Kate's phone pinged a text message. She glanced at it; it was from Jack. She blinked quickly back up at the judge, who was speaking. 'It goes without saying that I would have contacted you all immediately if any of this had set off alarm bells in my mind. I can't say I am aware of anyone in the gallery during the cases you've mentioned who might be threatening. I mean, these are all violent criminal cases we are referring to, Inspector. But in answer to your question, there is no stand-out person that I recall from the regulars in my courtroom.'

Jack wanted Kate to introduce Brian Jarvis into the conversation. 'What about officials?' she asked. There, it was out.

'I beg your pardon?'

'Is there anyone within the official courtroom or administrative staff whom you might consider suspicious or indeed capable of such violence?'

'I . . .' The judge looked knocked off balance. 'Do you mean someone on my team?'

'I do,' Kate said, nodding. 'For Courtroom Eleven in particular.'

'I must say, I'm shocked by that question.'

Kate frowned. 'Why? It has to be asked. Someone is targeting convicted criminals from your courtroom. We need to look at everyone who is familiar with the cases.'

'Well, I . . . I don't know what to think.' Kate waited while Judge Leland spluttered her way through, trying to regain her suddenly rattled composure. 'Good grief, no. I can't think of anyone from our Crown Courts who is capable of what you're suggesting.' Moira Leland picked up her fountain pen and put it down again. She blinked rapidly. 'Er, is that all, Inspector?'

'I'm wondering about Brian Jarvis.'

Now the judge just looked disturbed. Kate thought about the text message; what was Jack up to, weaponising her like this?

'Do you mean the clerk of the court from seven?' the judge said, her voice sounding unnaturally tight.

'I do. I gather he's clerked in your courtroom?' She kept the question open and light.

'Oh, well, once or twice. But I hardly know him. Surely you don't—'

'No, no, nothing like that,' Kate lied. 'Er, Mr Jarvis is helping us with our enquiries and I just wanted to be sure we were talking to the right person. He seems knowledgeable.'

'Well, he is,' Judge Leland said; the ground she'd lost during the topple from her high perch had been regained. Kate imagined her all but stroking down her ruffled feathers. 'He's been here an awfully long time and I suspect that if anyone can help you with queries around the North London Crown Court, Brian is your man.'

'Well, thank you, Your Honour. We were simply doing what we call due diligence. We've spoken to everyone behind the scenes, so to speak, and we left you till last, just in case you could give us any more insight than those who run the court.'

'Well, quite. You need to understand that as a judge I am entirely focused on proceedings; every nuance, every aspect of law presented and discussed, every question being asked, I must scrutinise and test. I don't really have time to be looking around and taking a measure of the people who have no bearing on the trial. And we are on trial for someone's life, usually, in these rather notorious and violent cases. I have a specific and demanding role. If I get it wrong, all hell breaks out.' She smiled. Kate noted that the lecture had allowed her to gather up her shock and tie it neatly back into a manageable place. It was also an unnecessarily long speech; she was working too hard to impress Kate.

'There would be a section of society that believes you do get it wrong.'

Moira Leland's gaze narrowed. Kate felt like a squirming fish on the end of a spear, but she knew she mustn't show any struggle to hold that stare. How many people on the stand had quavered beneath it?

'Are you criticising my judgements, Inspector?'

'Certainly not, Your Honour. Nor is my statement personal. It was a collective you, as in the judicial system; I am merely observing that you are one of the more liberal judges in this Crown Court and even you would have as many supporters as you might have critics.'

Judge Leland nodded, touching her perfect bob. 'That would be true. It's not easy being a sentencing judge these days, with crowded prisons, the howl for harsher sentencing . . . while the government is setting out plans for earlier and earlier paroles. It's actually a nightmare.'

Kate frowned, beginning to understand her better. 'Do you deliberately hand down more lenient sentences, then?'

The judge gave her a look of sympathy as though Kate was dimmer than she'd imagined. 'No. When we have a verdict of guilty, I must weigh up what sort of sentence will not be tampered with. It's too easy to let these violent perpetrators out believing them to be somehow rehabilitated. Take Davey Robbins from the trial that Brian Jarvis clerked for. He likely would have broken the law again – I saw only arrogance in that young man. If he's prepared to hurt someone as much as he did Amy Clarke, I have no doubt he would have hurt another woman in a similar fashion. It's such a grey area. Suffice to say, I handed down a sentence that should have kept Davey Robbins incarcerated for at least five long years. I could have gone for about seven or even eight, but you and I both know he'd have been out in five. I always aim to get it right the first time so no one fiddles with it, but the prison system in its wisdom thought otherwise.'

'It's happened a lot in your cases, though,' Kate observed.

The judge shrugged again. 'You need to talk to the civil servants at the Department of Justice who let violent men . . . women beaters, rapists, paedophiles, murderers, out earlier than the sentencing judge decided after much consideration.'

'I feel your pain,' Kate admitted.

'I suspect you do, Detective Inspector. Let's not forget that we're on the same side, you and I.'

Kate nodded. 'Your time's precious and I thank you for sparing me some of it.'

'I hope you find your man, although I'm sure many would disagree.' It was said as a casual remark.

'May not be a man,' Kate quipped and watched the judge frown. 'Or at least, not necessarily a man working alone. I'll see myself out, thank you again.'

Outside the judge's chambers, Kate passed another of the clerks of the court. 'Excuse me. Can you help me find my way out of this warren quickly?' She introduced herself.

'Ah, one of the police team. Such strange and frightening events. I'm Shirley. Were you just seeing Judge Leland?' Kate nodded. 'How was her mood?'

'Testy,' Kate admitted.

Shirley grinned. 'Nice understatement. She's very good, but she scares a lot of folk. I'm sure she doesn't mean to, but I think that insular manner comes from years of living alone.'

'Oh, I noted a wedding ring. There was a photo of—'

Shirley nodded and Kate let her talk. 'Yes, she was married. He died, some years ago now, I gather. You know Brian, don't you?'

There was that name again. 'Yes,' Kate lied; she'd not met this man that everyone else had.

'He knows Moira Leland quite well – they often take coffee together in the cafeteria – and tells me the judge's personality changed after her husband died. It was all very sad.'

'I won't ask.'

'No, don't, because I've already said too much – I only wanted to explain that she's exceedingly remote and can be touchy, but she's one of the best here. We all like working with her for her professionalism.'

'Is Brian Jarvis around?'

'I saw him talking to a journalist in the cafeteria but he might be in court now.'

Kate thanked Shirley and hurried away, now desperate to reach

Jack and let him know they had been lied to about the relationship between Judge Leland and Brian Jarvis.

Brian Jarvis reached for his phone and read the surprising text message. They were in a break in his courtroom's proceedings and he quickly sought out the defence team. 'What do you think?'

'We're going for a continuance.'

He nodded; he needed to act, and this break in the trial would help. He moved to Judge Lewis's chambers and knocked gently. 'Sorry to interrupt, Your Honour,' he said. When the judge looked up, he added, 'Continuance?'

'I thought as much. Yes. Fine.'

'I might take a few hours, Your Honour, as we're done for today.'

Judge Lewis grunted rather than answered, already lost to some paperwork he was reading.

Brian nodded and closed the door quietly. He sent a text back to reassure the recipient that he had everything sorted. Then he made the call. He had to catch the reporter.

'Er, I can, of course,' Brian heard Lauren Starling say. He could imagine her pretty face frowning. 'Have all your plans gone awry?'

'No, we decided to meet for lunch instead.'

'Halepi doesn't open for lunch, though.'

There was just a moment's hesitation. 'No, I know,' he lied. 'It's such a pity, but we've decided to stay close to her home all the same. She's not terribly well and I don't want her having to travel too far. Anyway, if you want to see me, I'll be in your neck of the woods in about two hours.'

'Definitely. I'll be waiting. Um, let me give you the address.'
Brian pretended to write it down, but he already knew exactly
where Lauren Starling's flat was. He'd seen her name on the list of
doorbells, heard her laughter filtering down from the rooftop and
he knew the person who had prompted that laughter was none
other than the man who was hunting him.

Maybe the time had come for Detective Superintendent
Hawksworth to see life through Brian's eyes, to understand what
it was to lose someone to an unfair and cruel killer.

'Thanks, that's easy enough. I know the street.'

'Great,' Lauren said. 'I'll have the kettle on.'

He smiled. 'See you soon.'

Just two errands to run. Both tasks required shopping and a
trip home. He hurried around collecting all that he needed from
beyond his four walls. The first package was seen off to its destination with a bike messenger. He knew the other bike messenger
would arrive hot on its heels and the note to go with it needed to
be written quickly. He'd settled on Pedro Ximénez San Emilio,
which was eye-wateringly expensive. The salesman assured him
the fruit was laid out in the sun after picking until the grapes were
all but raisins. Then, only a slow fermentation began before being
halted to hold all the natural sugars within. 'Aged for a dozen
years, this one,' the fellow said. 'Hence the price tag.'

'Ninety pounds,' Brian said, whistling.

'Worth every penny when you taste it.'

'It's not for me.'

Brian returned home and wrote the note to accompany his gift
while he awaited the messenger.

My dear Moira,

I've learned that the original Spanish grape grower of this family was
a secretary to the Court of Justice in Cadiz, which feels somehow

fitting, as I do know how much you love your daily nip of Pedro Ximénez. And this one is exceptional, as I'm sure you'll discover. Given we've shared many bottles of Pedro together, I wanted to make sure it was as good as the salesman claimed, so I hope you don't mind that I tasted it. They didn't have a sampler in the off-licence. Call me sentimental, but with its taste still on my palate, I can imagine it hitting yours and bringing the pleasurable relief I hope it will after one of your long days in court. Taste it soon and enjoy, knowing I am thinking of you as the first bonfire of syrupy delicious-ness hits.

Perhaps you're sensing farewell. You'd be right. I doubt we shall see each other again as I suspect my time is now very short, but you've been a bedrock through my grief and helped me to answer the call of true justice.

This is sent with only thanks and the love of caring friendship.

Justly yours, Brian

The messenger arrived as he was tucking in the flap of the card's envelope.

'Be careful with this, young man. It cost an arm and a leg.'

'Will do, mate,' he said and, having placed the bubble-wrapped bottle into his messenger bag on the bike, he roared off for the brief journey to the Crown Court.

Brian took a moment to savour this day. It was a perfect spring morning, sharp sunlight cutting through the trees, turning the dancing heads of daffodils and jonquils luminous. He inhaled the fresh air of the peaceful Conical Corner he had called home for thirty years or so. He felt as though he should be thinking about how much he'd miss this, but he'd made the decision to give up its beauty many years ago when he stepped onto the pathway of murder. The truth was that he wouldn't miss his life; it had been nothing but relentless grief for fifteen of those thirty years here. He'd forgotten what feeling happy was like. Instead, he pulled on his facade daily, acting it out for all those around him. Only Moira Leland understood.

He wondered when Hawksworth's team had put the pin into his name, into his photograph on the incident room board. Had to be that smart Sarah, spotting the iPod. His mistake. His only one, it seemed, in a string of deaths they would gradually begin to attribute to him, the courteous, willing, unremarkable clerk of the Crown Court. None of his colleagues would believe what they would read, finding it impossible, no doubt, to match up the killer in the news against lovely old Brian from Courtroom Seven. Now his name would appear in news articles as a terrifying murderer, a serial killer. But there would be many, he knew, who would privately applaud his hobby and acknowledge that Brian Jarvis was the only person in the legal system who was doing the law's true work, answering to its calling – Justice.

He would die with that thought in his mind. He had no intention of the charming and handsome Detective Superintendent Hawksworth putting handcuffs on him and marching him down to the lock-up. There would be no trial, no sentencing and no prison for him. No way. He'd go out killing and trust that someone would kill him in the process – in fact, he'd make sure of it.

He congratulated himself that he had left no loose ends, especially no one suffering on his behalf for his actions; he had no affairs to get in order. Everything was now neatly bedded down with his solicitors since the cancer had found him. Nothing had changed in his plan for his estate, the proceeds of which were to be donated towards setting up another home for battered women and children. If they had the courage to escape, then Brian had the means to provide them with somewhere to live for a while. It was the best he could do with what he had.

He stepped back into the house his wife had adored for one final walk around, allowing all the memories to flood him. It was an assault and his cheeks were wet, his woollen jumper damp from the tears that ran as he remembered. He hadn't meant to be sentimental at the end but, unlike his family, he'd been able to prepare for it. They'd just been wiped out. Their fragile bodies shattered. The twins had died holding hands. His wife's face had been unrecognisable despite the best efforts of the funeral parlour. He had not been able to see his daughter at all . . . the police had advised against it. Four lives snuffed out needlessly by a careless, drunken driver.

The man had got himself well and truly soused for no good reason, it seemed. He'd sobbed in court: he hadn't meant to hurt anyone . . . *boohoo*. He wished he could take his time back, he'd begged through his tears.

Kevin Dewsbury got just twelve years for his carelessness. He served eight and was dead within days of getting out . . . Brian had seen to that. He wondered absently if they'd ever find Dewsbury's body.

In each of the three bedrooms he paused to kiss the pillow where a girl he loved had once laid her light-haired head: Emily and Chloe, his granddaughters; Jane, his daughter; and Vivian, his wife . . . all taken too soon. Now they might be reunited if he could be forgiven for his sins.

'A few hours, girls, and we'll be together,' he promised.

Brian Jarvis pulled on his parka and flat cap, tapped his pocket to be sure and left his house in Enfield for the last time. He decided to treat himself to a taxi, which he hailed easily enough.

'Head for Paddington Station,' he told the cabbie. 'It's not far from there.'

29

Judge Moira Leland had no courtroom appearance today. The trial was delayed yet again because the prison had sent the wrong prisoner. How did that happen? She cursed quietly under her breath.

She stared at the tall bottle of sherry on her desk. She knew Emilio's brand of Pedro Ximénez well – ordered it in restaurants – but had never stretched to spending what she was sure was an alarming price tag for a whole bottle. Brian was a dear. They'd had to keep their close friendship a secret, but they allowed the staff at the North London Crown Court to see that they were friendly colleagues.

This was the result of the text she'd sent from the spare cheap phone she kept for that purpose. She had needed to warn him about what she'd learned from that Detective Inspector Carter; *how could they know about an accomplice?* She had panicked slightly but Brian had reassured her that he would fix everything and, with his imminent death – she presumed the cancer – he would die with her secret. She was not to worry.

He'd added that the car would be removed within forty-eight hours and scrapped by people who knew better than to mention it again. He suggested she get rid of the spare phone immediately, separating it from its special data card as she'd been taught and destroying that. She'd already done so with no little relief; this was obviously his goodbye.

She was surprised that the seal had been broken on the expensive bottle but it had made sense when she read his note, and she took no offence. Typical Brian . . . always so fastidious, but she was glad his time was over, if she was honest. He was a man lost to his grief. At the beginning it felt as though neither of them had anything to lose; he was grief-stricken and knew he was dying, while she was grief-stricken and not thinking too clearly, but time had passed. She had perspective on her loss and she was tired of the tension. Now, with the police beginning to close in, what she wanted suddenly was to retire and live out her life quietly . . . away from all things judicial. Perhaps she'd write a book. The thought made her smile.

She needed to get rid of the evidence of their link. Putting his card into the wastepaper bin, she set it alight with a match from a box she kept in her top drawer. She liked the odd cigarette but less and less these days, so this box of matches had lasted a long time.

Moira took the wastepaper bin to the window, which she opened, and watched the small card ignite and burn itself to ashes while the short billow of smoke was released into the open air. She checked there was nothing to be retrieved from the detritus and then covered the ashes with some other litter. The smell of burning paper would dissipate soon enough.

Sunlight was streaming in from the large picture window in her corner office. She rang the switchboard. 'Hold calls, please.'

'Yes, Judge Leland . . . until?'

'I'll let you know.'

She kicked off her heels and clicked the *Do Not Disturb* sign on her door, then moved to her cabinet and picked up a small crystal glass, which she filled with a generous couple of inches of Brian's sherry. It wouldn't hurt, and there was no public work for the rest of the day. She would go home shortly but for now she just wanted to sit quietly, let the light stream in and around her, and contemplate the end of a relationship and the beckoning of a new life.

She settled back onto the sofa, not resisting the urge to curl her long legs up. She rested on an elbow, looking out to where the trees surrounding the Crown Court dappled the sunlight that would soon be warm enough to bronze her skin. She held the glass and let the light glimmer through the rich raisin-coloured syrup, sparking the bonfire of its lustre as Brian had mentioned. 'To you, Brian Jarvis,' she said. Moira Leland sipped and sighed with pleasure that it tasted every bit as exceptional as he'd promised.

Jack and Kate were holed up in his office, waiting for the others to gather for the debrief.

'Do you know what's nagging me?' Kate said, leaning back in her chair.

'Go on.'

'The phone call that Mirror Man makes after killing Peggy Markham. Could be the same person who helped with the car after the Brownlow death . . . an accomplice?'

'Apart from the car business I don't understand why he needs one,' Jack said.

She shrugged. 'Someone who understands, helps with his conscience. Perhaps there's someone who sympathises . . .'

'And does what? Research?'

'Potentially.'

'The only valuable accomplice that a serial killer might need is another sympathiser, as you say, but that person has to be useful or they are simply a liability.' He shrugged. 'Logistics?' He shook his head at the thought. 'No. The accomplice has to be able to somehow deliver details of his victims to him before anyone else.'

Kate sighed. 'So that someone would have to be on the inside.'

'Not police,' Jack said, emphatically.

'No, but from the system. Jarvis would certainly need to know information from prisons.'

'He could find that out easily enough just using his own name.'

'Shall we test it?' Kate asked. 'How about you ring Paxton's prison? Can we find anyone who spoke to Brian Jarvis? I'll ring the prison for Robbins.' She left, leaving Jack to make the call. When she returned he looked back at her, resigned.

'No one knows the name Brian Jarvis, or at least no one's saying they do. I spoke to the governor and his third in command. They're going to ask the deputy governor as a matter of course. He's somewhere in the prison.'

'I drew a blank with the name at Wakefield. I mean, we could keep pushing down through the hierarchy?' She shrugged.

Jack shook his head. 'Okay, so let's say Brian Jarvis has an accomplice. What if—' His mobile rang. 'Hawksworth?' He listened. 'Does he recall who?' He sat forward and nodded at Kate. 'You're sure?' He paused. 'Okay, well, thank you. I, er, was just dotting some i's and crossing some t's,' he said, making it sound routine. He rang off and stared at Kate with a pensive expression. 'Apparently, Moira Leland spoke with the deputy governor at Pentonville.'

'Judge Leland,' Kate repeated, surprised. 'The accomplice?'

'Let's go through your meeting with her again. Facts aside, give me your feelings from that meet.'

Kate shook her head as if not wishing to believe where they were being led. She fought it. 'You really think a judge is involved in these murders?'

He held her gaze and his look said *why not?*

'Fuck, Jack!' Fortunately, she lowered her voice at the expletive.

'Is it so far-fetched?'

'But she's the one banging them up.'

'She's also the one giving the lightest sentences.'

Kate's look slid across him with a mix of awe as much as horror. She blew out a groan of disbelief. 'She fits the smudgy figure in the CCTV at Portsmouth.'

'Okay, let's go through it. We're alleging the Mazda was parked in Portsmouth and then picked up by a woman.'

Kate listened with obvious forced patience. 'Right.'

'What do we know about that woman?'

'Taller than Jarvis. Slim.'

'Leland?'

'Would fit that description . . . but then so would I.'

'I accept that. Next, according to Bernie Beaton, the killer rang someone – has to be some sort of accomplice – to let them know the ugly deed was done.'

'And how do you draw the line from there to Judge Leland?'

'Well, they haven't told the truth about how friendly they actually are, and because of something you said earlier. You described her as implacable, elegant, entirely in control.'

'Yes, qualities you'd anticipate in any Crown Court judge.'

'But our antennae should certainly twitch that she was as rattled as you describe at the mention of Brian Jarvis.'

'Couldn't it have just been shock? It would be like one of us learning that, oh, I don't know . . . Joan was under suspicion of serial killing.'

'Perhaps. You said she played it very casual about Jarvis, as if they barely knew one another.'

'True. She said she didn't know him very well but the other clerk . . .'

'Shirley.'

'Yes. She gave me the impression that they know each other well, often take coffee breaks together and so on.'

Jack looked away and sighed. 'So we've potentially caught her in a lie about her relationship with Jarvis; she fits the build of our shadowy figure on CCTV; we know he called someone.'

She frowned. 'All right. And we should add that she's super touchy about sentencing.'

'Go on.'

'It's her soapbox. I mean, I know it's ultimately her responsibility to pass the sentence, but I could tell she's determined not to let her sentences be interfered with once passed. So she leans towards being lenient, is quite public in her belief, and that means other officials are less likely to tamper with her already known to be lenient sentences.'

Jack watched her and let a silence stretch. 'Okay, let's flip that,' he said. 'She deliberately sentences as lightly as she dares. In order to . . . what?' He stared at Kate with such ferocity she could feel it like pressure within.

'In order to guarantee they'll be out as fast as possible – especially if they are given an early release.' Kate looked horrified by her own statement.

Jack wasn't finished. 'So that . . .?'

'Oh, come on, Jack.'

'All right, I'll say it. So that her accomplice, Brian Jarvis, can pick them off and render absolute justice that I suspect they both believe in for these offenders.'

Kate leaned her head onto one hand in despair. She needed a moment or two to process this terrifying notion they'd aired. She looked up. 'I liked her.'

He shrugged. 'I'm testing a theory with you.'

'Do you believe it?'

Jack nodded unhappily. 'Yes. The reason we're struggling is that, deep down and morally, we agree with her. I want us to look into Judge Moira Leland more closely.'

She nodded. 'I'm on it. What about you?'

'I want to find out more about the Jarvis family, plus I need to organise a farewell gift for my friendly criminal psych.'

Kate gave him a sad smile. 'Not seeing each other again?'

He shook his head. 'It's too hard.' He placed his hands on the desk with finality as if drawing a line under Anne McEvoy's involvement. 'Where are this elusive daughter and those grand-daughters of whom he talks so highly but has no photographs? Meanwhile, as far as the judge goes, let's explore the husband's death . . . anything suspicious, anything untoward.'

Kate stood, sighing at the damning juncture they found them-selves at. 'Fucking hell.'

A tin was rattled in the near distance.

'This has arrived for you, McEvoy,' one of the prison officers said, finding her in the library. 'The powers that be tell me I'm allowed to give it to you.'

Anne could see what they were immediately.

'Sorry we had to open the wrapping. Looks like your Detective Superintendent is genuinely a secret admirer, eh?'

Anne shrugged with a smile; she had no intention of sharing any truth with the prison officers. She had a good relationship with them, mostly because she gave them no lip, no trouble and could talk down an angry inmate with solid regularity. With that trust and reliability came certain easing of rules. 'I suspect this could be the last, so I don't think I'll be sharing these.' She grinned more widely. 'Unless you would like one, Officer Wright?'

'They're all yours and you could use the fattening.'

Anne smiled. There was no note, but only one person knew how much she loved Thorntons chocolates. While she waited for her group to assemble, she might just open them and enjoy a rare treat. She couldn't resist unwrapping the paper, inside which she found a gift box with a double layer of drawers that pulled out from the front once the lid was lifted. Inside was the premium collection of Thorntons' continental range. It was over the top – definitely a fond farewell from the only man she'd ever loved. She selected a favourite, one called Apricot Danish, which was a blend of the fruit with hazelnuts and croquant within a parfait. It was scrumptious. She couldn't stop at one as she moved around the library setting up for a group therapy session; she really didn't mean to eat quite as many as she did.

By the time her group arrived, there were half-a-dozen empty spaces across both layers of the chocolates.

'Come on in, everyone. Good to see you . . .' She felt behind her for her chair, landing not quite evenly on the seat. 'Gosh, I really shouldn't have been so greedy. The sugar's gone to my head.'

Jack made the decision that he would be arresting Brian Jarvis by tonight, with the hope of charging him with the series of murders. He gave the team three more hours to assemble sufficient evidence so he could feel confident in an arrest rather than simply formally detaining the clerk of the court.

At a knock, he looked up to see Ali. 'News?'

'Yes, sir. I've finally confirmed that Brian Jarvis is a lifetime member of the Tottenham Hotspur Football Club.'

Jack felt like Rocky for a moment when he stood, both fists in the air like a champion. 'Yes! Ali, good work!'

'Thank you, sir. He also did purchase the limited special edition holdall.'

He blew her a kiss. 'Excellent. Go and help Kate – she's on a mission and we don't have much time.'

Ali disappeared and Jack made a mental note to discuss her career trajectory with those who could influence it. She was diligent – a little terrier – and she was modest. She hadn't hung about for praise; he admired that. He would help her on that journey to Detective Constable, which he had already heard through Mal was her goal.

A familiar anorak moved past his line of vision. 'Sarah?'

'Yes, sir.' She arrived at his doorway.

'On the occasions you've met Brian Jarvis, did you notice his shoes?'

She blinked in thought and didn't seem for a moment to consider this an odd question. 'I noticed he was a smallish shoe size. I believe he was wearing a pair of brown shoes when I noted that.'

Jack dug around his desk, looking under files until he found the colour photocopy. 'Like these?'

She leaned in and nodded. 'Possibly. Yes, certainly that sort of comfy shoe.'

'Great. Right, Sarah, two things. First, can you find out where Jarvis's daughter lives? We need to talk to her about how her mother died. Can you also find out where Brian Jarvis is right now, please?'

'Will do.'

He stood and followed her out into the incident room. 'Mal?' Realising that Mal was speaking on the phone, Jack gave an apologetic gesture. He waited. 'Sorry.'

'Guv?'

'The blue Mazda hatchback?'

Mal nodded.

'Can you get the reg? And I think we should find out if Judge Moira Leland has a blue Mazda hatchback matching our description parked anywhere around, close to, or below her block of apartments. Kate has her address.'

'On it. By the way, that was confirmation from our friendly roadside chemist. He picked out Jarvis from three photographs.'

'Oh, bloody good work, Mal. Right, listen up, everyone,' he said loudly into the room. All eyes rested on him. 'Through your diligence, our net is closing fast around Brian Jarvis. I would say within the hour we will be arresting him. Just a few more comprehensive and damning items to gather in. Kate?'

'Nearly there,' she said, turning back to the phone call she was on. 'I'm just holding on for some info.'

He nodded and his phone rang. It was Lauren. 'Hello there. Everything okay?' He glanced at his watch. It was nearing five.

'Yes, all fine. How are you doing?'

'Pretty good, actually.'

'Oh, you sound chirpy.'

'I'll tell you more tonight.'

'Ah, that's why I called. Can we make it a tad later?'

'Sure. Better offer?'

'Hardly.' She laughed. 'I'm just doing one quick interview, which is conveniently in my own backyard of Bayswater, but it might run a little over.'

'It's not a problem. Look, I've got to dash – things are heating up. Text me when you think your interview is wrapping up.'

'Okay. Thanks, Jack. Can't wait.'

Kate nodded at him as he rang off.

'Gather round, everyone,' he called out. 'Kate?'

'Thanks. Well, the plot is definitely thickening. Judge Moira Leland's husband did not die of cancer as people have been led to believe. He was killed, aged forty-five.'

Jack blinked, feeling the tingler within tighten.

'Jeremy Leland was involved in a tragic hit-and-run in the early evening of July 1995. He was out jogging when a couple of joy-riders, high on drugs, were tearing up some rubber at the same time. Police gave chase, and Mr Leland happened to be running across the road at a pedestrian crossing as they ran the lights. He was smashed into the bollards in the middle of the road and died of massive internal bleeding before the paramedic team could reach him. According to the pathology report, most of the bones in his torso were smashed or fractured, his skull split as well.'

There was silence. Jack punctured it. 'What happened?'

'They actually handed themselves in, which helped their cause. The driver got eight years for dangerous driving and only served four. His companion got three years and was out in sixteen months. Judge Moira Leland gave up working for one year, returning to the Crown Court in North London to pick up her career again. She has famously been quoted as saying she didn't believe a harsher sentence would have served any purpose as it couldn't give her Jeremy back.'

Jack nodded. 'Okay, everyone, we are looking seriously at Judge Moira Leland as an accomplice to Brian Jarvis.' He quickly explained his rationale, which brought a taut silence to the room. 'We can certainly hypothesise that she has motive. Now we need proof of her involvement with Jarvis. We hear they are very friendly, but both deny it. We know he made a call to someone after killing Markham. Did Brian Jarvis call Moira Leland directly after Peggy Markham's death? Mal, any luck on that car yet?'

'Not yet, boss. We should hear back any minute.'

He nodded. 'Sarah, your turn.'

'Right,' she said, pushing her glasses up her nose. 'Brian Jarvis does indeed have a daughter and granddaughters, but they are all dead.' A gasp sounded around the room and Jack swallowed; he'd suspected something like this but to hear it confirmed was chilling. Sarah was always at her most blunt when she was excited, like now.

He cleared his throat. 'Go on, Sarah.'

'Um, I have discovered that the Jarvis family has always owned the house in Enfield but, when his daughter got married, Jarvis took up a position at Bristol Crown Court and he and his wife moved there and rented out their second home. His daughter and her eighteen-month-old twin daughters came for a visit from Hove and they all went out for an evening stroll around the local green. It was a cold, slightly misty night. Kevin Dewsbury, twenty-six, well over the limit on alcohol, cleaned them up in his Land Rover, hitting Brian's wife first. She was flung against a brick wall and succumbed at the scene to the main head injury she sustained. The twins died instantly, still strapped into their twin pram, when he reversed into them. As he drove away, he dragged Brian's daughter beneath the car for several metres. That happened in April 1992. Jarvis took leave of absence, as far as I can tell, and resurfaced in March 1993 back at the family home, taking up his present position at the North London Crown Court.'

Jack joined the dots. 'But he's obviously not shared this information with his colleagues. And because he took up a new role well away from his dramatic past, he was not recognised more than a year later.'

'There's more, sir. The drunk driver was a very well-known footballer and had a heavyweight legal team representing him.

They argued everything from his team losing two of its members
in a helicopter crash the previous fortnight, to the sudden infant
death of his newborn, to the misty night and the two women in
dark clothing as mitigating circumstances. He got a suspended
sentence and four-hundred hours' community work.'

Another gasp rippled through Jack's team. He looked down
with disgust at the news as Sarah continued.

'Finally, Brian's real name is Colin Jarvis, but he changed it by
deed poll in that interim period after his family's deaths, taking
his middle name of Brian to deliberately distance himself from
the tragedy, media attention, et cetera.' Sarah looked up from her
notes. 'So that added yet more space between his previous life and
the one he lives now. Unsurprising that none of his colleagues
seem to know his history.'

'Good work. Right, everyone . . . now we have motive.
It's thin, because not everyone who loses someone turns into a
killer, but I'd stake my life on it that both Jarvis and Leland are
highly motivated. They have both had very real trauma in their
lives that is relevant to their daily work and the criminals who
pass through the North London Crown Court. I believe firmly
now that Judge Leland has made it easy for Jarvis to pick off the
violent offenders. She sentences as lightly as she dares, while he
bides his time until the system either lets them out early, which
seems to be the norm today, or, if they do their full time, he
picks them off then.'

He'd noticed Mal taking a call while Sarah was speaking.
'Something for us, Mal?'

'Yep, guv. We've got the car, I believe. Blue 2005 Mazda 3
hatchback with cloth trim, registered and in good nick – obviously
used to be garaged. It's presently parked in an underground space
beneath Judge Leland's apartment building and in her spot . . .
apartment six.'

They blew out a relieved breath of excitement as one. Someone even clapped. 'Good stuff, Mal.'

'We can now add Judge Leland to our list.'

'Do we invite her to help with our enquiries?' Kate asked.

Jack shook his head. 'No, arrest her. You do it, as she knows you. Escort the judge to Belgravia nick and, of course, she'll want her solicitor present.'

'Who will advise her to say nothing,' Kate replied.

'Yes, true, but Judge Leland will know our intent by then and you'll be able to surmise plenty from how she responds to her arrest. It also buys us time, and we'll know she's the link if Brian Jarvis reacts. Speaking of which, Sarah, do we know where Brian Jarvis is?'

'I've left a voicemail for him, plus I'm waiting on a call back from one of the admin team, but I'm sorry, at this point no one at the Crown Court seems to know exactly where he is.' Jack's expression darkened. 'He was scheduled for a meeting at the Old Bailey, according to Shirley Attlee, his colleague. He told her he might be having lunch at a restaurant in Bayswater. That's all I've been able to hunt down.'

'Stay on it, Sarah.'

'Sir?' It was Ali again. 'The caravan was rented out to a Mr Derek Bryan. I think that's too close to be a coincidence, if you don't mind me saying so.'

'I don't, one bit. Right, everyone. I was going to wait until we could compare a sample of Jarvis's handwriting to the letter received by Amy Clarke, but I'm not prepared to wait any longer. Brian Jarvis is to be arrested on sight. Put out the call, Kate. I'll head to his home; Mal, you go to the courts with Kate – find him. Come on, Sarah. You can come with me. You too, Ali. Kate will escort Judge Leland and show her to her cell to await interview.' He gave Kate a glance. 'You'll be in charge. I'll let you start the first round of questions.'

Pleasure winged its way back to him from Kate's expression. She said nothing, only nodded, but that look said droves about having each other's back.

30

They drove in silence as they left the Scotland Yard car park but Jack realised Sarah and Ali needed more than his close-held rage. 'All right, here's what I'm thinking. Jarvis knows we're firmly onto him and he will likely take precautions to tidy up loose ends: the car, the iPod, anything else he might have that ties him directly to any murders, like train tickets, parking tickets, receipts, bookings on a computer. He's smart enough to cover his tracks.'

'I don't think he's trying to get away, sir,' Sarah hazarded.

He nodded. 'I don't either. But I'm concerned about whatever else he thinks he needs to clean up before we get to him. I don't want any ambiguity once we have him in our lock-up.' He glanced in the mirror at the ambitious and capable constable sitting in the back. 'Feeling ambivalent, Ali?'

'I'm not sure I know what that really means, sir,' she admitted, and her honesty made him like her all the more.

'Are you having mixed feelings?'

'I'm embarrassed to say I am, sir.'

'You'll discover more of this as your career progresses. It's normal. Ask anyone around you how many times they've felt torn. It speaks of someone with empathy and we mustn't lose that or we become robots. Brian Jarvis is a reflection of all of us, including the police force and our constant frustrations and despair at watching serious crims getting off on technicalities, and liberal views that wax and wane depending on the wind. However, take away the emotion and Jarvis is making a mockery of the very justice system he claims to uphold. He is taking lives. A vigilante may be popular but in our book he's breaking the same laws as those he hunts.'

She nodded. 'And the judge?'

'I think we could spend the rest of the day in a philosophical discussion about Judge Leland's involvement. Nevertheless, it boils down to the same thing. She's complicit in murder and she is defying everything she swore an oath to uphold.'

'I'm still . . . ambivalent, sir,' Ali admitted sadly and won a grin from Jack that she caught in the mirror.

He flicked on the blue lights behind the radiator grille. 'Best route?'

'Via Camden Road, sir,' Sarah replied. 'Otherwise roadworks will trap us.'

Jack knew she was right – how did she always know these things?

'Judge Leland asked not to be disturbed,' the lady at the reception counter explained with a sympathetic smile. She reached for a notepad. 'Perhaps I could take your—'

Kate flashed her warrant card and Mal followed suit. 'She'll see me.'

The woman peered at the cards. 'Oh, right. Er, well, let me call someone.'

'No, that's fine. I know where her office is; we can find our way.' Kate didn't wait for the receptionist to splutter a response about how unusual this was. 'Thank you . . . Hilda,' she said, reading the woman's badge.

Kate marched through the courtroom corridors with Mal, retracing her steps from the previous day until she found herself standing in front of the judge's office. She tapped on the door and waited.

There was no answer. Kate tapped again, a little louder.

'Judge Leland? It's Detective Inspector Kate Carter.' She waited, listening for a rustle or any sound of movement, but it was silent behind that door. Maybe she'd stepped out, gone to the bathroom or headed to the cafeteria.

Kate glanced at Mal, who nodded and she tapped again and this time twisted the door handle, tentatively opening the door. 'Judge Leland?' Kate peered into the familiar spacious room, glancing towards the empty desk. She felt a ping of disappointment as much as frustration that they would now have to get over to the judge's house in St John's Wood. Another half hour or more through traffic. It also meant a further delay; Jack would not want Judge Leland to go missing altogether.

Kate sighed and turned to leave. Just as she was closing the door, she caught sight of Her Honour Judge Moira Leland on the sofa, presumably having a nap.

'Ah, nearly missed you there,' Kate said, more loudly, hoping to rouse the woman, but Moira Leland didn't so much as shift position. Kate blinked.

Sunshine was streaming through the glass onto the judge's daringly short hair. 'Judge Leland?' she said, her tone much sharper than perhaps necessary. She didn't stir and Kate felt a current of alarm like electricity flooding her body. She leapt forward, throwing her bag down and crouching by the sofa. 'Moira?' She shook the woman who was lying propped up against plump cushions.

Moira Leland's head, which had been facing the warm sunshine, lolled forward.

'Shit!' she heard Mal yelp.

'No!' Kate groaned. She shook the judge again, already knowing it was hopeless. Her eyes were closed and her expression grave but serene; she looked all the more elegant in death, and this close-up hinted to Kate at the beauty she'd been several decades earlier.

Kate stood, her mind racing. She sped into the corridor and it was pure luck that she found someone walking by. 'Contact security and have them come to Judge Leland's room, please. It's urgent.' The young woman frowned, looking indecisive. Kate dragged out her warrant card from her pocket. 'I'm Detective Inspector Kate Carter and I need security here *now.*'

The woman nodded and hurried off down the hallway as Kate closed the door and retreated into the quiet of Judge Leland's death scene. Kate breathed out slowly, calming herself, and took in the surrounds.

'What do you want me to do?' Mal said.

'Organise the security. Check if the staff here have found Jarvis. I'll preserve the scene here.'

Mal departed.

She moved over to her bag and turned to a new page of her pad. Her mind was already reaching towards Tottenham: the CID office there would have to be called to secure the scene properly.

She scribbled down some early thoughts and reminders before finding her phone and triggering all the official responses. She would have to use the court's team to prevent contamination of the scene by distraught staff until the SOCOs arrived to start forensics, photographing everything, bagging and tagging.

With a loud tap at the door, a security guard appeared, looking as though he'd run down the hallways. 'Is everything all right, miss? A detective told me to hurry.'

She crossed the floor to prevent him going any further. 'I'm afraid everything is not all right.'

After briefing the shocked guard and insisting he keep details of what was in this room a secret for now, she posted him outside the door.

'No one enters until the scene-of-crime team arrives. They're on their way.'

She thanked him as she began dialling Jack to give him the alarming update.

As Kate's call came through, Jack was turning away from Brian Jarvis's front door.

'No one around the back, sir,' Ali said.

Sarah nodded. 'No sign of any movement. I don't think he's at home.'

'No, I don't believe so, either. We'll need our forensic team down here, though, so we need to secure the house. Sarah, can you ring North London Crown Court just in case he's gone in?' He looked at his jangling phone as Sarah nodded. 'Kate? How are you getting on?' he answered.

'Not good.'

'Oh? Can't find her?'

'No, I found her. I'm sorry to tell you, Jack, that I discovered Moira Leland dead in her office at the North London Courts.'

He paused, allowing Kate's news to zip around his mind like a pinball in a machine . . . it didn't make sense. 'Dead?'

'Not long gone. She's warm to the touch.'

'Fuck! How?'

'Nothing messy. Could have been a heart attack, an aneurysm, an overdose, maybe.'

'Suicide?'

'I can't confirm. There's no sign of any drugs around – no pills or blister packs. She'd been drinking sherry and the bottle is here.

If I had to take a guess, I reckon it was spiked, but forensics will confirm that soon enough.'

'Murder?' He sounded like it was an impossible thought. Both Sarah and Ali turned his way, anticipating the worst.

'Potentially,' Kate replied. 'There's no sign of a struggle, nothing out of place, but the security guard mentioned he signed for a courier arriving with a package for Judge Leland this morning. Soon after, she told the reception to hold her calls, and the way I found her, it looks like she just curled up on the sofa with her glass. I agree that sherry at lunchtime is unusual, but she had no more official duties today at the court.'

'It's Jarvis.'

'My thought too.'

'I'm sorry you had to find her, Kate.'

'I liked her. She looked peaceful, though. If he is responsible, then he made sure it was a quiet end.'

'Is Cook on his way?'

'Yes. He'll take her back to Westminster morgue. I might go with her.'

'Good idea. Let's get that sherry tested as a priority. See if you can find the wrapping, or some clue as to where it came from.'

'Right. How are you going?'

'No success with Jarvis. He's not at home.'

'Mal assures me he's not here either, Jack.'

'Okay. I'll keep you posted. Talk later.' He clicked off and faced his two companions.

'Judge Leland?' Sarah asked, still looking shocked.

'I'm afraid so, and probably Jarvis behind it.'

'Cleaning up,' Sarah stated.

He nodded. 'She was in knee-deep. Perhaps he felt he was doing her a favour. If Kate's right, then he's poisoned her, and in the process taken away the terrible decision he knew she'd have faced to either commit suicide or stand up as a criminal in the very courts she presided over for years. He knows she would have had to watch her stellar reputation crumble, give up her tailored clothes for prison-approved trackpants. Imagine it! She's a powerful person, has the respect of many, so the fall from grace is too much even for Brian to bear. Now he's made the difficult decision for her. He knows she wasn't a bad person . . . just a deeply bereaved one, like himself, trying to set the world right.'

'Does she have to be named, sir?'

'You want to keep her out of the murderous scenario?'

She nodded.

'That good heart of yours, Ali, will serve you well. But Judge Leland was complicit. We shall have to see; perhaps the government will want to avoid a scandal, but a crime is a crime, no matter one's best intentions.'

'What now, sir?'

'Get some eyes on Jarvis's house, Sarah, in case he returns. Kate says he's not at the courts, but I think we'll pay them a visit anyway. Someone might know something.'

'I am sorry, Detective Superintendent,' Shirley said, looking concerned. 'Is it urgent?'

'It is, rather,' he said, not wishing to reveal their intention.

'Oh dear, what a terrible day this is. Judge Leland's passing has been the most frightful shock for everyone. She was always so fit; she was like a beanstalk, ate salads, drank water . . . well, mostly. She was prepping for a big trial that starts in a fortnight.'

'Brian Jarvis is not answering his phone. Is that unusual, Shirley?' Jack asked, nodding at Sarah to make her way back to the car. Ali followed, wide-eyed.

'Yes, most unusual. Brian's very good at staying in contact but of course he might still be at the courts.'

'Courts?' Jack was confused.

'He was going to the Old Bailey today for a meeting and then I gather he was going for a luncheon, and then a meeting somewhere in Bayswater.' She glanced at her watch. 'He would already—' But she stopped at the alarm that suddenly gripped Jack. She turned as rigid as he appeared. 'Is something wrong, Detective Superintendent?'

'You said he was going to Bayswater? Why?'

'An interview.'

He clasped her arm. 'Shirley, was he doing an interview with a journalist for *Britain's Voice*?'

'I . . .' Shirley looked suddenly frightened by Jack's intensity. 'I don't know. I was told lunch, then some lovely young reporter wanted to talk to him about lenient sentences. They were meeting somewhere near Lancaster Gate.'

Jack closed his eyes momentarily. The nagging thought had finally clicked; he could almost hear a satisfying mechanical sound in his mind as it slipped effortlessly into his most feared scenario. He could see a figure in a grey parka. A man, and the hood of his parka was up as he retreated down the street from Lauren's apartment. So Brian Jarvis already knew about them, knew where she lived, probably presuming rightly that Lauren knew Jack as more than simply a contact on a police op. Jarvis had followed him, no doubt. Jack had led a killer right to her doorstep. No. It couldn't be happening again.

He reached for his phone as he began to run.

Joan walked into Jack's office, where Kate was seated behind his desk, lost in assembling all the evidence into a logical order to file and present to Martin Sharpe.

'There's a call,' Joan said.

'I'm presuming it's Dr Cook at the morgue? He said he'd call for me to come down.'

'It's not. It's the prison governor at Holloway. She was hoping to speak with Jack, but his phone seems to be permanently engaged.'

'Go via Sarah. She's with him.'

'No, Kate. I think you should take this one.' Joan stared over her half-spectacles at the flashing light on the desk phone.

Kate frowned and Joan nodded again. Kate picked up the receiver and pressed line one. 'This is DI Carter.'

Moments later, her mind spinning, she was pulling on her jacket. 'Get hold of Sarah, Joan. Find out exactly where they are and then let me know.'

'Dr Cook?'

'Redirect him to my mobile,' she growled over her shoulder. 'And I've told the prison not to call Jack again.'

Kate hit the button on the lift repeatedly even though she knew it made no difference. She gave in to her shock before she gave up and began hurtling down via the fire stairs, angrily wiping away the tears that helplessly came.

'Where are we going, sir?' Sarah risked the question. Jack knew he looked unnerved.

'To Bayswater,' he said. 'Seatbelts on. I won't be slowing.'

'Sirens?'

He flicked on the flashing lights. 'No. I don't want to warn him.' He began twisting and turning through the traffic, beeping now and then to ensure everyone realised a police car with emergency lights was trapped behind them. Traffic eased to the left and gave him sufficient room to navigate through the late-afternoon crush.

'Ali, keep trying that number on loudspeaker until you get through.'

They all listened to Lauren Starling repeat her voicemail message as Ali kept hitting redial . . . but Jack had the sickening feeling it was already too late.

Brian Jarvis arrived at Lauren's home and she buzzed him up, pleased he'd made it.

'How charming,' he remarked, swivelling to take in the flat.

'It's small but all I need,' she said. 'I'll just put the kettle on.' She disappeared. When she returned, Jarvis hadn't removed his parka. 'Can I take your coat?' she offered.

'No, it's okay. I promised myself I wouldn't stay too long.'

She frowned at him, understandably baffled.

'Um, some of these lovely old terraced buildings have rooftop gardens, as I understand it?'

'This one does!' she said, smiling.

'Really? How wonderful.'

'It's a lovely afternoon; we could have our tea up there if you'd like. We won't be disturbed. I think everyone in this building works in the city. Even I'm not normally home at this time of day.'

'What a nice idea,' he said. 'Can I help with anything?'

'No, the tea's brewing. Let me show you up and then I can fetch a tray. I'll bring all my notes now – would you mind if I record you?'

He shrugged. 'I don't mind. I can imagine it's easier than scribbling it all down.'

She smiled. 'I learned shorthand, but I've lost most of that skill as we tend to record all interviews now. This way. Follow me.'

Up on the roof he smiled back at her. 'I can imagine you'd want to spend the whole summer up here.'

'I haven't had that pleasure yet, but I'm sure I will.'

'And will you be inviting Jack Hawksworth to share those summer nights with you up here and in your bed?'

She faltered; blinked. Had she heard right? 'I'm sorry, I don't follow . . .'

'Why? I'm speaking the Queen's English, am I not?'

'But—'

'You are sleeping with Jack Hawksworth, isn't that so?'

All the smiles fled. Brian Jarvis was scaring her. 'No. I am not,' she said, her tone defiant.

'Oh? My mistake. You're certainly very friendly. You sounded like lovers the other day.'

'Other day? What are you talking about?'

'Oh, come on, Lauren. Please don't play the innocent. I followed your detective superintendent here. I heard you both.'

She heard her ringtone sound, not realising it would be the first of a dozen similar frantic calls. She looked towards the small table next to her notes where she'd put her phone, only to realise it was no longer there but in Brian's hand. 'Ah, I suspect this is Hawksworth now, ringing for you. No doubt he'll keep trying. We shall have to put up with its noise.'

'Can I answer it, please?'

'No, Lauren. Let's keep him guessing, shall we? You know, never be too eager, too easy. Are you sure you haven't slept with him? Those looks of his would open any woman's bedroom door.' He said this all conversationally. 'I've looked into him. Do you know what I discovered?'

She stared back at him. 'What is this about?'

'Oh dear, you really haven't connected the dots yet, have you? Well, while you do, let me tell you about your handsome policeman. He has a truly horrendous track record with his lovers – they all lose their lives.' He chuckled.

Lauren said nothing, remembering now what Jack had said about a previous friend.

'There was a beautiful Asian woman called Lily. She was killed while seeing our Mr Hawksworth, but far more intriguing is a woman called Anne McEvoy. Heard of her?'

Lauren refused to answer him.

'I like your defiance; I can see it building. Won't do you any good, though. Anyway, Anne McEvoy was a serial killer, like me. And, in fact, we share more than that – her motivations matched mine, as her victims were bad men who had done her a serious wrong. She wasn't after innocents; she only targeted criminals. In this we are birds of a feather, Anne and I. We both like Jack Hawksworth and we both kill the bad guys.' He smiled.

'You? You're the vigilante?' It was only now she noticed that he'd positioned himself between her and the door. She was trapped.

He smiled wider, took off his large, round glasses and flung them off the rooftop. 'I see perfectly well apart from needing reading glasses, but people make assumptions about someone who wears big glasses; it's as though we're somehow helpless.'

'If you only kill the bad guys, why are you threatening me?'

'Have I threatened you?'

She swallowed. 'I feel threatened.'

'I'm not trying to hurt you, Lauren, but you're in my way and you've tried to trick me.'

She looked back, confounded.

'John Murphy. I checked. He's not up for early release.'

'Jack asked me to say that. I never understood the rationale.' The phone continued to ring. 'Can we just answer that?'

He shook his head. 'I guessed Hawskworth was behind that little gem. I think I've been in his sights since his little sidekick Sarah made an unexpected visit to my home.'

'And do you have an accomplice?'

'I did,' he admitted. 'But I don't any longer.'

'What do you want to achieve, Mr Jarvis? How many more do you want to kill?'

'All of them, if I could. But you see, Lauren, my time's up too. I'm dying. I had hoped to die before I was caught, but I don't have long. And I don't have the strength to kill many more.'

'Are you going to kill me?'

'Why would I?'

'Then why are you telling me all this?'

'Because I want to see Jack's face, hear his wrath, feel his fury and despair but above all his impotence when he confronts me.' They heard a car squeal into the street. 'Ah,' Brian said. 'Take a look. I think the cavalry has arrived.'

She glanced over the top and saw the blue flashing light, doors flung open and Jack exploding from the car. He looked up.

'Lauren!' His lovely voice was filled with anguish.

'Answer him, my dear. Invite him up. Assure him I won't hurt you.'

Sarah was looking up as her boss yelled to the journalist. Her phone rang and, without taking her eyes off the scene, she answered.

'It's me. Where are you?' Kate asked.

'Er, Bayswater. Things have gone very south.'

'Give me the address.'

She did. 'Jarvis is here,' she added.

'I'm eight minutes away. Six with my lights on. Five with my siren. Tell him to wait for me before he confronts Jarvis. It's important.'

'Okay.' Sarah ended the call. 'Sir?'

'Not now.'

'Kate's five minutes away,' she murmured. 'She said it's important you wait for her before you engage with Jarvis.'

He swung round, angry. 'He's got Lauren Starling up there.'

'Jarvis said he won't hurt her.'

'Do you believe him?'

'I do, sir. I think his target is you.'

'Then I'm going up.'

'Please wait.' She sounded very firm . . . very Kate. 'She obviously knows something we don't.'

'What do you want me to do? Keep him talking?' This was said sarcastically but it was a good idea and she responded as such.

Sarah glanced at Ali. 'Get this street closed off, and some constables going door to door, keeping people inside.'

Ali nodded and got busy on the car radio.

Sarah raised her gaze to the rooftop. 'Mr Jarvis?' she called.

He looked over the edge. 'Hello, Sarah.'

'We're just securing the street. It may take a few minutes.'

He laughed. 'Why are you telling me?'

'I didn't want you to become alarmed if you see activity.' She glanced at Jack. 'I'm just playing for time, sir,' she murmured. 'Let's keep him talking until Kate gets here.'

'Brian? Can we use a phone please?' Jack held up his own.

His phone rang moments later.

'What do you hope to achieve with this, Mr Jarvis?'

'If I'm honest, I don't really know, Jack. I've never been a free-faller before. I feel like I'm making this up as I go along.'

'No more killing, Brian.'

'Just one more,' he replied.

'Please don't hurt Lauren. She has nothing to do with this.'

'She has everything to do with this, but I have no beef with Ms Starling.'

'Then who?'

'Well, you, for starters. I'd hoped to get a few more moved on to the next world before you caught up with me.'

'Kate's one minute away, sir,' Sarah murmured.

'Can I swap places with Lauren, then?'

Brian laughed. 'Yes, why don't you come and join us on the roof? It's lovely up here.'

'Moira Leland is dead.'

'Ah, that's good news. Swift and painless. I could ask for the same myself, but I don't think anyone would do me that favour.'

'Did she ask you to kill her?'

'Heavens, no. She had no idea. That's the best death, though. And I've been that generous with all of my victims. None of them knew it was coming; relatively painless for all except the wife-bashing Smythe, and of course Davey Robbins. I did hurt them, as they were particularly cruel to women. But generally, Jack, I'm a lot more merciful to them than they have ever been to their victims. None of them had worth, Jack.'

'But you are not their judge, Brian.'

'No, Moira helped me by fulfilling that role. But I *am* their executioner. I took it upon myself to rid the world of these bad people. My family were innocents, Jack. Good women, and my granddaughters would have grown up to emulate those good women. Their futures just ripped away. My life is a bonfire of ruin. I've followed the rules all my life; I've been a solid citizen, a reliable civil servant. I didn't deserve what life brought and I have come to the conclusion that there are too many innocents whose lives are changed through cruelty, carelessness, greed and thuggery. And too few of the perpetrators pay anything close to the price they should.'

'Here she is, sir.' Sarah gave a subtle nod towards a vehicle pulling up.

He watched Kate all but explode from the car.

'Ah, another of your brood, I see.'

'This is Detective Inspector Kate Carter,' Jack said.

'Mmm. I suggest that you both join us on the roof, or I will fling Lauren Starling over the top.'

Jack started. 'Okay, okay, we're coming.' He grabbed Kate by the arm. 'Come on.'

'Jack, I have to tell you something.'

'No time. Run!'

He was already sprinting towards the doorway.

On the rooftop, Brian looked Lauren's way and made a soothing sound. 'I didn't mean that. I promise I won't hurt you.'

'Are you going to hurt Jack?'

Jarvis shrugged. 'That depends.'

But he didn't say on what.

31

Kate couldn't keep up with Jack and those long legs that took the stairs two at a time. She was soon a whole flight behind. She watched from the bottom of the final ascent as Jack burst onto the roof, daylight streaming into the corridor where she was still struggling up the last flight. She too arrived, breathing hard enough to vomit, to be confronted by Brian Jarvis holding a long blade to Lauren Starling's throat. She watched Jack put up both hands.

'Don't.' He too was sucking in breath, with eyes only for Lauren.

'No tricks, Jack.'

'None,' he confirmed.

Kate really did feel like vomiting but that wouldn't help anyone. She swallowed repeatedly until she felt a measure of control.

Jarvis noticed her. 'Welcome. You must be DI Kate Carter,' he said warmly.

'Now what?' Jack said. 'What can you possibly do next that improves this situation for yourself?'

Jarvis shoved Lauren towards Jack. She squealed, fell against him, but quickly found her wits. Kate had a heartbeat of space to admire her composure.

'Go!' Jack said.

'Do as he says, Lauren,' Brian advised. 'Join the watchers on the street. There'll be action soon, as young Sarah suggested there would be.'

At Jack's silent urging, Lauren headed for the stairwell. She glanced nervously back at the two detectives and won a nod from Kate, encouraging her to get to safety.

'I hear you met Moira?' Jarvis commented.

Kate swung back around. 'And liked her,' she replied, knowing she needed to sound firm, unmoved by his threat.

He nodded. 'I promise you she will forgive me. What she would have faced after this would have been far worse than death. Like me, I know she welcomed the end, but she just didn't know how to do it. I removed that decision as it has been removed for me. Let me tell you what I mean by that – I'm dying, Jack and Kate. A few months left at best.'

Jack sighed, remembering what Anne had cautioned. 'We couldn't work out why the killings escalated, but health was a consideration.'

'You used a profiler?'

Jack nodded. 'Of sorts, yes.'

'Of sorts?'

'She's a guest of Her Majesty. But she's also a talented criminal psych. Her name is Anne McEvoy.' Jack said it defiantly.

'Jack,' Kate began. She felt he was suddenly like a gambler with the deck stacked against him; he had no idea of the ace that Jarvis had already put facedown on the table. But it seemed she would have to turn it over and reveal its presence.

'Oh, Jack, I think your colleague has something to tell you. Do you, DI Carter?'

She shook her head. 'No.' She would not explain on his terms and let him gleefully witness it.

Jarvis laughed. 'Oh, he'll find out soon enough. I'm surprised he hasn't already, to be honest. I thought the prison would have called him.'

Jack glanced between them. 'What are you talking about?'

'Nothing.' Kate looked desperately around to shift his attention by doing something physical.

'Oh, lovely Kate, trying to protect you. I think all the women who come into your orbit want to do that. Because heaven knows you can't protect them. Women on your watch get hurt, Jack.'

'What do you know, Kate?' Jack demanded and watched her shake her head in denial.

'We're talking about Anne McEvoy, Jack,' Jarvis said. Jack's attention snapped back to him. 'I rather admire her, actually. I was just telling Lauren that she and I have a lot in common.'

'What the hell?' Jack turned to Kate again. 'What is this?'

She shook her head again. 'Jack, listen . . .' she began gently.

But Jarvis, it seemed, had already tired of his own entertainment. 'I also told Lauren that I really want you to know what it feels like to be me . . . to learn that people you love are dead. No warning, no reason, just dead. Gone. Their lives snuffed out by someone who just didn't care.'

Jack looked towards Kate. Pain was written in her features. 'Kate?'

She had to be the one to do it; she would not let Jarvis have the pleasure. 'He's killed her,' she said, her voice flat and toneless. 'Sent her a box of poisoned chocolates, probably with the same drug he used in Moira Leland's sherry. She . . . she thought they were from you and so did the prison team. They let them through with only a cursory check.'

'Anne's dead?' He blinked as though trying to move the impossible thought away.

'Yes, Jack. Catch up, will you?' Brian said, lacing his tone with boredom. 'I used antifreeze for both. It's sweet and tasteless . . . and very effective. Blame yourself, Jack, my boy. You led me to her. I watched you, followed you. What a surprise to find you carrying a box of Thorntons chocolates into Holloway Prison. Of course, your journo friend helpfully filled in the blanks for me. Don't blame her, though. It's your fault. As I say, no woman around you is safe. That goes for you too, my dear,' he said to Kate. 'Just listening to you I sense a tenderness within you for this man. Get away from him while you can.' Jarvis watched Kate's horrified look. 'Or perhaps I'm already too late – you've fallen for the Met's poster boy. He's very senior and extremely handsome so—'

'Shut the fuck up, Brian!' Jack looked at Kate. 'Have you confirmed this?'

She nodded. 'She's gone, Jack. I couldn't reach you.'

Brian looked back innocently. 'Just like Moira, she probably died with a soft smile. No pain, I promise. Fell asleep and then her heart would have stopped.'

Jack raised his face to the sky and Kate could see all the tendons straining in his neck as he roared his despair. She watched the knife that Jarvis had held slack for minutes lifted again, unsure whether he was readying to protect himself or strike.

'Ah, that's it, Hawksworth. Let that pain come. I know that keening sound so well. I know she was your friend, but this agony suggests she was more. Was she more to you, Jack? Have I hit the right nerve?' Jarvis goaded, with an edge as sharp as the blade that glinted in the early evening sun. 'Or shall I threaten Kate, who seems to feel an enormous empathy for you?'

'Get behind me, Kate,' Jack ordered, returning his attention to them. His voice was low, menacing.

She did move momentarily but defiance as much as anxiety

kicked in and she disobeyed, certain that Jarvis had every intention of taking Jack with him.

Extreme fear combined with a flood of adrenaline in Jack's
body. His rationality told him everything was happening faster
than normal and yet time seemed to slow. He caught the subtle
movement of Jarvis's gaze sliding to Kate, who meanwhile had
strapped on her heroic cape and was clearly thinking of doing
something inadvisable. He knew this in the same nanosecond she
did by the tensing of her muscles; when he'd asked her to get
behind him, she had briefly, so that their bodies were touching. But
now he felt the gathering of energy that would propel her forward.

No way. Not Kate. He would not let her risk her life again
while he could help it. He heard her shout her intent as she
tried to angle in front of him. But he was bigger, stronger,
faster . . . and without a thought for strategy, he moved, launching
himself towards Brian Jarvis to cut her off. His body hit hers as he
elbowed her back and then collided with Jarvis as he sandwiched
himself between them. He had the time, surprisingly, to note Kate
snarling behind him and to turn and note the grin of satisfaction
on Jarvis's face.

It was only now, in this intimate moment of bodies clutched
unhappily together, that he realised his world had turned quiet.
Sounds were muted but colours were overly bright, the sun
dazzlingly sharp, the clouds so blinding in their purest white that
gradually his gaze felt like it was slipping. The light began to
refract and split into the spectrum as though he was losing focus.
Meanwhile, sensation felt raw. The blow had felt like a massive
punch to his belly. He was still shuddering from the force of it,
and then came a new sensation of toppling.

Blood bloomed on his body. Was it hers? 'Kate?'

'Oh, Jack,' he heard; her voice was strained and high, but her arms were around him, cradling him. Noise punctuated the silence as though the volume had been suddenly flicked on loud; he could hear police and ambulance sirens over a lot of yelling . . . was that Kate? Was she hurt? He could pick out the sound of pigeons disturbed from their rooftop nests as a jet made its approach to Heathrow and he idiotically wondered from where it was coming.

Jack could have sworn he was lifting up to float free from the rooftop, even from himself, which was odd but not unpleasant. There he was, finally able to view the scene with omniscient perspective. He hadn't expected to see himself mostly prone, lying next to the rickety table and chairs. His head and shoulders were propped up against Kate, her long arms protective. He saw her look up helplessly from the ground and he followed her gaze, both of them desperately seeking out Jarvis as he pulled off his parka.

'Jack, I'm sorry. I really didn't mean to bring you physical harm. I only brought you here because I wanted you to understand what it feels like to know helplessness in the face of someone who simply doesn't care about the people who matter to you. I assured Ms Starling I wouldn't hurt her. My aim was only to bring justice to those defying it.' He sighed, looked up towards the sun, then back at them. 'Here, Kate.' Jarvis flung his parka towards them. 'Keep him warm as the shock hits,' he said, before moving to the edge of the building. Then, using the small, creaking chair to get some height, he hauled himself onto the ledge.

'Jarvis, no!' Jack yelled, finally finding his wits, all of his senses switched back on to full focus. He tried to struggle from Kate's grip but it was no use. He looked down, expecting to see her rigidly clasping him but she wasn't; instead his belly and lap were a mess of blood. *Oh, for fuck's sake*, he thought. *We have to stop him*, and he pushed deeper to find some strength. *Move, Jack!*

He was suddenly trying to clamber onto his knees to reach towards Jarvis. Kate was screaming at him again and he was beginning to see stars.

'Can't let you have me, but you have my respect. Don't die, Jack. Don't want you on my conscience when I answer for my sins.' Jarvis gave them a friendly salute and jumped. He made no sound through the air, although they heard the crunch of his body hitting the pavement seconds later and the shrieks from Sarah, Ali, maybe Lauren, and other people below.

Jack had fallen forwards, raging with despair but also fading as he watched Kate scrambling to lean over the edge and look before she too slumped back down. Immediately, she was punching numbers into her phone.

'Sarah. Is he dead?' Kate demanded. Jack listened to her pause . . . his hearing was becoming distant, his sight beginning to narrow to tunnel vision as Kate blurred. 'Best outcome, I suppose,' he heard her say from far away. 'Listen, forget Jarvis. Ambulance on the hurry-up for Jack. He's been seriously hurt. Now!'

He frowned as he faded. 'Hurt? No, I'm . . .' The stain of blood was spreading across his shirt, even creeping up towards his chest.

Kate was back at his side, ripping open the shirt, buttons flying across the rooftop so she could see the state of his wound. She pressed on his belly. 'Jack, keep your eyes open. Please, Jack, please.' It took effort but he did as she demanded. He began to shiver, and she wrapped the parka around him, pulling off her jacket and placing it beneath his head. 'I won't leave you, Jack, but you mustn't leave me. Okay? Promise me.'

'I thought he'd stabbed you.'

'He got you instead because you're a heroic lunatic. Let me see.' She pulled back the parka. 'Shit!' She dialled again and snarled into the phone. 'Where's that fucking ambulance? Okay, thanks. Jack, they're coming up now . . . it's a lot of stairs and hopefully they're as fit as you. I need to put some pressure on the wound. It will hurt.'

'Fuck!' he yelled as she pressed warm hands onto his skin and then harder still. 'Don't tell Joan. FUCK!'

'She'll never know how much we owe her, I promise. Now, keep those eyes open for me. They're beautiful and I want to keep looking at them.'

He was cold suddenly, but the shivering sensation was waking him back up. Now he could feel the pain of the stab wound. He noted Kate didn't have a drop of colour in her complexion. *This is what shock looks like*, he thought, knowing he probably appeared the same. He groaned as a searing seam of agony sliced through his body.

'Good. Stay awake,' she said, sneaking another glance at his wound. Somehow she hauled him against her again, leaning back at a flattish angle against the wall and clasping his wound so tight he yelled again. 'You'll make it, Jack. I can hear them.' She kissed his thick hair. 'It could be worse.'

'Could it?' he heard himself bleat from far away through his panting. 'This shirt is from Savile Row. You find my buttons!'

They both found his remark far funnier than it probably was, and when the paramedics arrived, staggering under the weight of their equipment with Sarah not far behind, gasping for breath, they found Kate and Jack laughing together in each other's arms, like they were at a summer picnic.

Kate watched the man she still desired stir and work out that he was in a hospital bed and she was holding his hand. He was unshaven, hair messy, wearing a crumpled hospital gown. He looked splendid.

'There you are,' she murmured, squeezing his hand and shifting out of her chair to perch on the side of the bed.

'Here I am,' Jack said, voice husky. She helped him to sip through the straw of a nearby beaker of water. 'Thanks.'

'You saved my life, Jack. Do you remember that?'

'Because you were aiming to save mine.'

'It was probably my turn.'

He looked back at her, confounded. 'I'm not keeping score.'

'Are you in pain?'

Jack shook his head. 'I'm sure I should be.'

'Morphine's a wonderful thing. Enjoy it – it's legal in here,' Kate quipped.

'Where is here?'

'St Mary's. I'm very sorry about Anne, Jack. It's my fault that she came into Jarvis's frame.'

He shook his head. 'No, he followed me, remember.'

'Yes, but it was my idea for you to consult her.'

He held a brief silence. 'You know, I had time in the ambulance, distracting myself from fear while the emergency team put me through my paces, to consider the ruin of her life.' He gestured for another sip of water as his foggy mind became clear. 'She'd only done two years of prison and she was already a ghost of the woman I remember. She was going to fade in there. She was trying to stay positive because she knew it was for the rest of her life – no reprieve, no chance to see her daughter, who would potentially never know who her mother was and how much she loved her. And even though I could see that she was using her skills to help others, I felt only relief when she said it was probably best we didn't see each other again. I didn't *want* to see her again – that's the truth of it.'

'And now you won't have to face the guilt?'

'No, it's not that. I think if she could have worked out how to check out in a non-messy, non-suffering way, she would have. Jarvis took a difficult decision away from two suffering women, guilty of crimes that were in the public's interest but had to be punished. In a way I guess I could be grateful to him for that. Anne's free now.'

'Who is sorting out her funeral?'

'I guess I will. She has no one.'

'I'll help. You're not going to be doing much at all for a while. I've let Geoff know. He'll call.'

He nodded. 'Jarvis?'

'Dead on impact. Best decision he made.'

'Lauren?'

'Seems fine. When we were packing you up into that ambulance, I sensed Lauren was more excited than fearful.'

'Truly?' Now he did laugh and then groaned from the pain it prompted. 'Yes. Imagine how she's going to dine off that . . . up so close and personal with the country's most hunted man of recent times? Her feature story will be devoured. She deserves it.'

'Sharpe is impressed,' Kate said, tiring of his admiration for the other woman. 'We did exactly what he set us up to do and saved the Met the usual press circus.'

As if he'd been cued, there was a knock at the door, and they could see Martin Sharpe's face as he lifted a hand to wave through the glass.

He stepped inside. 'Not interrupting?'

'No,' they said together.

'Morning, sir,' Kate said.

'Sir,' Jack echoed, struggling to lift his head from the pillow.

'Be still, Jack,' Sharpe said, waving away protocol. 'Good grief, what a pair you two make – you're the talk of the Met.' He clasped Kate's hand before shaking Jack's and then, surprisingly, touching his cheek as a father might with a son. 'How are you doing?'

'Sounds rather epic to say I've survived a stabbing.'

'You were both heroic. And I'm certainly grateful. Well done to all in the team. This could have all got ugly. Mirror was slickly handled and brought to a close faster than I could have hoped. The media is only just waking up to it and your Ms Starling has the scoop.'

'Thank you for giving her the exclusive, sir.'

'Well, it's my last formal interview.'

'Going shopping for deck shoes instead, sir?' Jack wondered.

'Your day will come, Jack,' Sharpe groaned. 'My wife is determined to kit me out, so I stop looking like – in her words – an ageing plod, and more like a retired gentleman. What a load of old arse,' he grumbled.

Both Kate and Jack laughed.

'Don't do that, sir. It hurts,' Jack moaned.

'I'm recommending you for a promotion, by the way,' Sharpe said, addressing Kate.

'Me?' She sliced a glance Jack's way, making the presumption he was behind it.

'Yes. My last act before I leave. You've earned it, DI Carter. There's a lot of respect for you out there, not least from this fellow who holds you in such high esteem.' He prodded Jack gently.

Kate blushed. 'Thank you, sir.'

'Right, you need some sleep – I hear you haven't left his side.'

She looked down, embarrassed.

'Go on, he'll still be here when you wake up. He's getting the best care.'

Jack smiled at Kate. 'Thank you.'

'I'll come by tomorrow.'

Sharpe waggled a finger. 'And Joan says she's going to make a guess at how many pound coins you both owe after what happened on that rooftop.'

Kate gave a dramatic sigh. 'Right, I'm dialling Joan to tell her to empty out that wretched tin, and as soon as Jack's allowed out we're all going to celebrate with the proceeds.'

She bundled Sharpe out the door and looked back at Jack, giving him a bright smile. 'Be well.'

He nodded. 'By the way, Kate . . .'

She turned back.

'Dr Cook has been asking about you . . . and not in a professional way, I might add.'

'If you weren't so weak, I'd fling a pillow at you, Jack.'

He blew her a brief kiss and then she was gone. As she left, she saw him reach for his phone. She knew with a helpless pang that it would be to call the very lucky Lauren Starling.

'Jack!'

'How are you doing?'

'Just stopped shaking, I think,' Lauren admitted. 'I've been to the hospital twice now but they won't let me onto your ward. That Detective Inspector Kate Carter is quite protective.'

He grinned. 'You'll have to get used to that. Where are you?'

'Here, drinking awful hospital coffee and lurking in the main reception.' There was a pause and he hoped she wasn't crying, that he had read her wrong. He didn't think she was the weepy sort. He was right. Her voice was steady when it came to reassure him. 'I really want to see you, Detective Superintendent Hawksworth.'

He laughed. 'Well, what are you waiting for? I'm all alone now and helpless in bed, wearing a frock of sorts that has no ties at the back. Come and take advantage of me.'

The sound of her laughter through the phone felt like a balm, exactly what he needed right now. 'Give me a few minutes,' she said.

The pain of Anne's death would take a while to lessen but he already believed that she was in a better place; he felt strangely content knowing she was no longer that beautiful caged bird.

He would honour his promise to her as her farewell, hoping that by the time he was well enough to organise her funeral, he would know of Samantha's whereabouts. He would whisper it to her mother's coffin and, as Anne was cremated, perhaps her spirit could travel to where her daughter lived in what he hoped was the love and security Anne had wanted for her.

But right now his focus was on healing, and the best sort was to be found in the arms of a bright, smart woman, especially the one who had just arrived in the doorway to smile widely, a takeaway coffee in her hand from one of the new coffee shops in Paddington.

'I'm assured this is the best three-quarter-full latte in London,' she said, bursting in.

And Jack's groan was one filled with gratitude.

ACKNOWLEDGEMENTS

Without a retired Australian detective called Mick Symons, this book would never have come to fruition. I knew it would be an impossible story to write unless I had someone on the ground in London who was well versed in the procedures of Scotland Yard at a senior level during the early 2000s. Mick, an old friend and colleague of my husband, immediately put the word out through his networks and a retired senior detective, Mike Warburton, put his hand up. I remain very grateful to him.

Mike and I began to correspond and then, in early 2019, I flew to London and gave him a brief outline of my ideas and we were off. We spent the next few days with our heads bent over a couple of very good bacon butties in Wood Green Crown Court and the story began to come together. Mike caught on fast to my character of DCI Jack Hawksworth and helped me to bed down my police protocols. He took me into the public gallery for day one of a trial of three men accused of drug crimes. I found it particularly chilling watching the jury being sworn in; so many of them looked unnerved by the men staring straight back at them and the other intimidating folk in the public gallery and I didn't envy them the task of deciding their immediate future. The case wasn't relevant to my story but the surrounds were and I began to 'feel' the atmosphere of a British criminal court and all of its players.

We roamed all around Enfield area, walking the streets that the characters do and choosing locations that worked for the story. We visited the Alexandra Palace – known fondly as the Ally Pally by locals – on a stupendously cold day but I just couldn't work it into the story. Next time! Mike and I met once again in Portsmouth, this time chatting for hours over several pots of tea in the faded surrounds of a once glorious hotel that formerly welcomed the well-heeled and glamorous, but now its seafront tearooms welcomed mostly pensioners coming in from the cold for a mid-morning treat. It set a perfect mood for a key scene with the wind whistling across the shingle beach and a lot more education on the subject of a concerted police operation. Mike continued to be invaluable through the year of Covid-19 restrictions when I could no longer visit or tramp across locations with him, and I know how fortunate I am for our early work together and his ongoing commitment to the project throughout 2020, including numerous reads of chapters.

Few of my books these days are written without my hilarious, brilliant fellow writer in Britain – Alex Hutchinson – at my side. She writes under the pen name of Penny Thorpe but she's one of Britain's well-known archivists and is regularly called upon by broadcasters and TV hosts for her historical knowledge, particularly of chocolate. Alex and I tend to frequent a lot of chocolate shops while researching! She is the very best location expert and without Alex I would not have thought to go to Finsbury Park or found the particular spot where the character of Bernie Beaton hid. She can always find exactly what I need for the story – she's been doing this since 2015 – so I now look forward to our jaunts all over London as we hunt down the perfect place for various scenes. This was the first time she'd helped me with a contemporary novel and it was a lot of fun, especially investigating an old bowling alley we found near Finsbury Park, visiting Southwark, roaming Borough Markets, walking London Bridge. She moves me around on foot because we never know when I'll find just the right alleyway or shop, the perfect cafe or street. Penny Thorpe has written two novels about Quality Street and, now fully recovered from her own bout of Covid-19, she is busy working on her third. I miss not being able to move around Britain with her and I look forward to hopefully being reunited in 2022 . . . we have books to research.

Thanks to all the usual suspects in the Penguin Random House team – especially my publisher, Ali Watts, for giving me the opportunity to answer the determined campaign by readers to bring back DCI Jack Hawksworth in a new story. I doubt it will be his last. And a special nod to my editor, Amanda Martin, for her diligent and ever cheerful work on the manuscript – you are such a pleasure to work with.

Finally, a big kiss for Ian McIntosh. When I was first coursing about for a new crime story, the premise of this tale came at his suggestion, emerging out of his ongoing frustration – which I'm sure is shared by many – for the lenient sentencing given to convicted criminals and/or the early release of criminals due to the squeeze on our prison system. It's an old chestnut that is hard to crack and I suspect we'll wrestle with it constantly: I'm sure most of us appreciate that rehabilitation through incarceration is rare, yet none of us want to share our world with hardened criminals. And of course we want justice for the victims. I think we had one of those conversations of 'What would you do if . . .?' and out of it came the vigilante idea; hardly new but always intriguing and divisive and a perfect platform for a compelling story, which I hope you've enjoyed.

Fx

Want more DCI Jack Hawksworth?

Two heart-stopping thrillers from a
powerhouse Australian author